MW01126081

Praise for Simon Tolkien

"In epic fashion worthy of his namesake, Tolkien crafts a remarkable novel of an American boy swept up by love and circumstance and cast into the crucible of the Spanish Civil War. Intense, vivid, and moving."

—Mark Sullivan, bestselling author of *Beneath a Scarlet Sky* and *All the Glimmering Stars*

"[A] delight to read and deserves the success [he] will surely achieve."

—*The Washington Post*

"Simon Tolkien knows how to keep a story moving, and he does it well."

—NPR

"Written with great surety and absolutely compelling."

—*Booklist*

"Tolkien . . . proves himself worthy—and then some—of his literary pedigree."

—*Richmond Times-Dispatch*

THE PALACE AT THE END OF THE SEA

ALSO BY SIMON TOLKIEN

Final Witness

The Inheritance

The King of Diamonds

Orders from Berlin

No Man's Land

The Theo Sterling Duology

The Palace at the End of the Sea

The Room of Lost Steps

THE PALACE AT THE END OF THE SEA

A NOVEL

THEO STERLING: VOLUME 1

SIMON TOLKIEN

This is a work of fiction. Names, characters, organizations, places, events, and incidents are either products of the author's imagination or are used fictitiously.

Published by Lake Union Publishing, Seattle

www.apub.com

EU product safety contact:
Amazon Media EU S. à r.l.
38, avenue John F. Kennedy, L-1855 Luxembourg
amazonpublishing-gpsr@amazon.com

ISBN-13: 9781662528620 (hardcover)
ISBN-13: 9781662528644 (paperback)
ISBN-13: 9781662528637 (digital)

Cover design by Shasti O'Leary Soudant
Cover image: © ClassicStock / Alamy; © Jag_cz, © Dmitr1ch / Shutterstock

Printed in the United States of America

First edition

For my beloved wife, Tracy, who has supported me in all my creative endeavors throughout our marriage and has given me the courage and self-belief to carry them out

PART ONE

NEW YORK CITY

1929–1932

Der mentsh trakht un Got lakht.

(Man plans and God laughs.)

—*Old Yiddish Proverb*

1

KIDNAP

He was eleven when he was taken. On a day of early summer from almost outside his apartment house out into the bustle of the Village, and then east across Third Avenue under the webbed iron feet of the roaring El into regions of the great city that he had never seen before, smelling of garbage and horse dung and thick, acrid smoke.

And all the time, the old man held Theo's hand in an iron grip and kept up a quick pace, pulling him along the sidewalk, so he had almost to run if he wasn't to fall over. He had seen the old man several times in recent weeks, waiting under the spreading chestnut tree at the corner of his street in the early evening. He'd stared at Theo and his mother as they went past with his eyes glowing like coals under the rim of his battered old derby hat, which he wore as if it were an upturned soup bowl, pulled down over his ears like Charlie Chaplin.

He had the hat on now and the same long black alpaca coat, shiny at the elbows, which he was wearing over a clean but frayed white shirt buttoned to the collar with no tie, and Theo could see that in the side of his scuffed shoe there was a small hole that opened and closed as he walked, as if it were another beady eye.

He told Theo that he was his grandfather, speaking slowly in a thick guttural accent, and Theo thought he probably was. He didn't look like someone who told lies, and besides, there was something about the old man that reminded Theo of his father. Four days before, they'd been walking home and his father had stopped hard in his tracks, telling him sharply to get on home to his mother. But Theo had turned back at the stoop and had seen his father arguing, waving his hands in the air but seeming to have no effect on the old man, who stood there as immobile as the tree behind him. And maybe it was then that Theo had noticed the resemblance.

Afterward, his parents had talked in hushed voices and his mother had cried as she often did, and his father had gotten hot under the collar and said that there were laws to stop people being harassed in the street, and that he had a good mind to complain to the authorities if it happened again. *Authorities* was one of Theo's father's favorite words—he was a great believer in law and order. But it seemed like there was no need to get them involved this time. There were no further sightings of the old man, and today Theo's mother had woken up with another of her terrible headaches—the curse she called *la jaqueca*—and had sent him to the pharmacy on MacDougal with a quarter to get some more of her yellow pills. And on the way, without any warning, it had happened.

The old man had not been in his usual place under the tree; instead, it was as if he had appeared out of nowhere like a circus magician, and Theo was so surprised that he didn't try to resist, at least at first, allowing himself to be led away with his small hand still clutching his mother's coin, all enclosed inside the old man's huge calloused palm.

His grandfather could have been sixty or seventy or eighty, a hundred even. Theo couldn't tell. He knew only that he was taller than anybody he had ever seen and that his flowing white beard made him look like one of the Old Testament prophets in the illustrated Bible that his mother had given him the year before to celebrate his First Communion. Moses, perhaps, leading the people of Israel across the desert, or Jonah, who got swallowed by the whale; although most of all he reminded Theo of crazy Abraham, who was ready and willing to sacrifice his son until God stopped him on the top of the mountain, just in the nick of time. That picture was one of the scariest in the whole book, and Theo, closing his eyes, could see the long, glittering knife that Abraham had ready for the awful deed, raised high above his shoulder while he held Isaac pinned in place on the stony altar with his other hand.

Now, suddenly, Theo was terrified, and at the next corner he used all his strength to try to break free.

"Help!" he shouted, but he couldn't shake the old man's iron grip and his cry froze in his throat, coming out as a sort of croak to which no one passing by paid any attention.

"Where are you taking me?" he asked, looking up into his grandfather's strange but familiar face. The eyes were different from his father's: narrow yet penetrating, set back amid the hollows of a wrinkled face, but the thin, determined mouth and the jut of the chin were the same.

"I am taking you to meet your *bubbe* . . . your grandmother," the old man added, seeing Theo's look of incomprehension. "It is nothing to be scared about—it is . . ." He stopped, and the wrinkles in his forehead bulged as he searched for the English word. "An adventure!" he finished and smiled, a quick movement of his lips that was fleeting but nevertheless enough to make him seem more human, so that Theo didn't resist when the old man resumed their walk. Slower now, as if to reassure the boy.

"Why do you talk funny—like you don't know the words?" Theo asked.

"Not like your father, you mean?" the old man replied sharply.

"I guess," said Theo defensively. He was frightened again, thinking that he might have upset his grandfather with the impertinence of his question.

"Because I come from another country. Far away across the great sea. Just like your father, but he has forgotten that. He has turned his back on who he is, become something he is not," the old man added harshly and picked up his pace.

But he couldn't go much quicker because the city had changed and the sidewalks were packed with the laden pushcarts of peddlers that overflowed out into the street, where horses and delivery trucks and dirty automobiles mingled in a maelstrom of pent-up, impatient movement. The drivers blew their horns and crept forward at a snail's pace, cursing through their windows at impervious pedestrians who weaved their way between the wheels, wrapped in trails of gassy exhaust smoke that made Theo's eyes water.

On the opposite corner, a traffic policeman stood on a box and waved his white-gloved hands with self-important, theatrical gestures, but Theo knew there was no chance the cop would hear him above the din if he shouted, and he realized with surprise in the next moment that he didn't want to shout. He wanted to meet this *bubbe*, who was waiting for him somewhere among the gray-brick tenement buildings that towered up on both sides of the road. Narrow and tall with the sloping iron fire escapes clinging to their sides like a multiplying species of parasitic insect.

They turned a sharp, unexpected corner onto a smaller, quieter street, leaving the traffic behind. It was hot under the climbing sun and the asphalt of the sidewalk felt like it was bubbling under their feet, and Theo's head began to swim as he looked longingly across to where a group of shaven-headed children were holding hands and dancing with quick steps around a squirting fire hydrant, singing songs in a language he couldn't understand.

Abruptly, Theo's grandfather stopped. In front of them, a humpbacked old woman with a wart-covered face, partially concealed by a red kerchief, had parked a baby carriage across the sidewalk, and now she challenged them in a high-pitched screech to "buy, buy, buy," eagerly pulling back a frayed checkered cloth to reveal not a baby but a pot of steaming black-eyed beans.

"Not now, Rachel," said the old man impatiently and, stepping around the carriage, he pushed open the door of the tenement building behind her and, still holding Theo's hand, began climbing the steep winding stairs, which spiraled up and around above their heads into a shadowy gloom. It was cool inside, and in the semidarkness Theo felt as if they were going down and not up—into an underworld lit by small gaslights on the dreary landings. They flickered in the draft from a door that opened and closed somewhere above their heads, releasing a burst of voices speaking in that same strange language that he had heard outside on the street.

Up and up and around and around with the smell of urine and worse clinging to the crumbling lime-green plaster walls, until they were almost at the top. And then on the last-but-one landing, just as Theo thought that he was either going to be sick or collapse or both, his grandfather halted in front of a low door with a brass number 9 nailed slightly askew to the outside. He let go of Theo's hand and extracted a key from a pocket somewhere deep inside his coat and unlocked the door, ushering Theo inside.

Inside into another world, or that was how Theo thought about it afterward. He was suddenly hot again. It wasn't from the sun, which was no more than a dim glow through tiny, dirty windows shaped like portholes at the back of the long room that they had just entered, but rather from a large kitchen stove, halfway down the right wall, that was giving off heat like a furnace. Iron pots were boiling on the top, similar to Rachel's down below, and a woman with a blue scarf tied around her hair was using what was left of the surface to heat a pressing iron that hissed and spat like a live creature.

There were people everywhere. Theo thought he had never seen so many in one room, sitting in corners or in a tight group at one end of the long kitchen table. They were working at sewing machines or cutting bundles of cloth, which seemed to be piled up on all sides in a dazzling array of colors and shapes, including a few feet away from the door, where they were stacked high enough to make an improvised bed upon which a small boy half Theo's age lay fast asleep.

So many sensations he felt all at the same time: the smell of unfamiliar food, the stifling heat of the stove, hands touching him from all sides, and a cacophony of voices talking over each other in that same language he couldn't understand. He was excited and curious but not frightened, which surprised him afterward because he thought he should have been. Perhaps it was because he felt he belonged, but how could he, when everything was so alien? It made no sense to him then or later, when he often thought about this moment, turning it over in his mind.

A voice cut in, louder than the rest, telling the others in heavily accented English to "leave the boy alone, let him breathe, let me see my grandson."

They pulled back and there she was: his *bubbe*. Short and round—the opposite of his grandfather—with a yellowish face pockmarked and double-chinned under a halo of iron-gray curly hair, but transformed by enormous, wide-open, emerald-green eyes that seemed to drink him in and look straight down into his heart.

She put her hands on his head, pressing them slowly down over his ears and then, as if satisfied by what she found, drew him to a chair at the table, where he saw that there were different dishes already laid out on gleaming white porcelain plates. They were small and delicately made and all the colors of the rainbow. Standing over him like a sentinel, she watched him eat each one, telling him the names in halting English: pastries called *blintzes* with goat cheese inside that came from the blind dairyman on Hester Street, who kept his own animals out in Bronx Park; kraut and potato knishes; pickled tomatoes grown by his grandfather up on the roof—the best in all the Lower

East Side, better even than what the Italians produced and "nobody has green fingers like them"; and last but not least a sponge cake made with quince jam—quinces that were good, she said, but not as good as they used to be in the old country in the springtime, when she and her sisters were young and climbed the trees like squirrels and came home exhausted, with the precious fruit tied up inside their coats.

Theo ate with concentration, intoxicated by the variety of exquisite tastes he had never before experienced, and when he had finished, his grandmother called to the woman in the scarf to bring more: stew and beans from the pots on the stove. "It is cholent," she said, and made him repeat the word, pronouncing each syllable separately. "Jews have eaten it always. We cook it on Fridays so we can eat it hot on Shabbat."

"Shabbat?" he asked. "What's that?" He felt drowsy and more than a little nauseated. He had eaten too much already, and he looked longingly over at the sleeping boy in the corner, hoping he might join him on his bed of cloth. But he couldn't because he could see there were tears in his grandmother's beautiful eyes and he knew he'd said something wrong, but he did not know what it was.

It was his grandfather who came to the rescue. "It doesn't matter, Leah," he said gently, putting his hand on his wife's shoulder. "The boy will know these things in time, but it is us that he needs to understand now. Who we are, who he is. It is what we spoke of before."

The old woman sighed and nodded, and going over to Theo, she took his head again between her hands and kissed him once on the forehead and then retreated back toward the stove. And Theo's grandfather took off his coat and sat down on the other side of the table, fixing his pale-blue eyes on the boy, just as he had when Theo had first seen him, standing under the tree at the end of the street in the twilight.

"There's not much time," he said quietly. "Your father will be here soon."

"Why? How do you know?" Theo was afraid again now, but not of his grandfather. He feared what his father would do when he came, and whether he would bring the authorities with him to punish the old man and his wife. Theo didn't want that.

"He will know it was me who took you," said his grandfather simply. "And when he comes, you will leave and you will not be allowed to come back.

Perhaps you will never see us again. But you will remember. What is inside your head—that no one can change."

Theo nodded. He knew instinctively that his grandfather was right. He would never forget. Each moment, his eye and his brain were recording, selecting items for preservation: the stenciled gold of the inscriptions on the black Singer sewing machines, the cotton spools, the colors of the cloth, the smell and taste of the food so lovingly prepared, the faces and the bodies of his grandparents so much a part of him and yet so fleetingly known.

"What is your name?" asked his grandfather.

"Theo," he said, surprised. It shocked him that this man should be his grandfather and yet not know his name.

"Thee-o," repeated the old man slowly. "What kind of a name is that?"

"It's short for Theodore. Like the president. That's who Dad named me after. The one who killed the elephant."

"Which was a terrible thing," said his grandmother, vigorously shaking her head. "Devil's work."

"Quiet, woman!" said Theo's grandfather, raising his hand for silence but keeping his eyes on Theo. "We have no time. I told you that."

"And what is your last name?" he asked, returning to his questioning.

"Sterling. Like sterling silver. Dad says it's a solid name that people can rely on in business," Theo volunteered. It was a favorite saying of his father's, so often repeated that it had become like a family mantra.

"Solid, perhaps, but not true," said the old man. "Your name is not Sterling; it is Stern. Your father changed it because he denies who he is and who you are. He can do this for himself, but not for you. You have a right to know."

"What is Stern?" Theo felt confused again now, and anxious, and his voice was faint.

"It means *star* in our language, in Yiddish. It is a beautiful name—for the star that guides us. I am Yossif—Joseph Stern."

"Like Joseph, Jesus's father," said Theo, thinking of the bearded, kind-faced figure in the blue cloak and sandals that his mother put out beside the crib before Christmas with Mary and the baby. Up on the mantel in a miniature Bethlehem, before the shepherds and the kings who came after, each on their appointed day.

"No, like Joseph, Jacob's son, who was sold into slavery in Egypt and yet found his way to prosper and help his brothers, without ever forgetting who he was and where he came from. Perhaps one day you can be another Joseph," said the old man and smiled suddenly in that same unexpected way he had on the street when he had promised Theo an adventure. "Look," he said, reaching up and taking down an old battered photograph album from a shelf behind his head. "These are your ancestors. In Poland, where the winters are colder even than here and the goyim are cruel."

The old man slowly turned the pages, and Theo saw a succession of sepia faces. Men and women and children posed in their best clothes, looking trustfully forward into the camera lens. In one picture, there was a dog with a ribbon seated on a chair and a boy standing beside it dressed in a sailor suit, and there were several of a long wooden house with two smoking chimneys and people standing in front of it, lined up against a paling fence. They meant nothing to Theo and perhaps his grandfather sensed this, because his tone became more severe.

"They were killed. Not all of them, but most. This was my house—where I was born, and where my mother and father died," he said, pointing at the pictures.

"How did they die?" asked Theo in a whisper.

"Fire," said the old man, pronouncing the word as if it was a curse. "My parents tried to come out but the goyim would not let them. They burnt them alive and danced around the flames, singing songs. Everywhere they did this. Sometimes before, they would say, 'You can become Christian, be baptized, and live,' but the Jews refused. They had no choice: they had to be true to who they were. Because without that you are nothing, worse than nothing. Do you understand?"

Theo nodded even though he didn't understand and didn't want to. He was terrified now and wanted the adventure to end; he wanted his father to come and rescue him. And as if in response, a violent knocking began at the door and he could hear his father shouting, demanding to be let in.

"Quicker even than I thought," said the old man with a sigh, closing the book and replacing it on the shelf behind him.

The spell was broken. "Let him in, Leah," he told his wife. "What must be must be."

She opened the door and Theo's father crashed into the apartment, losing his balance and falling on the sleeping child in the corner, who promptly woke up and began to cry.

But immediately Theo's father was back on his feet and pulling Theo up from his seat with one hand, while his other fist was clenched, drawn back as if to hit the old man, who had remained in his chair throughout the commotion, just as immobile as he had been under the chestnut tree.

"How dare you! You had no right!" Theo's father spoke breathlessly. Theo had never seen him so angry.

Theo's grandfather briefly replied, but Theo couldn't understand what he was saying because he was speaking in that foreign language that he had heard earlier: a harsh jangle of sounds that made Theo even more scared. He clung to his father, burying his face in his shoulder.

"Speak English!" Theo's father shouted at the old man. "We aren't in Poland anymore, however much you'd like to think we are. And no, I won't take the boy and go. I'm not here to do your bidding."

But Theo's grandfather said nothing. Just stared blankly at his son, as if challenging him to do his worst. Behind him, Theo's grandmother had begun to cry, but her husband raised his hand again as if in warning, and she was quiet. Now, for the first time, Theo sensed the old man's true power: nobody in the whole room stirred or made a sound.

Theo could feel his father trembling, and it made him remember the Christmas before last when it had snowed so hard that the automobiles almost disappeared and he'd held on to his father so tightly as they'd pushed through the blizzard, coming back home from the store. It had been hot in the apartment, but he had had the same sense of an overpowering force field pressing against them.

Then, suddenly and unexpectedly, his father laughed and unclenched his fist, dropping his arm to his side, while keeping his other around Theo's shoulder.

"You old fool!" he said, spitting out the words to underline his contempt. "Thought you could take my son and make a Jew of him in a couple of hours! A few plates of herring and pickled onion and some cholent stew and he's yours for life. Is that it?"

Theo's grandfather shook his head but said nothing.

"No, even you aren't that stupid, are you? Jewish blood comes from the mother, not the father. Theo's a Catholic like his mother and there's nothing you can do to change that, however hard you try."

The old man nodded, an almost imperceptible movement, keeping his eyes fixed on his son.

"So why did you have to take him and put him through all this? What was the point?" Theo's father's voice rose as his anger threatened to get the better of him again.

"Because he's all we have, Leah and I," said Theo's grandfather quietly, framing each word with care. "No one here is our blood. And when we are gone, he will be the only one left to know. So I must tell him what you won't. Who we are, where we came from, who we left behind . . ."

"We! What about me? I know all that. I'm your son, aren't I?"

Theo thought he could hear an appeal in his father's voice, breaking out from behind his fury, but it had no effect on the old man.

"You're an apostate. A Jew who preys on his own people like a wolf in the night."

Theo could hear the venom in his grandfather's voice, coming from a place where there was no possibility of forgiveness.

"I'm not ashamed of what I do," said Theo's father, refusing to be cowed. "I work hard and try to get ahead because I believe in this country—it's my promised land. But you—you are here but not here. Living like animals, packed ten to a room with rats in the ceiling and garbage on the streets. Overflowing toilets on the landings. I know: I lived here long enough. And nothing has changed for you since you hauled your calico seabags up from Ellis Island. And nothing will because you won't let it. That's why I left."

Silence. The old man made no response, just stared through his son as if he weren't there. Theo felt his father's hand quivering on his shoulder, and then he lifted it and put it under Theo's chin, tipping his head up so that he could look into his eyes.

"Do you know why they treat me like this, son?" he asked. "Like I don't exist? Did they tell you that?"

Theo shook his head.

"Because I married your mother. That's why. I married a goy."

"A *goy*?"

"A Christian. Someone who is not a Jew. I married for love, not because one of their matchmakers had found me a woman. And for that they sat shiva for me. They covered their mirrors and swayed from side to side and muttered their crazy prayers, and at the end of seven days I was gone. Dead even to the woman who bore me," he said, looking over at his mother, who hid her head in her hands and started crying again.

"And now, now I am a ghost," he went on, raising his voice. "I am not here. I don't exist. None of this is happening."

Still with his arm around his son, Theo's father turned and pulled down a small wooden object shaped like a finger that was hanging by the doorpost. Theo hadn't noticed it until now. In his father's hand, he could see there was writing in strange letters on its side.

Theo's father held it for a moment and then very deliberately threw it on the ground, where it broke open, revealing some form of parchment.

With a cry, Theo's grandfather jumped up from his chair and, rounding the table, went down on the floor to gather the broken pieces together in his shaking hands. His son looked down on him with an expression Theo had never seen on his father's face before: despair and exultation, sorrow and contempt, all mixed up together in a rictus of extreme emotion.

"I'm no Jew and nor is my son," he said, spitting out the words. "We're Americans." And pushing Theo in front of him, he pulled open the door of the apartment and left without looking back.

They walked quickly, turning north when they reached Broadway and not pausing until Theo's father branched off to the left and went into Washington Square, where they sat down on a bench. Now they were back in familiar territory. His father often brought Theo here on Sunday afternoons to watch the chess hustlers play under the canopy of the oak trees, while the fountain sprayed its jets high in the center of the park, and sometimes a saxophone or trumpet player would send melancholy tunes winging on the air out through the arch toward Fifth Avenue, while his upturned hat lay on the ground in hope of recompense.

Theo's father would stand beside the tables, avidly following the players' moves, never tiring of seeing the hustlers getting the better of their social superiors; and then afterward, as they walked home, he would talk admiringly of how anyone could beat anyone in America because it was the land of the free (another of his favorite phrases) and the opposite of the country he had come from, where the common people were born into servitude and no one could get ahead unless they were born with a silver spoon in their mouth or saved or stole enough money to buy a steerage ticket on a boat to New York.

But now he was silent, gazing off into space and sometimes shaking his head, as if he were continuing the conversation he had just held with his unforgiving father.

"What was it you threw on the floor?" asked Theo. The events of the day had left him feeling traumatized, and he needed the reassurance of his father's voice.

"It was a mezuzah. The Torah—the Bible, I mean—instructs Jews to write the words of God on the gates and doorposts of their houses. The mezuzah is the container; the words are written inside."

"On the paper?"

Theo's father nodded. "I broke it because that's the only way I could get my father to react. I needed him to show some emotion, something to make me feel I exist. There's nothing worse than when your father looks through you like that. I won't ever do that to you. You understand that, don't you, son?" he asked, becoming emotional suddenly.

Theo nodded, frightened by his father's intensity.

"What did he say to you? Before I came?" Theo's father had his eyes fixed on his son's.

"That I'm not called Sterling. I'm Stern. Like a star. He showed me pictures," said Theo, becoming upset.

"What pictures?" his father pressed.

"Pictures of dead people," said Theo, his voice now no more than a whisper.

His father nodded, thinking. And then suddenly smiled, as if he'd made a decision. "You must forget," he said, snapping his fingers. "Forget all of it, like it was a bad dream. He will not bother you again, I promise. We have the future to think of now, not the past, yes?"

Theo nodded.

"Good. So you promise?"

Again, Theo nodded, and his father, obviously pleased, bent down and kissed him on his forehead. "You will be following in my footsteps at the factory before too long—Sterling and Son of New York City: Now that's got a good ring to it, hasn't it?"

Afterward, in the weeks that followed, Theo wished that he had asked his father more questions about his grandparents, but by then it was too late. He had agreed to a compact of silence, and he and his father never spoke of the kidnapping again.

2

ELENA

Theo could see his mother long before she saw him, a small figure dressed all in black standing out in the street, looking rapidly to right and left. Her dark eyes, which Theo had inherited, were weak and she needed thick glasses to read, but she would not wear them outside, whether through vanity or defiance, and distant objects were a blur.

"Run on ahead," Theo's father told him, pointing up the street. "She must be worried sick."

Theo was a fast runner, but now his legs held him back. He had longed for his mother when his grandfather took him, but now he wanted to avoid her unrestrained emotion and the inevitable interrogation that would follow once they were back inside. He had no intention or indeed capacity to simply forget his adventure as his father had instructed, but he also had a deep wish to keep what had happened to himself, to hug the experience close and keep it a secret.

His father understood none of this. "What's wrong with you?" he said impatiently. And when Theo didn't respond, he took hold of his son's hand and, quickening his pace, force-marched him along the sidewalk toward their apartment building. Theo stiffened even more: the physical sensation of being pulled along reminded him of how he had felt when his grandfather had taken him through the unfamiliar eastside streets earlier in the day, and he suddenly felt an intense, aching sense of loss that brought hot tears to his eyes.

Now Elena saw them. And with a cry she hurried down the street, catching Theo and enfolding him in her arms. He smelled her familiar scent—gardenia flowers and soap—and felt her warmth, and his legs gave way beneath him.

His parents were arguing. Lying on his bed, Theo could hear their voices in the next room through the half-open door. He listened, not moving, alarmed but also fascinated, because they never quarreled. In the abridged story Theo's father often told of his life, the accidental meeting with his future wife in Penn Station in the cold winter of 1914 was the changing moment: the day that he had first felt that sense of manifest personal destiny that had never left him since.

Theo knew the story by heart. In the first chapter, his mother, the young Elena, had arrived in New York alone and exhausted and almost penniless, on the last leg of a journey that had begun in Guadalajara a week before. She had, written down, an address of an uncle by marriage whom she'd never met, and she had hoped against hope as the train wound its way through the green hills and valleys of this new alien country that he would be there to meet her, but instead there was no one. Just the hard black platform and a great bustle of people coming and going all around her. She was invisible, stranded beside her suitcase, which contained everything she owned in the world: three dresses; her missal, Bible, and rosary; a silver hairbrush; and several faded photographs of her murdered parents.

A porter took pity on her, or perhaps just wanted to move her out of the way, and carried her bag over to a stone bench, where she sat, bewildered by the cacophony all around her: chatter and loudspeaker announcements echoing off the mighty granite walls in a language that she found hard to understand. She had learned English at school in Mexico, but it had been badly taught, and she had not applied herself to her lessons as she should have done.

She was so small and the station was so grand and vast. She had never seen anything like the girth of the huge Corinthian columns rising so gracefully up to the arching glass-and-steel roof that let in the bright November sun in a constant play of light and shadow. It dumbfounded her, this cathedral with no God. Its grand impersonal immensity dried up what hope she had left, and she bowed her head and began to cry.

Which was how Michael found her. He was hurrying across the concourse to catch his train, and the crowd parted for a moment just as she looked up, catching his eye. In a flash, he took in her perfectly shaped oval face, ghostly pale beneath a pathetically small cloche hat, dented from travel, that had drooped over to the side of her head, revealing the unruly mass of her jet-black hair, which was escaping from its pins and beginning to fall down over her shoulders. Hair that matched her luminous dark eyes, wet with tears and wide with fear of the unknown.

He wanted to stop her pain. Needed to, as if it was his own. He could feel it—a band tightening across his chest as he pushed past the people in his way, deaf to their angry protests. And when he got to her, he instinctively went down on one knee to offer her his handkerchief, reducing himself to her height while he told her over and over again that everything was going to be all right and that she didn't need to worry anymore. Until she finally stopped crying and began to laugh instead at the crazy hand signals he'd resorted to, to try to make her understand. And her smile was like sunlight emerging from behind clouds at the end of a rainstorm. Fresh with the promise of a new beginning.

Afterward, Michael called their meeting love at first sight, and within a month they were married and set up in an apartment of their own, impervious to the anger of his estranged parents sitting shiva for him in their sweatshop tenement over by the East River.

He said that he had been hit with a bolt of lightning that day in the station, and the electrical charge stayed with him, convincing him that he was lucky, that they were lucky, destined for some kind of golden greatness. In a stroke of supreme irony, he turned his back on the chosen people because he felt chosen himself. By whom, he couldn't say. Not God, not Christ—it was a source of lasting sadness to Elena that her husband showed no interest in her religion. America, perhaps—Michael Sterling was not a religious man, but he had an unswerving faith in his adopted country.

They never argued, because they had no reason to argue. Michael deferred to his wife in the house, treating her like a queen, and she didn't interfere in any way with his business other than to praise him for his success.

Sometimes he called her "his little flower," referring to her beauty but also to her fragility. Something had broken inside Elena when she left Mexico. Concealed behind a door in the hacienda, she had heard her parents cry out and die, and in New York she couldn't truly heal. The migraines she regularly endured—*las jaquecas*, as she called them—were a symptom of her broken state, and Theo's difficult birth had exacerbated her ill health. She lacked energy and rarely went out except to the Spanish church by Gramercy Park, and this suited her husband well. He had no reason to be jealous and he felt she was safe at home, surrounded by the best that money could buy: a Kelvinator refrigerator, a Westinghouse electric range, and stylish French furniture from Bloomingdale's.

When he came home from work bearing roses or other small presents, she would take his coat and listen to the story of his day, praising and sympathizing with small clucking noises where appropriate. And later she would cook him wonderful Mexican meals with ingredients purchased at the local market that didn't include pork or shellfish, and agree with him when he praised the government's laissez-faire economic policies and heaped invective on the Communist Party and the unions that wanted to stop hardworking citizens like Michael Sterling from getting ahead. Elena hated the Communists even more than her husband. The godless bandits who had killed her parents had called themselves Socialists, which amounted to the same thing—a flag of left-wing convenience to justify their reign of terror.

Oftentimes, during these conversations, she would turn to Theo sitting between his parents at the table and tell him to listen closely so that he wouldn't miss the pearls of wisdom his father was delivering. And Michael would glow, preening in the candlelight like a well-fed peacock.

They were perfectly happy with each other, but their happiness was built on a fundamental lack of connection between them. Michael knew nothing of his wife's alternately vengeful and merciful God, who was as real to her as his factory was to him, and she had no idea of the struggle that he had gone through to climb from poverty to comparative wealth, stepping down hard on the heads and shoulders of his people to get there.

Elena had never visited her husband's factory, and he had been to her church only once—for Theo's baptism, when they had stood together, proud parents by the font, as Father Juan named the baby, with Michael sure that he was Theodore for the great president who perfectly embodied the unbridled energy of his adopted country, and Elena equally convinced that her son was named after the semi-mythical Saint Theodore of Amasea, who slew a dragon and was martyred in a furnace for his beliefs somewhere near the Black Sea early in the fourth century. The saint's icon, purchased through a mail-order catalog, had pride of place in the elaborate shrine Elena kept in her room, lit by sweet-smelling votive candles, and he was as real to her as the twenty-sixth president was to her husband.

Michael knew no more than a few words of Spanish—yes, no, and a few mispronounced endearments—and she had never heard him speak Yiddish. And their son did not bridge the gap between them. Instead, he shuttled backward and forward between their two separate worlds, speaking Spanish with his mother and English with his father, listening to her endless stories of Mexico and talking baseball and Babe Ruth with his father, who had promised to take him to Yankee Stadium to see the great man on the day Theo turned thirteen and became a man (Michael didn't let on, but he had in mind a kind of all-American secular bar mitzvah).

Michael and Elena lived in a perfectly separated alignment like two heavenly bodies orbiting each other with an equal gravity. They loved each other with a happy superficiality, and so when conflict arose, as it had now, they lacked the tools to find resolution and instead crashed against each other until they were spent.

"You do this. You. It is your fault. You see him standing there night after night and you do nothing. Nada!" Elena shouted, her voice shrill and angry and her always heavily accented English becoming confused as it often did when she was excited.

"I didn't know he would do that. How could I?" Michael was on the defensive, but Theo could also sense exasperation in his voice.

"It's your job. You are the father."

"I brought Theo back, didn't I?"

"No, you did nothing. Nada!" she spat out the word again. "It was San Antonio who brought him back. I knelt and I prayed and I begged and at last the holy saint heard me. Praise be to God! But next time we won't be so lucky. Next time, that old devil will take him away. I know it. To Chicago or Buffalo: somewhere you won't find him. And I will never see my son again. *¡Nunca jamás!*" She was crying now, almost hysterical.

"He won't. He can't. He's got no money. You should see the way they are living over there. Worse than when I was a boy."

"You see—you are thinking of them, of being the good son again. Your heart is with them. I know it."

"No, Elena, it isn't. You know it isn't. They are dead to me and I to them. You and Theo are my family. All that I need. You know that."

There was silence then, just the sound of crying, and looking through the half-open door of his bedroom, Theo could see his father holding his mother by the shoulders as she shook, her body convulsed with sobs. She seemed to be clinging to her husband but also beating against his chest with her fists. The spectacle frightened Theo, and he backed away into his room.

And when his mother came in later and stood by the bed, he pretended to be asleep, ignoring her soft repetitions of his name until she gave up and left. But afterward, he regretted letting her go. He felt alone and panicky. Was she right? Would his grandfather come again and take him away, for good this time? To Chicago and Al Capone—the two were forever associated in Theo's mind since reading in his father's newspaper about the Saint Valentine's Day Massacre back in February. The photograph of the dead men lying with their limbs splayed out at odd angles beneath the bullet-ridden brick wall of the anonymous garage had given him nightmares for days afterward.

He tried not to think about Chicago; instead, he imagined himself Robinson Crusoe counting his stores or King Arthur naming his knights, going around the Round Table once, twice, three times. But it was useless. He couldn't sleep. The pale moon shone balefully through a gap in the drapes and the mahogany clock ticked away the hours on the mantel, until finally he fell into a half-waking dream in which he was back on the street to which his grandfather had taken him. Just as before, the shaven-headed children were there, skipping and singing the same song in their strange language, and his grandfather was pulling him along the sidewalk past the beggars and peddlers to where the old woman, Rachel, was waiting with her perambulator. "Buy, buy, hot and fresh!" she cried, but this time Theo's grandfather didn't step around her. Instead, he stopped, pushing Theo forward as she pulled back the checkered cloth with her bony hand, and he found himself staring down not at black-eyed beans but at himself, trussed up and unable to escape.

On Sunday, Theo went with his mother—just as he always did—to the Spanish church behind Gramercy Park. Elena held his hand tight, darting her head from side to side as they walked down Park Avenue. Dressed in black from head to toe and wearing a mantilla veil, she stood out from the bejeweled ladies in ermine coats and high-heeled shoes, sauntering past the glamorous shopfronts with their beaux, but she had no eyes for them, only for the tall prophet-like figure of whom she was so terrified. But there was no sign of him—just as there hadn't been in the three days since he took Theo.

The priest, Father Juan Carlos, was Elena's best friend in New York—not that she would ever have thought of him in that way. He was her father confessor and spiritual guide, the appointed intermediary between her and her God. But he also understood and liked her, and his clerical robes enabled her to relax and speak her mind when she was with him in a way that she never could with her husband.

In his early forties, he had a lean, ascetic face topped with a mass of unruly black curly hair that Elena would secretly have liked to cut and comb: a wish that she would never have admitted to anyone, least of all in the confessional. If it hadn't been for his lopsided nose, broken in a schoolboy fight, he would have been handsome.

He had beautiful hands, and Theo remembered how when he was young, the priest used to kneel down beside him after Mass with his cassock spread out across the floor like a pool of black water and interlace his long, tapering fingers to become the church, before he raised the index fingers in an arch for the steeple and opened his thumbs to reveal the people inside. The simple rhyme had delighted Theo, and he had always responded by clapping his own hands and asking the priest to "do it again; do it again" until his mother intervened and told him that Father Juan had more important things to do than play games with children who should mind their manners.

Theo had gotten older and the games had stopped, but not just for that reason. In the last two years, Father Juan had lost his sunny disposition, becoming careworn and preoccupied. His infectious laugh was rarely heard, and his hazel eyes had a haunted look, as if they were forever straining to catch a glimpse of a far-off place that remained always just out of sight.

In the presbytery where the priest and the most loyal members of his congregation drank thick black coffee out of tiny porcelain cups after Mass and munched sweet biscuits baked lovingly by Elena in her Westinghouse oven, they talked of nothing but Mexico. They were all exiles in a foreign land, and America only interested them to the extent of its government's rumored complicity in the brutal war being fought in the Jalisco highlands between the Mexican army and the Cristeros, the Catholic peasantry who had risen up in rebellion against President Calles's ruthless attempt to suppress their religion and secularize the country.

In a repeat of the violence of 1914 when Elena had lost her parents, fleeing across the open fields from the monstrous spectacle of her burning home, Catholics were being murdered and driven out of the country, and Father Juan regularly hosted refugees as they passed through New York. Many had harrowing stories to tell, and the parishioners of the Church of the Sacred Heart, desperate for news from home, flocked to hear them.

This Sunday, there was an even larger turnout in the church than usual. A well-known Catholic businessman had recently arrived from Mexico City and was touring the United States on behalf of the Knights of Columbus, raising money for the rebels.

Father Juan introduced him as Don Andrés, and he spoke to the congregation at the end of Mass from the lectern at the side of the altar, speaking Spanish fluently but with a trace of a foreign accent.

Don Andrés was older than Theo's father—he had to be, because he was silver-haired with a creased, weather-beaten face, giving him the look of someone who had lived in many different climates, and yet to Theo he seemed strong, with a wiry athletic build and an air of relaxed confidence. He looked nothing like anyone whom Theo had ever seen at the church—tall, pale, blue-eyed, and immaculately dressed in a morning suit, which was obviously tailor-made because it fit him so perfectly. Afterward, when looking back on this first meeting, Theo remembered that his strongest first impression of Don Andrés was that he looked like a man used to getting his own way.

He spoke well—he knew how to hold his audience's attention. He told them that Mexico had become the belly of the beast, that churches were being used as stables or even makeshift cinemas, that holy statues were used for target practice and altars for dining tables. Nothing was sacred, not even the lives of the priests.

"Have any of you heard of Father Miguel Pro?" Don Andrés asked, looking out at the congregation.

Here and there, a few people began raising their hands, and Theo felt a rising tension in the church, running like an electrical charge through the packed pews, reaching his mother. She said nothing, but he could see how she had become rigid and was twisting her hands in her lap. The compulsive movement frightened him and he put his hand on her elbow to stop her, but she pulled her arm away.

"Good," said Don Andrés, nodding his head. "Well, then you will know he was a righteous man, possessed of an extraordinary courage. For two years he lived in hiding in Mexico City, visiting the houses of the faithful, disguised in workmen's overalls or beggars' rags, to marry and baptize, give communion and hear confessions. Sometimes, he even dressed as a policeman and slipped unnoticed into the prisons to bring the blessed sacrament to those condemned to die. Priests like Father Miguel are keeping the faith alive in Mexico, and that is why President Calles hates them so much.

"Many times, Father Miguel's superiors advised him to flee, but always he refused, and the Virgin of Guadalupe watched over him. But in the end even she could not protect him, and he was arrested."

He paused, and a woman in the front pew, clearly agitated, stood up, holding out her shaking hands: "What happened to him, señor? Please—for the love of God—tell us what happened!"

"The *federales* shot him like a dog in the prison yard. He refused the blindfold; he showed no fear. He blessed his executioners before they raised their rifles, holding his crucifix in one hand and his rosary in the other, and at the last moment, just before they fired, he shouted: '*Viva Cristo Rey.*'"

As one, the congregation leaped to their feet and repeated the rallying cry of the Cristero rebels, looking up past Don Andrés to the sanctuary where their life-size Savior hung bleeding on a huge wooden cross suspended on two iron chains from the chancel ceiling. Theo had always found the cross terrifying, but he had succeeded over the years in shutting it out of his consciousness by refusing to lift his gaze to its level. Now, involuntarily, he looked up at the crucified Christ and felt a jolt of fear and revulsion, intensified by the fierce grip with which his mother had suddenly taken hold of his hand as she pulled him up to stand beside her. Turning toward her, Theo was horrified to see that she was openly crying, with thick sobs shaking her small body.

Slowly the congregation resumed their seats, waiting for Don Andrés to continue. But instead of doing that, he bent down and opened a small black doctor's bag that was on the ground near his feet. Theo hadn't noticed it until now, and he was surprised by how scuffed and worn it was—a contrast to its owner's elegant clothes. Carefully, Don Andrés took out a brown manila folder from which he extracted a photograph.

"President Calles had copies of this made to frighten the faithful. But now he wants to get them back because he's realized that the picture of Father Miguel inspires our soldiers and makes them fight harder," said Don Andrés, coming out from behind the lectern and walking into the central aisle of the nave.

There were gasps as he passed slowly up and down between the pews, holding up the photograph for everyone to see. Turning, almost against his will, Theo saw a thin young man in a cheap suit standing in front of a wooden fence with his arms stretched out on either side, resting on two bullet-riddled dummy figures that had clearly been used for target practice by trainee firing squads. Like a clothed Christ, Theo thought.

At that moment, death seemed more real to Theo than it had ever been before. The certainty of it was monstrous and yet inescapable, and he hated his mother and this stranger for making it so tangible. He longed to be gone, to be out in the fresh morning air away from the cloying smell of incense and cut flowers, but he was trapped in the pew with no possibility of escape.

And Don Andrés had not finished. Back at the lectern, he reached down into his bag again and held up a dirty piece of cloth. "They used this at the morgue to clean Father Miguel's body, and afterward an attendant gave it to one of the faithful. This is Father Miguel's blood," he said, raising his voice for the first time and pointing to several dark reddish-brown stains on the material. "Blood shed for the church, shed for Cristo Rey. Martyr's blood!"

A collective sigh passed through the congregation as they gazed at this new relic, real in a way in which the thumb of a lesser-known sixteenth-century Spanish saint kept behind the altar and brought out on holy days was not. Theo wondered if some of them were looking at the bloody cloth not with horror but with cupidity, hoping that Don Andrés might give it to their church and so immeasurably raise its prestige in the city, but such thoughts were clearly far from his mother's mind. Beside him, she continued to weep, staring up at Don Andrés and turning to follow him with her eyes when he left the church.

Theo was embarrassed. He was sure that everyone could see the exhibition she was making of herself, and of him. He wanted to say something, but he thought she might shout at him if he did, and that would make their humiliation worse, so he remained silent, wishing himself anywhere but where he was.

Afterward, in the presbytery, Theo was surprised to hear Father Juan and Don Andrés talking in English. They both spoke with an accent, but Theo detected at once that, unlike the priest, Don Andrés was a native speaker. He didn't sound like an American, and so Theo thought logically that he had to be British, particularly as Father Juan kept addressing him as Sir Andrew. *Sir* was the same title that all the characters had in *The Boy's King Arthur*—currently Theo's favorite book, which he had already read three times start to finish. Bad and good, they were all called *Sir*—except the king, of course, and Merlin.

"Is he a knight?" Theo asked his mother in Spanish, leaning close to her and speaking in a whisper.

But at the moment he spoke, there happened to be a pause in the general conversation, and Don Andrés, clearly possessed of razor-like hearing, answered Theo's question himself, speaking Spanish too.

"Yes, but without the armor, I'm afraid," he said, smiling. "Do you like knights, young man?"

Theo nodded, his face hot with embarrassment. Father Juan and the parishioners of the Sacred Heart were kind, but they never included him in their conversations about politics and religion. And now here they all were, suddenly focused on him, craning their necks to hear what their illustrious visitor might be saying to Elena's young son.

"And who is your favorite knight?" asked Don Andrés, persisting with his questions, notwithstanding Theo's evident discomfort.

"Answer the gentleman," said Elena.

Theo could hear the urgency in his mother's voice. He knew she would think it a stain on the family honor if he was rude to such an important guest in front of Father Juan and the church elders, but he remained tongue-tied until she pushed an invisible finger into the small of his back, forcing out the answer, "Lancelot," with a sudden expulsion of held-in breath.

"Lancelot, eh?" said Don Andrés, stroking his chin. "Even though he betrayed his king?"

Theo nodded. His eyes were held unwillingly by the curious stare of the Englishman, who seemed a different person now to the impassioned speaker in the church. There was an irony in his voice and an amused expression that hadn't been there before. And Theo felt, too, the strangeness of the moment—that he and this foreigner should be discussing a subject about which his mother and the others in the room were completely ignorant.

Abruptly, Don Andrés laughed. "I may not approve of your choice, but I can understand it," he said. "Lancelot was certainly glamorous, even if he was disloyal. He was the Douglas Fairbanks of Arthur's court. No wonder the queen couldn't resist him. You have a clever son, señora . . ."

Don Andrés paused, looking expectantly at Elena, whose turn it was to blush as Father Juan stepped in to introduce her.

"Señora Sterling," he said. "And her son is Theo. You're right that he is a clever boy. I can vouch for that."

The Englishman smiled at Theo and then returned his attention to Elena, bowing slightly to acknowledge the introduction.

"Sterling," he said, repeating the name. "A good name, strong and sound like my country's currency, but not Spanish. You are married to an American, señora?"

Elena swallowed, twisting her hands nervously again like she'd been doing in the church. Ever since they'd arrived in the presbytery, Theo had been conscious of his mother's suppressed excitement. Several times he'd thought she was going to speak, but now—presented with the opportunity—her natural shyness got the better of her and all she could do was nod.

"Elena came here from Mexico in 1914. Her parents were killed by the Socialists," said Father Juan, coming to her rescue.

Don Andrés grimaced, but he didn't take his eyes off Elena. "I am so sorry," he said. "Have you ever been back?"

Elena shook her head. She was rigid—an outward sign of the effort she was making to control her emotions.

"That must be very hard," said Don Andrés, and Theo had the curious sense that the Englishman was taking in and experiencing his mother's pain: an intimacy that he instinctively resented but was powerless to prevent.

Perhaps his sympathy gave Elena courage, because she suddenly started to talk, her words tumbling out in a flurry of disconnected sentences: "I met the priest. The one they killed," she said. "I thought I recognized his name, and then I knew it was him in the photograph. He hadn't changed, even though he was much younger, a novice, when he came to our house. There was a Jesuit symposium in the town and everyone took in someone. He was our guest. My father sent me to his room in the evening with a bowl of hot water, and he was standing by the open window looking out at the sunset over the hills with his hands raised, palms out. Like this," she said, demonstrating. "And I was ashamed of interrupting him at such a moment. I put down the water and backed away. I was going to leave, but then he turned and beckoned me over, and his smile . . ."

Elena stopped, overcome by the intensity of her recollection, but Don Andrés urged her to go on. He was sitting forward in his chair with his eyes fastened on her, and it felt to Theo as if he and Father Juan and the parishioners had somehow receded so that his mother and the Englishman were now the only people in the room.

"What about his smile?" Don Andrés asked.

"It was radiant. Coming from somewhere deep inside, from his soul. Somewhere I can't reach, however hard I try . . ." said Elena, searching for the right words. "I went and stood beside him, and we watched the last red arc of the sun sink down out of sight, and it was the most beautiful thing I'd ever seen, even though I'd seen it a hundred times before. And then he said it."

"What?"

"'Praise him!'"

Don Andrés gazed intently at Elena. It was as if he was holding his breath until he sighed, as if letting go.

"Thank you," he said. "Thank you for telling me that. I only met Father Miguel once, but I had the same impression as you. He knew God. It would have been what gave him such strength at the end. Here," he said, reaching down into the bag by his feet and extracting the manila folder containing the photograph he had displayed in the church. "I would like you to have this, señora."

Elena flushed, clearly embarrassed. "I couldn't," she said. Her voice was quiet now, barely audible, as if she was shocked and embarrassed by how much she had said and by how much attention she'd drawn to herself.

But Don Andrés wouldn't take no for an answer. "I insist," he said, getting up and putting the folder in her hands. "Father Miguel would have wanted you to have it. And don't worry. I have several other copies."

Resuming his seat, Don Andrés looked around at Father Juan and the silent parishioners and smiled. It felt to Theo as if the Englishman had gone away somewhere with his mother and had now returned, smugly pleased with the experience, and the thought infuriated him, blocking out any other response he might have had to her moving description of her long-ago meeting with the dead priest.

What right does he have to talk to her like that? he said to himself, before the next thought came unbidden into his mind: She encouraged it. It's her fault even more than his.

He clenched his fists and swallowed hard, straining to control his anger, but no one was watching. Their focus was on Don Andrés, who was speaking again in that same authoritative voice he'd used to such effect in the church. "Make no mistake, my friends," he said. "President Calles and his henchmen are servants of the Devil. Who else would kill a saintly man like Father Miguel in cold blood? This battle being fought now in Mexico is a struggle between good and evil, and it is our Christian duty to support the priests and the Cristeros in every way we can, even from afar. We can all be knights," he said, glancing back at Theo with a sudden disarming smile, "Knights of Columbus standing together behind Cristo Rey."

Everyone in the room called out their agreement. This is what they had come to hear. The Englishman's conversation with Theo's mother was now a forgotten interlude as they took out their money to give generously to the cause that was so dear to their hearts.

Outside, Theo and Elena had reached the other side of Gramercy Park when she realized that she had forgotten the tin in which she had brought the biscuits.

Because she was thinking about Don Andrés! thought Theo, looking down at the manila folder in his mother's hand, but he agreed to go back, leaving her sitting on a bench under an ancient elm tree whose branches twisted out from inside the locked gates of the park and over the sidewalk.

At the presbytery, he passed two parishioners who were leaving through the front entrance, and then stopped dead in his tracks in the narrow hallway. On the other side of the half-open door, Don Andrés was talking in English:

"There is a Raphael Madonna in the National Gallery in London near where I live that reminds me of her—the same quiet reserve and beauty, the same knowledge of death and pain, and yet transcending that, an inner certainty of faith that can't be broken—the same quality that she recognized in Father Miguel all those years ago. What a coincidence—that she should have known him! I wish I could show you the painting, Father. You would know what I mean. She . . ."

Theo turned and ran out the door. He couldn't stand to hear any more. He was angry, but ashamed, too, in a way that he couldn't understand. He'd heard his father speak of his mother's beauty countless times, but this was different. The Englishman's praise made Theo think of her in a way he never had before. It was as if a window had opened in his mind on something ugly and dangerous, and he knew even as he ran that running would make no difference, because the window could not now be closed.

He stopped at the corner of the park, trying to compose himself and prepare a lie to explain why he had come back empty-handed, but he needn't have worried. His mother didn't seem to care. Talking about the past seemed to have taken a weight off her shoulders, and she insisted they take the bus home as a treat, climbing up to the top floor of the double-decker so that they could look down on the bustle of Fifth Avenue. "I'm proud of you," she said, using her fingers to comb Theo's hair—a habit she had when she wanted to convey something important to him. "Father Juan knows you are clever, but you heard how Don Andrés saw it too. Fancy that only he and you had read about those British knights! Did you see how Señora Castaneda was looking daggers at me? And well she might: her Franco can barely spell, let alone read a book."

Theo pulled away, unable to contain his irritation.

"What's wrong?" she asked.

"I don't know. I didn't like him."

"Why not? I don't understand."

"I told you I don't know," he said, flattening his face against the window. There was no way he could ever tell his mother what he had heard Don Andrés saying about her in the presbytery, but he resented that he had to keep it a secret. She'd thrust herself forward to gain the Englishman's attention. She ought to be ashamed of herself, not sounding so exuberant.

"You don't know because there's no reason for it," she said angrily. "He is a good man, trying to help my country, a man of God. You say these things to make me unhappy. I don't know why I deserve it."

Theo could hear his mother beginning to cry again and his anger evaporated, just as it always did when she became upset. Now he wished he could take his words back, but a barrier had come between them that he did not know how to overcome.

Elena took a handkerchief out of her bag and blew her nose. And they passed the rest of the journey in uneasy silence.

3

COACH EAMES

The experiences of those tumultuous few days that had begun with the walk across the city with his grandfather and ended in Gramercy Park with his mother had a profound effect on Theo, but not one that was visible to the outside world, because he did not speak about them to anyone. Beneath the cloak of silence, however, his reactions to the events in the tenement and those at the presbytery were very different. He longed to forget the intense connection he'd witnessed between his mother and Don Andrés, and the Englishman's words of admiration he'd overheard behind the door, but however hard he tried to bury his memory of what had happened, it still kept creeping back into his consciousness, filling him with a clinging sense of unease that felt like shame.

It made no sense because he had done nothing wrong. His only cause for guilt was that he had broken his promise to his father to forget his grandparents. Just as hard as he worked to consign Don Andrés to oblivion, he hoarded his memories of the Lower East Side, and the effort caused him not even a twinge of remorse. In bed at night, he took them out and examined them one by one, as if they were treasures: the hot, stuffy room; the photographs of another country in the old, battered book; his grandmother's hands on his head. Touching his own hand under the coverlet, he felt the tight clasp of his grandfather's calloused palm, and closing his eyes, he recalled the power of the old man reaching deep down into him, as if in search of his soul.

It was not necessarily a power of good. He understood that, taking just as much care to remember what his father had told him about the reasons he had become estranged from his parents. That, too, was part of his whole experience of that day, which had been his grandfather's gift to him. *"Perhaps you will never see us again. But you will remember. What is inside your head—that no one can change."* In the darkness, he whispered the old man's words aloud, committing them to memory, because a sixth sense told him that they were true and that his grandparents had gone from his life.

Weeks passed, and however hard he looked, peering into the shadows, there were no tall figures waiting in the evening twilight at the end of the street. He had no way of knowing then or later whether his father had taken steps to keep his grandfather away, or whether such measures had proved unnecessary because the old man had chosen not to return, having accomplished in that one day all that he had set out to do, leaving the seed he had planted to germinate in his grandson's head and heart.

There were a thousand questions Theo would have liked to ask his father about the Jewish world he'd glimpsed that day, but the promise he'd made in Washington Square held him back, and he avoided the subject with his mother, too, because he knew how much it upset her. He was guarded with her now, watching his words. The secret of what he had heard at the presbytery door weighed upon him, keeping them apart.

Elena, too, said nothing more to her son about *el secuestro*, the kidnapping—her word for what had happened—hoping that he would forget. But with her husband it was different. She was insistent that they should move. Only that way could she regain her peace of mind, she told him—with no trail left behind for his crazy, wicked father to follow.

Michael liked their home, but he didn't like his wife's distress. The tears in her eyes were irreconcilable with happiness and success—his vision of where they should be. And so he set to work and found a bigger apartment close to Union Square, this time on the ground floor with a patch of garden at the back. The rent was almost twice as much as before, but it was worth it to see the immediate change in Elena.

She loved the garden. It didn't matter that it was practically the size of a postage stamp and that the high roofs of adjacent buildings meant that it got only a few hours of sunshine each day. The garden's best feature was an old apple tree with a twisted, gnarled trunk that had survived against the odds amid the urban sprawl, and there was enough shade beneath it for two small chairs and a table where Elena could sit and drink coffee, overlooked by innumerable envious neighbors. To her delight, a pair of Baltimore orioles soon took up residence in the high branches, and she would hush Theo so they could listen to the male's flutelike song and watch for the flash of its bright-orange markings as it flew out to forage in the bird feeder that she kept stocked with cherries and grapes.

As the summer went on and fledglings were born, Elena became terrified that a predator would find the nest, and Theo would often catch his mother looking anxiously up into the canopy of the tree. Sometimes, catching sight of danger through the open window, she would run out into the garden, waving a brush or even on one occasion a frying pan to frighten away a squirrel or one of the mangy neighborhood cats that prowled the roofs and often kept Theo awake at night with their wild caterwauling.

The fragility of the birds and their young unsettled Theo, although it was really his mother's love for them that he found upsetting. He did not want her to be hurt, but at the same time he resented that she should allow herself to become so vulnerable. As the months passed, he longed for the ordeal of her anxiety to be over, and it was a relief when one morning she told him they were gone.

But he was unprepared for her happiness. "I saw them fly away," she told him. "I woke up early. I don't know why. And went to the window and it was as if they had waited for me." She smiled, taking his hand. "And in three weeks, perhaps less, they will be home."

"Home?"

"Yes, in Mexico. I loved the orioles when I was a girl. They came in September—I thought it was always on the same day, although of course it wasn't. The air would be suddenly filled with their song, and I'd lie on the ground out in my father's coffee plantation under the Inga trees, looking up to listen. I thought it was the music of heaven."

She was silent, and Theo sensed his mother's yearning for her homeland. "Can we go there?" he asked, embracing the sudden unexpected connection he'd felt spring up between them. "For a visit?"

"*Tal vez*—perhaps," she said, but her eyes were full of tears, and he knew she did not believe she would ever return.

After the orioles left, Theo started at a new school. It was the final installment of Elena's determination to leave their old life behind, but unlike the house move, it was not a success, or at least not initially.

Father Juan and Don Andrés had been quite right that Theo was clever, but it wasn't an attribute that won him any friends among his new classmates, who had known each other through grade school and were suspicious of all new arrivals, particularly when they spoke fluent Spanish and knew all the battles of the Revolutionary War and their dates.

They asked him about his weird name, and when he told them that he'd been called it after Theodore Roosevelt, they agreed he was putting on airs and needed taking down a peg or two.

And it got worse in class when Theo put his hand up to answer the teachers' questions.

"Correct! It seems the Good Lord has chosen to cast a pearl among the swine this semester," said Monsieur Perrin, the French teacher known throughout the school, including to the other masters, as Pompous Perrin or Old Pompo. The nickname had been cruelly bestowed on him by the class of 1912 and had stuck ever since. Perrin knew about it and was fully aware that the boys were laughing at him when his back was turned, and Theo's cleverness presented a rare opportunity to get back at his tormentors.

His method was simple but effective. He would ask the stupidest of his students to answer difficult questions, usually involving irregular verbs, and then, after making a great show of sighing and shaking his head, would turn wearily to Theo at the front of the class. "Please put us out of our misery, Mr. Sterling. Our friend, Mr. Binns, wouldn't know the answer even if it was staring at him on a plate. Like the head of John the Baptist!"

It didn't matter that Theo had done nothing to cause this serial humiliation of his classmates; he still got the blame for it. Expertly fired spitballs hit his cheeks or neck as soon as the teacher's back was turned, and glue was smeared on his chair. But the class's chief bullies, cousins called Billy and Paddy O'Donnell, who excelled on the football field but at little else, decided that such petty revenge was not enough.

On the chosen day, they lay in wait for Theo at the lunch break—the best opportunity for attack, as all the teachers were eating too—and set upon him as he went to his locker to get his books.

Without warning, Theo felt himself violently pushed from behind and fell over. The older O'Donnell, Billy, aimed a kick at Theo's side but only half connected as his foot scuffed over the books that had fallen out of Theo's hand. Acting on instinct, Theo rolled away and got up. He felt a hand claw at his shoulder and heard the material of his jacket ripping as he took off down the corridor and out onto the playground.

His pursuers were right behind him as he spun his head desperately from side to side, searching for an escape route. The school gate was locked, and everywhere there were walls, doors, more walls. Except back the way he had come. He stopped and turned, letting the boys get close, and then at the last moment sidestepped, evading their outstretched flailing arms as he ran back through the main hall, down the steps, and out onto the athletic ground.

He crossed the cinder track that encircled the playing fields and then headed out onto the muddy grass, where he twice almost slipped. Now he could hear only one of the boys behind him and, looking to his right, he saw that Billy was running across to the far gate behind the goalposts to cut him off. He was going to get there first, and then Theo would be trapped. Billy saw the look of panic on Theo's face and laughed, drawing his finger across his throat with a theatrical gesture.

Theo veered to his left, running toward the athletic pavilion, a whitewashed wooden structure with a black-creosoted, pitched roof where equipment was kept and the scorer turned the numbers on match days. But this was no refuge. The pavilion had windows but no door, and inside there would be no one to help him. What a fool he'd been to run to the loneliest place on the school grounds, he thought hopelessly as he reached the other side of the grass with his heart hammering inside his chest and sweat pouring down his face.

His side hurt from where he had been kicked, and he feared what further blows would feel like, even as he also shook with impotent rage against the two bullies. As he approached the pavilion, he thought the word *please* over and over again, as if he were shouting it into his own inner ears, praying for a miracle.

And then one happened. A voice close by said: "Mind where you're going, son. You'll hit a wall if you're not careful."

Theo stopped in his tracks. There, standing in front of him in the doorway of the pavilion, where just now there had been nobody, was Mr. Eames, the athletics director, dressed in a tweed jacket with colored tie, plaid pants with plus fours, and a pair of brightly shined two-toned shoes. This was his standard getup, so that he permanently looked as if he were about to play golf, even though that was not a sport offered by Saint Peter's and Mr. Eames had never been seen in the company of a niblick or a mashie.

"Not so fast. You two come here," said Mr. Eames. He wasn't looking at Theo anymore but over his shoulder to where Billy and Paddy had skidded to a breathless halt in the middle of the cinder track and were about to turn tail.

"So what happened?" he asked, switching his attention back to Theo, who dropped his eyes and didn't answer. The two bullies deserved a whipping, but that didn't mean he was going to sneak to a teacher to get them their just deserts.

"You're new, aren't you?"

Theo nodded.

"And this was going to be some sort of initiation rite, is that it?" he asked, turning back to the cousins. "A good old Irish welcome to Saint Peter's, administered inside my hut? Far from prying eyes, so that no one would be the wiser?"

They were silent, too, shifting from one foot to the other.

"Well, we'll see about that," he said. "You—what's your name?"

"Theo—Theo Sterling."

"All right, Theo Sterling, you go and sit on that bench over there," he said, pointing to a dilapidated set of bleachers on the other side of the sports field. "I'll be wanting to have a talk with you once I've finished with these two."

Theo did as he was told. And five minutes later Mr. Eames emerged from the pavilion with Billy and Paddy in tow and walked over to where he was sitting.

"Say your piece," Mr. Eames ordered, looking at them sternly.

Solemnly, with their eyes fixed on the ground, each one mumbled that he was sorry and then walked quickly away.

Mr. Eames sat down beside Theo and lit a cigarette, looking out across the track at their retreating backs. "They won't bother you again," he said, without offering any explanation of what he had done to them inside the pavilion to secure that result.

Theo nodded. His heart was still racing, and he was finding it hard to swallow. He bit his lip, frightened that he might lose control of his emotions and start to cry. He realized that he terribly didn't want that to happen in front of Mr. Eames.

The athletics director glanced over at Theo and pulled out a small silver flask from an invisible inside pocket of his jacket, unscrewed the top, and handed it to Theo, who looked down at it uncertainly.

"Go on, drink," said Mr. Eames. "It won't do you any harm and it might make you feel better."

Theo drank and snorted and swallowed some of the golden liquid, and after the initial shock to his system, it did make him feel better—warm and giddy, which was certainly an improvement over what had gone before.

"Useful in an emergency, but best kept on the q.t.," said Mr. Eames, taking back the flask and restoring it to its hiding place. "Need-to-know basis, if you know what I mean?"

Theo nodded, even though he wasn't quite sure he did.

"Good," said Mr. Eames, flicking away his cigarette onto the cinder track, where it lay, sending up a straight line of blue smoke. "Now, Theo, tell me—do you know what you are?"

Theo shook his head, feeling even more confused.

"Well, I'll tell you then. You're a runner. That's what. Those two knuckleheads are a disgrace to the Emerald Isle, but they're not bad footballers, and if you can outrun them in those shoes"—he glanced down with a shake of his head at Theo's clunky footwear—"then I'd say you've got the gift. What you do with it, of course, is another matter entirely. But if you're prepared to work, I think I can make something of you. So what do you say?"

Theo nodded. At that moment, he would have agreed to almost anything Mr. Eames proposed, but the idea of making something of himself was exciting. Better that than becoming a good Catholic or a successful American or the other prepackaged destinies his parents seemed to have in mind for him. And, besides, he liked running. When he ran, he felt alive.

"Good," said Mr. Eames. "Well, that's settled then. You'll start tomorrow at three o'clock. Don't be late."

The athletics director was as good as his word. From that day on, the bullying stopped. Theo's enemies did not become his friends, and his classmates continued to regard him with suspicion, but he was left alone, and for Theo that was enough. As an only child, he was used to his own company, and he soon came to love the running that he practiced on the cinder track every day after school.

Mr. Eames was a good coach. His flamboyant dress belied a methodical approach to his work, which began on the first afternoon with an unexpected question.

"Are you going to run fast or long?" he asked. They were inside the pavilion and Mr. Eames had his back to Theo, rummaging among a pile of equipment.

"I don't know."

"Yes, you do. Dig down inside yourself and think. Sprinters run on nerves; distance athletes run on heart and guts, and on brains too. They have to measure their opponents, watching for their moment. Not too soon, not too late . . ."

"Distance," said Theo. "Definitely distance."

"Good," said Eames, smiling. "That's the answer I was looking for." He rummaged some more and turned around, holding out an old pair of running shoes, each with three spikes on the bottom.

"What are they for?" asked Theo doubtfully, pointing at the spikes.

"Traction, speed—you can't run without them. If you were going short, there'd be more of them, because sprinters run on their toes. But for distance, you need a heel. These aren't perfect, but they'll do for now. Try them on."

To Theo's surprise, they fit beautifully, and by the end of the afternoon he had fallen in love with his new shoes. The spikes, or *pins* as Mr. Eames called them, gripped the old cinder track, propelling him forward, and the extraordinary lightness of the shoes allowed his feet to fly.

"Breathe with each stride; measure the exhale and the inhale so each part of your body is in tune with the rest. Breathe deeper so you can feel your diaphragm rising and falling. Up and down, in and out—whichever way you sense it. Breathing is the key, and you mustn't ever forget it." The instructions that

Mr. Eames gave him made Theo think about his body and mind in new ways; and as he ran, he felt a vast sense of potential welling up inside him. As if he could do anything.

On Tuesday and Thursday afternoons, the other school athletes trained, and on alternate Saturdays, there were meets where they competed against other teams in the city's Catholic League.

These other boys were older than Theo, but there was none of the petty jealousy that he had encountered in the classroom. They were united by a shared passion for their chosen sport and a fierce loyalty to Mr. Eames, and they welcomed the addition of a talented distance runner who increased the team's chances of success.

On match days Mr. Eames drove the school coach, known to the boys as the *battle bus*, a rectangular blue vehicle with a flat roof that looked as if it dated back to the first years of the internal combustion engine. It had a sign on the side that read **St Pe e 's**—the result of some forgotten wit having painted out the *t* and the *r*—and it wheezed and chugged as it rolled across the city with Mr. Eames at the wheel. But it never broke down, and inside it, bouncing up and down with his companions on the extraordinarily uncomfortable seats in which the springs were just below the leather, Theo tasted his first experience of true happiness. He was part of a team, united in doing something they loved, and striving to fulfill their potential.

In competition he learned patience: the art of biding time, watching and waiting for the right moment to take the lead. At first this had made no sense to Theo. "If I'm at the front, then surely I can leave the others behind," he said.

"Set the pace, control the race? Is that the idea?" his coach countered.

Theo nodded.

Eames laughed. "I wish it was as simple as that," he said. "But distance running's about using your brain as well as your legs. I told you that before. It's the hounds that control the race, not the hare. The front-runner cuts the wind for everyone behind him: on average it takes eight percent more energy to lead than to follow. And staying back means you can see when it's the right time to make your move. It's about seizing the moment but also knowing when the moment's right."

Theo listened and he began to win. He watched his opponents and began to develop a sixth sense about their strengths and weaknesses. And his own too. In some races it came down to who was prepared to endure more pain and who believed in themselves the most. It was a voyage of self-discovery in which Theo forged an inner strength that was to stand him in good stead in the hard years to come.

He was happy, unexpectedly happy, and the only dampener on his enthusiasm was that his parents weren't involved in his success, although this was his own doing. Elena had been enthusiastic about the school and had been eager to attend an evening for new parents and pupils held in the main hall in the second week of the semester. She arrived early, wearing her best dress and a green silk hat adorned with a silver floral brooch that she had bought specially for the occasion, and insisted on sitting in the front row, from where she put up her hand to ask the headmaster a series of questions about the religious-instruction curriculum while Theo squirmed in embarrassment beside her.

After his experience with the O'Donnell boys, Theo's overriding concern was to avoid anything that would draw attention to himself. It didn't matter that his classmates weren't present and that the headmaster seemed happy to answer his mother's questions. He still worried that other parents would talk about the small woman with the funny accent who wouldn't stop asking ungrammatical questions about Jesus, and that this would provide a spark for the classroom persecution to begin again.

Afterward, he said nothing to his mother but vowed to himself that he would do everything in his power to keep her away from the school henceforward. And so, when the race meets began, he said nothing about them to her or to his father.

It hurt him that other parents turned out to support their children and that his weren't there, but he found a strange pleasure in the pain. The constraint that he'd felt with his mother ever since the encounter with Sir Andrew in the presbytery persisted, and he blamed both his parents for shutting his grandparents out of his life, even though he knew that it was his iron-willed grandfather who had begun that estrangement.

He was determined to keep the running for himself. It satisfied the need he had begun to feel for a life separate from his parents, who seemed to see him as an adjunct to themselves rather than as a person with an identity in his own right. He told himself that his mother could not relate to him outside the bounds of the claustrophobic Mexican world that she inhabited with her fellow exiles in Gramercy Park, and he knew for a fact that his father saw the school as nothing more than an irrelevant interlude needing to be filled in before Theo was old enough to join him at the factory and fulfill the family destiny that Michael had had mapped out for his son since the day he was born.

Theo was determined not to allow either of his parents to dent his new, hard-earned sense of self-worth and, as the weeks passed, he developed a growing affection for Coach Eames, who cared passionately about the success of his athletes but without seeming to want anything from them in return, other than their industry and commitment.

On a Tuesday at the end of October, there was a different kind of athletic event. Mr. Eames drove the battle bus uptown past Central Park and out into the hills beyond Harlem, where the team dismounted into a world of Gothic towers and crenellations constructed in a dazzling mix of gray schist rock and brilliant white terra-cotta.

WELCOME TO THE CITY COLLEGE OF NEW YORK, proclaimed a sign at the entrance gate. "And it *means* welcome," said Mr. Eames enthusiastically. "Welcome to Black boys and to Jewish boys—and girls, too, before long, if what I hear coming down the grapevine proves correct. This'll be a different kind of challenge for you all today, believe me."

"What kind of challenge?" asked Theo, running to catch up with his teammates after he had dawdled too long, gazing up at the crazy panoply of gargoyles, grotesques, and florals that seemed to cover every inch of the soaring facade.

"The boys you'll be up against today know how to run," said Mr. Eames with a grin. "You'll see."

The meet was in a stadium across the road from the campus—an echoing mausoleum full of empty seats rising in tiers up toward an overcast sky. A banner at the finish line was emblazoned with **Labor Sports Union of America**, and before the events began, there was a call for silence and those who were wearing hats took them off, and everyone except the boys from Saint Peter's sang a song that sounded like a hymn but didn't mention God.

"Arise, you prisoners of starvation! Arise you wretched of the earth." Looking over at his coach, Theo was surprised to see him singing the words with a rare fervor at odds with his usual detachment.

"What's the song?" Theo asked his teammates, but none of them seemed to know, and it was only years later when he heard the song being sung by strikers outside his father's factory that he discovered it was "The Internationale."

Before the 1,500 meters race, Coach Eames came over as he usually did to check Theo's spikes. But he wasn't alone. There was an older man beside him. He had a leathery face with the skin stretched tight over the bones and a pencil-thin silver mustache, and he looked Theo over from head to foot with cool gray eyes, as if taking inventory.

"This is Mr. Booker, Theo," said Coach Eames. He sounded nervous, Theo thought with surprise. He'd always seemed so self-contained and sure of himself, and the change made Theo look at the stranger with curiosity as he put out his hand to greet him.

Booker ignored it. "You say he's fast," he said to Coach Eames. "But how fast? That's the question. Is he faster than Ledley over there?"

"Maybe," said Eames. "Maybe not—he's just starting out. But he's got the gift, Charlie. I know that much. He's the first one with it that I've seen at Saint Pete's since I started working there, and that's a good four years now."

"High praise indeed!" said the old man, looking unconvinced. "Do you believe in God, son?" he asked, speaking to Theo for the first time.

"Yes, I think so, sir," Theo stammered, taken aback by the unexpected question.

"You don't sound too sure," said Booker with a harsh laugh. "But don't worry. I'm no God-fearing man either. If anyone's up there, I reckon he's washed his hands of us or forgotten we exist, which amounts to the same thing."

He paused, looking Theo up and down as if waiting for a response. But Theo said nothing. He felt as if the old man was probing him for weakness, and he was determined to give nothing away.

"You're wondering why I'm asking, aren't you, son?" Booker said, keeping his eyes fixed on Theo.

Theo nodded. It was exactly what he was wondering.

"Well, I'll tell you. You see that boy over there?" The old man pointed to a tall Black boy two lanes to the right, who was kneeling on the track, although whether in prayer or readiness for the race Theo couldn't tell. "That's Ledley Clay, and he's a true believer. Do you know what that means?"

Theo shook his head, confused. The old man was strange—not like anyone he'd ever met before.

"It means that when he runs, he feels the power of the Almighty in his legs and his arms—hell, in his goddamn balls, too, probably, pushing him down the track like it's his own personal Henry Ford Model T combustion engine. And that makes him nigh on unstoppable. Do you think you can compete with that, son? With that Jesus charge?"

"I don't know, sir," said Theo, feeling overwhelmed by the old man's torrent of blasphemous phrases. And then realizing he'd given the wrong answer, he quickly added as Booker was turning away: "But I'm going to try, sir. I'm going to give it all I've got."

Booker kept walking, and Theo didn't know if he'd heard him or not. He hoped he had, because at that moment there was nothing in the world Theo wanted more than to impress the cantankerous old man.

Theo ran harder and faster that race than he had ever run before, but it wasn't enough.

Clay took the lead from the starting gun, and with an apparently effortless stride, he had soon left all his competitors except Theo behind. After each circuit of the track, he was farther ahead, but Theo refused to give in, digging down deep through searing pain into some essential part of himself where he could find the strength not to surrender. For a few minutes, it worked. He even seemed to be reeling Clay in, and at the turn he caught him looking back over his shoulder, measuring the distance between them. Theo interpreted this as a sign of weakness and drove himself forward until suddenly his legs buckled and it was all he could do to stop himself from falling. For the first time he had come up against the end of himself, and hot tears started in his eyes as Clay faded from view into a blur up ahead, and he was reduced to jogging the rest of the race.

But finish it he did, and it was only then that he heard the cheering and felt Coach Eames's arm around his shoulders.

"I'm sorry," he said. "I tried. I tried, but—" And then he broke off because there were no words to describe what had happened at that moment when he'd reached his breaking point.

"You tried your best," said Eames. "Just like you said you would. And it was almost enough. Clay was winded, too, and if you'd got to him then, it might have been different. Even old Book had to admit that. And next time, if you work hard, you're going to win. I know you will. I'm proud of you, Theo," he told him, squeezing his shoulder.

Theo felt a rush of sudden euphoria—one of those moments in life when anything seems possible. He was like a vessel long becalmed, starting forward across the sea as the long-prayed-for wind suddenly fills its sails. Looking up at his coach, he felt a profound gratitude to this man whom he had known only a few weeks, for believing in him and his talent. The real person he was and might become—flesh and blood and viscera and will—not an idea of him, like his father clung to.

Theo didn't realize the danger he was getting into as he made this comparison, paying no heed to where such thoughts might lead.

Coach Eames drove the battle bus back down Broadway, beating out a rhythm with his free hand on the dashboard while his team sang "The Battle Hymn of the Republic," trampling out the vintage in high, raucous voices that hadn't yet broken into manhood. Outside, under the blazing streetlights, girls not much older than them, with thickly painted faces, stood in lines outside the taxi-dancing ballrooms. They shivered in long, thin, three-dollar shop dresses that clung to their unformed figures as they called out invitations to the passing trade, trying to lure clerks and store assistants inside for dime-a-time dances—a squeeze and a whirl and a few moments of forgetfulness under the low lights as the band played hot Dixieland jazz without pause into the early hours.

Through the open windows of the bus, Theo thought he could faintly hear the music: the pounding of a tin-pan piano and the cry of a trumpet driving the melody, half drowned out by the shrieks of the street hawkers selling hot dogs and pretzels, and the endless horn blowing of the bustling yellow cabs trying to find a way through the snarled-up end-of-day traffic.

At Forty-Ninth Street, they came to a complete halt. It was twilight now and the sky had begun to drizzle. Eames pulled the bus off the road and got out to see what was happening. The boys followed him, snaking their way through the crowds until they got into Times Square, which was bright with neon light. All around, the big electric signs glowed, blinking at each other across the glistening wet roadway as they flashed their messages in vast white letters, advertising Turkish cigarettes and Pepsodent toothpaste, special revues and billiards, and dancing, dancing, dancing with the loveliest, prettiest girls in all the world. But no one was paying any attention; instead, the upturned eyes of everyone in the densely packed throng were fixed on the news ticker on the facade of the New York Times Building, spelling out not the end of the world but something that felt very like it:

BLACK TUESDAY. WALL STREET IN PANIC AS STOCKS CRASH. DELUGE OF SELLING OVERWHELMS MARKET . . .

"They're jumpin' out the windows down by the Exchange," said a fat, red-faced man in a tall trilby hat who was half blocking Theo's view of the ticker. Even out in the open, Theo could smell the reek of cheap alcohol on his breath. "Saw 'em fall with me own eyes."

"The wages of sin are death," called out another onlooker standing even closer to Theo—a bareheaded octogenarian whose remaining strands of wispy hair had been pasted by the rain into thin gray lines across his white scalp. His skin had the pallor of death, but his mad black eyes gleamed in their hollowed-out sockets, defying the Grim Reaper's scythe. "Behold, they shall be as stubble, the fire shall burn them," he intoned, and then, staring down at Theo, he yelled: "Shall burn as an oven, and all that do wickedly, shall be stubble! Malachi 4:1."

Terrified, Theo pulled away from the fanatic and was only just caught from falling off the curb and under the rattling wheels of a trolley bus by Coach Eames's quick-thinking intervention.

"Shut up, you old fool!" shouted the coach, but the old man paid no attention, continuing to broadcast his message of hell and damnation at the top of his voice.

"Don't listen to him," said Mr. Eames, setting Theo back on his feet. "He doesn't know what he's talking about."

Theo nodded, but he wasn't so sure. *Stocks* and *markets* were words from a foreign language, incomprehensible and unrelated to the narrow boundaries of his daily life. But the rapt gaze of the crowd and the fear so clearly apparent on their upturned faces told a different story, filling him with a sense of foreboding that the world had indeed changed that night, leaving them all exposed and defenseless in the face of an approaching wave of destruction.

Theo's father didn't see it that way. He assured his wife and son that there was nothing to worry about. The crash was a just punishment for the stock market speculators who had thought they could get rich quick by treating life as a betting game. They had never done a proper day's work in their lives and deserved to be ruined. But for those like Michael who worked hard, managed their money well, and used their initiative to get ahead, the rewards would continue to flow, just as they had been doing for him through all the years since he left his father's sweatshop and labored night and day to set up his own business. They had to, because this was America: the land of opportunity, where you could make your dreams come true.

And Michael took comfort that the government, his government, agreed with him. He had been first in line at his local polling station to vote for Herbert Hoover the previous year and had celebrated Hoover's election by going out to purchase a photograph of the new president in a sterling silver frame. This now hung in pride of place over the mahogany highboy radio console that Michael had bought for Elena at the time they moved. He had purchased one of the most expensive RCA radios on the market as a way of demonstrating to her his growing financial success, but she had shown little interest in the new machine once she realized that the programs were in English, and Michael now monopolized its use when he was home.

Every evening after dinner, he settled himself in his padded armchair positioned directly across from Hoover's picture and listened to the NBC news, nodding sagely in agreement with the reassuring comments about the economy, emanating from the president and his cabinet. And then, after the news had given way to dance music, he carefully unfolded a pair of gold-rimmed pince-nez spectacles onto the bridge of his nose and read snippets aloud from his copy of *The New York Daily News*, apparently unconcerned that neither his wife nor son were listening to him. Sometimes, indeed, he would address his remarks directly to the president's photograph, as if he were present in the room.

"'"Any lack of confidence in the economic future or the basic strength of business in the United States is simply foolish," President Hoover told business leaders today,'" Michael read out. "And you're right on the money there, Herbert," he told the photograph, looking up. "This depression's a temporary setback, that's all. We've got to keep our heads down and not listen to those damned Communists who want to go around handing out relief because they know that that's the way to make people dependent and break their spirit. Aren't I right, Elena?"

"Yes, Michael," his wife agreed, shouting across the room from the kitchen. "God preserve us from those devils!"

4

SKYSCRAPER

The Depression—as President Hoover christened the economic collapse in an attempt to make it seem less catastrophic than it was—got worse. Unemployment rose and businesses failed, but the spreading malaise did not daunt Michael Sterling. To the contrary, it just stoked his determination to insist that everything was going to be fine in this best of all possible worlds. Almost every day he quoted the president's assurance that "we have now passed the worst and with continued unity of effort we shall rapidly recover."

There was a decided quality of religious fervor about Michael's faith in the future and, like all religious enthusiasts, he felt the need to proselytize—convincing others had the added benefit of helping him convince himself. And he didn't need to look far for evidence to support his belief. Up above, the soaring new skyscrapers of Manhattan bore testimony to the confidence of their creators. They were the cathedrals of commerce, a statement forged in steel that New York City was the beating heart of a new world of limitless potential.

One building in particular captured Michael's imagination. As the months passed, he watched the white-and-gray brickwork of the Chrysler Building rising floor by floor on the corner of Lexington Avenue and Forty-Second Street, each one with matching rows of gleaming glass windows reflecting the noonday sun. Oftentimes he would get up early and take the subway to Grand Central and then linger near the building site to try to strike up conversations with the construction workers before walking on to his factory in the Garment District. If successful, he would come away from these encounters armed with mind-numbing statistics that he would memorize and then repeat back to his family at dinner: that the building would require more than three million bricks and nearly four hundred thousand rivets, and that if the electrical wiring was laid out end to end, it would stretch all the way from New York City to Chicago! *"Chicago,"* he would marvel. "Imagine that!"

Michael told them that Walter Chrysler was sparing no expense because this was going to be the tallest and most beautiful building in the world. A monument to the power of human ingenuity and endeavor. His admiration for the automobile tycoon knew no bounds. He was sorely tempted to buy a photograph of Chrysler to hang next to Herbert Hoover and refrained only because he felt that it would be disrespectful to the president. So it came as no surprise that he insisted on Elena and Theo accompanying him on a tour of the building on the first weekend after it had officially opened to the public.

The great day dawned auspiciously bright, and they arrived outside the main entrance ten minutes before opening time. Craning their necks, they gazed up the side of the soaring tower to where the terraced arches of the crown rose through a sunburst pattern of triangular windows to a stainless-steel spire thrust like a spear into the cloudless blue sky.

"The spire was Chrysler's ace in the hole," said Michael, pointing upward excitedly. "It's how he won the game. None of them saw it coming!"

"What game?" asked Elena, disapprovingly. Like all good Catholics, she abhorred gambling. The Roman centurions had drawn lots for Christ's clothes at the foot of the cross.

"The race to the sky, of course," said Michael impatiently. "Haven't you been listening to anything I've been telling you these last months? All this year he's been in a battle with the Bank of Manhattan to see who can build the highest skyscraper in the world. Taller than the Eiffel Tower, taller than . . ." Michael searched for another suitably impressive comparison and came up a blank. But this didn't faze him, and he returned to his story with redoubled enthusiasm: "So a month ago, the people at the bank were sure they'd won. They even held a victory party over on Wall Street to celebrate, but they'd reckoned without old Walter. A few days later, he hauled his spire up through the roof and won the race in an hour and a half. He'd had it hidden in there the whole time, the sly old goat. The whole building's one thousand and forty-five feet from top to bottom. An honest-to-God miracle—that's what it is!"

Michael stared up, awestruck—he might as well have been gazing up at the roof of the Sistine Chapel—but Elena didn't follow suit; instead, she raised her perfectly symmetrical arched black eyebrows and shook her head and sighed. The building didn't seem like a miracle to her at all, but rather a blasphemy. A narcissistic attempt by a vain industrialist to masquerade as God that could end only in disaster. She'd come on the expedition reluctantly, unable to say no to her husband's pressure, but that didn't mean she was going to pretend to enjoy the experience.

Theo had his head thrown back, too, like his father, gazing up and imagining what it would be like for someone to fall head over heels in slow motion past each of the seventy-seven floors to a certain death on the sidewalk below, looking in as he fell at the people at their desks carrying on with their work, oblivious to his cries.

Michael called Theo out of his daydream. The gigantic steel doors were opening, and he hurried his family forward and into the lobby. Theo was completely unprepared for the shock of its beauty. He had expected something loud and brash and monumental, but instead it was intensely quiet inside—an extraordinary contrast to the roar of Forty-Second Street—and the thick walls of African red-and-orange marble made the dimly lit interior seem like a pagan temple. The doors to the elevators with Egyptian designs decked out in elaborate wooden marquetry were like entrances to magical tropical kingdoms straight out of *King Solomon's Mines*.

"Walter has his own special elevator, of course, going up to his private apartment at the top. I hear it's furnished like a sultan's palace with gold everywhere, even in the bathroom," said Michael knowingly.

"Which elevator is it, Dad?" asked Theo.

"One of those over there," said Michael, waving vaguely toward the opposite end of the lobby. "He takes his Ziegfeld girls up there after the show. They say he's just bought his favorite one a diamond necklace from Cartier, and she wears it at the revue for everyone to see."

"Michael!" said Elena sharply. "Don't talk like that in front of Theo. What's the boy going to think?"

"He's old enough to think for himself," said Michael, but he sounded sheepish in the face of his wife's angry criticism and was temporarily silenced while the elevator operator, a magnificent factotum dressed in a gold braid uniform with a gold-colored mustache to match, inspected their tickets and then pulled back the iron gate to usher them inside.

"Prepare yourself for the longest vertical ride on earth," said Michael with a return of his earlier excitement. "And the fastest too! Nine hundred feet a minute, if you can believe it!"

It was unimaginable to Theo, but true—he watched the second hand on his father's watch and yes, it literally took no more than a minute for them to reach the seventy-first floor, where they stepped out onto the observation deck and peered down through the triangular-shaped windows at the great city below.

"Look, there's my factory," said Michael, but Theo couldn't distinguish the lead roof his father was pointing at from all the other lead roofs tangling for space in the Garment District out beyond Seventh Avenue, and he was similarly unsuccessful in picking out his home and school. And now, instead of a fantasy of falling, he felt the city's towers pushing up toward him from out of the canyon-like avenues, as if they were a multitude of hungry, needle-headed insects, each striving to draw clear of its rivals. Only the still blue water of the Upper Bay, stretching out wide and indifferent beyond the Battery, provided relief from the seething mass of construction on all sides.

Behind him, Michael had followed Theo to the south-facing windows and now took hold of his shoulder with one hand, fixing him in position, as he pointed with the other out toward the bay. "Look, son—over there on the Jersey side, just before you get to the Statue of Liberty. That's Ellis Island, where they took us from the ship. We had to get through there or be sent back. Do you see it, like a square with the middle bitten out?"

"Yes," said Theo, shrinking from his father's intensity, but curious too—his father had never spoken to him before about how he got to America, always preferring to look forward rather than back.

"I remember how the government inspectors were watching us when we went into the big hall and I willed myself to stay upright, which was hard because my body was still rocking with the ship and we were weak and hungry after all those weeks in steerage. And frightened too: more than you can imagine," said Michael in a faraway voice, as if he'd crossed time and was reliving the experience again. "Everyone was scared. You could smell the fear—it stank worse than the dirt on our bodies—but we knew that if you gave in to it, then they'd say you were sick and chalk a big *X* on your coat, and maybe you'd have to go back across the sea.

"They came at us with buttonhooks and pulled our eyelids back to check for trachoma. It hurt and my father got angry and that was nearly the end, but I think the inspector we had felt sorry for us, and moved us on, and suddenly there we were on the ferry heading across the bay down there, and I looked up at the towers of Manhattan and the stars blinking and I was happy, happier than I have ever been in all my life, except for the day I met your mother."

Michael beckoned to his wife, opening his arm wide to invite her into the family embrace, but Elena refused to come forward. Today, everything her husband said seemed to irritate her.

Though embarrassed by his father's schoolboy exuberance, Theo was moved, too, by his rapturous love for the great city spread out beneath them, and he was angry with his mother for throwing a dampener on the day. She was being unfair, and Theo felt a keen awareness of the contrast with the efforts she made with her baking and her appearance when she knew that Don Andrés was going to be at the church for Sunday Mass.

Theo had hoped that the Englishman's visit to raise money for the Knights of Columbus the previous summer would be a one-off, but in this he had been quickly disappointed. Don Andrés had returned at regular intervals since then and made sure to single out Elena for courtly attention whenever he did so, while Theo sat beside her, gripped with an impotent resentment of which the Englishman appeared completely unaware.

Recently, Theo's irritation had reached a point where he could stay silent no longer, and he'd asked his mother why Don Andrés was such a frequent visitor, but she'd brushed aside the question, saying that he had business in the city.

"So why didn't he come before?" Theo had asked.

"Because he didn't know about the church," Elena had reasonably replied.

"Or about you," Theo had been sorely tempted to shoot back, but he'd restrained himself, not wanting to precipitate the already existing tension between himself and his mother into open warfare. And he worried, too, that voicing his suspicion could make it come true. He'd seen how animated and talkative his mother became when the Englishman was there. Different from how she was with the other parishioners or with her husband.

Returning to the elevators, Michael stopped in front of a glass case containing an open wooden box of metal tools—calipers and spanners and wrenches—with the name W. P. Chrysler engraved in gold lettering on the front.

"He made most of them himself when he was starting out as a railroad mechanic in Kansas, earning a nickel an hour," said Michael, gazing reverently at the box. "Do you know why he's put them here?" he asked his son.

Theo shook his head.

"To show people like us what you can do in this great country if you use your talents to the full. You can build this," he said, throwing his hands out wide. "You can achieve anything, even if you come from nothing. That's the point."

"But what shall it profit a man if he shall gain the whole world and lose his own soul?" said Elena, pronouncing the words slowly, almost as if she was uttering a prophecy or a curse.

"What's that?" asked Michael, turning to his wife, surprised by her interjection after she had maintained a brooding silence all day up to now.

"It's the Gospel. It's what the Lord Jesus told his disciples." Theo could see that his mother's small fists were clenched, and he sensed both her anger and the effort that it was costing her to speak out against her husband.

"And if Jesus said it, it must be true. Is that what you're saying?" asked Michael. Theo could hear the edge of mockery in his voice.

"Yes," said Elena simply. "I think this place is like the Mount of Temptation that Satan took Christ up to in the desert, where he showed him all the kingdoms of the world and offered them to him if he would just kneel down and worship him. But Jesus refused. Tell your father what the Lord said, Theo. He needs to know."

But Theo shook his head, refusing to be drawn into this battle between his parents, which made him feel like he was being torn apart inside.

"Very well," said Elena. "I will, then. Christ said: 'Get thee hence, Satan: for it is written, thou shalt worship the Lord thy God and him only shalt thou serve.'"

For all his irritation at her for spoiling the day, Theo couldn't help but admire his mother. She was small and delicate, but she had set herself like a boxer with her hands on her hips and her chin jutted forward, refusing to be cowed by the force of her husband's personality.

Michael met his wife's stare, and then glanced back down at Walter Chrysler's tools for a moment before he spoke, softly this time: "You seem to forget that your God is not my God, my dear. Your Christ is not my Messiah. And in case you've forgotten, I gave up a great deal to marry you."

Theo saw his mother's face go rigid, as if she had sustained a blow, but he understood that it also reflected a determination not to respond, and both his parents remained stonily silent as they rode the elevator back down to the lobby and made their way home. Sitting between them on the subway train, Theo felt both angry and bewildered. He wanted to restore his father's high spirits and his mother's placidity, but he was powerless to do either, having no key to unlock the mystery of their marriage.

The Chrysler Building didn't hold the title of the world's tallest building for long. As Theo and his parents walked the observation deck on that spring day in 1930, work had already begun ten streets away on the Empire State Building, destined within a year to eclipse Chrysler's gleaming spire by more than two hundred feet. But the wealthy's insatiable thirst for aerial construction couldn't hide the reality of what was happening in the suffering city down below, where the Depression had started to exert a viselike grip on the lives of the inhabitants.

Out on Fourteenth Street—the nearest thoroughfare to the Sterling apartment—there was still the same crazy noise. Phonographs in the dime record shops with horns hung over their doorways blared hot jazz out onto the sidewalks where street peddlers were still hawking their wares, yelling out rock-bottom prices for rayon socks and candy bars and worthless watches in black leather bags, all striving to be heard above the roar of the traffic. And outside the department stores, pullers were still urging passersby not to miss out on bargain prices, pointing back at the heavily rouged girls in the show windows behind them as they slowly circled their narrow, gilded cages in dresses and furs, opening them out at each pass to display beautiful linings and an enticing glimpse of leg.

But there was a sense that they were all going through the motions. Consumer confidence had evaporated, and not just in the stock market. Watching the barkers, Theo sensed that they shouted until they were hoarse not just to attract customers but also to try to convince themselves that things were not as bad as they seemed. But behind them, the stores were half empty and the cash registers were silent, and in the windows the girls' faces beneath their makeup were pinched and pale with anxiety. Every worker in the city feared that the next payday would be their last and that they would soon be returning to their families with the dreaded pink slip clutched in their shaking hands.

Those who'd lost their jobs trudged the streets, looking for work until their shoes were worn to shreds. For some, selling apples provided a small temporary hope that they might stay on their feet. They could make a dime if they sold a crate, but even that soon became impossible when so many were doing the same, and this pathetic last attempt at self-reliance gave way beneath them like the last rung of a broken ladder as they joined the long queues for bread and soup snaking around the decayed street corners of the Bowery. There was no dignity to be hoped for there, except perhaps in death. Louis Armstrong's rasping voice and soulful New Orleans trumpet ran through Theo's memory of those years, telling the truth in "St. James Infirmary Blues" in a way his father never could:

When I die, want you to dress me in straight-lace shoes
Box-back coat and a Stetson hat
Put a twenty-dollar gold piece on my watch chain
So the boys'll know that I died standin' pat.

Theo's father still kept faith with his beleaguered president, but for many in the city, the name Hoover had become a term of abuse. Hoover blankets were the sheets of old newspapers that the homeless wrapped themselves in to keep warm, Hoover leather was the cardboard they used to cover the holes in the soles of their shoes, and Hoover flags were their empty pants pockets turned inside out—the visible proof of their destitution as they held out their hands for alms. And at night they slept in Hoovervilles—shantytowns made of cardboard, tin, and scraps of broken wood. There was even one in the old drained reservoir in Central Park, where Theo ran sometimes with his teammates in the afternoons.

In the winter evenings, coming back from school, Theo saw these ragged men, and women and children too, pawing over the contents of restaurant garbage cans set out for the sanitation trucks—or, on one occasion, fighting like animals over waste lumber being given away on a half-finished building site. Mostly, however, they seemed too tired and cold and beaten to fight, standing around makeshift fires in empty ash cans, stamping their feet to keep warm, and periodically taking off their old battered hats to hold them over the blaze before quickly clamping them back on their heads, sighing as they felt the momentary heat penetrate their frozen skulls.

Beside the stop on Fourteenth Street where Theo got off the bus on his way back from school, a gun shop called attention to its wares with a huge imitation black revolver hanging upside down over the sidewalk. Each time Theo passed beneath the jet-black barrel, he shuddered, feeling its inhuman, pitiless aim down through the center of his head.

Only the Socialists preaching Marx from atop their soapboxes in Union Square seemed to have a solution to the general malaise. "Which side are you on?" they shouted, and Theo wasn't sure. "Why do five percent of the population own ninety-five percent of the wealth?" they asked, and Theo didn't know. "Look up above your heads! See what the rich waste their money on while the poor starve," they cried, pointing up at the skyscrapers, and Theo did as they said, wondering whether his father was right. Were these buildings a triumph of the human spirit, as he claimed, or an obscene exercise in narcissism by selfish men who had more money than they knew what to do with, fiddling like modern-day Neros while Rome burned?

"Capitalism isn't working anymore," the Communists thundered. "Anyone can see that. It's labor that produces wealth, and therefore wealth should go back to labor." Theo could see the raw justice in that, although he had sense enough to keep his thoughts to himself. His parents were united in their hatred of the Reds.

But united in little else. It took all Michael's energy to maintain his belief in his own capitalist destiny when the half-empty clothing stores spelled ever fewer orders coming in to his factory, and he was quick to take out his frustration on his wife when he came home, complaining about overspending on the household and even implying that the headaches that he'd begun to suffer from were a contagion that she'd infected him with.

In response, Elena withdrew further into herself and spent more time at the Spanish church, where Don Andrés remained a regular visitor. In December, he brought Theo a big vellum-bound copy of *The Romance of King Arthur and His Knights of the Round Table* illustrated by Arthur Rackham. On the flyleaf, it was inscribed in beautiful calligraphy:

For Theodore Sterling from Sir Andrew Campion-Bennett with best wishes for Christmas 1930

Theo loved books, and this was the most beautiful one he had ever seen. The haunting pictures, alternately romantic and sinister, stirred his imagination in a way he had never before experienced, but that didn't make him grateful to Sir Andrew for the present. He had given the Englishman no reason to like him in the eighteen months since they had first met, and he was sure that the gift was designed to curry favor not with him but with his mother. Theo felt used, and he regretted now that he had not refused the book when Sir Andrew gave it to him. But there had been no time, which Theo realized must have been Sir Andrew's intention, because he had put it in Theo's hands just as he was leaving the presbytery, and he had not been back since. Father Juan said that he had gone back to England.

Theo knew that the gift compromised him, particularly after he agreed to his mother's request not to show it to his father. He understood her motives: the book's rich binding made its value obvious even to an intellectual philistine like Michael Sterling, and Theo was sure that his father would start asking questions as soon as he saw it. Questions that would lead to suspicion of his wife, which would further poison the already febrile atmosphere in the apartment.

Theo had his suspicions, too, and keeping the book secret felt like a betrayal of his father. So much so that he gave serious thought to telling his mother that she needed to take the book back to Father Juan to give to Sir Andrew, but each time he was about to broach the subject with her, the words dried up in his mouth and he continued to keep it hidden in the back of his wardrobe, from where he took it out at night to turn the pages and gaze spellbound at Rackham's pictures with the aid of a flashlight.

He worried about his father, and not just because of the book. Now, instead of listening to the radio after dinner, he would sit hunched over his bureau in the corner of the living room, muttering to himself as he puzzled over invoices and bank statements and added up columns of figures again and again in the hope of finding more dollars to pay his creditors.

One evening he asked Theo for help. "You have a go, son. My eyes are strained. I can't tell my sixes from my eights," he said, standing up and running his hands through his thinning hair in exasperation.

Theo had no such issues but, try as he might, he couldn't make the numbers change. He was expecting his father to become angry, but instead, to his surprise, Michael patted him affectionately on the shoulder. "We're going to make a good team, you and I," he said. "'Sterling and Son'—it's got a nice ring to it, doesn't it?"

Theo went rigid. They were almost the same words that his father had spoken to him in Washington Square on the day he was taken by his grandfather. Back then he'd still been half a child, and the prospect of working in his father's factory had seemed unreal, part of a future that had no relationship to his eleven-year-old life. But now all that had changed. Soon his father would have the right to take him out of school, and Theo knew that there would be no more books and no more running once he had become the *son* in Sterling and Son. It would be the end of everything that made his life his own.

Still gripping his father's pen, he swallowed and his heart hurt where it beat against his chest, and he had to shut his eyes to stop the tears from leaking out onto his cheeks. He felt he couldn't breathe, but he knew he had to say something. He had to protest. Not to do so would be to acquiesce. And it had to be now—before his oblivious father withdrew his hand and moved away.

"I want to stay at school," he said at last. The words came out half choked in a dry whisper as his fear of his father squeezed his throat.

"What's that?" Michael said, not understanding.

"I want to run. My coach, Mr. Eames, he says that I've got a talent, that I can be special. I—"

"Run? What are you talking about?" Michael looked bewildered. Theo had never mentioned running to him before.

"I run for the school. In competitions. And I win my races too. All of them."

"I don't care if you win them or lose them," said Michael angrily. "Running doesn't matter. You can run from here to Philadelphia and it won't make any difference. It won't put food on the table; it won't pay the rent." His voice had risen dangerously as he started to take in the fact of his son's defiance. "You need to grow up, young man, and get your ideas in order, and stop listening to idiots like this Eames man. If that's what they're teaching you in that school, then the sooner you're out of it the better. Do you hear me?"

Michael was holding Theo's shoulder again, but the gentle touch of before had been replaced by a fierce grip.

Theo had no strength left to argue, but he stayed mute, refusing to give way until Michael reached down with his other hand and seized his chin, twisting it up and around so that he was looking his son in the eye.

"I said: Do you hear me?" he said, spitting out the words between his teeth.

Theo looked into his father's staring eyes and quailed. And when his father let go of his head, he did what he had to do and nodded.

Once, but once was enough. "Good," said Michael, relaxing. "And now we'll hear no more about it."

Released from his father's grip, Theo got up from the desk, accidentally scattering the pile of papers onto the floor. He couldn't help crying now. Thick, wrenching sobs jolted his body. All he felt was the need to get away into his bedroom and shut the door. Nothing else mattered. But in his blind rush, he almost collided with his mother, who'd heard the raised voices and come into the room to find out what was going on.

"Stop," she said breathlessly, catching hold of Theo's arm. "What's happened? What have you done to him?" she demanded, turning on her husband.

"Nothing," said Michael defensively.

"It's not nothing; it's something," Elena shot back. "He wouldn't be crying like this otherwise. What did you say to him?"

"I said he was going to come and work with me in the factory when he turns fourteen in the fall, just like we always agreed. But he said no; he wants to stay at school and run."

"Run?" It was Elena's turn now to look bemused.

"Yes, he says he's got a coach who's been taking him to competitions and filling his head full of crazy ideas. It's the first I've heard about it, and it looks like the first you have too. But I set him right, which is what matters. Running—I've never heard anything more ridiculous!" Michael snorted.

"But I want to run," said Theo, plucking up courage again, now that his mother was in the room. "And it's not just that: I want to learn, too, and make something of myself."

"Make something of yourself! Which you wouldn't with me, I suppose?" said Michael bitterly. "Having a business, supporting your family—that's worthless, is it?"

"He's not saying that," said Elena. "There's nothing wrong with having ambition."

"Maybe I could go to college—Coach Eames says I might get a scholarship," said Theo, hoping to further enlist his mother's support.

"Coach Eames this; Coach Eames that! The boy talks about him like he's some kind of know-it-all Svengali who's got an answer to everything," said Michael, starting to lose his temper again. "But he's just a stupid athletics coach. That's all. And he's not your father; I am. You'd do well to remember that, Theo."

"Don't shout at him. Can't you see he's scared?" said Elena, angry now too. "Theo, go to your room. We can talk about this some other time when everyone's calmed down."

Theo didn't have to be told twice. Released from his mother's hold, he ran into his room and slammed the door before collapsing on the bed. He could hear the sound of raised voices outside, but he didn't want to hear what they were saying and pulled the pillow over his head, covering his ears. He felt as if he'd ventured all he had and lost, and now he had nothing left except despair.

5

MICHAEL

Theo awoke late. It was a Saturday and he'd been allowed to sleep in. He opened his door nervously, worried that the hostilities of the night before might be continuing, but to his surprise, he heard the sound of singing coming from the kitchen.

Crossing the living room to investigate, he caught sight of his father with his arms out and his head thrown back, giving an impassioned impersonation of Enrico Caruso, singing *"O Sole Mio"* to his wife, who was standing at the sink with a dripping dishmop, trying not to laugh.

Michael broke off when he saw his son. "The sun is shining," he said, waving expansively toward the golden glow coming through the open window. "And not just on your mother's beautiful face; it's shining on Manhattan and on Brooklyn and on Coney Island too."

"Coney Island!" Theo repeated the name incredulously.

"Yes. Coney Island. Where you and I are going, just as soon as you get dressed and eat those eggs that your mother's cooked for you."

"Why?" Theo asked, sitting down. He felt utterly confused. Last night his father had hurt him and reduced him to tears, and now for no apparent reason he was taking him to Coney Island, of all places.

"Your mother's got housework to do and she wants us out of the way. And I've been thinking that we don't spend enough time together, you and I. There's more to life than work, you know."

Theo nodded. There was nowhere in the world he wanted to go more than Coney Island. It was his personal pot of gold at the end of the rainbow. He'd been there twice before, each time for his birthday, and the most recent expedition had been spoiled before it began when a thunderstorm had come up out of nowhere, closing the rides and sending everyone scuttling back into the subway, from where they'd traveled back to Manhattan, packed miserably into the train like wet sardines.

But would going with his father mean that he was caving in again? Agreeing to give up on his school and his running? He'd given in the night before, but only because he'd been forced to, and he remained determined to try to find a way to change his father's mind.

"What? Don't you want to go?" asked Michael, looking surprised himself now.

"Of course I do. I just—" Theo broke off.

"Going has nothing to do with anything else," said Elena, intuitively understanding her son's anxiety. "It's a chance to do something fun with your father. That's all. Other things can wait."

Theo looked over at his father, who nodded encouragingly. He was not one to admit he'd been wrong, and Theo realized that this was as close as his father was ever going to get to an apology.

The subway train was full, but there were straps to hang on to as they crossed the Manhattan Bridge and were carried swaying through Brooklyn until they reached its southernmost tip, where they joined the tide of visitors pouring out onto Surf Avenue and surging forward from there into a razzle-dazzle wonderland of sight and smell and sound.

So many people, so much noise. Theo could hear thousands of clamoring voices, mechanical pianos mimicking the up-and-down whirl of the golden carousels, hucksters bellowing invitations through their handheld megaphones, and closer to the boardwalk, the sound of crackling gunfire, from which he instinctively recoiled until he saw that it came from the roadside shooting galleries where hawkeyed boys with thin, narrow faces peered down the sights of real rifles at pockmarked tin targets, watched over by their forgotten girls.

They began with food, queuing at Nathan's Famous for nickel red hots and, at Michael's insistence, knishes—potato cakes flavored with onions and fried in deep fat. *Knishes*—Theo remembered both the word and the taste, taking him back to the hot tenement kitchen on the day he was taken and to his grandmother standing over him, naming the dishes on the table and telling him where each one came from. His grandmother with the emerald-green eyes. His father's mother, whom his father never saw. Theo tried to imagine what it would be like to never see his mother and wondered how his father could stand it, or his grandmother either. This easy capacity for estrangement was mysterious to him. It made his father seem alien, which scared Theo and made him remember his contorted, angry face the night before, thrust up against his own. What would his father do if he defied him? Would he turn his back on Theo too?

The compact of silence that his father had sworn him to in Washington Square eighteen months earlier weighed heavily on him. The invisible, unspoken-of past felt like a malign silent force, guiding the present and the future, and Theo instinctively looked for a way to open it to the light and break its hold.

"Did you eat knishes when you were young, when you were . . . ?" Theo's voice trailed away as his courage abandoned him.

"A Jew?" Michael finished his son's sentence. To Theo's surprise, he looked amused, not angry.

"Yes."

"I did," said Michael. "And I eat them now when I'm not one anymore. Just like I loved Coney Island when I was a kid and love it now just as much—especially the knishes." He laughed, taking another bite.

"Did you come here with your father?"

"Of course not!" said Michael, laughing even more. "You've met him. He'd rather have died than be seen here. 'Sodom by the Sea' was what he used to call this place. He'd have beaten me with his belt if he'd known where I was going."

"But you still went?"

"Yes, whenever I could borrow a nickel for the subway ride. I had more freedom than you, I suppose, and less school. Maybe that was bad. I don't know. I could have used some more learning. But one thing I was sure of was that this place was Paradise by the Sea, not Sodom. Everyone could have a good time. It didn't matter where you were from or who you were, and it still doesn't. Coney Island's about families having fun, not starving themselves and wailing to

Jehovah all weekend. It's about people who work hard all week having a chance to let their hair down and eat hot dogs and relish and apple pie and enjoy the sunshine . . ." Michael stopped, smiling at his own verbosity. "It's America, I suppose. I felt it here when I was a kid, and that's why I loved it. It's what I'd crossed the sea to find, what I was hungry for, couldn't get enough of . . ."

He broke off again, looking out toward the ocean.

Theo suddenly felt a great wave of affection for his father. It was as if he was glimpsing another person buried beneath the driven, angry man his father had become. He wanted to know more, but before he could think of any more questions to ask, his father snapped out of his reverie, and the moment was gone.

"Enough of the past; enough of me!" he said, getting up. "This is your day, son. Not mine. Where do you want to go first?"

Theo didn't know, and so his father chose for him. They went to Steeplechase Park and paid the quarter admission and stood with their heads thrown back, watching the roller-coaster riders flying up and down in tight, stomach-lurching loops. Theo felt a guilty excitement as he stared up at the legs and underwear of the shrieking girls whose summer skirts billowed up in the wind as they were thrown this way and that.

He looked down and saw his father laughing again. "Don't worry. I was young once, too, you know," Michael shouted. And Theo had to smile, even though he felt ashamed.

The ride his father loved most and kept returning to was the steeplechase. He and Theo rode gaily painted wooden horses on parallel steel tracks that ran around the whole of the park. They went up and over a miniature lake, and then stretched forward, running neck and neck down the slope, inspired by the speed and the rush to believe that they were real jockeys whipping their horses toward the finishing line. But twice running, a fat man sailed past them on the inside track and claimed the victory.

"You want to know my secret?" he asked, leaning into Theo with a leer as they climbed down from their horses.

Theo stepped back and shook his head, appalled by the rancid smell of the fat man's breath.

"Well, I'll tell yer anyway," said the fat man, undeterred. "It's me weight takes me down quicker. Laws of gravity that's what it is. Just like ol' Isaac Newton told it. Young scrawny lad like you ain't got a chance against a big bloke like me."

The fat man laughed unpleasantly and disappeared into the crowd, leaving Theo feeling deflated. But he kept the information to himself, not wanting to spoil his father's illusions.

Or his father's mood. It was as if Michael was determined to be happy and for Theo to be so too. He spent money extravagantly and insisted that they try everything: from the blue-sparking Dodgem cars to the penny arcades to pitting his wits against Mr. Memory, who knew more facts than anyone in the world, according to the sign outside his tent. Michael knew a fair number, too, but he was unable to get the better of Mr. Memory with his questions and left a dollar poorer, although still in high spirits.

"He'd be competition for your know-it-all Mr. Eames," said Michael, digging his son in the ribs.

But the wounds of the night before were too raw for Theo to see the joke, and Michael quickly changed the subject, plying his son with more hot dogs—from Feltman's this time.

It was hot and humid and Theo was glad that they hadn't come to swim, wearing thick, itchy woolen costumes beneath their clothes like so many of the other pleasure-seekers. From the elevation of the boardwalk, they looked down at the multitude of people on the beach—so many bodies packed together across the expanse of sand that from a distance they didn't seem human at all but instead a vast impersonal patchwork of cloth and flesh, deprived of individual meaning. Beyond the incoming waves, in utter contrast, the ocean faded into an empty blue horizon toward which the early-evening sun was now slowly setting.

Walking back up Surf Avenue, they passed the freak show, glimpsing through half-open tent flaps Laurelino, the man with the revolving head, and the "Woman without Limbs"—and name, too, it seemed. Where did the freaks go when the day was done? Theo wondered. Did they have a home? Was there any mercy in the dark world left over for them?

Luna Park was lit now with a myriad of colored lights—fifty thousand of them, according to Michael, ever ready with a statistic. But Theo could see that many of the bulbs were broken and that the paint was peeling on the candy-colored cupolas and domes. All day he had willed himself to match his father's mood and be happy, struggling to deny this tinseled melancholy that had had its hand on his shoulder since the morning, and now held him tightly in its grip. He looked around at the ragtag crowd heading back toward the subway and understood that Coney Island wasn't real. It was an escape and nothing more from the reality of the Depression that still held the city and its inhabitants in its cruel maw, refusing to let them go.

Weeks passed and Theo's unease grew as his fourteenth birthday got closer, and his father still made no reference to Theo's future. He was torn between a reluctance to raise the subject for fear of provoking another violent outburst and a wish to force the issue and be done with the anxious suspense that was eating away at him.

Michael, in contrast, had seemed much happier since the expedition to Coney Island and frequently referred to their shared experience. Whole dinners would pass with Michael describing to Elena the thrill of the steeplechase or his failure to get the better of Mr. Memory, while Theo squirmed in impotent frustration, answering in monosyllables when his father reminded him of particular highlights. Elena sometimes became irritated by Theo's reticence, telling him to "sit up straight and answer your father," but Michael appeared unaffected, happily continuing with his stories. There was a new opaque quality to his father that Theo couldn't penetrate, and he felt sometimes as if he were being played like a fish on the end of an expert angler's line.

At school, Mr. Eames noticed the change in his star pupil.

"You're thirty seconds slower," he said, holding out his stopwatch accusingly as Theo finished his practice run, too out of breath to respond.

"Something's changed. You've lost energy and concentration. You're not going through the gears; you're grinding them, acting like they don't exist. Forcing the pace and then having nothing left. It's like you've forgotten everything I've taught you."

Each rebuke hit Theo like blows to the solar plexus, but he said nothing, keeping his head down so that Mr. Eames couldn't see the effect his words were having.

"You can't get away with going at this half cocked. I don't know how many times I've told you that. Some meets you can still win because there's not the competition, but when we go back to City College, you're running against the best—athletes that have a chance of representing their country one day. And the way you are now, they're going to eat you for breakfast. I don't want Charlie Booker to see that. Not after what I've told him about you. Not after how I've built you up."

"Don't you think I know that?" said Theo, forcing himself to answer. "Don't you know how grateful I am? I want to do well; I want to repay you, it's just . . ."

"Just what?"

"My father . . ." Theo stopped. Talking about his father to Mr. Eames felt like a betrayal. He could hear his father's voice on the night of the argument: *"He's not your father; I am. You'd do well to remember that, Theo."*

"What about your father?" asked Eames insistently.

"He says I have to leave school when I'm fourteen and go to work in his factory. He says running doesn't matter, or school either."

"Ah," said Eames, letting out a deep sigh. "Now I see."

The next day Mr. Eames asked Theo to remain behind after practice. They sat on the bleachers like they did on the first day they met, when Mr. Eames saved Theo from a beating by the O'Donnell boys, and just as he did then, Eames lit a cigarette and watched the blue smoke rise into the still late-summer air. He stayed silent for a long time.

"I spoke harshly to you yesterday and I'm sorry for that," he said at last. "You're not one to slack off, and I should've seen that something must've happened."

"It doesn't matter," said Theo, looking out across the cinder track to the brick wall of the school with the lead roofs of the classrooms rising beyond. Everything seemed monochrome—empty and forlorn.

"But that's where you're wrong. It does matter," said Mr. Eames passionately. "You have a rare talent and I think—no, I know—you have a chance of doing something special, and I don't want you to lose that opportunity."

"Neither do I," said Theo flatly. "But I don't see what I can do about it."

"How about if I talk to him? Maybe I can get him to see what's at stake."

"Would you?" said Theo, suddenly excited. "Would you do that for me?"

"Of course I would," said Mr. Eames, clapping Theo on the shoulder. "It'll carry more weight coming from me."

It was amazing the effect that a little hope had on Theo. Or perhaps it was having an ally, somebody who would speak for him. He wanted to believe that his father would see reason, and he was encouraged when both his parents proved receptive to the idea of Mr. Eames visiting.

"You must keep an open mind," Elena told her husband. "We must think of what is best for Theo."

"You can rely on me for that, my dear," said Michael, smiling broadly. "I'm looking forward to meeting this man whom I've heard so much about."

At any other time, his father's apparent change of attitude to Mr. Eames would have rung alarm bells for Theo, but his newfound optimism made him take everything at face value, and he happily reported back to his coach that six o'clock on Friday would work very well for his visit, and that both his parents would be there to hear what he had to say.

Elena was not used to having visitors and spent the whole day cleaning the apartment, dusting in invisible corners and scouring every surface not once but twice with disinfectant, so that the rooms smelled more like a hospital than a living space by the time she had finished.

"Nothing but the best for our friend, the coach," said Michael, raising his eyebrows when he returned from work. But he seemed amused, not angry, as he settled into his armchair to await their guest's arrival.

The doorbell rang at precisely six, and Theo felt a surge of gratitude to Mr. Eames as he went out into the hall of the apartment building to greet him, knowing the importance that both his parents attached to punctuality. And he was encouraged, too, by the effort that Mr. Eames had made with his dress. Gone was all trace of his usual extravagant getup, replaced instead with a gray, off-the-rack suit and a conservative navy-blue tie.

"Best not to smoke," said Theo as he led the way down the corridor. "My mother doesn't like it. And my father's a Republican, but you've probably guessed that already. He's got a picture of the president on the wall."

"And I've got a picture of Joe Stalin in my bedroom," said Mr. Eames.

Theo stopped dead, looking back at his coach, open-mouthed.

"Come on! I'm joking," said Mr. Eames, laughing. "The point is, none of that matters. I'm here to talk about your running, remember? Not what I think of Herbert Hoover."

Theo nodded, but now, at the last moment, he was seized with a terrible misgiving. He thought of the change in his father since the night of the argument. He was planning something. Theo was sure of it. His father wasn't the type to give way, and Theo knew how much he wanted him at the factory. The running meant nothing to him. "Ridiculous"—that's what he'd called it.

Theo wanted to run, and so he had wanted to believe he could. That had been his mistake. He'd built up his hopes like a castle in the sand on Coney Island's beach.

He turned to his coach, searching for a way to explain. But it was too late. He didn't even know how to begin. And like an automaton, he opened the door of the apartment and let the different halves of his life collide.

"Now, Michael, listen to what Mr. Eames has to say," said Theo's mother, having settled their guest in the other comfortable armchair across from her husband and the radio console.

"I certainly will, Elena. I'm all ears," said Michael, who had courteously gotten to his feet when Mr. Eames came in, shaken his hand, asked him how he was, and wished him a cordial good evening.

So far, so good, thought Theo, perched beside his mother on the edge of the couch, positioned between Mr. Eames and his father. But then he immediately thought again that it was all too good to be true, and his nervous anxiety grew to match his mother's.

Elena had convinced herself that Mr. Eames was going to spill some of his iced tea on the carpet. She had moved an occasional table close to his right knee, but he had not taken the hint and kept his glass in his hand, where it tipped dangerously from side to side as he made hand gestures to support his arguments. Elena stared at the movement of the liquid, willing him to put the glass down.

Finally, Eames was done, wrapping up with a rosy description of Theo's prospects for athletic glory if he kept training hard and preserved his focus.

"What are you saying?" asked Michael. "That he could represent his country, go to the Olympics?"

"Yes, it's certainly a possibility," said Eames. "Theo's got the talent; it's just a question of how hard he's prepared to work at it."

"He's always worked hard," said Elena. "He's a good boy and we're very proud of him, aren't we, Michael?"

Theo's father nodded, but said nothing. He was looking hard at Eames with a quizzical expression on his face that Theo couldn't interpret.

"I'm sure you are," said Eames, glancing from one parent to the other. "You've every reason to be."

"I'll give it everything I've got," said Theo earnestly. He had never heard his coach speak about the Olympics before. In five years, at the Games in 1936, he'd be turning nineteen, which would be the perfect age. For a moment he was there, imagining flags, a crowd like in Yankee Stadium, the touch of his feet on the track accelerating into the bend . . .

And then it was gone. He was back on the couch, watching his father, who was talking in that same even tone that Theo so much distrusted.

"Well, all this sounds very exciting," he said. "But I do have a couple of questions."

"Of course," said Eames. Theo thought for a moment his coach was going to say *shoot* or *fire away* like they did on the radio, but thankfully he didn't.

"Well, first off, is this just your opinion that our son's so special? I don't mean to be rude, but you're just a high school coach, and I'm sure there are plenty of other teachers in your position all over the country who think their pupils are star prospects, but that doesn't mean that they are."

"No. It's a fair point, Mr. Sterling, and you're right to make it. But the fact is that I've got a second opinion from a coach who's far more qualified than me, and he thinks just as highly of Theo as I do."

"And who might this person be?"

"His name's Charles Booker. He runs the program at City College, and he organizes some of the interstate competitions too. He's got a lot of experience."

"Ah, yes. City College," said Michael. "That's in Harlem, isn't it?"

"Overlooking Harlem."

"And they have Black athletes there, don't they?"

"Yes. They have everyone. That's how you find out who's the best."

"So I'm assuming Mr. Booker must have watched our son to form his assessment of his capabilities. Would you mind telling me where he did that, Mr. Eames?"

"At City College."

"How many times?"

"Twice, I think."

"And that's something Saint Peter's knows about, is it? That you've been taking their kids over to Harlem to compete?"

"No, I don't need to ask them. It's left up to me to design the athletics program," said Eames, starting to sound defensive.

"Well, I think it's something we would have liked to know about. Don't you agree, Elena?"

Theo's mother nodded, a frozen expression on her face. One Hundred Tenth Street was a boundary between two countries as far as she was concerned. Anyone who went north of there was risking their life, and Michael knew full well that she would be appalled that Eames had taken their son to such a dangerous place.

"Now, Mr. Eames, you can see how shocked my wife is," said Michael. "And you may be wondering why I'm not too? I can assure you it's not because I approve."

Eames said nothing, but Theo could see from the rigidity of his pose that he was holding himself in.

"Let me explain," said Michael. "When Theo told me about these ideas you've been filling his head with, I thought I should make some inquiries."

"Inquiries!" repeated Eames angrily. "Have you been spying on me?" He put his iced tea down, and Theo could see that his fists were balled up and his face had gone red.

"I wouldn't want to call it that," said Michael. "I just wanted to know who I was dealing with. That's all. I make no apologies. I think any father would have done the same when their son's future is at stake. And I'm glad I did do some digging, because some of what I heard back worried me. I was about to talk to Theo and Elena about it, but then when I heard you were coming over, I thought I'd wait and let you give your side of the story."

"What story?" asked Eames, speaking through clenched teeth.

"The story about you and Mr. Booker both being signed-up members of the Labor Sports Union of America. Do you deny that, Mr. Eames?"

Eames said nothing and Theo's father laughed. "Well, there's not much point in you pretending it's not true. Two months ago, you wrote an article for their magazine, *Sport and Play*, about the next Olympics. I've got it over there in my bureau. I congratulate you, Mr. Eames—it was very well written, full of interesting ideas."

"I don't understand, Michael," said Elena, looking confused. "What is this Sports Union?"

"It's an organ of the United States Communist Party," said Michael. "And the Olympics Mr. Eames is wanting to train our son for isn't the Olympics you know about, Elena; it's the Workers' Counter-Olympics. The next one's in Chicago. He's training our son up to be a Red. That's what he's doing, and the joke is that Theo doesn't even know it."

But now Theo did. He remembered the big banner across the finish line the first time they went to City College and the song they'd sung before the races, echoing around the empty stadium, and how Coach Eames had looked—the fire in his eyes as he sang. It was all true, what his father was saying. Every bit of it.

"We must tell the school," said Elena, standing up. The color had drained from her face and she was trembling.

Eames was standing, too, looking down at Theo's father as if he was of a mind to strike him. "Is that what you intend to do?" he demanded. "Because if so, why did you have me over here? Why put us all through this ridiculous charade? Just for your own cheap amusement, is that it?"

"No, it was because I wanted my wife and son to see who they were dealing with. I wanted them to understand why Theo needs me to watch over him while I teach him my business. And, to answer your question: No, I won't tell the school if you do what I ask."

"Which is what?"

"Give up the Communist Party and stop seeing my son."

"Why should I? I've done nothing wrong," said Eames, blustering. "There's nothing illegal about being a Communist."

"No. But I don't think the school will see it that way. Do you?"

Eames looked away, breathing deeply, and then nodded. "I'll stop seeing your son," he said. "But the rest is my business."

Eames settled his hand for a moment on Theo's shoulder. "I'm sorry," he said. "This isn't what I wanted for you." And then, picking up his hat in the hallway, he fixed it on his head, opened the door, and was gone.

All weekend, Theo felt hope and belief leaving him like air escaping from a slowly deflating balloon. It drained him of strength, even more when he tried to resist the process.

At breakfast the next morning he had a brief confrontation with his father. He was angry with him, angrier than he had ever felt at anyone, but he was fearful of him, too, and of what he might do.

"You're upset now," said Michael, coolly regarding his son as he sat between his parents with his eyes fixed on the tablecloth, studiously ignoring the huevos rancheros—his favorite dish, of fried eggs on tortillas with a salsa of cilantro and tomatoes, that his mother had cooked for him specially that morning. "But one day you'll thank me. That man was leading you astray."

"Astray!" Elena cried. "He is a devil, a ravenous wolf!" She banged her fist on the table. "One of those that Our Lord warned us against—false prophets who come to us in sheep's clothing. It is monstrous—we send our son to a Catholic school, and they deliver him to a Communist."

"They didn't know," said Michael reasonably.

"They need to know now," she fired back. "I'll tell them if you won't."

"No!" yelled Theo. The sudden violence of his outburst, breaking his morning silence, shocked his parents into momentary silence themselves. "We made an agreement with my coach—here, last night—and we aren't going back on it now. If you do, I'll run away," he said, turning furiously on his father. "I'll do what you did to your parents."

"Be quiet! Don't you dare speak to me like that!" Michael shouted at his son, half rising from the table. It was the first time he'd looked shaken and Theo felt a momentary empowerment, knowing his shaft had hit home.

Michael sat back down, making a visible effort to control himself. "I think it's best we don't tell the school," he said. "We can't take Theo out until he's fourteen, and this way there'll be no trouble."

"You're going to put your faith in a Communist?" asked Elena, shaking her head in disbelief. "You fool. The first chance he gets, he'll be pouring his poison into our son's ear again."

"No, he won't. He knows what will happen if he does that. And besides, Theo won't listen," said Michael. "Will you, son?" He looked hard at Theo, waiting for an answer.

Theo shook his head: a quick, almost imperceptible movement that didn't satisfy his father.

"You need to tell us you won't talk to that man again. Yes or no: we need to hear it, Theo," demanded his father.

"Yes! I told you I won't if you leave him alone. He's the only one who cares about me because of who I am. Not like you and Mama. You just want things from me," Theo shouted as he got up from the table, pushing his uneaten food away.

On Sunday, he went to church with his mother. It felt easier to go than to say no. There was a cold, unseasonable wind blowing through the old trees in Gramercy Park, and as they passed the iron gates, a cloud of black rooks flew up over the roofs of the tall town houses, circled chaotically in the gray sky, and then settled back down into the high branches, cawing raucously to each other. Elena smiled, looking up, but Theo shivered, wishing he could throw a stone and stop their hoarse cackling.

At Mass this time, Theo forced himself to look straight into the eyes of the crucified Christ hanging down over the chancel of the church. He stared up, taking in the nails, the cruelly bent knees, the crown of thorns, and the INRI inscription scrolled across the apex of the cross. He tried to understand what his mother felt about this man who stood at the center of her world, reaching out into all she saw and touched, and wondered how she could be so certain about events that had happened nineteen hundred years ago in some distant land that she had never seen, things that made no scientific sense.

Christ lived and died. That Theo could readily accept, looking up at the cross. But then he'd risen—rolled away the stone sometime on the Saturday night or Sunday morning and walked out of the tomb. And saved the world.

But how could he believe that? People who died were dead. Like the old man with the shock of white hair who was hit by the garbage truck on Twelfth Street the year before. He'd gone out into the road without looking and slipped on the ice, and then he was lying there right in front of Theo with his limbs all out at a funny angle and his eyes staring and nothing behind them. Nothing at all—Theo had had time to see that for himself before his mother pulled him away, hurrying off down the street, shaking and crying. And he'd known then just as he knew now that there was no coming back from that. No chance.

Theo looked at his mother standing beside him in the pew with her black veil falling over her shoulders, reciting the Creed with such triumphant certainty in her voice, and he understood with sudden intuition that her faith came from her heart, formed whole and unbreakable as a diamond crystal in her earliest consciousness in that hot southern country that he had never seen. She felt Christ and he didn't. Felt the presence of the living God in the trees and the rooks and the orioles when he saw only what he saw, nothing else. That was the difference between them—inevitable, perhaps, when she had grown up on a coffee plantation in rural Jalisco, where religion infused every facet of daily life, while he was a child of New York City, where everything was man-made, and what you saw was what you got.

And yet on this Sunday morning, Theo wanted to believe because he needed some outside power to appeal to that would intervene to stop his father from ruining his life by imprisoning him in his dreary factory manufacturing ready-to-wear women's garments. A prison sentence without parole. And so Theo looked up at the crucified Christ and prayed.

Outside, afterward, Sir Andrew came up to them, taking off his hat as he bowed to Elena. Theo inwardly groaned—he hadn't seen him at the Mass, so he must have been sitting somewhere behind them. And he hadn't expected to see him either. Sir Andrew had not been at the church for several months, and Theo had privately hoped that he might be gone for good.

"You've grown, young man," said Sir Andrew. "You'll be as tall as me soon."

Theo nodded, keeping his eyes on the ground.

"How old are you now?"

"Thirteen."

"He'll be fourteen in October," said Elena, trying to make up for her son's taciturnity.

"An important birthday," said Sir Andrew. "I shall have to bring you another book illustrated by our friend, Mr. Rackham."

"No, you mustn't," said Elena.

"Why mustn't I?" asked Sir Andrew, playfully imitating her. "I hope Theo liked *King Arthur*?"

"He loves it; looks at it almost every night, don't you, Theo?"

Theo said nothing. He felt furious with his mother, but he couldn't contradict her, given that what she said was true.

"So what's the problem then?" Sir Andrew asked her, smiling.

"It's too much. It gives him ideas when he's got to keep his feet on the ground. He's leaving school soon and going to work in his father's factory."

"At fourteen? Isn't that a bit young? A bright lad like your son could do well with an education behind him."

"His father knows best," said Elena, injecting into her voice a note of finality that Sir Andrew was quick to pick up on.

"Of course," he said, backing off. "Please forgive me, señora. I didn't mean to intrude."

It was too much. For a moment Theo had thought that Christ had found a way to answer his prayers. The English nobleman would make his ignorant mother see the error of her ways, and she would go back and tell her husband that Theo was staying at school because it would be a waste of his talents to be sent to the factory. And his father would have to give way because he didn't want to cross his wife. It was for her benefit, after all, that he'd put on that charade with Coach Eames. He'd needed to get her on his side.

But the flame of hope died again as soon as it had been lit. Sir Andrew didn't care about him. Of course he didn't. He talked to him and flattered him and gave him books because it allowed him to engage with Theo's mother. And her son's presence beside her meant she could flutter her eyes behind her veil without anyone being able to accuse her of impropriety. Except Theo, of course. It was too much. He couldn't bear it anymore.

"Stop it! Stop flirting with him," he said viciously, finally letting go of all the anger he had pent up inside.

"What?" asked Elena, astonished. "What did you say?"

"You heard me," said Theo defiantly.

Suddenly, without warning, she brought her left hand back and slapped her son hard across the cheek. Her wedding ring caught him on the lip, which began to bleed.

In the ringing silence that followed, Sir Andrew took a handkerchief out of his pocket and gave it to Theo. "You should apologize to your mother," he said gravely. "What you said is beneath you."

Theo looked Sir Andrew in the eye, refusing to be cowed. "I should have said it to you, then," he told him. "I know what you were doing."

Sir Andrew flushed with anger, but he had no chance to respond. People were gathered around them now, asking questions, trying to understand what had happened. Elena was crying, and Father Juan had taken her arm and was leading her toward the presbytery. Theo followed, clutching the handkerchief. He'd like to have run away, but he knew that that would only make things worse. He hated himself for what he'd done to his mother, and he hated her for what she'd done to him. Once inside, he sat down in a corner and closed his eyes, overcome by a black despair.

At home, nunlike, Elena withdrew into herself, making no reference to what had happened. She couldn't without naming the vile allegation Theo had made, and she felt instinctively that that would be in some perverse way to acknowledge it. And she knew, too, that talking increased the risk that her husband would hear of it. She was frightened of that and worried, too, that Theo would say something to his father if she provoked him.

She had searched her conscience both alone, kneeling before the shrine in her bedroom, and with Father Juan in the confessional, and she knew she had done nothing wrong. And Father Juan had assured her that Don Andrés was guilty of nothing improper. He had just been polite and courteous—the way well-bred English gentlemen are known for being with ladies of their acquaintance.

Elena could think of nothing her son could have done that would have wounded her so deeply, and she could not understand how he could think such a thing, let alone say it in public, humiliating her in front of her countrymen, whose good opinion she cared about so much.

Father Juan had suggested that she might prefer to come to church on Wednesday evenings instead of on Sundays, at least for a while, but she would have none of it, walking up the nave to her pew with her head held high. She went alone, however, having told Theo to remain at home, excommunicating him until he had repented of his sin.

But he did not repent. He was as angry as his mother, and he cared nothing about being denied the sacrament because he was angry with God too. He had prayed to the crucified Christ and nothing had happened, and now he wanted to know if that was because God didn't care or because he wasn't there. Theo strongly suspected the latter and decided to make an experiment to prove his hypothesis. The fact that it would involve further punishment of his mother only served to provide him with a stronger incentive to proceed.

Two Sundays after the debacle at the church, he got his chance. His father had a meeting in the Garment District after breakfast, and when his mother left to go to Mass, he had the apartment to himself.

He went into his mother's bedroom. The window was a little open, and a slight breeze was rustling the half-drawn drapes. The sun had risen above the rooftops, and its slanting beams shone through the gap down onto the gray rug and as far as the side of the pretty Mexican quilt drawn tightly up over the bed. Theo remembered his mother embroidering it years before, amazed in the end at how something so vibrant and colorful could come from so many hours of delicate threading.

In the shadows on the bedside table, Theo caught sight of a photograph of his grandparents: a middle-aged man with wide-awake eyes in a high collar and tie with his layered hair brushed back from his forehead, and his wife, who looked diminutive and shy and unmistakably the mother of Elena. He turned away quickly. His business was not with them.

Across from the bed, out of the light, was the shrine. Small half-burned votive candles set in brass holders stood on either side of a low altar surmounted by Christ on a wooden cross. He was much smaller here and without the horror of the hung body in the church. Below, a tall rectangular picture of the olive-skinned Virgin of Guadalupe held pride of place with a glass vase of drooping pansies picked from the garden and small pictures and statues of Elena's favorite saints closely arrayed on either side. There was the icon of Saint Theodore holding his dragon-slaying lance, a tiny reproduction of Giotto's picture of Saint Francis feeding the birds, a wooden Saint Anthony of Padua that she had prayed to for Theo's safe return when he was taken by his grandfather, and, over to the side, a porcelain statue of Christ in a blue robe with a benevolent expression on his bearded face. Theo had been with his mother when she had bought this last from a street vendor on Fourteenth Street years before. She'd haggled over the price, and Theo had thought at the time how strange it was that Christ should have been standing there on the ground between piles of neckties and candy bars.

He would have preferred the cross, but it was wooden and would not break, and the Christ figure was an acceptable second best. He picked it up carefully but then half stumbled over his mother's needlepoint kneeler as he stepped back, righted himself, and then walked over to the tiled fireplace.

Now, glancing back at the shrine, he didn't want to carry on. He was disgusted with himself, but ironically it was his sense of the enormity of the crime he was about to commit that forced him on. If Christ existed, then he would surely find a way to punish him for smashing his effigy, and then Theo would know. Once and for all, he would have his answer.

Slowly opening his hand, he allowed the statue to fall onto the hard tile, where it broke into several pieces, but not as many as if he had thrown it on the ground as he had originally intended.

He looked down at Christ's broken head and immediately realized the absurdity of his act. What had seemed of vital importance a moment before now felt cheap and sordid. It proved nothing except his own meanness born of his need to hurt his mother. Because why would Christ care if a boy broke a dollar statue mass manufactured somewhere over the river in New Jersey? He had infinitely worse things to worry about, with people starving and out of work. If he was up there at all, which Theo now realized he was never going to know.

What mattered was that Theo was alone. That was what he needed to understand. Nobody was going to stop him going to his father's factory when he was fourteen and, given that he was too young to run away, he'd better get used to the prospect and learn to adapt.

He went over to the fireplace and carefully picked up the broken pieces of the statue and replaced them one by one on the altar, and then he went into the kitchen to wait for his mother. He would tell her that he'd picked Christ up and taken him over to the light to get a better look and then he'd slipped. He'd say it was an unfortunate accident and that he was sorry, and that when he went to work in his father's factory, he would save up his earnings to buy her another statue of her Savior—even more beautiful than the one she'd lost.

On the last day of school Theo went over to the sports pavilion in the afternoon. It was a half day after prize-giving and almost everyone had gone home, so he thought he would be alone.

It was full summer now and the sun shone down hard and relentless on the cinder track, and inside the pavilion the familiar smells filled his nostrils, intensified by the heat—moist towels mildewing in half-open lockers, ankle tape and unwashed socks, decomposition. Beyond the silence, Theo fancied he could almost hear the voices of his teammates shouting encouragement to each other across the room as they got ready to go out. The sensations pained him. He'd been a fool to come.

A shadow fell across the doorway, and he instinctively backed away into a corner. But the newcomer sensed his presence immediately and stopped awkwardly just inside the threshold. Theo saw that it was Coach Eames.

"Oh, it's you," said Eames. "What a strange coincidence—I was thinking of you, just a moment ago as I was walking over, and now here you are. How are you, Theo?"

"I'm all right, I guess," said Theo guardedly. "I was just looking . . ." He stopped, realizing he had no real explanation for his presence in the pavilion. "Anyway, I'm going now. We're not supposed to talk, you know."

"I know," said Eames, stepping aside. He looked dejected. Like a runner coming in from a defeat, Theo thought.

Theo walked out into the sunlight and started back toward the school. He felt his memories clutching at him like tentacles, and he balled his hands into fists, pushing them deep down into his pockets, repelling grief with anger. He knew that he needed to be tough now if he was going to survive, and wallowing in the past was a stupid way to begin.

Behind him, Coach Eames was calling his name. He stopped, turned around, hesitated a moment, and then walked back.

"You forgot these," said Eames, holding out Theo's spiked shoes. "You don't know when you might need them again."

Turned over in Theo's hand, the silver pins shone in the sun and he remembered Mr. Eames holding the shoes out to him in the pavilion on that first day and how they had felt out on the track, propelling his feet forward in effortless strides.

He started to walk away, but then turned back. There was something he needed to say, but he didn't know how to say it, and so after a moment he just held out his hand. And Eames, with a smile, took it.

"Thank you," said Theo. "Thank you for believing in me."

"I still do," said Eames. "Nothing's changed about that."

6

FACTORY

Michael took Theo to Yankee Stadium for his fourteenth birthday (making up for not having done so on his thirteenth), and Babe Ruth hit a home run off the third pitch of his last inning, fired by the Red Sox pitcher low and inside.

Theo never forgot the moment: the score deadlocked and all those tens of thousands of people around him silently concentrated on that one distant figure in the blue cap and striped number 3 jersey, willing him to give them what they all craved. Everything frozen, and then the flash of the action: the pitcher's arm drawn back and Babe pulling away from the plate and stepping in to connect with such violence and exquisite precision.

The ball sailed high into the azure late-afternoon sky and descended in a sweet arc straight toward Theo high up in the bleachers. He stood with his hands extended, certain in that moment that he would catch it, that it had to be, but then it passed over his head and was gone.

And the game was over. The waves of cheering flowed through the stadium as Ruth trotted around the bases and tapped his foot on home plate. He looked up, took off his cap with a theatrical gesture, waved it to the crowd, and disappeared from view.

Afterward, in the crush of bodies leaving the stadium, Theo looked over at his father and saw his eyes were shining.

"Wasn't he magnificent?" Michael said.

Theo nodded.

"Think of it: he had nothing—went to a reform school, for God's sake—but out there he fears no one, takes second place to no one, and there's nothing he can't do," said Michael with wonder in his voice.

"But not for much longer," said a man standing behind them. "He's thirty-six, almost over the hill. Enjoy it while you can, son. Nothing lasts forever."

"The Babe will," said Michael defiantly, but the man was gone, taking the magic of the day with him.

And two days later, Theo went to work at his father's factory.

They took a bus up Broadway and got off in Herald Square because Michael said he wanted to walk the rest of the way. Theo dawdled, slowing their pace. He felt as if a door was closing in his life and that once he reached the factory, it would close forever, shutting off all connection to a past that he was still finding it hard to let go of.

But Michael showed no signs of impatience. He was excited but kept level with his son by stepping sideways and then forward, almost as if he were waltzing. And all the time he kept up a constant stream of chatter like a verbally incontinent tour guide. He seemed unaware of his son's misery, or at least had made a decision to appear so, following a strategy determined in advance. Whichever was the case, his father's insensitivity riled Theo, whose resentment against him was still as strong as ever. Days out at Yankee Stadium were no more than a temporary sticking plaster over a wound that had not healed, and it was only fear of his father and a sense of realism—a quality that Theo possessed in advance of his years—that kept him from further protest.

"This whole district used to be called the Tenderloin," said Michael, waving his arm expansively. "Do you know why?"

Theo shook his head glumly.

"Well, I'll tell you. It used to be a bad neighborhood. Worse than Harlem, worse than Hell's Kitchen even. The locals called it Satan's Circus, if that gives you an idea of what it was like. There was every kind of vice here—saloons, gambling houses, you name it—and when this police captain called Williams—Clubber Williams, he was known as, for the way he used his billy club—got transferred here, he rubbed his hands together and said: 'I've been eating chuck steak since I've been on the force, now I'm going to have me some tenderloin!'"

Michael imitated the rubbing for a moment and then stopped and slapped his side, laughing uproariously. But Theo looked puzzled. He'd become interested in spite of himself in what his father was saying, but now he didn't get the joke.

"Don't you get it?" said Michael. "Clubber was talking about how much money he was going to make from taking kickbacks. And boy, he did! He was a millionaire by the time he died, and nobody could lay a finger on him."

"He was a crook," said Theo.

"Yes, of course he was. But that didn't mean he wasn't a successful one," said Michael with a sly smile. "It's not easy to make a million, you know."

Now they were on Seventh Avenue, passing high art deco loft buildings with elaborately patterned marble facades. At the intersections, the traffic was heavily congested with delivery trucks double- and even triple-parked on the cross streets, while they were being loaded and unloaded by sweating warehousemen. Push boys threaded their way between them, wheeling metal racks laden with swaying dresses and coats. And all the time, Theo's father was shouting above the cacophonous noise, pointing out landmarks and telling Theo who owned what and whether they were going up or down in the world.

Michael was going up, or at least that was what he told Theo to explain his recent move to the building that they had now reached. And, at least initially, Theo believed him. They crossed a large entrance hall with a wide staircase and several elevators, and Michael opened a door in the corner with **MICHAEL STERLING** engraved in gold capitals on the frosted glass. Inside, a middle-aged lady wearing bright-pink lipstick and thick horn-rimmed glasses interrupted her typing to greet Michael and be introduced to Theo.

"This is a red-letter day, Mrs. Hirsch," said Michael, keeping his hand proprietorially on Theo's shoulder.

"Indeed, it is," said the secretary, beaming at Theo, who managed a weak smile in return. "I'm sure young Master Sterling will be an asset to the firm."

"Thank you. I believe he will," said Michael, obviously pleased. "And now, don't let me interrupt you further. I'm going to show the young master around."

Beyond Mrs. Hirsch's room was a long gallerylike showroom with built-in mahogany sample cabinets and a double row of tailors' dummies hung with an array of garments in different styles, from shimmering evening gowns flowing to the floor to bias-cut, body-skimming dresses and smart summer suits.

"This is where we bring the customers," said Michael proudly, stroking a satin sleeve. "They come in from all over the country. Penn Station's just down the road, you know."

Theo nodded. He was impressed, but past his father's chatter he sensed a stillness in the room, a museum-like quality that was at odds with the picture of busy commercial activity that his father was trying to convey.

Behind the showroom was Michael's office, which was as untidy as the showroom was neat. Papers and account books overflowed from open filing cabinets onto chairs and other surfaces and mounted to a tottering pile on his big desk at the back.

"Don't worry. There's order in the chaos," said Michael, seeing his son's surprise and looking around the office as if for the first time. "But that doesn't mean I can't do with some help. This is where you'll be, at least to start with, while you're learning the ropes," he said, pointing to a smaller desk under the window, currently the only uncluttered surface in the room, with only an inkstand and blotter on the top.

Outside in the street, more of the ubiquitous push boys were at work, and a rack of pink dresses with elaborate ruffles kept pace comically with a man in a pinstripe suit, distracting Theo for a moment from the weight of the world, which he felt settling down on his slight shoulders.

It wasn't until the afternoon that Theo got his tour of the factory.

"It's best to wait for Frank," Michael had explained. "You'll like him."

And, rather to his surprise, Theo did. Frank Vogel had been Michael's manager for a long time. They'd been together when Michael was running sweatshops in the Lower East, and it was obvious that Michael trusted him completely. Theo could see why. There was an openness about Frank that was instantly appealing and he spoke plainly, telling the truth as he saw it.

He shook Theo's hand and then stood back, looking him up and down. He was a tall, heavy man with strength in his arms and penetrating green eyes that reminded Theo of his grandmother's—the kind that look deep down into people and assess them for who they really are.

"How old are you?" he asked.

"Fourteen." Theo felt annoyed with himself that he sounded so jittery, almost stuttering over the word.

"Well, I was two years younger than you when I started, and I remember I felt as nervous as a long-tailed cat in a room full of rocking chairs. But I soon got used to it. And you will too."

"Thank you, Frank," said Michael a little testily. "But my son's not a cat and he's got no reason to be nervous, so don't go putting ideas in his head. Shall we show him round?"

"Right away, boss," said Frank, standing aside for Michael to lead the way and winking at Theo as he followed him out of the door.

To Theo's surprise, the factory was not in the same building as his father's office. Instead, they crossed the street and went in through a warehouse entrance diagonally opposite to the window above Theo's desk.

At the back, a big man in a dirty white singlet that bulged out over his stomach was standing with a metal rack of dresses, waiting for the elevator to descend. A sign on the gate read **Goods Only**.

"Wait up, Easey," said Frank. "We'll ride with you."

The big man grunted. When they got closer, Theo could see in the dim light that his head was shaped like a cannonball: completely round and bald with two small bullet-like eyes above a mouth and nose that were twisted as if from an old injury, freezing his facial expression into a permanent scowl.

The elevator arrived, settling in place with an alarming noise of creaking and clanking, and Easey pulled back the iron grille and pushed his handcart inside. Theo noticed that he limped as he walked. The rest of them fitted uncomfortably into the small space that was left.

Easey was now hidden behind the dresses, but looking down below their hemlines, Theo could see that the shoe on his left foot was much bigger than on the right. It was more like a boot. Theo thought of the man's deformed clubfoot inside and felt ashamed of the instinctive revulsion that led him to shrink back against the elevator's grille.

"What's the problem with the dresses, Easey?" asked Frank. "I thought you were taking them over to Kramer's."

"They said they weren't right. Alvah needs to look at them again." Easey's voice was unexpectedly high-pitched, squeaky even, but its mean tone fitted with the impression of the man that Theo had gotten from seeing his face in the warehouse down below.

"Alvah needs to get it right the first time," said Frank.

Easey didn't answer. The elevator had reached the sixth floor, and he was already pushing out his handcart as the others got out. Theo felt a scrape on the back of his heel, which caused him to lift his foot in pain, but Easey had already turned a corner and was out of sight before he could say anything. The clubfoot clearly didn't stop Easey from moving quickly when he wanted to, and for the rest of the day, Theo was limping too.

Although it was much bigger, the factory initially reminded Theo of his grandfather's sweatshop. There were the same bare bulbs hanging down from the high ceilings, the same overpowering heat in the humid, fiber-filled air that made it hard to breathe, and the same black-and-gold Singer sewing machines at which lines of women in headscarves were hard at work, their fingers moving like lightning as the needles punched hundreds of stitches every minute through the fabric.

But as he walked around the factory floor, Theo soon realized that there were far more people here than in the sweatshop and many more machines. His father, ever the tour guide, named the different workers and their occupations as they moved from one area to the next, but soon they all blurred in Theo's mind and the whole place seemed a mass of basters and trimmers and spreaders and pressers, of Jacobs and Nathans and Isaacs, all indistinguishable from each other.

Theo was left with a general impression that, away from the sewing machines, most of his father's employees were men, and most had Jewish names and wore yarmulkes on their heads. But beyond that, he garnered no real understanding of what they were doing, just that they seemed to have no great affection for his father. They barely looked up when Michael told them who Theo was, remaining grimly intent on keeping up the pace of their work. Michael, however, seemed blissfully unaware of their hostility, glowing with pride as he took Theo around.

"And now I've saved the best for last," he said happily, stopping outside a closed wooden door in a plywood wall that had been used to partition off a corner of the factory floor, creating a separate room inside. He knocked, which surprised Theo, and then went in.

The cutter's room was very different from the rest of the factory. Theo sensed that immediately. The ventilation was clearly better, because he could breathe easier and it wasn't so hot. It was quieter, too, and the big window was sparkling clean.

At least half the floor space was taken up by a large rectangular table covered with paper patterns in different shapes, inscribed here and there with notes written in the same careful hand. Over toward the window, pieces of muslin were pinned to two tailor's dummies hung with tape measures, while to the sides of the room, shelves along one wall were crammed with portfolios labeled in the same handwriting. Two electric fabric-cutting machines with sharp blades were ranged against the other, but neither were in use when they came in.

At the center of the table, a man was working. He was wearing a waistcoat and his shirtsleeves were rolled up above his elbows, exposing the thick black hair on his forearms. Theo could see his face in profile: the carefully groomed mustache and small goatee, the long aquiline nose, and the curly dark hair oiled into place. Theo guessed him to be in his early thirties.

In his hand he had a pair of long silver scissors that he was using to cut a piece of pale fabric, and he did not look up from his task when Theo and the others entered. Instead, his thumb and middle finger continued to operate the scissors, moving with an even rhythm that was machinelike in its precision. The level of concentration required was extraordinary, and it wasn't just Theo who was aware of it. Michael had begun to speak when he came in but stopped, remaining where he was until the cutter finally put down his scissors and looked up, and it was only then that Theo became aware that there was another person in the room.

"That'll be all, Easey," the cutter said. "I'll see you later."

The warehouseman had been invisible behind the opened door, but now he came out of the corner where he had been standing and pushed past Theo on his way out. Theo felt an elbow in his side. It didn't hurt, but he felt dirtied by the contact and then immediately afterward experienced that same sense of shame he had felt in the elevator.

"What was that all about, Al?" asked Frank. "If there's a problem with Kramer's, then you need to talk to me—"

"No, he doesn't. Not now," interrupted Michael, sounding irritated. "This is much more important. Al, I want you to meet my son, Theodore. He's going to be working here with us, learning the ropes. Theo, this is our chief cutter, Alvah Katz."

Michael had put his hand on Theo's shoulder as he spoke, and now to Theo's surprise and discomfort, his father pushed him slightly forward toward the table.

For a moment the cutter looked intently at Theo, examining him in the same way he would a garment on one of his dummies. There was no warmth in his gray eyes.

"Pleased to meet you," he said when he was done, extending his hand, which Theo took. But as soon as there was contact between them, Alvah withdrew, turning his attention back to Michael. "I do have a question, Mr. Sterling."

"Yes, what is it?"

"You introduced your son as Theodore, but is that what you would like him to be called? Or would Mr. Theodore be better, or Master Theodore, or even perhaps Master Sterling, to distinguish him from your good self?"

"I don't know," said Michael. "I hadn't thought about it. What do you suggest?"

"It's not for me to suggest," said Alvah. "But perhaps it will depend on what role your son will be taking on."

"As I said, he'll be learning the ropes. He's going to be helping me in the business."

"So, will he be your deputy, your number two? Vice president of the company?"

"Yes, eventually. When he's ready."

"I see," said Alvah, looking grave.

"You see what?"

"Just that some of the workforce may not be very happy about having a teenager put in charge. It doesn't seem right, somehow, particularly when he's so inexperienced."

"He's learning the ropes. How many times do I have to tell you that?" said Michael, getting angry. "And the workers will do what I tell them to do or take the consequences. They should be grateful for having a job at all, with what's happening in the country."

"I'm afraid I don't agree. I—"

"I don't give a damn whether you agree," shouted Michael, cutting him off. And then stopped suddenly, passing a hand through his hair and taking a deep breath. "God, Alvah, you never give up, do you? Twisting everything I say, always looking for trouble, like you can't help yourself. No, don't bother answering," he said, raising his hand. "You'll just make it worse. You can call my son Master Sterling. It'll do you good to show some respect."

Michael left the room without waiting for a reply. But Theo caught Alvah Katz's eye as he turned to follow his father and saw that he was smiling. A mean, sardonic smile with no humor in it. Theo sensed the man's powerful malice and his capacity for cruelty, and suddenly felt frightened for his father.

Two days later, Theo had another encounter with the cutter, this time in his father's office.

It was midmorning, and Theo had been trying with very limited success to impose some order on the nearest of his father's chaotic filing cabinets. His mind had started to wander and he was idly looking out of the window, observing Easey Goldstein, who was leaning against a lamppost on the other side of the road, smoking the butt of a cigarette. There was something repulsive about the way he greedily sucked in the smoke that made Theo want to look away but at the same time kept him watching, fascinated to see whether he would keep going to the point where the butt burned his fingers.

Just as Easey finally dropped the butt on the ground, Alvah Katz emerged from the warehouse and stopped beside him, talking rapidly. He gesticulated several times as he spoke, pointing back inside, and Theo had the strong impression that he was giving instructions. Easey appeared to say nothing in response, but his usual hostile scowl was replaced by a look of intense concentration as he listened, which made Theo smile—it was somehow absurd on the warehouseman's moonlike face.

After a minute Easey nodded twice and went back inside, while Alvah crossed the road, coming straight toward Theo's window. Theo dropped his head, surprised at how much he wanted to avoid another encounter with the cutter. Sensing that Alvah was coming to the office, he thought of making an escape to the restroom, but then glanced over at his father, sitting looking careworn behind his desk, and changed his mind.

Less than a minute later, Mrs. Hirsch ushered in Alvah, who waited in the doorway with a faintly disapproving look on his face while the secretary cleared files from the chair across the desk from Michael and piled them on top of a cabinet.

"Sorry about the mess," said Michael pleasantly. "Theo and I are doing some spring cleaning. But we'll be organized in no time, won't we, son? The boy's already proving a great asset to me, Alvah. He's got a good head for figures. Gets it from his mother, I expect."

Theo was surprised at his father's friendly tone. He appeared to have completely forgotten the angry scene in the cutter's room.

"Now, what can I do for you?" Michael asked. "What brings you down from your aerie?"

Alvah smiled coldly at the banter. "What brings me down here, Mr. Sterling, is the discovery that, as of this morning, my colleagues upstairs are unable to leave the factory floor during work hours, or at least not without applying to Mr. Vogel. I think we all agree that it's simply not acceptable."

"Not acceptable. I see. Well, let me tell you what's not acceptable," said Michael, leaning forward across the desk. "People are leaving without permission when they're supposed to be working, and some of them are stealing. You know this because I've complained about it before. But nothing's happened and it still goes on. I don't know how they're doing it, but I'm going to get to the bottom of it, I can assure you of that. And in the meantime, the doors stay locked. That needn't apply to you, of course. I will arrange for you to have a key so that you can come and go, but I will need your assurance that you're not going to give it to anyone else."

"I can give you no such assurance," said Alvah primly. "I wish to be treated exactly the same as everyone else."

"Well, more fool you then," said Michael. "Do you want to be paid the same as them as well? That would certainly save the firm some money!"

"You're being absurd," said Alvah. He was silent for a moment, fingering his hat in his hands, and then he turned to look at Theo. "May I ask if you approve of this new policy of your father's, Master Sterling?"

Theo wilted under Alvah's scrutiny, saying nothing because he didn't know what to say.

"Perhaps it might help you to have a little background," said the cutter affably. "Years ago, when I was about your age, maybe even a little younger, I lived in the Village, and one fine day there was a fire in a garment factory over by Washington Square. Someone had dropped a cigarette in a scrap bin and whoosh—the sky was black with smoke and the bells of the fire engines were ringing, racing to the rescue from all over Manhattan. My mother and I went to look; everyone in my neighborhood did. The firefighters had their ladders up against the building, but they weren't high enough; they could only reach the seventh floor. There were girls at the windows of the upper floors, screaming. And then, all of a sudden, they started jumping. I remember some were holding hands. The firemen held up life nets but they weren't strong enough, and the girls fell through them. They died right in front of me, smashed to pieces on the stone pavement, and when the rest of the girls saw that, they didn't want to jump, but they had to because they were burning—their hair, their clothes . . . they were like living torches when they fell."

Theo gasped and Alvah paused, allowing his words to sink in.

"The owners had locked the doors. That's why that happened," he finished, keeping his eyes fixed on Theo.

On the other side of the desk, Michael slowly clapped his hands. "Quite a story!" he said. "I'm impressed, Alvah. You're always surprising me with your talents. But what happened twenty years ago has got nothing to do with our situation, as you well know. Frank has keys to the stairs, there's a well-maintained fire escape on the front of the building, and there's the goods elevator, too, if needed. But they won't be needed because there's not going to be a fire: no one's allowed to smoke and there are sprinklers in the ceiling that are checked every week."

Alvah didn't respond. He was still looking at Theo. "What do you think, Master Sterling?" he asked. "Should your father be locking the doors?"

Theo shook his head. It was almost an involuntary movement, an instinctive reaction to Alvah's terrible story.

"Thank you," said Alvah, getting to his feet and finally turning his attention back to his employer. "Mr. Sterling, I urge you to listen to your son," he said. And then, putting on his hat, he walked out of the office without waiting for a response.

Notwithstanding his father's oft-repeated assertion that he was there to learn the ropes, Theo remained downstairs in the office, except in the afternoon when he accompanied his father and Frank Vogel on their daily tour of the factory. And this also seemed to be the only time when Michael went up there as well, which surprised Theo, given the way his father had waxed lyrical about his company as a living, growing expression of himself throughout Theo's childhood.

Theo could see from some of the documents he had been set to organize that his father was being pressed by creditors on all sides, but he was no accountant and his father didn't talk to him about the firm's overall financial health. Michael's default setting had always been optimism, and he still seemed able to turn on the faucet of his self-belief when buyers' representatives came to the office. On these days he would dress in his best Brooks Brothers suit and tie and take the rep out to a three-course lunch at the Roman Gardens with a stop afterward at a speakeasy behind Penn Station, leaving Theo "in charge," as he put it. But these days were few and far between, and dust continued to gather in the showroom.

Apart from Frank, the only other regular visitor to the office was the man from the Pinkerton Detective Agency. His name was Marty Meagle, and he was always looking about himself, as if convinced he was going to find something important lurking in a corner. He had a shifty and unscrupulous appearance—just how Theo imagined a fraudster might look, instead of someone tasked with investigating crime. But Theo never got the chance to find out if his impression was correct because his father always sent him out for half an hour as soon as Marty arrived, so that the two of them could talk together confidentially.

By the time Theo got back after a coffee and roll in the Automat, Marty would be gone and Michael would be looking energized, letting fall that Marty's report had been very interesting and that progress was being made, although to what end he did not make clear.

The detective's visits, however, had the opposite effect on Theo, who felt sure that it was Marty who had dug up the dirt on Coach Eames. They reminded him of what he had lost and of how he had been railroaded into working at the factory, where he was learning nothing except how to organize a filing cabinet, and rekindled the impotent anger against his father that was forever smoldering inside his chest.

Two weeks after Theo began work, a buyer arrived at short notice from Philadelphia and Michael went out to lunch, leaving Theo in the office. Shortly afterward, Frank appeared, looking for Michael.

"Maybe he'll give us some work. God knows we could do with it!" said Frank after Theo had told him about the buyer.

Theo could hear the weariness in Frank's voice. "How bad is it?" he asked.

"It's tough to make ends meet. I sometimes think that my job's a bit like what that poor Greek sod had to put up with, pushing a massive boulder up the hill all day only for it to roll back down again just when he'd got it to the top."

"Sisyphus," said Theo.

"That's him!" said Frank, smiling. "Did you learn that in school?"

"Yes. I liked Greek and Latin, especially the history."

"I bet you did. And that's where you should be now, learning your verbs and pronouns and getting ahead. Not stuck in here with the likes of us, heading up shit creek without a paddle."

Theo didn't say anything. He felt a surge of gratitude. No one since Coach Eames had shown him any sympathy or understanding for what he had been forced to give up, and he was also pleased that Frank was prepared to use such a vulgar expression in front of him. It made him feel grown-up.

"Your dad sees everything his way," said Frank after a moment. "It's his strength and his weakness, and it doesn't make life easy for the rest of us. You especially."

"Why's it his strength?"

"Because it's what gives him his drive and his self-belief. It's the reason we're sitting here in a swanky office off Seventh Avenue instead of working our fingers to the bone in some filthy sweatshop over by the East River. That's where I came from, too, just like him, and I know for a fact I'd still be there if it wasn't for your father."

"How did he do it?" Theo was sitting forward in his chair, alive with curiosity. Nobody who knew his father had ever talked to him like Frank was doing now.

"He refused to give in," said Frank. "He saved money, borrowed some, too, and got his own shop. And then he bled his workers dry, forcing them to work day and night for practically nothing, and used the money he made to buy equipment and rent more space. Dog eat dog, on and on, up and up, year after year, until one day he told the Lower East to kiss his ass and set himself up over here with the big boys."

"And then?"

"Then? Then the Crash. It's the Depression that's killing him. He hasn't got an answer to it and so he denies it's there, but that's not going to work for much longer. Self-belief will take you a long way, but it doesn't drive an automobile through a brick wall. I wish it did." Frank laughed hollowly. "We're overextended here. That's the problem. The rents are too high. It was worse before we moved, but it's still not good."

"You moved because of the rent? My dad said it was a move up, not a move down."

"Well, we went to a higher floor, but that's about all the up there was in it," said Frank, laughing again. "The trouble is we're neither a sweatshop nor a proper factory. We're something in between—a subfactory, I suppose you could call it. The other factories round here, places like Weiss and Kramer, they've got a proper capital base, but we're not like that. We've got some work of our own—your father's always been good with the buyers. He can charm the birds off the trees when he wants to, but there aren't so many birds around these days, and we need the subcontract work the other factories give us, so it doesn't help that Alvah keeps rubbing them up the wrong way."

"How? What's he doing?"

"He cuts the fabric his way instead of the way they want it, and then they send it back and we have to start over. You saw it yourself the other day. I call him out on it, but he doesn't care. He thinks he could walk into another job at the same money or better if Michael fired him, and he's probably right. He's a prize schmuck, but that doesn't mean he's not a good cutter."

"Why doesn't he go, then?" asked Theo.

"I don't know. Maybe he likes being a big fish in a small pond. He can make more trouble that way."

"I don't like him," Theo blurted out. It was as if he felt he couldn't just keep asking questions, but needed to say something himself.

"Me neither," said Frank, smiling. "And I'd like nothing better than to see the back of him. But that's not an item on your father's agenda. More's the pity."

"Why not?" The answer made no sense to Theo, having seen firsthand how the cutter treated his father.

"Because Alvah's important to your father. Much more important than I am, even though me and him go back a lot further and even though I'm loyal and Alvah's a snake. Alvah allows him to dream," said Frank slowly, as if he was searching for the right words. "And it's dreams that keep your father going. They're his food and drink.

"Sorry, I'm talking in riddles," he went on, seeing the look of mystification spreading across Theo's face. "The point I'm trying to make—badly, I know—is that your father believes that Alvah isn't just a great cutter but a great designer and patternmaker too. He thinks that Alvah could have made a career in haute couture, designing dresses for Greta Garbo and Jean Harlow . . ."

"Could he?" asked Theo, awestruck. He'd been in love with Garbo ever since he sneaked into the Paramount to see *Anna Christie* after school the year before and kept going back for an entire week.

"No. I very much doubt it," said Frank. "If Alvah was a genius, he'd be in Paris now, instead of working here. But what matters isn't what I think; it's what your father thinks. Up until recently, he used to pay Alvah to go to the movies and sketch the dresses that the stars were wearing, and then Alvah would make designs and patterns and Michael would manufacture and sell them. They were doing pretty well, and it got even better when Alvah made friends with a warehouseman who worked on the loading dock over at Saks. Then he could see the designer dresses for himself when they came in. Until the man got fired, that is."

"Was he Easey Goldstein—the guy at Saks, I mean?"

"Yes," said Frank, looking surprised. "How did you know that?"

"I didn't. It was just a guess. Easey's in the warehouse, and I've seen him and Alvah together a few times, talking."

"Have you now?"

"Yes, over there," said Theo, pointing through the window at the warehouse entrance on the other side of the street. "It looked like Alvah was telling him what to do."

"Interesting. I can't prove it yet, but I'm sure Easey's involved in these thefts your dad's stirred up about, and I wouldn't put it past Alvah to have his finger in the pie too. I've always thought that that's what got Easey fired from Saks, although Alvah said it was because they'd found out he was showing him the clothes, which is why Michael hired him, even though I was against it. One favor deserves another, was how Alvah sold it to your father."

"Do you know about Pinkertons?"

"Marty Meagle, you mean?"

Theo nodded. "My dad's got them investigating the thefts, although I don't know what they've found out."

"Nothing," said Frank. "You can bet your bottom dollar on that. Marty's as dumb as a doornail when it comes to detective work, but he knows how to play your father. Michael loves anything cloak-and-dagger, so Marty serves it up to him by the bucketful and charges him an arm and a leg every time he makes a report. It's another expense we can't afford when Michael should be leaving the whole thing to me. It's my job to keep the workers honest."

"I don't think it was right to lock them in," said Theo. "I'm glad you've put a stop to that." He wouldn't have been so forthright before, but Frank's easy confidences had emboldened him.

"No. I didn't like it either," said Frank. "It was your father's idea, and I'm sure he got it from Marty. I told him it wasn't legal, but he wouldn't listen. And it was a gift to Alvah. I heard all about how he came over here, telling you about the Triangle Factory fire, stirring up trouble between you and your dad. And you can be sure he's been doing the same up on the factory floor. He fancies himself a union leader now that he can't be the world's next great designer, and he's got a ready audience up there, I can tell you that."

"But maybe the union's right," said Theo. "I mean, I've seen what some of the workers here are being paid—ten dollars or less for a sixty-hour week—and it's not enough to live on. I know it's not."

"So that gives them the right to steal. Is that what you're saying?" asked Frank, looking annoyed.

"No, of course not," said Theo, quailing a little. "I just think they should be paid a bit more. That's all."

"But the firm hasn't got more. You can't get blood from a stone. And maybe it's better to have a job earning something than go home with a pink slip and have nothing."

Theo nodded, unconvinced. He could see what Frank meant, but it didn't make it right. He was aware of Frank looking at him, but he still did not raise his eyes.

"You're right," said Frank after a moment, sounding conciliatory. "It's not a living wage. The workers know that and we know that, and that's why they're angry and listening to Alvah and not me when he stirs the pot. It'll end badly, I warrant, unless the Depression goes away, and I don't see any signs of that."

"How will it end, then?" asked Theo anxiously.

"I don't know," said Frank. "We'll think of something. You're a good kid, and I'm sorry for laying my burdens on you. I've got a bit carried away. I can see that."

"No, don't be sorry. Please," said Theo, getting up from his chair. "Nobody ever talks honestly to me. Not like you've been doing. My coach used to at school, but I'm not allowed to see him anymore, and you're right—my father won't listen to anything he doesn't want to hear."

"But maybe he will. Maybe if you speak to him. He's lonely, you know. That's why he's brought you here. And he's changed these last few months. He's gotten taut as a bowstring, keeping everything in. I'm worried he could break."

"Is that why you talked to me?"

"Yes, I suppose so. And I think you've got a right to know too. You seem older than fourteen, and you're not a dreamer like your father. Maybe, between us, we can get him to see some sense."

"And do what?"

"Replace Alvah. That would be a start."

Frank smiled, but over on the other side of the road, Theo saw that Easey Goldstein had come out of the warehouse and was standing with his back to the wall, staring across the road in his direction.

7

STRIKE

Theo wasn't learning much about the business, sitting in his father's office day after day doing mundane clerical work and looking out of the window, and he felt ashamed of his ignorance when he reluctantly joined his father and Frank on their afternoon tours of the factory floor. He could see in the workers' eyes that they identified him with his father, and sometimes he would look back over his shoulder and catch an emaciated seamstress or button maker singling him out for a particularly venomous glare.

Theo was sure that Alvah Katz was stoking their resentment by constantly reminding them that a fourteen-year-old boy with no experience had been put over them, and he longed to double back and tell them that he'd been forced to work here against his will and that he wanted nothing to do with a regime that was paying them starvation wages. But of course he didn't, dutifully following his father up and down the aisles instead, like a dog on its master's leash.

Oftentimes the cutter's room door was half open and he would catch Alvah watching their progression, smiling his trademark sardonic smile, and at such moments Theo was sure that the cutter knew exactly what he was going through and was enjoying every minute of his misery. Alvah was always careful to treat him with exaggerated courtesy, addressing him as Master Sterling just as he had been instructed, and it added to Theo's frustration to see how his father was pleased by this sham show of respect.

Downstairs, when not distracted by his mounting troubles, Michael enjoyed nothing more than sitting back in his chair and looking over at his son by the window. "Sterling and Son," he would say happily, rolling the words around on his tongue. "This is what I always dreamed of, ever since the day you were born." His apparent obliviousness to his son's misery, willful or otherwise, infuriated Theo even more.

But, in spite of all this, he tried to remember all that Frank had told him about his father—how hard he had worked and dreamed and how everything he had built was now teetering on the edge of collapse because of the Depression. He willed himself to overcome his anger and speak to his father as Frank had suggested, but when he tried, his father refused to listen. Theo's concerns, like Frank's, broke like feeble waves against the tide wall of Michael Sterling's eternal optimism. The bad times were almost over, he insisted, and prosperity was just around the corner. "Trust me!" he said. "I know."

At least twice a week, Michael visited his bank—a branch of the proudly named Bank of United States, with impressive Corinthian columns supporting its limestone facade facing out onto Sixth Avenue. He was one of the bank's best customers, and they treated him well. The manager, Mr. Friedmann, made a point of coming out from his back office to greet Michael and shake his hand, exchange pleasantries about the weather, and inquire after his family, as he ushered him to the principal cashier's desk to conduct his business.

The bank made Michael feel prosperous, even if he wasn't, and he enjoyed going there, which was why he would not delegate the task to anyone else in the firm, not even Frank. He had taken Theo there on his second day at the office, and had beamed with pleasure as Mr. Friedmann had expressed himself delighted to at last make the acquaintance of young Master Sterling, about whom he had heard so many good things.

"They've been with me through thick and thin, gave me my first loan when I was starting out," Michael had told Theo as they were walking back to the office. "The one thing you can trust Jews with is your money. They know what they're doing when it comes to business."

Theo had been surprised by this unexpected exception to his father's otherwise wholesale rejection of his Jewish heritage, but he'd kept quiet at the time, having no inclination to spoil his father's good mood.

Now, on a cold Wednesday afternoon in December, Michael came back from the bank, looking breathless and flustered. He summoned Frank to the office and immediately launched into a rambling account of what he'd just experienced.

"There was a crowd there," he said. "Spilling out into the road. They were pushing and shoving, shouting that the bank was in trouble."

"What kind of trouble?" asked Frank.

"I don't know. Like I said, they were yelling, and it was hard to make sense of anything. But then Mr. Friedmann must have seen me, because he came over and said it was all because some fool trader over in the Bronx had gone round telling everyone that the bank had refused to sell his stock, which was untrue. He told me there'd been a riot at the branch over there with people demanding their money."

"A riot!" Frank repeated the word, sounding incredulous.

"Yes, that's what he said. They had to bring in mounted police to control the idiots."

"Did they give them their money?"

"Yes, if they wanted it. But Friedmann said a lot of them saw reason when the manager came out and talked to them. Everyone's so jittery. That's the trouble. One stupid rumor and they're rushing around all over town, banging on the doors of the banks like chickens with their heads cut off. The mayor needs to do something before it gets really out of hand."

"Do you think there's any substance to it?" asked Frank.

"The rumor? No, of course not. The bank's got two hundred million in deposits. It's one of the biggest in the country, for God's sake. They financed half the building work round here. There wouldn't be a Garment District without them. You know that."

Michael continued to pace backward and forward across the office. It was as if he didn't believe what he was saying, because his agitation was getting worse, not better.

"I don't know," he burst out. "Perhaps I was wrong; perhaps I should have cashed out. I was thinking about it, I can tell you that. But then what Friedmann said made sense. If you can't trust the banks, who can you trust? I mean—there'd be nothing left." He threw up his hands and then pushed them back through his hair.

"Do you want me to go back with you and talk to Mr. Friedmann?" asked Frank quietly. "I can't advise you on what to do without hearing what he has to say."

"No, it's too late now. They'll be closed," said Michael, glancing at his watch. "I'll go in the morning. But you know, the more I think about it, I'm sure he's right, and this whole panic will turn out to be a tempest in a teapot. I've just got to stay calm and not let crazy people get inside my head. That's what matters."

Theo could see the effort his father was making to regain control of his emotions, giving himself instructions and taking deep breaths between sentences. And by the time he had finished speaking, he was almost back to his normal self, with the mask of confidence back in place again. But its momentary slippage had unnerved Theo and he found it difficult to sleep that night, waking up in the dark with a cold sweat on his brow, fearful of unseen demons.

Michael was unusually quiet on the way to work the next morning and went straight on to the bank after dropping Theo at the office.

Frank came in soon afterward, looking worried. He didn't seem in the mood for conversation, either, and he and Theo sat together silently, waiting for Michael to return.

It didn't take long. Michael burst through the door and immediately began cursing, using language that Theo had never heard his father use before. "Son of a whore!" he shouted. "All that big money talk and it turns out he's just a fucking two-bit shyster."

"Who?" Frank asked.

"Friedmann. He lied to me. They're thieves—the whole damn lot of them. They've been using our money, my money, to speculate, buying up risky mortgages. The bank's built on sand."

"How do you know?"

"Everyone's saying so, and their stock's falling. I saw it on the ticker. It'll be worth next to nothing by tomorrow."

"Did you talk to him?"

"No. How could I? There's a padlock on the door, and a notice outside saying the bank's been closed by order of the state superintendent, whoever he is. People were shouting and screaming like yesterday, but it won't do them any good. I don't think there's anyone inside."

Michael sat down heavily in the chair behind his desk and drummed his fingers on the surface.

"Why did I listen to him? Why am I so stupid?" Michael punctuated each question by punching his right fist into the open palm of his left. "It's the Jews coming back to bite me. That's what it is. My father's revenge for me turning my back on them."

"No, it isn't," said Frank. "You need to get a grip on yourself, Michael. You're acting like you've been possessed by some crazy dybbuk. What do you think your son's going to think, seeing you like this?"

Michael was silent, gripping the edge of his desk as he worked to get control of his breathing like he had on the previous day. But he was worse this time, and Theo worried that his father might be going to have a heart attack or a stroke of some kind.

"We can weather this," said Frank. "The bank will have to pay out eventually and, in the meantime, we've got the stock and orders coming in."

"Do you think so?" said Michael, eager for reassurance. He seemed like a child, Theo thought. Swinging wildly from one emotional extreme to another.

"Yes," said Frank. "But we'll need to tighten our belts, and the employees will have to take a pay cut."

"They won't agree to that. Alvah won't let them."

"Maybe we shouldn't give Alvah the chance. Maybe it's time to let him go. We can find another cutter."

"I don't know," said Michael, running his hands through his hair again. "I can't think about that now. But you're wrong if you think a pay cut's going to be enough. We're going to need money for cash flow. We need another bank."

"Not a Jewish one," said Frank.

"No. Over my dead body," said Michael, and unexpectedly laughed.

He seemed, with Frank's help, to have come back from the brink. It had been horrible for Theo to witness these glimpses of his father without his faith in the future. It had felt like watching a dynamited building imploding and falling and crumbling to dust right in front of his eyes.

Michael got up from his chair and put on his hat and coat. "I'm off to find me a goy banker," he said with a grin. "Wish me luck."

But he was gone before they could.

At the end of the afternoon there was no sign of Michael, and Theo decided to walk home, hoping that the fresh air would clear his head. It was getting toward nightfall and a cold breeze was blowing across Sixth Avenue, circling as if trapped between the tall buildings on either side. Theo hunched his shoulders, shivering even in his winter coat, as he pushed forward.

Lost in his thoughts, he almost collided with a scarecrow-like man who had been standing over a grating in the sidewalk, absorbing hot air up through the legs of his pants from the subway down below. "Sorry," Theo said, putting up his hand. "I didn't see you." But the man had gone before he had finished his sentence, vanishing into the gloom.

Above Theo's head, the squat iron supports of the El curved away, throwing intricate black shadows down onto where the road and sidewalk were lit by the streetlights. As he passed underneath, the wind died away, replaced by a clinging, dripping mist that seemed to seek out his hands, chilling the bones of his fingers even as he forced them deep into his pockets. He wished he had brought gloves and hurried on, crossing into Broadway, where a sound of feel-good music came wafting out to him through an open door. Inside, he caught a glimpse of a long, narrow speakeasy, lit by gas lamps that hung like white balloons over air thick with dense tobacco smoke, blue as sea fog. Theo stopped, moving instinctively closer, listening as the voices of the Carter Family sang out in melodious unison—"Keep on the sunny side, always on the sunny side / Keep on the sunny side of life"—but then ceased as if they had never been when the door closed, shutting Theo out into the night.

What if there is no sunny side? he wondered, as he resumed walking. Where does a man go then?

For Theo it was Union Square, where he stopped at the subway entrance and bought some roasted chestnuts from an old man in a battered fedora, who had been about to pack up his gear but had time for one last customer. Theo looked down into the little charcoal fire, greedy for warmth, and watched as the vendor shook his tin pan so that the nuts would bake evenly, and then took them to a bench in the park to eat. They burned his chilled fingers, but he ate them anyway, careless of the pain.

There were few people around. A bootblack called over to him from the flagpole: "Shine 'em up, Mack? Shine 'em up, five cents," but his appeal was halfhearted and he didn't persist when Theo shook his head, and soon he shouldered the tools of his trade and walked past Theo with his pale knees bizarrely visible in the lamplight through the holes in his ragged pants, worn away by a life of kneeling and shining on the cobbled sidewalks.

The moon had come out from behind the clouds, shining down on the bronze statues bordering the park—George Washington on his charger and Abraham Lincoln looking out across the centuries toward the crazy bustle of Fourteenth Street and Theo's way home. But he lingered where he was, alone except for a down-and-out sleeping on a nearby bench, huddled in his Hoover blanket of old newspapers.

From far away, Theo could dimly hear the sound of boats' foghorns calling out to each other through the murk as their prows passed in the harbor or out on the Hudson, but drowned out now by the chimes of the clock in the bell tower of the public utilities building as it struck the hour. He looked up toward it and then across the skyline to where the electric advertising boards flashed their brilliant white messages into the night, with the darkened buildings below catching their glare and giving off dull reflections.

EARN WHILE YOU SLEEP BECAUSE THE PILE GROWS WITH US urged the sign above the bronze doors of the Union Savings Bank, and Theo shook his head in disbelief, thinking of his father, whose pile—such as it was—had disappeared while he slept. The Bank of United States had been built on sand, his father had said, and everything seemed that way to Theo now. Nothing held, nothing could be relied upon as the flood tide of destruction rushed in.

A figure emerged out of the trees, interrupting his reverie, and formed itself into a policeman, walking the beat. He stopped beside the sleeping man and tapped several times on the back of the bench with his nightstick.

"Move on now," he ordered. "You know the rules."

"All right, all right. I hear you," said the man, getting slowly to his feet, like Lazarus emerging from a shroud of newspaper. He wiped his watery nose on the hard, glossy sleeve of his shabby overcoat, gathered his meager belongings into a sack bag that he swung over his shoulder, and stumbled down the path toward Theo, where he stopped for a moment, looking up at the signs that Theo had been reading a minute before.

"It's a fucking joke," he said eventually, pronouncing the words slowly and precisely as if they were a judgment. "But you know what, son—I'm done laughing."

And then without further comment, he shuffled away past Washington's horse and was lost to view.

"Tell them the truth! Tell them you've got no choice. And don't try and pretend what you're asking them to do isn't hard . . ."

"Yes, yes, stop sounding like an old woman," interrupted Michael impatiently. "Be satisfied we're doing it your way with the big speech, Frank. And I'm not firing Alvah. I told you that."

Out of sight behind Michael, Frank rolled his eyes at Theo, and then almost fell forward onto him in the next instant as the goods elevator juddered to a halt.

"We need to fix this thing," said Michael irritably, pulling back the grille and getting out.

But he'd forgotten about the elevator by the time they'd gotten out into the corridor. "All right then, let's get this over with," he said, taking a deep breath before he pushed open the door to the factory.

Frank went around, calling for quiet and gathering everyone in a semicircle in the empty area at the center of the floor. Theo noticed that Alvah had come out of the cutter's room and was standing at the back, but there was no sign of Easey Goldstein.

"Please pay attention," said Frank. "Mr. Sterling's got something important to tell you."

And at first it was okay, or at least it seemed that way to Theo. He wished his father hadn't waxed quite so lyrical about his achievement in finding another bank to take their business, but at least he was trying to treat his employees with respect, and they seemed to be listening to what he had to say.

But he hadn't yet got to the hard bit about the pay cut, and when he did, some of them started murmuring and several looked over toward Alvah.

"So it's just until we get over this hump," Michael told them, trying to sound hopeful. "The bank has got to pay out, and then we can go back to where we were. And we're all in this together, you know. I promise you that."

"No, we're not," said Alvah, speaking for the first time and pushing his way to the front, so that he was standing directly opposite Michael. "You're sitting down in your fancy office with your boy there," he said, pointing an accusing finger at Theo. "Going out to expensive lunches whenever you feel like it, but we're half starving up here on what you're paying us."

"That's nonsense, Alvah," Michael snapped back. "You're paid ten times what they are and you know it."

"That doesn't change what you're paying them," said Alvah, not missing a beat. "They can't feed their families, and now you're going to cut their wages by a third. They won't stand for it, I tell you."

"And I say they will," said Michael, getting angry. "I've already told you I've got no choice."

"Yes, you do. You could sell something or get a loan from this great new bank you've found. It's not for me to tell you how. It's you who's supposed to be running this company, and you've been making a god-awful job of it up to now. That's plain as the nose on your face."

"Shut up, Alvah," said Michael, beginning to lose his temper. "You've got no right to talk to me like that. Not here. I built this company from nothing."

"And nothing is what it's going to be again until you start listening to us. Yes, we've got demands too," said Alvah, taking a piece of paper from his pocket and handing it to Michael, who started reading them aloud:

"Fifty percent increase in wages, no work on the Sabbath . . ." He stopped, looking up. "Haven't you heard a word I've said?" he asked, staring at the workers. "The bank has failed. If you don't take a pay cut, this business will fail, too, and you'll have nothing. Is that what you really want? Nothing?"

"We want justice," said Alvah. "And until we get it, we're not working."

"You're going on strike?" There was disbelief as well as anger in Michael's voice.

"That's right. Now who's with me?" Alvah asked, looking around.

About twenty hands went up—maybe half the workforce—and Theo thought he caught a flash of disappointment on Alvah's face, although it was too quick for him to be certain.

"Anyone who walks out of here now isn't coming back," said Michael. He spoke slowly, forcing himself to stay calm because he wanted his threat to be taken seriously.

But Alvah wasn't going to back down. Not now. Not when he'd come this far. "Keep your hands up," he told his followers, turning around to look at them as he raised his, clenched now in a fist. "And repeat this after me: 'If I turn traitor to the cause I now pledge, may this hand wither from the arm I now raise.'"

Some of the voices were loud, some barely more than murmurs, but Alvah didn't seem to have lost any support as a result of Michael's threat, and straightaway, everyone who'd raised their hands began gathering their belongings and filing out the door. Theo could hear them going down the stairs.

Alvah was the last to go. "See you on the picket line," he said.

"I'll see you in hell, you ungrateful son of a bitch! I'll make sure you never work again," Michael shouted furiously, screwing up the list of demands and throwing it at Alvah's back.

But he was already gone, and the paper ball bounced harmlessly off the swinging door.

They took the stairs themselves to go back down—Michael and Frank in front, and Theo bringing up the rear—as Michael said he no longer trusted the elevator. Theo felt shocked and fearful and strangely excited, all at the same time. Fearful for his father and the future, but excited by the courage of the strikers, refusing to accept a cut to their already meager wages. He'd been moved by the way they recited their unfamiliar oath, even as he hated Alvah for leading them down the path of destruction. Because Theo was sure his father was right. They'd end up with nothing, sleeping rough under Hoover blankets and standing in line for soup in those long queues that snaked around the cold street corners of the Bowery. Dying on their feet.

Theo could hear his father up ahead, talking to Frank in short, scattergun sentences: "Did you get a list of who's left? Good. It could've been a lot worse, but we need to hire replacements today, not tomorrow. We've got to keep the place running and fulfill the orders. That's what matters."

"It won't be easy finding another cutter at this short notice." Frank sounded somber, fearful even.

"We will. Even if we have to comb the whole of the Lower East, we'll find somebody," said Michael defiantly. "And you're the one who wanted me to get rid of Alvah, Frank, so I don't know what you're complaining about," he added irritably.

"Yes, I wanted you to fire him, but that was months ago when we'd have had time to hire a proper replacement and before he turned half the workforce against you. He's been working on them up there every day while you've been messing around with Pinkerton."

"Shut up. Damn you. Shut up," Michael shouted, losing his temper again. "I'm this close, Frank. Do you hear me? This close, without you rubbing it in."

Theo couldn't see what his father was that close to, but he guessed he meant to breaking. He remembered that that was what Frank had told him he was worried about when he said that Michael was taut as a bowstring. And his father's voice was tenser now than Theo had ever heard it. What would happen if he did break? What would that mean? For him and his mother? For all of them?

They reached the bottom of the stairs and walked out into the street at the same time as Easey Goldstein was coming up the sidewalk, pushing a double rack of women's evening gowns.

"I'll take that," said Frank, putting his hand on the rack to stop Easey's progress.

"What the hell! Let go of it. I've got to get these in the warehouse," said Easey. Surprise had made his squeaky voice go up at least another octave.

"No, you let go of it," said Frank. "And you're not going in the warehouse either."

"Why the fuck not?" Easey demanded, coming out from behind the crepe de chine and approaching Frank.

"Because you're fired," said Michael. "That's why."

"What for? I've got a right to know," said Easey, standing his ground.

"You know what for. You've been stealing, robbing me blind."

"Says who?"

"Never mind who. It's enough that we know. Now get along. You've got no more business here."

"It's him, isn't it?" said Easey, pushing Frank hard in the chest with both of his meaty hands, almost sending him over. "He's been on my case ever since I got here, he has. And after all that lowdown from Saks I gave you before. Where's the gratitude? That's what I want to know. Where's the fucking gratitude?"

With each verbal salvo, Easey pushed Frank again so he could not get his balance back and finally ended up sprawled half in the road, half on the sidewalk.

Theo watched, horrified, as the big man lifted his heavy boot with obvious intent, but then seeing what he was about to do, Michael took hold of Easey's arm and pulled him back—and, responding instinctively, Easey swung around with his free hand and punched Michael hard on the side of the face.

Michael staggered back against the dresses, raising his hands, and Theo could see blood seeping out between them.

Easey looked back at Michael and laughed defiantly. "That's nothing. Just you wait until Alvah's finished with you. He's going to bleed you dry, you'll see."

And with that Easey turned on his heel and limped quickly away toward Seventh Avenue. Looking after him, Theo was amazed at how quickly the big man could move when he wanted to, even with his clubfoot.

Alvah and Michael were both as good as their word. Early next morning, the strikers were standing on either side of the entrance to the factory, forming a small picket line, and the twenty workers who'd resisted Alvah's call to down tools succeeded in passing between them, joined by a similar number of new recruits, including an ancient cutter with a bent back who looked like the picture of Methuselah in Theo's illustrated Bible.

The strikers shouted abuse at their replacements, calling them scabs and finks, and waved their homemade placards. But Marty Meagle's Pinkerton men were on hand to force them back when they pushed too far forward and seemed to have the situation reasonably under control.

Theo watched through the window of the office and provided a running commentary on what was happening to his father, who remained behind his desk and so out of view of the street.

Theo didn't think his father had slept at all the previous night. He'd woken several times to hear him pacing and talking, and when he looked out from behind his bedroom door, he'd been alarmed to see no sign of his mother, which meant that his father had to have been chattering away to himself.

And Michael's state of nervous excitement continued throughout the day. When he wasn't talking to Marty Meagle or Frank on the telephone, he was conducting a muttered monologue about the revenge he was going to exact on Alvah and Easey, although Theo had noticed that not only did his father not want to show himself at the window, but he'd also sounded mighty relieved when Theo reported that there was no sign of Easey on the picket line.

Michael's cheek and jaw were heavily bruised where Easey had hit him, and he constantly ran his hand up and down over the injured area, as if to keep reminding himself of the reality of what had happened. The movement seemed odd and compulsive to Theo. He had the impression that the punch had unhinged his father in some way, undermining his sense of invulnerability and puncturing the thick shell of his self-belief.

The confrontation outside the factory was much more vitriolic at the end of the day. The strikers' rage against the scabs who had taken their jobs had intensified with each passing hour, and they swarmed around the exit when the first workers started coming out, led by Frank, who tried unsuccessfully to keep them walking. Instead, they froze and then turned tail as one and rushed back inside. Several of the strikers tried to follow them, but Theo could see that Frank had the door locked.

Now the Pinkerton men waded in, indiscriminately hitting out at the strikers with their billy clubs. But, to Theo's surprise, the strikers stood their ground, using their placards to fight back. Several even succeeded in overpowering the Pinkertons and turned the batons on their attackers.

The Pinkertons were outnumbered and soon had to beat a ragged retreat to the other side of the street, leaving the enraged strikers to resume hammering on the door of the factory. And they might have gotten in had it not been for the sudden arrival in the street of several police vans, accompanied by a wail of sirens.

They parked outside Theo's window and so his view of what happened next was blocked, but when they pulled away a few minutes later, there was nobody left in sight. The workers had gone home and the strikers had either run away or been arrested, leaving only their broken placards littering the gutter and the sidewalk as evidence of what had occurred.

And soon they were gone too. An old woman in a tattered overcoat came tottering down the street in the twilight, wheeling a battered baby buggy, and stopped outside the factory. Methodically, she bent down and picked up the cardboard signs and sticks. As Theo watched, **WE ARE NOT SLAVES** followed **NO TO WAGE CUTS** and **BETTER TO STARVE QUICK THAN STARVE SLOW** into the covered interior of the carriage. Then, once everything was safely stowed away, the old woman resumed her slow progress, pushing on toward Broadway.

"She's done well for herself. That'll make for a good fire tonight," said Frank, chuckling. He'd just come into the office and was looking out of the window over Theo's shoulder.

"I wonder what she makes of all those signs," said Theo.

"I doubt she even reads them. She's surviving. That's all. It's a full-time occupation these days."

Behind them, Michael was muttering again, paying no attention to their conversation as he shuffled papers across his desk.

"Everyone got away safely," Frank told him. "But whether they'll be back tomorrow, I don't know. It was touch and go out there before the police arrived."

"They'll be back," said Michael, without looking up from what he was doing. "They need the money."

"They're scared. That's all I'm saying."

"And you? Are you scared?" Michael asked, fixing his gaze on Frank so that he could gauge the truthfulness of his answer.

"I was when I was out there. I'm not anymore."

"Yes, that makes sense, I suppose. But for me it's different. I never used to be scared of anyone or anything, and now I'm nervous all the time. I can't sleep. I'm like a cat on hot bricks. I hate it." As Michael talked, he had gone back to stroking his jaw and cheek.

"You should get that looked at," said Frank. "Easey packs quite a punch. I've heard he worked in a slaughterhouse over in the Meatpacking District when he was starting out, rolling heavy barrels and stacking great slabs of meat on racks thirty feet high. You don't lose that kind of strength."

"His kick would have been worse than his punch," said Michael.

"I know," said Frank. "Don't think I'm not grateful."

Michael put up his hand in acknowledgment and then dropped it wearily, looking over toward Theo with a trace of a smile. "Quite a time we're having of it, aren't we, son?"

Theo nodded, unable to think of any more adequate response.

"It's not what I wanted," Michael said. "I wanted . . ." He stopped, unable to put what he was trying to say into words. "For it to be better than this," he finished lamely.

"It will be," said Frank. "We've got to keep going. That's all."

"Yes, you're right," said Michael, taking a deep breath and sitting up in his chair. "I built this factory, and I'm not going to let that bastard Alvah destroy it." He thumped the surface of his desk with the bottom of his fist, and a pile of papers fell on the floor.

Behind Frank there was a knock on the door, and Mrs. Hirsch appeared in response to Michael's loud *"Come in."*

"Mr. Meagle's here to see you," she said.

"Good. Yes, show him in," said Michael, getting up and coming around from behind his desk to greet the detective, who performed a strange physical double take as he extended his hand and then immediately withdrew from Michael's warm clasp of it, just like Alvah had done with Theo when they were first introduced back in the fall. "Thank you, Marty," Michael told him. "You've done us proud today."

Theo was shocked at his father's sudden change of mood, veering from weariness to energetic hand-shaking in less than a minute. But then he recalled how much his father enjoyed his cloak-and-dagger dealings with the detective and felt less surprised at his enthusiasm.

"Our success has come at some cost, I'm afraid," said Marty, looking as solemn and mournful as a professional pallbearer. "Several of my men have incurred injuries, which require hospital treatment."

"Your success!" repeated Frank, scoffing. "Your lot ran away; it was the cops who made the difference."

"That is not my understanding of what happened," said Marty, drawing himself up and radiating righteous indignation.

"Well, you weren't there."

"All right, Frank. That's enough of that," said Michael. "You know what they say, Marty: you can't make an omelet without breaking some eggs. Or heads, for that matter," he added, smiling.

"I have my report if you'd like to go over it," said Marty frigidly. He tapped his briefcase and looked askance at Frank and Theo.

Michael nodded. "Frank, why don't you take Theo out for something to eat?" he said. "It's on me. You deserve it, after all you've done today. Good work, both of you. Good work!"

Theo followed Frank out of the door, and as he was closing it, he heard his father asking: "Have you got it, Marty? Have you got it?" There was no mistaking the eagerness in his voice.

"What was that about?" Theo asked Frank as they got out onto the street.

"I've no idea," said Frank. "But whatever *it* is will cost money, that much you can be sure of. I dread to think what old Marty's charged us for today, but whatever the figure is, we can't afford it. That much is guaranteed. He'll bleed us dry by the time he's finished."

"That's what Easey said Alvah was going to do."

"Yes. Him too. They're damn vultures, the whole lot of them," said Frank angrily. "But for now, I say we forget about them. I don't know about you, but all that violence has made me hungry. I vote we go to the best steakhouse in the Tenderloin. What do you think?"

"Sure," said Theo. "I think I can manage that."

If Michael had hoped that the combined brutality of the police and the Pinkertons would deter the strikers from returning, then he was sadly mistaken.

Next morning, they were back, but in greater numbers, and Alvah, now wearing a flat worker's cap, had brought a loudspeaker to encourage them. They had also made new, bigger placards to replace the ones they had lost. **NOT MICE BUT MEN** one of them proclaimed, and Theo couldn't help but admire their bravery.

"Marty says the new ones are from the union, but I'll bet a dollar to a doughnut they're Communists," said Michael bitterly. "The Reds are always ready to cause trouble whenever they see a chance, pushing their dirty noses into other people's business. But they won't stop us. Marty's got more men here today. It won't be like yesterday."

But it was. Only worse. The fighting began again as soon as the workers started to arrive. The Pinkerton men forced their way to the door, where Frank was standing on the inside with the key, ready to open, and then tried to escort the workers down the makeshift corridor they had formed between their two lines, while the strikers surged against their backs, some using makeshift clubs that they had concealed inside their coats.

Some of the workers got through, but as many others turned tail and ran back toward Seventh Avenue. The strikers made no effort to pursue them, concentrating all their attention on laying siege to the door of the factory, and Theo could see the workers who'd escaped standing at the corner of the street, talking to each other and watching anxiously to see how everything would turn out.

Michael, meanwhile, was talking to the police department on the telephone, venting his frustration on the desk officer at the other end of the line, who kept telling him that help was on the way. In response to a sign from his father, Theo opened the window and Michael held the mouthpiece out toward the street. "Hear that?" he shouted into the telephone. "No sirens; nothing! So where the hell are your men?" But his protests made no difference, and when he asked for the precinct captain and lieutenant by name, he was told they were busy and that they would get back to him later in the morning.

"Busy!" Michael spat out the word as he crashed the telephone back down on its cradle. "Someone's got to them. That's what's happened. Paid a big slice of dough into their benevolent fund. Bastards!"

Near the door of the factory, the groups of picketers and Pinkerton men began to separate. There was no need for further violence, now that no one was trying to get through the door. Up at the corner, the workers who hadn't made it inside began to drift away. None were prepared to run the gauntlet of the picket line again.

Watching them go, the strikers held up their placards in triumph and began to sing. After a moment, Theo recognized the tune and was at once borne back on a tide of memory to the empty, echoing stadium opposite the City College on the day of the Crash. In his mind's eye, he could see the men and boys, black and brown and white, standing ramrod still and looking up into the clouds while they sang the workers' anthem with such extraordinary fervor.

Theo turned away, overcome by shame that he was the enemy of these poor people who were asking only to be paid a living wage for their ceaseless, mind-numbing work. He thought of them bent over their machines, ruthlessly exploited by men like his father from the dawn of their lives to a premature dusk, enslaved in all but name. He felt disgusted with himself and wished he was anywhere but where he was.

Michael, however, was impervious to his son's soul-searching. "See, I told you so," he said furiously, pointing through the window. "That's 'The Internationale' they're singing. They're Communists, every last one of them."

Bad news came thick and fast after that.

Frank came down from the factory and crossed the road. Theo was surprised that the strikers let him pass without incident, but then he thought it was of a piece with the way they had not protested outside Michael's office. They were obviously under instructions to leave the management alone—perhaps because Alvah wanted to make sure Michael retained a ringside seat to watch the destruction of his business.

"What's happening?" asked Michael when Frank came in.

Frank shook his head. He looked beaten, Theo thought—a shadow of the man he'd had dinner with the night before.

"If you've come over to tell me we haven't got enough workers to keep the factory running, then you can save your breath because I know that already," said Michael bitterly. "I saw them for myself, the cowards, scurrying away at the first sign of trouble. Not even waiting to see if Marty's men could help them through."

"They're scabs," said Frank. "We were never going to find heroes in half a day, were we?"

"No, I guess not. But that doesn't mean we can't find more," said Michael. He stopped talking, looking hard at Frank. "There's something else, isn't there?" he said. "Go on. Spit it out. I can take it."

"The managers at Kramer's and Weiss's called. They're canceling their orders. All of them. They won't do business with us until we take everyone back."

"Why?"

"They said they've got no choice, that they'll have strikes, too, if they don't cut us loose."

Michael sat back hard in his chair. He looked like he had taken a physical blow to the body, one that had knocked the stuffing out of him.

"Maybe it's them who warned off the police," he said.

"Probably," said Frank. "I didn't ask them. What do you want to do now?"

Michael shrugged. "Does it matter?"

It was Frank's turn to stare. "We've got to do something," he said.

"All right. What?"

"You know what. We've got to get Alvah in here and do a deal."

"He won't. It's all or nothing with him. Always has been. He won't listen to reason. Too busy playing to the gallery."

"Okay, maybe you're right. But if he won't talk, we'll have to give him what he wants, and hope something turns up. You never know."

Frank waited for a moment, but Michael did not respond. "I'll go and get him," he said and went out of the door.

"Do you want me to leave? Go to the Automat or something?" Theo asked, looking over at his father, who had remained where he was since Frank left, sitting back half slumped in his chair, staring at the floor.

"No, stay," said Michael, looking up with a wan smile. "There's no point missing the ending when you've sat through the play. And there's lessons to be learned here. Lessons you wouldn't learn in school."

"What lessons?" Theo asked. He felt he'd learned quite enough already and wanted to go somewhere he could be alone, away from all the pain and misery he'd witnessed over the previous few days. Running in Central Park like he used to do, running away from all this.

"Life lessons," said Michael. "How men like Alvah destroy other men's dreams, everything they've built, brick by brick. Until there's nothing left."

The door opened and Frank came back in. "I've got him outside," he said. "Shall I bring him in?"

Michael nodded. Frank beckoned, and Alvah appeared in the doorway.

"So you haven't brought your loudspeaker, I see," said Michael, looking his enemy up and down from head to toe. "With that and the cap and the beard, you looked just like Lenin. Did you know that, Alvah? Was that what you had in mind?"

"No," said Alvah. "I hadn't thought of it. I've been too busy fighting your goons and beating back your scabs, trying to get you to pay your workers a decent wage."

"Oh, spare me your speeches!" said Michael contemptuously. "You don't give a damn about them. You're going to be fine at the end of this. You're a good cutter and you'll walk into another job, but they won't. They'll lose everything because they listened to you."

"They'll have dignity and they'll be paid what they deserve," said Alvah. "They're not your slaves."

"No, they're pawns in this game you've been playing with me. Pawns you've sacrificed so you can win. We both know that." Michael waved his hand dismissively. "But what I don't understand, and what I want you to explain to me, is why you're playing it in the first place. What do you hope to accomplish with all this destruction? Tell me that. Please. I really want to know."

"I don't know what you're talking about."

"Yes, you do. Are you a Communist, Alvah? A Lenin? Is that it?"

Alvah turned to Frank. "This is pointless," he said. "You told me he would listen."

"I am listening, Alvah," said Michael. "I'm waiting for you to answer my question."

"All right, I'll tell you what I am," said Alvah, finally getting angry. "I'm a Jew. Not a God-believing Jew with a yarmulke on his head, but a Jew who's proud of it, not ashamed like you. I'm a Jew who tries to look after his own people. But you—you suck on their blood like a vampire and stop them from observing the Sabbath. You've been betraying your people for years—in the Lower East and now here. And someone needs to call you to account. Now will you agree to our demands?"

"If I do, the business will fail," said Michael.

"No, it won't. You'll find a way."

Michael shrugged his shoulders and sat back in his chair. "I'll sign what you want," he said. "It doesn't matter. You deal with it, Frank. I'm tired."

8

DEFEAT

For the rest of the morning, Michael was listless and kept wandering out of the office and coming back in again, as if forgetting why he had left. On several occasions Theo saw him outside on the sidewalk, gazing up at the windows of the factory, where work seemed to have resumed, but he made no move to cross the street. All the time, he kept stroking his cheek and jaw, backward and forward where Easey had hit him, as if he was trying to understand something that made no sense and failing in the attempt.

Theo felt jittery. "Are you okay, Dad?" he asked when his father had come back into the office for what seemed like the tenth time.

"Yes, yes. I've got a lot on my mind. That's all. Get on with what you were doing. I'll be all right."

"But you said we wouldn't be. You said the business would fail. You said—"

"I said a lot of things," Michael interrupted testily. "But that doesn't mean they're going to happen. You just need to give me some room to think. Why don't you take the rest of the day off? It'll do you good to get some air—maybe you can run a bit, like you used to? It's not raining."

"How can you say that?" Theo burst out.

"Say what?" asked Michael, not understanding.

"About my running, when you're the one who stopped me. You took me out of school and ruined everything. Or have you forgotten all that?"

"No, I haven't forgotten!" Michael shouted, angry now too. "It's you who are forgetting, Theo. Your manners, the respect you owe me. I'm your father, goddammit!" He thumped his fist on his desk and stopped, breathing hard and struggling to collect himself before he went on in a firm, controlled voice: "I'm sorry, son, but you need to do as I say. Marty's coming and Frank, too, and I need the office to myself. Go home now and I'll see you this evening."

Theo got up, gathered his things, and put on his coat. His pride was like a chain holding him in check as he moved slowly toward the door, hoping that his father would call him back.

He turned as he went out and his father was staring at him, or rather through him, as if he was seeing something or someone in the empty showroom beyond.

"Are you sure you're all right?" Theo asked.

"Yes, of course," said Michael, snapping out of his trance with a shake of his head. "Tell your mother . . ." he began, but then stopped. "No, it's better it's me who talks to her," he went on. "I'll see you both this evening. We can talk then. Close the door."

And those were the last words that Theo ever heard his father say.

There was no sign of Michael in the evening, but this didn't much surprise Theo, notwithstanding his father's promise to come home and talk. He assumed his father was still busy trying to find a way out of his troubles.

Elena was as lacking in curiosity as ever about her husband's business. She had continued to accept his optimism at face value, and in the last few days he had told her nothing of the bank's failure or the workers' strike, and had passed off the bruising to his face as an accidental injury he'd suffered from falling over in the factory.

Theo might have spoken to her himself, but the breach between them that had fissured at the church when he'd accused her of flirting with Sir Andrew was still there. Neither she nor Theo had suggested that he should resume accompanying her to Mass.

And so Theo was surprised when his mother knocked hard on his bedroom door in the morning, calling him to come out. He was dressing to go to the factory but ran out to her in his underwear because of the urgency in her voice.

"Your father's not been here all night. His bed's not been slept in. Do you know where he is?" Elena had taken tight hold of Theo's arm, and she spoke breathlessly in short, staccato Spanish sentences as she looked up at him.

Theo shook his head, but inwardly he trembled. He felt her fear spreading through him like a deadly contagion.

"I'll call the office," he said. "Maybe he's still there. There's been trouble at the factory."

"What kind of trouble? What are you talking about? Why didn't he tell me? Or you? You could have told me; you would have known too."

Ignoring his mother, who was becoming more hysterical with each question she threw out, Theo went to the telephone in the hallway, but it rang just as he was about to dial. He froze with one hand on the earpiece and the other on the stand, seized with a premonition that something awful awaited him if he took the call. He felt, illogically, that he could prevent it from happening if he remained utterly motionless. Not even breathing.

But the telephone went on ringing, and when Elena saw that he wasn't going to answer, she walked over and grabbed it out of his hands.

He watched her listening to the voice on the other end of the line—it sounded like Frank's—and watched her hand holding the earpiece drop limply to her side. She was saying something, but he couldn't make it out. And then she said it again: "Your father's dead. He's killed himself."

Theo heard it but he didn't believe it. "No, he can't be. He was fine when I left him yesterday. There's some mistake. I know there is. I'm going over there," he told his mother, running back to his room to put on the rest of his clothes.

"What are we going to do?" she called to him frantically as he rushed back past her, but he wrenched open the front door of the apartment without responding and started running down the corridor outside. Behind him he could hear his mother's voice shouting again: "Come back! We need to talk!" But he was hardly listening as he burst out of the building and ran to the bus stop.

He waited for what seemed like hours and then took off down the road, running, dodging between pedestrians. And almost immediately a streetcar came up from behind and passed him, and he could not outrace it to the next stop. He reached out wildly with his flailing, beseeching hands as it pulled back out into Broadway and left him in its wake.

He thought of going down into the subway or running on, but forced himself to wait, knowing that a bus or streetcar would be quicker if he could just stay patient. But that was hard, unbearably hard, because all the time he felt he was in a race against the clock, even though another voice in another repressed part of his brain was whispering to him that this was absurd. His father was dead and everything was changed and there was no going back.

On the bus, he closed his eyes and clenched his fists and tried to stop his knees swinging from side to side as he willed the vehicle forward, past traffic lights and intersections, trying to shut out the babble of indifferent voices all around him, talking about Christmas and the chances of snow and the sale that day at Klein's. Instead, he listened to scraps of conversations swirling in his head like litter blown up in a wind: *"I'm worried he could break"—"The Depression's killing him"—"I'm this close"—"I'm tired"—"tired"—"Close the door . . ."*

He got off at Thirty-Sixth Street and ran up the road and into his father's building on the corner, where he stopped short, narrowly avoiding a collision with Frank, who was standing guard outside the office. The winter sunlight streaming in through the high windows of the vestibule lit up the gold lettering of Michael Sterling's name stenciled on the closed door behind him.

"Get out of the way! I need to go in," said Theo angrily. He thought if he could just get inside, then maybe his father would be there and all this would be like a dream from which he could wake up and start over.

"You can't. The police are here," said Frank, barring the way.

"I don't care," Theo shouted, trying to push past Frank, who held his ground and took hold of Theo's wrist in an unexpectedly strong grip, forcing him back.

"It's bad. Really bad," he said, looking into Theo's eyes, trying to make him understand. "I won't let you see it. Maybe I'm wrong, but someone has to look out for you. Someone has to make a decision."

All at once Theo gave way. He sagged, and Frank had to put out his other hand to hold the boy up.

"Let's go somewhere and talk," he said. "I know a place."

It was quiet. Only two blocks away, and afterward Theo couldn't remember how they'd got there. Just that he was sitting by the window opposite Frank, with two white coffee mugs and a pitcher of water and a pair of cloudy glasses lined up between them on a small wooden table patterned with innumerable pale overlapping circles made by thousands of previous hot mugs drunk by thousands of previous customers come here to talk about their troubles.

"I saw him at five when I went home," said Frank in a matter-of-fact tone. "So he did it sometime after that. And he was all right when I left or I wouldn't have gone, obviously. I told him that everyone was back at work and he seemed happy about that, although both of us knew that we couldn't pay them. And then today when I came in, he was in his chair and the gun was on the desk, and—"

Frank broke off and looked out of the window, trying to compose himself.

"Are you sure . . ." Theo began.

"He was dead?"

Theo nodded. He had hard hold of the underside of the table, as if readying himself for Frank's response.

"He blew his brains out, Theo. He must have put the damned thing in his mouth."

Theo gasped. The room turned and he thought he was going to be sick, but then he felt Frank's hand on his arm and the room righted itself.

Frank poured out a glass of water, and Theo took it with both hands and drank it all.

"I'm sorry," said Frank. "I shouldn't have said that. It's just I thought you needed to know because I didn't let you see him. There wasn't any doubt. None at all."

"Why?" Theo asked. He meant to say "Why did he do it?" but he found it hard to speak and managed only the first monosyllabic word of his question.

"I can't tell you exactly. He didn't leave a note, even though there was paper on the desk, lots of it. I think he just sat there and it got dark and something in him broke. He'd tried and tried to hold everything together, and he couldn't anymore, for some reason. He'd just reached that point. And he'd got the gun in the drawer, locked up with Marty's reports. Loaded and ready to use when he needed it."

"How do you know?"

"I called Marty before you came and he told me. He got the gun for Michael because Michael asked him to, and then he saw him put it away. And when I went in, the drawer was pulled open with the reports still in there, and the key was on the desk. It all added up."

"Why did he want the gun? So he could do this?"

"No, I don't think so. Marty said he didn't tell him what he wanted it for, but my guess is protection. He didn't feel safe after Easey punched him. He was . . ."

"Like a cat on hot bricks," said Theo, remembering his father's phrase.

"Yes, that's it."

Frank was quiet now, drinking his coffee and looking out through the window at the people passing by on the sidewalk outside, wrapped up in their winter coats.

"It's Alvah's fault," said Theo, leaning forward across the table. "He's killed my dad with his stupid strike. He knew he couldn't pay—"

"No. Alvah didn't help, but the truth is we were going under when the bank failed or even before that maybe," said Frank, shaking his head. "The business couldn't cope with the Depression. Michael fought against it as long as he could, but—"

"But what?" interrupted Theo bitterly. "Just because your business fails, it doesn't mean you have to kill yourself."

"For Michael it did," said Frank. "The business was everything to him—his life's work, his whole identity. You of all people shouldn't need me to tell you that."

"Because he forced me out of school to join it, you mean?"

Frank nodded.

"You're right," said Theo slowly. "My dad was selfish—selfish through and through. He never thought of anyone except himself. Not once. Just the business, always the business: Sterling and Son—you know, saying those words makes me sick. Because Alvah was right and so was my grandfather. Do you know what he said?"

"Your grandfather?" Theo nodded and Frank shook his head. "I never met him," he said. "He was before my time."

But Theo wasn't listening, borne along now on the rushing torrent of his emotion. "He said my dad preyed on his own people like a wolf in the night. That's why everyone hated him—you could see it in their eyes when we walked round the factory. That's why he wouldn't go near the place without you there. I'm happy it failed. He got what he deserved."

"No, he didn't," said Frank fiercely. "Nobody deserves to die like that. God knows, your father had his faults. But I loved him. And I think you did too."

Theo's head dropped and he began to cry. Memories came flooding through the open breach in his defenses: his father standing with his head thrown back in Lexington Avenue, gazing spellbound up at the glory of the Chrysler Building; his father shiny-eyed at Yankee Stadium after Babe Ruth hit the home run and won the game. He was so real and alive, so how could he now be dead?

Frank handed Theo a napkin and he held it hard to his eyes, blotting out the visions, and fought to reassert his self-control. It was an effort of will that felt like an act of violence, stamping down hard on his emotions.

"What are we going to do?" he asked when he could trust himself to speak. He could escape the past but not the future, and he saw it now, opening out in front of him—a desolate plain stretching away into darkness. The prospect filled him with fear and foreboding.

"There's no point in me sugarcoating it for you. It's going to be bad," said Frank. "The business is finished. I sent everyone home, and they won't be coming back. And once the news is out, the creditors will move in and seize the assets. I doubt there'll be anything much left, even if the bank pays out, and that could be months away."

"But what about my mother, the apartment? Are you saying there's going to be nothing?"

"Pretty much," said Frank. "I've not met your mother. Can she work?"

"No, she wouldn't know where to start," said Theo with a hollow laugh. "She left everything to my father. He liked it that way."

Frank nodded. "I'll try to help," he said. "But it's not going to be easy. I've got to find work myself. You mentioned your grandfather. Do you know where he is?"

"Somewhere in the Lower East. I could try and look for him. But it's a long time ago that I went there. He's called Joseph Stern. He told me that."

"All right, I'll make inquiries. You should go to your mother now. I can deal with what's left over here."

Outside the coffee shop, Theo swayed and leaned against the wall. His eyes hurt and his legs felt heavy and he swallowed hard to keep from starting up crying again. He didn't want Frank to leave, and he didn't want to go home and face his mother. But he forced himself to put out his hand. "Thank you," he said. "I know this is hard for you too."

Frank took Theo's hand in both of his and looked into his eyes. "Don't give up," he said. "Just because he did doesn't mean you have to. I believe in you. Remember that."

There was no time for Theo to think, let alone give up, in the topsy-turvy days that followed his father's death. Everything seemed to fall apart. There was no money even for the funeral, and Michael would have gone to a pauper's grave in the potter's field if Frank hadn't scraped together enough for a cut-price send-off in a crowded Jewish cemetery in Brooklyn, where he still had to pay extra for them to overlook that Michael was a suicide.

Elena refused to attend or to have anything to do with the arrangements. She told Theo that her husband had betrayed them, lied to them, abandoned them, and murdered himself, listing his crimes one by one on the fingers of her hand. Suicide was a mortal sin against God about which the Catholic Church's teaching was clear and unambiguous. He could not lie in consecrated ground, and so the manner in which his body was disposed of was an irrelevance. He could be burned on a pyre by the Hindus for all she cared, she said, because it wouldn't make any difference to his true fate, which was already well underway in the pits of hell, where he was suffering richly deserved eternal torments inflicted by an elite squad of devils.

Theo thought all this was medieval nonsense, only adding to his sense of alienation from the Church, but his mother's absence from the funeral hurt him hard as he struggled to stay upright in the driving wind and rain, standing graveside between Frank and Mrs. Hirsch. The rabbi was a very old man with a querulous voice, and Theo could hardly hear what he was saying. A task made more difficult not just by the noise of the wind but also by the presence of a professional mourner, who beat his breast and wailed loudly in incomprehensible Hebrew. Frank told Theo afterward that the mourner had not been an optional extra but was part of the package including the cheap pine coffin supplied by the funeral home. But he clearly expected to make most of his fee from tips and pulled importunately at their wrists like a professional beggar afterward as they made their way back to the car.

Theo kept looking around, irrationally hoping to see his grandparents. But, of course, they weren't there. He was curiously satisfied, however, that his father had been taken back by the Jews at the end, notwithstanding the ramshackle nature of the ceremony and the fact that it had required a bribe to make happen. He remembered his grandfather's pronouncement: *"He has turned his back on who he is, become something he is not."* And now perhaps his father had become himself again: Micah Stern, who had worked and loved in a new country and fought against fate until the struggle proved too much for him and he fell.

Theo hoped that maybe one day there might be enough money for a headstone to give his father's name and dates, but for now there was nothing. Worse than nothing, in fact, because it quickly became apparent in the days following the funeral that Michael owed money on almost everything in the apartment, and this mountain of debt now fell on the heads of Theo and Elena like an avalanche.

They sat on the French armchairs and watched helplessly as heavy men in gray overalls trooped in and out, removing the Kelvinator refrigerator and the Westinghouse electric range, and the next day other similarly dressed men came for the furniture, too, and a city marshal served them with an eviction notice stating that the rent on the apartment hadn't been paid for three months.

Without Frank, they would soon have been homeless. "I've found you somewhere on the Lower East Side," he said. "It's not what you're used to, but you'll be together, and it's the most I can afford. Thank God, Weiss has given me work or I couldn't even do this."

"Thank you," said Theo. He felt frustrated at the inadequacy of the words to express his intense gratitude, but then to his surprise his mother came to the rescue.

"You are our Good Samaritan," she said, walking over to Frank and taking hold of his hand. "I wish Michael had brought you home to meet me. We are lucky to have you as our friend."

Frank blushed and stammered to find a reply, but it didn't matter. Theo knew him well enough to know that he was pleased and was grateful to his mother—a feeling at odds with the slow-burning resentment toward her for refusing to mourn his father, which he carried inside him, locked up with the other grudges that had kept them apart for so long.

Frank was right. Their new home bore no relation to anything that they were used to. It was in the same Jewish neighborhood where Theo's grandparents had lived, but the tenement building was in worse condition and the apartment was far smaller.

They had to climb six flights in the semidarkness to reach it, holding on to each other to avoid tripping on broken stairs or falling over hunks of plaster that had fallen from the ceiling and been left to lie. The only light came from small gas burners in the halls, flickering in the gloom behind their dusty mantles.

On each floor there were four apartments, two at the front and two at the back. Theirs faced the back, where the building was separated from another tall tenement by a narrow lane, so that no sunlight could come in through the small windows, and access to the gray light on offer meant opening up their rooms to the prying eyes of the occupants of the apartments across the way.

A woman and her husband lived directly opposite with their young son, who had bulbous eyes and a shaved head. The man was gone during the day, working somewhere, and came home drunk at night and shouted at his wife in incomprehensible Yiddish. He may have hit her, but Theo and Elena never saw that, and the boy sat and stared out of the window for hours at a time, a picture of misery.

Theo never got used to the woman. She was young but old, and her face was blotchy and yellow, stretched tight across the bones. Sometimes he lay on his bed and watched as she came out onto the fire escape, carrying bundles of wet clothes, and the wind whipped up her heavy skirts, revealing cheap cotton stockings with holes all over, the size of quarters, and red, bony knees.

Day and night the rancid smells of cooking and garbage were trapped in the stale air. Some of the residents on the higher floors could not face the long journey up and down the stairs and dropped their refuse bags from their windows like bombs that often burst open on the cobbled ground by the trash cans in the lane. There, a group of terrifying wildcats permanently lurked, fighting over the garbage. They seemed to Theo to be of a different species to the domestic cat, huge and hideous with scars and open wounds and bristly torn fur smeared with filth. They were rumored to use the fire escapes to steal babies from their cribs at night, and their caterwauling in the small hours was enough to freeze the blood.

Inside, Theo and Elena's apartment consisted of four small rooms—a cramped bedroom for each of them, a tiny kitchen with a gas stove, and a living room with a fireplace that didn't draw properly, so that the price of a little warmth was being enveloped in a thick black smoke that made them practically invisible to each other as they coughed and gasped for air.

They shared the toilet with the other three apartments on their floor. It was cramped and windowless and there was no electric light, so visits required crossing the hall with a candle. Horrors awaited if it went out, as enormous cockroaches and worse lived in there, waiting to latch on to defenseless victims as they crouched.

They were prisoners, Theo thought, captive like the pigeons that the caretaker kept in coops up on the roof. Sometimes he followed the old man up there and watched from behind a smoking chimney stack as he let them out to fly and then stood on a cornice, sinister against the skyline, and waved his black pole like a necromancer to call them back.

But to Theo's surprise, his previously fastidious mother refused to be discouraged. She laughed at the smoke and the cockroaches and at the mice that ran in and out of holes in the wainscot, skillfully evading the traps she set for them each morning, and with Theo's help, she bargained for vegetables and penny pinches of rice and butter with the peddlers and shopkeepers on Orchard Street, and concocted meals that were the highlight of their weary days.

The best dishes she reserved for when Frank came to dinner once a week. She rightly regarded him as their savior and constantly expressed her gratitude to him, which made him blush beet red and squirm with embarrassment as he stammered that he wished he could do more, but that he also had responsibilities to his old mother, with whom he lived in a small apartment over on Hester Street.

"You have opened my eyes, Frank," Elena told him. "I had thought ill of the Jews before because my husband's parents refused to accept me. In fact, they pretended he was dead after he married me." Elena shuddered, and there were tears in her eyes as she recalled the memory.

"I know," said Frank sympathetically. "Michael told me."

"I hated them," she said, warming to her theme. "But they weren't done. When Theo was eleven, Michael's father took him. It was the worst day of my life. I cried, I tore my hair, I was in despair until San Antonio answered my prayers and restored my son to me. And now that we have moved to this neighborhood, I worry that the old man is here still and will try again. I lie awake at night, thinking about it."

"I think it's all right," said Frank soothingly. "I've asked around and I've found no trace of him. There are so many of us here. People come and go all the time and leave nothing behind."

"But I don't understand. Why would you be looking for him?" Elena asked, staring at Frank with sudden suspicion.

"Theo asked me to. After Michael died."

"Is this true?" asked Elena, turning to her son, her eyes wide with alarm.

"Yes," said Theo. "They're my grandparents. I thought they might help."

"They wouldn't. Don't you know that? They would take you away from me and make you live with them," said Elena, almost hysterical now. "Promise me that you won't go looking for them again. Swear it."

Theo nodded reluctantly. The move to the Lower East Side had had the same effect on him as his mother, making his father's family seem within reach, but unlike her, he wanted desperately to find them. He still remembered the authority in his grandfather's voice—that sense the old man had conveyed that he could explain the world if he was just given enough time—and the feel of his grandmother's hands as they slid down over his head, as if she was memorizing him. He longed to see them again and to be told that he was a part of their family.

He was like the survivor of a shipwreck, scanning the horizon for land. Released by his father's death from his promise to forget, he had already gone looking for his grandparents several times since the move, trying to recognize the streets the old man had taken him through on that long-gone summer afternoon, but all the tenement buildings looked the same. Once, he'd been convinced that he'd caught sight of Rachel, the hunchbacked peddler whom they had encountered outside his grandfather's building, but when he ran across the street, dodging the traffic, and went up close, he found the woman looked nothing like her and that there was a real child, not beans, inside her baby carriage.

The disappointment had hurt like a body blow, and he felt the same now, hearing that Frank had found no trace of his grandparents. The promise to stop looking for them extracted by his mother felt like another door closing, shutting out the light.

Elena breathed deeply, trying to regain control of her emotions. "I'm sorry, Frank," she said, reaching out and taking hold of his hand. "Michael's death has unnerved me. Nothing feels safe anymore. But it's better when I don't think of him. Much better. With your help, Theo and I are trying to start anew."

"It's not better for me."

"What?" Elena looked up from her sewing, not understanding.

Theo had been replaying the dinner conversation in his mind ever since Frank left, and now his long-suppressed anger toward his mother burst out from him like a flood tide breaking the walls of a crumbling dam: "It's not better not thinking of my father. It's worse. It's like you're killing him a second time, pretending he didn't exist. Frank's too polite to say so, but he feels the same. I know he does. He loved Dad, just like I did. Like I do!" Theo added, raising his voice.

"I don't know what you mean," said Elena, flustered.

"Yes, you do," said Theo harshly. "How do you think I've felt listening to you talking about him burning in hell this last month? And then leaving me to go to the funeral alone? Do you know how old I am?"

"Fourteen."

"Exactly. And you think that's right? You think that's how a mother should treat her son?"

"He did this to us. He disgraced us, left us with nothing. He put us here. Have you forgotten that?" said Elena, fighting back now that she had recovered from the initial shock of Theo's attack.

"He didn't want to. He worked like he did to succeed, to make us rich and give you the best that money can buy. But he was defeated by the Depression, by Alvah . . . God, you don't even know who that is, do you?" said Theo incredulously, seeing the uncomprehending look on his mother's face.

"No, I don't. Who is it?"

"A snake who organized the workers against him. One of your Communists." Theo laughed humorlessly. "It doesn't matter. The point is that you had no idea what Dad was having to deal with at the factory."

"He didn't tell me, and nor did you, for that matter."

"You could've asked. You saw the stress he was suffering from."

"Stop! Please stop!" Elena pleaded, putting her hands up to her temples.

"All you care about is yourself!" he shouted. "I don't exist, just like Dad didn't."

"What are you talking about? I love you. You're my son."

"I'm talking about my school. I was happy there, and you took it away from me. Destroyed my hopes."

"Your father did that."

"He couldn't have without you. That's why he went through that charade with my coach. To get you on his side. And God did he succeed!"

"Your coach was a Communist. He was training you up to be a Red."

"Rubbish. He cared about me, wanted me to make something of myself. Not like the two of you."

"The Communists killed my parents. Your grandparents. Have you forgotten that? They took away everything from me. My home, my country . . ."

Elena had started to cry, but Theo steeled himself to go on. He had to. He felt his life depended on it.

"Coach Eames wasn't like that and you know it," he told his mother. "Don't you dare tell me he was a wolf in sheep's clothing like you did before."

Elena was silent. She looked crestfallen, and Theo wondered in a corner of his brain if she might be going to apologize, but he'd gone too far to stop now and escalated his attack further, going to the forbidden place that he had tried without success to obliterate from his mind. It was as if he had been headed there from the beginning and only realized it now when it was too late to turn back.

"You were thinking about yourself, just like you always do," he said slowly, deliberately. "About what happened to you. About your church and your parents, about Don Andrés . . ."

"What are you talking about?" Elena looked genuinely incredulous at the sudden turn in the conversation, but that didn't deter Theo.

"You encouraged him."

"I did no such thing."

"Everyone could see it. Why do you think he kept on coming back?"

"Because he likes the church. He didn't know about it before. But that stopped because of you. I hope you're pleased with yourself."

"You bet I am. I should have told my father about that stupid book he gave me. He was using me to get at you, and I let him. It makes me ashamed."

"He was not. He was being kind, even though you didn't deserve it with the way you treated him. You were rude and ungrateful. You made *me* ashamed."

"You're blind," said Theo, shaking his head. "He's been after you since that first day he came to the church. When I went back to the presbytery, I heard him talking with Father Juan. He said you were like a painting. A Madonna. He said you were beautiful and that you had faith like that priest that got shot. The one you knew."

Theo's voice slowed as he said the words that he had kept bottled up in his head for so long. Aloud, they didn't sound so ugly or dangerous. Maybe because they were true.

"Why didn't you tell me?" Elena asked.

"I don't know," said Theo softly. His anger had evaporated, replaced now by a cold emptiness and a pricking behind the eyes.

"I haven't done anything wrong," said Elena. "I swear it on all that is holy. Not for one moment did I think of Don Andrés in an impure way, and it pains me that you could believe such a thing." It hurt Theo to see that she had her hand on her heart.

"Maybe you didn't know what you were feeling."

"I knew. My conscience is God's most precious gift. More valuable than life itself. Do you think I would sully it like that?"

Theo shook his head. Now the idea seemed crazy, when he had been certain it was true a minute before.

"You humiliated me that day, Theo. And yes, you're right: it hurt even more because I loved that church. It was the last link I had to where I came from, to what I had lost. I tried to carry on going because of that, even though it wasn't the same. People looked at me differently. They knew you weren't with me and that Don Andrés had stopped coming. But I wouldn't give in, until I had no choice, after what your father did. And I didn't deserve it. None of it. Just like you didn't deserve what happened to you, for which I'm sorry. More than I can say."

Theo wanted to run away and he wanted to embrace his mother all at the same time. Instead, he sat rooted to his chair, weighed down by the silence between them. Words dried in his throat, where before they had come rushing out uncontrolled. He felt exhausted, more tired than he could ever remember.

Elena began to get up and he forced himself to speak. "I'm sorry too," he said. "I don't want to hurt you. I know it seems like I do, but I don't."

She leaned down over him and stroked his hair, just as she used to do when he was a boy. "I've always found it so hard to get beyond what happened to me," she said, and her voice was quiet, almost a whisper. "I wasn't much older than you, and it's stayed in my head. In my dreams. The shots, the screams, the fire. That they should have died like that." She paused, breathing deeply, gathering herself before she went on: "Michael made it better. He made me feel safe, but then he took it away. And it was as if I'd lost everything all over again. But I hadn't. I have you. My beloved son."

Theo was crying. He reached up blindly and took his mother's hand. Outside, it had begun to rain and the torrent of water running down the dark window glass felt like a stream washing away the barriers that had for so long kept them apart.

In the days that followed, Theo was buoyed by the improvement in the relationship with his mother that followed their conversation, but the new openness between them did nothing to help his ongoing struggle to make sense of his father's death, which his mother understood even less than he did.

He searched constantly in his mind for his father, but Michael was as elusive in death as he had been in life. Theo's memories fragmented if he looked at them too closely. He remembered words, but not how they had been spoken; times they had shared together, but not how those moments had felt. He had often been told that he looked like his father, and he took to gazing at his reflection in the mirror for minutes at a time, trying to find traces of the dead man, but he remained forever just out of sight.

One night Theo imagined that if he died, too, then he might find his father waiting on the other side, ready to explain everything, but the thought frightened him and he backed away, squeezing his temples with his fingers to expel the idea from his mind.

He was haunted by the image of the big imitation revolver hanging upside down outside the gun shop on Fourteenth Street. He knew why: the gunshot had been his father's final message. Brutal and simple, it told them that he did not love his wife and son, because he had been prepared to abandon them to destitution, and that the world was a terrible place from which he had had to escape. But that message was the polar opposite of everything he'd always said about himself and about them. It contradicted his constantly repeated assertion that they had been chosen by destiny. Was life meaningless? Was that what he was telling them? Had he been lying all along?

Theo needed to find his father to ask him why he had blown his brains out. And to punish him and even perhaps to forgive him. But he could do none of these things. And every morning he rose exhausted from his broken dreams to face the life of grinding poverty to which his father had condemned them.

Soon it got worse. On a night in March a blizzard blew over the city. Snow swirled in the light of the arc lamps and settled on window ledges and fire escape treads. Down below, the garbage disappeared under a white cloak, and Theo's face lit up as he looked out in the morning on this magical transformation of ugliness into beauty that had occurred while he was asleep.

But with the snow came a new kind of cold that spread through the tenements in the days that followed, grasping the inhabitants in a hypothermic vise. Theo and Elena could not afford the dollar sacks of coal that the street vendors sold, and so Theo had to join thousands of others who roamed the streets with their makeshift carts, foraging for wood.

Beneath the thin layer of snow was ice. A horse slipped in the road outside their tenement building and lay quivering in agony for hours until a policeman finally arrived to put it out of its misery. And people began dying, too, carried out of the tenements in cardboard coffins and stowed in the back of morgue vans whose gassy exhausts filled the frosty air with clouds of choking black-and-blue smoke as they drove away.

Elena began to cough. At first Theo thought it might be because of the damp steam from the wet laundry that they had had to hang inside, draped across the furniture because of the weather, but the cough persisted and got worse. It racked her thin body, and Theo became terrified that he would lose her.

She lay in bed, holding Theo's hand, and gazed at the shrine on the opposite wall. She had carefully packed up all its pictures and statues when they'd left the Fourteenth Street apartment and had set them up here in exactly the same arrangement, with the wooden cross up above. Only the porcelain Christ that Theo had broken was missing from the assembly. Amid all the troubles at the factory, he had never gotten around to replacing it as he had intended, and there was a space on the side of the shrine where it had once been.

Suddenly, Theo felt an overwhelming need to confess. He had to tell her. It was as if the untold sin undermined the power of the shrine like short-circuited electricity.

"I broke it," he told her, the words spilling out of him in a rush before he knew he was going to speak. "Christ, I mean. Because I was angry at you, and because I wanted to know what would happen. I'm really sorry . . ." He broke off because he was crying and couldn't say any more.

"I know," she said, looking up at him and taking hold of his hand. "I knew all the time, and it doesn't matter. God forgives you if you are sorry. He always does."

"Will he forgive Dad?"

"No, I don't think he can," she said sadly, looking up at the cross. "Your father's not sorry."

She closed her eyes and he said no more, not wanting to upset her. Soon she fell asleep and he stayed beside her all night long, anxiously watching her labored breathing until he, too, slept where he sat, as the gray light of the early dawn began peeping in between the thin cotton drapes.

In the morning Frank came and brought an old Jewish doctor with a long, doleful face that grew longer as he took Elena's temperature, stared down her throat, and listened to her chest through his stethoscope. He moved the chest piece up and down her rib cage, while her wide-open garnet-brown eyes stared up into his.

When he had finished, he looked over at the shrine. "You're a Christian," he said. "A stranger in a strange land here!"

"Yes," she whispered. "Innocents abroad."

He smiled and his face lost its lugubriousness, almost as if it was a party trick. "The shrine's beautiful," he told her.

"Thank you."

"Do you pray a great deal?"

"Yes. The saints are watching over us, me and my son."

"Good," he said. "Because you must pray to them now for life, you hear me? Not how you Christians say—'thy will be done.' Your son needs you."

"I know," she said and squeezed his hand as he got up to leave.

Theo and Frank followed him out of the room. "It's touch and go," the doctor told them, writing out a prescription on the table in the living room. "This medicine may help, but we need the weather to change. It's too cold for the poor and the weak—Christians and Jews. And she needs to fight, which is hard because she's delicate."

Whether it was due to Elena's prayers or just a favorable adjustment in the movement of the continental jet stream, the unseasonable weather did change on the day after the doctor's visit, and the long-delayed New York spring suddenly arrived with a burst of sunshine breaking through the overhanging clouds. The high walls meant there was little change in the light at the back of the tenement, but the warmth in the air soon had a beneficial effect, and Elena began to rally.

On his next visit, the doctor recommended air and exercise, so every morning she and Theo walked in the neighborhood, going farther as Elena's strength grew. One day they crossed the Bowery and found themselves in Little Italy. It was like entering a new country where the pushcart vendors sold eggplant and plum tomatoes and olives, instead of the Jewish food they had been used to. They called out their wares in Italian, and Elena half understood. It wasn't her language, but the people were of her world and she felt the hair on her skin quivering as she stood stock-still on Mulberry Street and tried to take in everything around her—the signs on the shops and in the windows, the dress of the people, the infectious chorus of a Verdi opera being played through a loudspeaker outside the entrance of a phonograph shop, the smell of pizza and oil, and another Latin world stronger in her nostrils than anything she had experienced since she first came to America.

And then, around the corner, came the Virgin Mary. Borne by six handsome young men in open-necked shirts on a platform of shimmering silk and flowers—roses and lilies and marigolds—she floated at head height with a beatific, serene expression on her curiously fleshlike face. Elena was ecstatic. Gazing up, she saw not a statue but a vision of the Holy Mother herself, like the one the peasant Juan Diego saw in Guadalupe five hundred years before.

Without a word, she joined the procession and began to follow the float down the street in the wake of the golden-robed priest and his acolytes. Theo pushed his way through the crowd to keep up with her. All along the sidewalks, people were kneeling and smiling and crossing themselves and even breaking into song.

"Today is the Annunciation when the angel came to Our Lady," Elena told Theo, shouting over the noise. "At home there was fiesta and nobody worked, not even my father. We danced instead!"

The procession wound its way up Mulberry Street, turned and turned again, and entered a small church filled with incense and saints in alcoves and awash with deep color from the sun's illumination of the stained-glass windows.

Theo saw that his mother was crying. "What is it?" he asked fearfully. "Why are you upset?"

"I'm crying for joy," she said, taking his hand. "God is here. We're going to be all right, Theo. I know it."

9

THE LOWER EAST SIDE

From that day on, Elena was happy, setting forth in the mornings from their apartment and walking to the Church of the Most Precious Blood on Baxter Street for the daily Mass.

The resident priest, Padre Paolo, had been in Mexico for a time and spoke some Spanish. He welcomed Elena enthusiastically into his flock and took her into the sacristy to show her a reliquary containing a fragment of the tibia of Saint Anthony of Padua, whose intercession had saved Theo from his grandfather three years before.

With the padre's encouragement, she was able within a few weeks to overcome the language barrier sufficiently to be allowed to join the group of devout ladies that cleaned the church and arranged the tall vases of flowers that were displayed on almost every free surface. Everyone complimented Elena on her arrangements—she had a natural talent for the work, they said.

The Italians gave Elena back the sense of belonging and purpose that she had lost when she left the church community in Gramercy Park. She had thought that she would never be free of the disgrace that her husband's suicide had brought down on her, but here she could make a fresh start with people who shared her faith.

But for Theo it was different. He did not belong. It was his mother's religion, not his, and the Mass was an empty vessel without the spark of faith to give it life. He was grateful to the Church for reviving his mother, but that was a superficial response. Underneath, he continued to nurse a grudge against an institution that taught that those who committed suicide would rot in hell and forbade them burial in consecrated ground. He told his mother that he didn't want to go with her to Mass and, rather to his surprise, she did not object.

Theo's break with the Church pained Elena, but she was relieved that there was no possibility of him revealing their past history to the Italians and embarrassing her like he had done at the church in Gramercy Park. Her illness had taken a severe toll on her health, exacerbating her sense of her own fragility, and she could neither bear to lose this new, unexpected happiness she had found, nor cope with quarreling with her son, who was such a powder keg of emotions. They were getting along better now, but there was no guarantee that his anger would not burst out again, just as it had before. In the long run, she believed that time would heal Theo's wounds and that he would return to Christ, but for now she was determined to keep hold of what she had and not rock the boat.

They spent less time together, and while Elena worshipped, Theo struggled with his demons. As the weeks passed, he was overcome by a creeping numbness, which was his body's attempt to build a protective wall around his tortured emotions. It spread like a thin film across his consciousness, so that nothing felt fully real and his memories started to seem as if they belonged to another person.

One day he pulled out his suitcase from under his bed and took out the few objects that he had brought with him when they moved. Slowly, he turned the leaves of *The Romance of King Arthur*, the beautiful book that Sir Andrew had given him, and looked at Rackham's magical pictures. What would the great illustrator have made of their filthy tenement? Theo wondered.

Across time, he heard a faint echo of Sir Andrew's aristocratic voice, promising *"to bring you another book illustrated by our friend, Mr. Rackham."* He remembered how angry he had been on that day at the church when his mother had slapped him and Sir Andrew had given him his handkerchief to stanch the blood. There it was in the suitcase, too, with the scripted initials *ACB* embroidered on the corner. Black on white. He didn't know why he'd kept it. For the monogram perhaps: a knickknack from a distant land where men had titles and spoke English with strange nasal accents.

Theo dug down farther and found the running shoes that he was looking for at the bottom of the suitcase. He turned them over and ran his fingers over the silver spikes and across the thin white leather, remembering how he had thought in the early days that they were magic shoes, gripping the track and propelling him forward in a perfect rhythm that had felt like flying. He closed his eyes, trying to recall the sensation, but it eluded him. It had been so long now since he ran that he had forgotten what it was like.

The next morning he crossed the Bowery and went back to his old school. He had no wish to see any of his old classmates, so he went in through the back gate on the far side of the running track and crossed over to the sports pavilion. There was a man inside, sitting at a table, cleaning a baseball bat with linseed oil.

"Can I help you?" he asked, looking up at Theo standing in the doorway.

"I'm looking for Coach Eames," said Theo diffidently.

"He's not here anymore. I'm the coach now. Why do you want him?"

"He helped me with my running. I wanted to talk to him about that."

"Well, I wish I could help you, but he was gone before I got here," said the man kindly, as though sensing Theo's disappointment. "The headmaster might know where he went, I suppose, but I doubt it, somehow. My understanding is that Eames left under a bit of a cloud, although what that cloud was, I'm not sure."

Theo muttered his thanks and hurried away, breaking into a run as he left the gate. But he hadn't exercised in months and he soon stopped, doubled up and winded. Then, as he was catching his breath, he realized to his surprise that his gasps were cries too. He was crying for what he had lost. That year at school, on the cinder track and in the battle bus, had been the only time Theo had felt he truly belonged anywhere. Coach Eames had given him that, and his father had taken it away.

Theo wondered now whether one of his parents had told Saint Peter's about the coach's politics, but he rejected the idea as soon as he thought of it. His father had said he wouldn't, and nothing had happened since to change Theo's belief that he'd been telling the truth. Theo thought his father had been a selfish but not a spiteful man, and he didn't think that his mother would've done something so radical without her husband's agreement or without telling her son what she'd done. The school must have found out Coach Eames was a Communist from some other source, but the result was the same. He had disappeared into the great city, gone now where Theo could not follow.

The visit to his old school left Theo restless. He needed distraction, and he found it at the movie theaters that were dotted all over the Lower East, paying a dime to sit in the cheapest seats at the back of the balcony and watch the double features. He enjoyed Bela Lugosi and the Marx Brothers, was irritated by the escapist rags-to-riches fantasies in which the boy got the girl and everything ended up hunky-dory, and returned again and again to watch the Chicago gangster movies that had become popular since the Depression hit. They paid lip service to the idea that crime doesn't pay with their antiheroes dying in a hail of bullets at the end, but they also glorified the gangsters' rejection of hard work in favor of brute force, and poured scorn on the American values that Theo's father had preached.

Theo liked Edward G. Robinson in *Little Caesar* with his vicious smile and the way he said "See!," poking his finger or his gun into his victims' chests to impose his will on them. But the movie he loved the most was *The Public Enemy*. He watched it again and again, mesmerized by James Cagney's portrayal of the young hoodlum turned bootlegger who murdered his way to power. Even from the back of the theater, Theo experienced a visceral response to Cagney's burning eyes and snarling voice, his merciless contempt for all weakness, and his terrifying volatility. The character's raw rage forced Theo back in his seat, ripping through his defenses. Cagney made him feel.

Afterward, walking back, he felt cleaned out—a kind of empty contentment, ephemeral but soothing. He looked up at the blackened tenements lining the streets and laughed at the irony of his father's tireless attempts to escape the Lower East, only to end up plunging his family back into the same cesspool, and he tipped his cap to the spire of the Chrysler Building shimmering in the distance.

However, the cinema cost money—money they did not have. And now that his mother was better, Theo began to look for work. He had low expectations and wasn't surprised when he was turned away wherever he applied, but then to his astonishment, he was handed a job almost without asking.

Once a week, sometimes alone and sometimes with his mother, Theo went to the public bathhouse on Rivington Street, carrying a towel and a piece of soap wrapped in newspaper. Inside, he got a ticket from the attendant and sat with a crowd of men and boys on one of the long wooden benches in the waiting room. No one moved—they all had their eyes fixed on the big black hands of the clock on the back wall, counting out the minutes until the bathers emerged shiny-faced from the showers.

Then, when the attendant was ready, he shouted, "Next batch!" and the next in line stampeded through to the booths, desperate to get there first so as to avoid the showers where the faucets didn't work properly and the water came down in all directions, soaking their clothes where they'd hung them up on the pegs.

They were allowed ten minutes before the attendant turned off the water and made his rounds, hammering on the doors with his stick, and calling out "Time's up. Everyone out." Then they would get dressed and emerge clean and blinking into the sunlight, while more bathers rushed past them to take their turn.

It was in one of these stampedes that Albie the attendant slipped on a bar of soap and broke his leg. Theo, who liked Albie, stopped and knelt beside him, forgoing his shower, and then went to summon help. And Albie, suitably grateful, recommended to his employers that Theo would be an excellent replacement until he could return to his duties. All Theo had to do was fill out a form and lie about his age and the job was his, at least on a temporary basis.

Theo loved the work. The bathhouse was one of the only joyful places in New York City. It delivered on its promise: men came in dirty and went out clean, and in between sang bawdy songs as the hot water splashed over them and washed away their sins. Some even left him penny tips in the saucer he was allowed to keep by the door.

The Lower East began to seem less alien, now that he had a place in it. As he walked to and from work, people recognized him and patted him on the shoulder because he was a part of the baths where many of them spent their happiest ten minutes of the week.

Only a few doors down from the baths was a brothel, providing a different kind of service to the residents, and the whores kept him a chair on the sidewalk where he ate his lunch, supplemented by bootleg beer that they kept in a zipped-up bag, concealed from official eyes. They called themselves Greta and Jean and Claudette, as if they were movie actresses, and dressed in old flowery kimonos covered with pictures of waterfalls and cherry trees and Confucian philosophers, with virtually nothing on underneath. They sprawled indolently, indifferent to passersby stumbling over their meaty legs. Occasionally they would pull at the coattails of possible customers, but most of the time they soaked up the sun and gossiped and knitted shawls. The middle of the day was not their busy time.

Theo was their mascot, just as Genesis the Goat was the mascot for Jake's Saloon across the street—dry at ground level but one of the Lower East's most popular speakeasies down in the cavernous basement. Genesis had gilded horns and a collar encrusted with rhinestone gems and could do no wrong, wandering the local streets and wantonly stealing food from the pushcart vendors like a sacred cow in India, while Jake, his owner, puffed on a perfecto cigar and ruled as the king of Rivington Street, protected by the cops whom he paid handsomely for the privilege.

Theo walked tall in the sunshine, feeling the jingle of coins in his pocket. Good fortune had rained down upon them in the last weeks: a church for his mother and a job for him falling from a radiant sky, and Providence still had more gifts to bestow. On a Saturday in June, Frank announced at dinner that a little money had at last come through from the Bank of United States, enough for them to be able to move to new accommodations. He had already spoken to the landlord, who had offered them an apartment facing the street on the second floor. There would be more space and light, and they would be sharing a toilet with just one other family, who were known to be the cleanest in the building.

Elena was ecstatic. She jumped up from her chair, kissed Frank on both cheeks, and told him he was their guardian angel, and went off to say a prayer of thanks at the shrine in her bedroom.

"It really seems like your luck's changed," said Frank, smiling and raising his glass.

"You sound like my father," said Theo, for whom luck was a dirty word. "But, yes, I'm happy and grateful too. You've been a good friend to us, Frank."

"I owe it to your father. He helped me, so it's only right that I should try and help you. He wasn't all bad, you know."

"Just toward the end," said Theo with a wry smile. "And he had Alvah to contend with then, as well as the Depression, so I guess we should make allowances."

Theo was surprised at his own magnanimity. He wouldn't have been able to talk about his father with any such detachment a month ago, and now here he was, making allowances. It was amazing what a job and a little good fortune could do.

"Michael loved Alvah, even though he didn't deserve it. And I guess now, looking back, that I was jealous of that," Frank said thoughtfully. "Alvah was part of the dream he had—"

"Like me," said Theo, interrupting.

"Yes, like you, although he hadn't worked out your role in the way he had with Alvah. And so it hurt him when Alvah turned on him, hurt him more than I understood at the time," Frank said, twirling his glass. It was almost as if he was talking to himself.

"Where is Alvah?"

"He got another job in the Garment District, paying more, probably. But I don't know if he'll last. He's a powerful figure in the union now, and his employers won't like that."

"Is he a Communist? Dad said he was. Do you remember—at the end?"

"Maybe. I don't see him, so I don't know. But whatever he is, it's not because he believes it, but because he thinks it's the best way to get people to follow him. Alvah's what Alvah cares about."

"Yes, you're right," said Theo. "It's funny—I used to want to find him and shoot him down like in the movies, but now I don't know when I last really thought about him."

"You're growing up, becoming a man. You've built something here, something to be proud of."

Theo smiled and was about to reply, but at that moment his mother came back into the room and Frank got up to go. "Move-in date's in a week," he said. "I'll be here to help you."

The new apartment was a vast improvement over the old one. Like day and night. No longer were they looking out into a foul-smelling, airless vault with the neighbors' weird son gazing at them with his vacant stare from only a few feet away. Instead, the sunlight streamed through their open windows, and outside they heard not quarreling and caterwauling but the infinitely varied noises of the street: traffic, peddlers calling out their wares, shouts, snatches of song. Theo felt its energy and even at night, when all was quiet, he sensed the living pulse of the Lower East, breathing deep like a vast creature, readying itself for the day.

The Monday after they moved was Independence Day and, in the evening, Theo walked with his mother down Essex Street to Seward Park and watched the fireworks display. Catherine wheels fizzed on gigantic poles; Roman candles popped red, white, and blue stars; and rockets flew on golden wings over the tenements. Then, at the end, everyone held sparklers in their hands and sang "The Star-Spangled Banner," and a few wild young Italians fired revolvers into the sky.

On the way back, Theo felt an infectious joy. "Wasn't it wonderful?" he said.

"Yes. But sad too," Elena replied wistfully.

"Sad! Why?"

"Because it reminds me of my home when I was young. No country does fireworks like my country. On Independence Day, on the Virgin's Day, on all the great saints' days, we would have castles of fire and bulls bursting into fiery colors. The church bells would ring, and the saints would go through the town like on Mulberry Street, but not like that, because there were so many people there, more than you can imagine, and all of them singing hymns, praising the Lord."

"You make it sound beautiful," said Theo, moved by his mother's description. "But you can't be happy if you're always looking back, always comparing what you have to what you don't have. We're here now; not there. Isn't that enough?"

"Yes, of course it is," said Elena, laughing. "I promise you I'm happy here with you. Happy in our new home. Happy that God has taken me back. I shan't have much left to pray for if the Lord keeps on giving like he has."

She stood on her tiptoes and kissed her son on the cheek. "I love you," she said. "You know that, don't you?"

Theo nodded, too filled up with emotion to be able to respond. And they walked on without saying anything more, a small lady in black and a young man towering over her, artificially slowing his pace and reducing his stride to match her smaller dainty steps.

At home, Theo couldn't settle, so he went out wandering the streets. It was late now, but there were still drunken revelers about, determined to extract the maximum indulgence from the few hours left of the holiday. Theo felt uneasy, remembering the revolvers in Seward Park, and turned for home.

But then, coming around the corner of a street two blocks from his apartment, he stopped dead in his tracks. There, standing on the sidewalk only a few yards away, was a man he instantly recognized, but had never expected to see again. As Theo watched, Sir Andrew went up the steps into a tenement building and disappeared from view.

After waiting a moment, Theo followed. The door was still ajar where Sir Andrew had pushed it open, and Theo put his head around the side for a moment and looked into the hallway. The pale yellow-green flame of a small gaslight in the crumbling ceiling flickered in the draft, providing a dim light, but it was enough for Theo to see that there was no one there. Cautiously, he stepped inside and went over to the foot of the staircase that spiraled up around a central well, ascending into darkness. Up above, he could faintly hear the sound of voices, although he couldn't make out what they were saying because they were too far away.

Theo thought of leaving, but he didn't. His curiosity was too great, and he went up as far as the first bend in the stairs. Above his head, someone else was climbing, too, going up to the third floor, and Theo followed, stopping on the landing below. A corridor with a series of closed doors on either side opened up to his right, poorly lit like the hallway.

On the floor above, there was the sound of knocking and light streamed out into the stairwell.

"What the hell do you want?" demanded an angry male voice. "Do you know what time it is?"

"Yes, ten o'clock. And I'm very sorry to disturb you, but I was wondering . . ." It was without question Sir Andrew—Theo instantly recognized his upper-class English accent, so bizarrely out of place in this dingy building.

"What?" interrupted the first voice, angrier now.

"I was wondering if you might know of a Mrs. Sterling who may be living in this building. She has a son, Theodore. They speak Spanish."

"No one speaks Spanish here. This is the Lower East, not Mexico City, you dummy! Now get the hell out."

The door slammed, and Theo heard Sir Andrew sigh. And then, down below in the hallway, there was someone moving and Theo ducked away into the corridor, just in time before a powerful flashlight shone up the stairwell.

"Hey, you. What are you doing up there?" The light and the hard, accusing voice meant it had to be a cop, and Theo flattened himself against the wall.

"I'm sorry, Officer. I was looking for a friend of mine. That's all." Theo could hear Sir Andrew going past him, descending the stairs.

"All right, keep your hands out of your pockets where I can see them and get outside. I hope you've got some papers to go with that funny accent of yours."

"Yes, of course, Officer."

The door below shut, and Theo was left alone. His heart was hammering and he couldn't keep pace with the thoughts that were rushing through his head. He'd been scared of being found by the officer and accused of being a burglar, and he was worried now that one of the residents would come out and find him and call the cops again. But then he wasn't thinking about that anymore, just about Sir Andrew. Why was he looking for them? What did he want? Only Sir Andrew could answer these questions, but Theo didn't want him to find them. Sir Andrew would try to interfere and change everything, just when their lives had gotten better and they'd found a little happiness.

But if he didn't go after Sir Andrew, Theo would never know what he was doing here, banging on doors, searching for them in the dark. And what were the chances of finding him like this? Didn't that have to mean something?

Theo went down into the hallway and opened the door a fraction, peeping out. There was no one in sight. Sir Andrew had gone and he'd missed him, just the same as with his grandparents and Coach Eames. Gates had closed one after the other into houses he might have entered . . . The narrowing and constriction of life suddenly felt intolerable to Theo. He pulled open the door and ran down the steps.

Up at the end of the street, he saw a tall figure about to turn the corner and he took off after him, running like he used to run, as if his life depended on it.

"Stop!" he shouted. "It's me, Theo. Wait."

He swung into Orchard Street without slowing and crashed into Sir Andrew, who had stopped, hearing the shouting behind him. The force of the collision knocked them both off their feet.

Theo was momentarily stunned, and when he looked up, trying to stop everything spinning, he found himself staring into the round black barrel of a revolver, pointed between his eyes.

"Theo!" The gun wavered and dropped, and a strong hand reached down and pulled Theo up to a sitting position.

"I must say I've had quite a few surprises in my time," said Sir Andrew, squatting down on the sidewalk beside him. "But I think that just about takes the biscuit!"

Takes the biscuit! Theo started to laugh at the strange phrase, and then the laughter made him cough and he clutched the side of his chest, feeling the hurt where he'd hit the ground.

"Why are you looking for us?" he asked once he'd gotten his breath back.

"Because I want to marry your mother if she'll have me. And take care of her, and you too. I've been looking for you ever since I heard—" He stopped, putting his hand on Theo's shoulder. "I'm sorry about your father, Theo. That was a terrible thing."

"Not for you it wasn't," said Theo furiously, pushing Sir Andrew's hand away as he tried and failed to stand up. He had to have hurt himself more than he realized when he hit the pavement.

"Try not to be so angry," said Sir Andrew. "It makes you say things that are unjust, like you did at the church the last time I saw you. You shamed your mother then when she had done nothing wrong, and I stayed away after that because I didn't want to make it worse for her."

"How honorable of you!" Theo sneered.

"So I had no idea what had happened until a few days ago, when I met Father Juan and he told me," Sir Andrew went on, ignoring Theo's insult. "But all he knew was that you had gone to the Lower East. If I had known before, I could have saved you from all this. It must have been terrible," he said, waving his hand at the crumbling tenements rearing up on all sides in the moonlight.

"No, it isn't . . ." Theo began, but then he stopped, remembering the winter and how his mother had almost died.

"I've been knocking on doors, but no one has heard of you, and tonight, I have to confess I was close to giving up when you jumped on me," said Sir Andrew. "Why did you do that, Theo? If everything is good, then why did you come after me?"

Theo was silent, biting his lip because he realized he had no answer to the question. He already regretted going after Sir Andrew, but at the same time, he thought he'd have done the same if he could turn back the clock. He could make no sense of himself.

Sir Andrew gave Theo his hand and helped him gingerly to his feet. They began to walk, but Theo could take only small steps because of the pain from his fall.

"She won't have you," he said.

"We'll see," said Sir Andrew placidly. "I'm not such a bad catch, you know."

Theo felt another surge of fury and would have liked to have punched Sir Andrew for his arrogance, and maybe he would have done if it wouldn't have hurt him so much to draw back his arm.

Sir Andrew left Theo at the door. "I'll be back in the morning," he said. "And I'll be bringing a doctor."

Elena was asleep when Theo got back in, and he didn't wake her. Instead, he lay on his bed, going over in his mind all that had just happened.

He was furious with Sir Andrew. What right did the man have to come barging into their lives, turning them upside down like he and his mother were playthings? He thought of waking his mother up and inventing some story to persuade her that they had to pack their bags and leave, but he couldn't think of anything even halfway believable, and besides, where could they go? Frank was still paying most of the rent, and the few dollars Theo earned at the bathhouse wouldn't even cover the cost of the grim apartment upstairs that they'd just managed to escape from. They were prisoners of their poverty, defenseless against Sir Andrew and his money.

And what would his mother say? He'd believed her when she'd told him that she'd been innocent of any impurity toward Sir Andrew, but that had been before her husband died. Now everything was changed. She was free to love again, and the church would bless a marriage with a fellow Catholic, especially an important one like Sir Andrew.

What a fool he'd been! He'd created the whole situation by chasing after Sir Andrew. He hadn't needed to, so why had he done it? Was he looking for a way out of their poverty himself? No! He rejected the idea out of hand. He was no mercenary.

Theo's side hurt, and his head ached with all the conflicting questions his mind kept throwing up without providing any satisfactory answers. He couldn't stay still anymore, and so he got up and began to pace about, and the noise woke his mother, who came out into the kitchen in her nightdress, rubbing her eyes.

He told her the truth, the whole truth. When it came to it, it wasn't even a choice. She was shocked, sitting down hard in her chair and gripping the edge of the kitchen table as if to try to keep hold of reality.

When he was finished, she was quiet for a while and he started up pacing again, until she asked him to repeat what Sir Andrew had said.

"Which bit?" he asked.

"What he said about me and you," she said.

"I already told you. He said he wanted to marry you."

Elena smiled. It was just for a moment, gone in an instant, but Theo was sure about what he had seen, and he erupted in anger.

"It's his money, isn't it?" he shouted. "Just like with Dad at the railway station. You're down on your luck, so you hitch a ride with the first nice car that comes along."

This time Elena didn't slap Theo but just went back into her bedroom and closed the door.

In the morning Theo left for work without waiting for Sir Andrew and his doctor. He was damned if he was going to take any favors from the interloper.

All day, he was upset. The bathhouse with its shouts and steam suddenly seemed precious to him, and the whores, too, who teased him at lunch that he had a bug up his ass and wanted to know if he'd like them to remove it. Even the beggars and the peddlers and the pretzel sellers—Theo saw everyone and everything with a new intensity born out of an intuition that they might soon be gone.

At home at the end of the afternoon, Sir Andrew and his mother were waiting for him, sitting across from each other at the kitchen table. Sir Andrew looked ridiculously out of place amid their poverty, with his pearl-gray flannel suit, two-tone wing tip shoes, and the panama hat that he held in his hands: a picture of self-possession. His presence made Theo see the apartment through new eyes: yes, it was an improvement over the old one, but it was still cramped and shabby, reeking of the privation that he and his mother had grown accustomed to over the last six months.

"So, have you decided?" Theo demanded, standing in the doorway with his hands thrust deep in his pockets.

"No," Elena said. "I want to know what you think."

"It's not up to me," said Theo.

"No, but it would mean changes for both of us."

"What kind of changes?"

"We would be living in England—"

"Count me out."

"Please, Theo. Don't be like that. There are things that would be good for us. Surely you can see that. You could go back to school—one of the best—and you could start running again. Andrew says that England's wonderful for athletics, don't you, Andrew?"

"Yes, indeed. It's the home of running, but I'm sure Theo knows that," said Sir Andrew, smiling.

"I don't want to run," said Theo flatly. "I'm done with all that." It infuriated him that his mother was trying to placate him now with the offer of schooling and running, when she had backed his father over destroying all of that the year before.

"And we wouldn't have to worry about money," she went on, warming to her theme. "We can't carry on relying on Frank. It's not fair to—"

"That again! Is that all you can think of?" Theo cut in furiously. "You're not something to be bought like one of his houses."

"Don't talk to your mother like that!" said Sir Andrew. His tone was sharp, almost threatening, and Theo wanted to hit back hard because he felt passionately that Sir Andrew had no right to come into his home, the home that he'd built so painstakingly with his mother, and tell him what he could or could not do. But he held his tongue, not because he was intimidated, but because he was ashamed of what he'd said. He thought of the whores on Rivington Street and hated himself for comparing his mother to them.

Elena took a deep breath. "I like Andrew," she said. "I wouldn't be talking to you about this if I didn't."

"Then that's settled," said Theo bitterly. "There's nothing else to talk about." He turned to go, but Sir Andrew called him back.

"This isn't a good place for your mother. Surely you can see that. She told me that she almost died here in March, or have you forgotten that?"

"It's our home," said Theo stubbornly. "We made it together."

"Yes, you did, and I admire you for it. But what's going to happen next winter when you've got no money for coal or proper food?"

Theo said nothing—he had no answer, and Sir Andrew shook his head. "This is ridiculous," he said, turning to Elena. "It's your decision, not his. We could be happy. You know that. And Theo will come round in time, once he sees what England has to offer."

"I'm staying here," said Theo.

"Living on the streets, throwing your life away. That's stupid and you know it."

"Better that than being a piece of baggage brought along because my mother can't leave me behind. Part of the package—you get her, but you have to take the son too. No, thanks!"

Sir Andrew sighed and got up from the table. "You must decide, Elena. I love you with all my heart, and I hate this. It's not what you deserve." He waved his hand, taking in the apartment, the street outside, the Lower East. "When should I come back?"

"Tomorrow morning," she said with a wan smile. "I'll know by then."

"Very well," he said, putting on his hat. "Theo, I hope you will do the right thing," he added as he went past him and out the door.

Sir Andrew's parting shot was well aimed. Theo hated what he had said about their life in the Lower East, but that didn't mean he didn't agree with it. He didn't know how his mother would get through another winter, and the prospect terrified him, the more he thought about it. He'd lost one parent and he couldn't stand to lose the other.

He could also see why his mother would like Sir Andrew. It wasn't just the money and the security. He shared her faith and her language, and he knew and loved her country. All the things that had been missing with Theo's father. Theo hated the Englishman for having what his father didn't have, but he also recognized what that could mean for his mother.

He knew, too, that it would be easy for his mother to leave America. She had never had an investment in the country that his father had believed in so passionately. He vividly remembered her rejection of Walter Chrysler's brazen materialism on top of the skyscraper. Ever since she left Mexico, she had been looking for echoes of home: in the Spanish church in Gramercy Park and now at the church in Little Italy. New York was where her husband had shamed her with his suicide. She would sail away from it without a backward glance.

But for Theo, it would be a rupture he could hardly contemplate. The city was all he knew. It was his home. It was all he had left of his father. Leaving would mean parting with Frank, who was his only friend and the only person who had really known his father—the only one he could talk to about him. He had lost so much already; how could he bear to lose what he had left?

And yet . . . and yet the pain of such a schism attracted him, too, in a way he could not explain. Perhaps it was that same desire to escape numbness and to feel that had taken him to the movies to watch Jimmy Cagney over and over again.

In the end, he kept returning to the fact that he had willed all this to happen by going after Sir Andrew. He could have avoided the whole sorry mess if he had just stayed put outside that tenement and let him disappear around the corner and out of their lives forever. But instead he'd run after him. Why? Was it because he was thirsty for adventure, like the knights in the old book Sir Andrew had given him? Was that it?

He went over to the window and looked out into the street. Everything was defined in the early-evening light—a black cat with white paws sitting on the turn of the fire escape opposite, grooming itself with elaborate precision; two fat men arguing in Yiddish directly underneath the cat but entirely separated from it, gesticulating wildly with their hands but somehow never touching each other; the three brass balls of the pawnshop on the corner swinging gently in the breeze; and a flock of birds above the tenement roofs circling in the pale sky before they flew away. Theo breathed it all in once, twice, three times, and then turned away. He went over to the door of his mother's room and knocked.

She was praying at the embroidered kneeler, her hands tightly clasped together.

"You can stop that now," he said. "I'll go with you if that's what you want."

She started to get up, but he closed the door without waiting for her to reply and left the apartment to wander the streets again until long after nightfall.

Sir Andrew and Elena were married in the Church of the Most Precious Blood with no one present except Theo and Padre Paolo and Frank, whom Elena had insisted on inviting. Afterward, they had lunch at the Waldorf Astoria and Sir Andrew treated Frank with an elaborate courtesy, which pleased Theo even though he wasn't prepared to admit it.

Frank looked like a fish out of water, which was what he was, having never been in a Catholic church or a hotel like the Waldorf before, but he was happy too. He had become very fond of Elena over the past six months, and he was delighted about the sudden change in her fortunes. He kept referring to her as Lady Campion-Bennett and laughing, and then she laughed, too, as if the humor was infectious.

He was delighted, too, for Theo, telling him how wonderful it was that he was going to be rich and go back to school and have the life that his father had tried to deny him. Theo grinned and bore it until he couldn't stand it anymore and then lashed out at Frank as soon as they were alone.

"Do you think I want this?" he shouted. "Do you think I want to leave New York?"

"No, I guess not. But whatever you get on the other side of that ocean is going to be a whole lot better than what you've got now. You can bet your bottom dollar on that much," said Frank, standing his ground. "You're clever—way cleverer than me—and it's a crime to waste your life working as a shower attendant and living in a slum."

"It wouldn't always be that way. I'd find a way out," said Theo sullenly.

"Like your father? That didn't pan out so well, did it?" Seeing Theo wince, Frank went on quickly, "No, I'm sorry I said that. It wasn't fair. But this is a golden opportunity for you, if you're willing to take it. Sir Andrew seems like a decent man to me. He'll do his best for you if you give him the chance."

"He'll do what he has to do to please my mother. That's who he cares about. When I get on that ship tomorrow, it'll be like I have nothing left."

"It's scary. I can see that. But it's still the right thing to do."

Theo shook his head, as if in disbelief. "Don't you care that I'm going?" he burst out. "It's thousands of miles away. We may never see each other again."

"No, I think we will," said Frank, unruffled. "One day, a few years from now, I'll be down there in the harbor, waving my hat, and you'll be coming down the gangway looking like a million bucks with a beautiful girl on your arm."

They left from Chelsea Piers the following afternoon, traveling first class on a White Star Line steamship bound for Southampton. It was a vast behemoth the likes of which Theo had never seen, and the first-class staterooms looked like a floating extension of the Waldorf Astoria. He stood on deck as the liner moved slowly out of its moorings and down the Hudson, waving to Frank until he disappeared from view.

Then they were out in the bay and passing Ellis Island, and he could hear his father's voice in his ear, clear as a bell above the sound of the turbines: "*We had to get through there or be sent back . . . Everyone was scared. You could smell the fear—it stank worse than the dirt on our bodies . . .*" Theo looked across at the huge redbrick and limestone hall glittering in the sunshine. There was no one there now, and yet in his mind's eye he could see a crowd of people on the steps with his father and his grandparents in their midst, hurrying up to where the doctors and inspectors were waiting for them with buttonhooks and chalk. Their lives hanging in the balance, dependent on what was about to happen to them inside this palace at the end of the sea.

Farther out, passing the Statue of Liberty, he could hear his father again: "*I looked up at the towers of Manhattan and the stars blinking and I was happy, happier than I have ever been . . .*" Theo looked back and there were the same towers—and new ones, too: the Chrysler Building and the Empire State—but they were receding as the steamship picked up speed, and he was losing what his father had come so far to find.

They passed through the Narrows into the Lower Bay, and Manhattan Island was lost to view. Theo crossed to the other side of the deck. Ahead, the blue emptiness of the ocean stretched out to the horizon, but behind the ship, he caught sight of the great Ferris wheel on Coney Island. It was getting toward dusk and the colored lights were on in Luna Park and he could hear his father again, although more faintly now: *"It's America . . . I felt it here . . . it's what I'd crossed the sea to find . . ."* Theo glimpsed him, wild-eyed on the horse in Steeplechase Park, his shoulders arched forward and his hair streaming back as he rose and fell with the rails, and he saw the child in the man, too, with all the driving force and energy that had taken him up and up like a magnificent ocean wave until it crashed down upon the empty shore and was gone.

The ship was picking up speed now and Theo felt the sea spray on his cheeks, unable to distinguish it from tears as he wiped it away and turned to face his future, filled with that same tinseled melancholy he'd felt on that day he'd spent with his father on Coney Island a year before.

PART TWO

ENGLAND—SCHOOL DAYS

1932–1934

10

THE LEDGE

They drove down to the school on a hot and humid day in mid-September. It turned out to be a longer journey from London than Sir Andrew had anticipated, because they were delayed first by an accident on the highway and then by a convoy of farm vehicles piled high with tottering bales of newly cut hay. They moved at a snail's pace along the narrow, winding country roads in a drawn-out procession that Causier, Sir Andrew's chauffeur, couldn't get around. His angry honking had no effect on the drivers in front, who carried on at a precise ten miles per hour, until Sir Andrew instructed Causier to desist.

"If we're late, we're late," he said. "It's not our fault. Father Philip will understand."

"I hope so," said Elena nervously, clasping her hands together inside her stole. "We do want to make a good impression."

She glanced unhappily over at Theo, who sat morosely silent with his head turned away from them, staring out of the window at the slowly passing hedgerows, just as he had throughout the journey.

But behind his fixed expression, Theo was feeling a welter of conflicting emotions. He was angry about being sent away to boarding school, but that was nothing new—he'd been furious ever since his stepfather had told him about it at breakfast three weeks earlier. Now, however, a growing anxiety about what he would have to face at the end of the journey had added to his inner turmoil, and he welcomed the delay caused by the farmers' stolid defiance of the Rolls-Royce behind them, even if it meant having to endure more of the uncomfortable chafing of his tight new uniform suit against his sweating skin.

"Stop fiddling with your collar," his mother told him, reaching out to pull on his arm. "You'll ruin it if you carry on like that, and there won't be time to change when we get there."

"It's too tight," said Theo, pushing her hand away. "I can hardly breathe with it on."

"I remember I hated Eton collars, too, when I was your age and first had to put them on. *Chokers* we used to call them at my school," said Sir Andrew sympathetically. "But you'll get used to it in a couple of days. Everyone does."

"Like slaves do with their iron collars? They forget they're there—is that what you mean?" asked Theo, seamlessly transferring his irritation over onto his stepfather. They were the first words he'd addressed to him all day.

"Of course not," said Sir Andrew mildly, refusing to be provoked. "You're a schoolboy, not a slave. All good schools have uniforms. It fosters a sense of identity. Makes everyone feel they're part of something bigger than themselves."

"Slaves aren't given a choice, though, are they?" said Theo, sticking to his theme. "They have to do what their masters tell them. And that's exactly what's happening here, isn't it?"

"No," said Sir Andrew. "You're going to school because it's what boys your age do. It's for your own good."

"And yours too. I know you both want me out of the way. And where better than this godforsaken place, stuck out in the middle of nowhere?"

"Theo, please," said his mother. "I can't stand it. It's the opposite of godforsaken. Andrew says it's the best Catholic school in the country." She had started to cry, the tears shaking her chest as she fumbled in her handbag for her handkerchief.

Immediately, Sir Andrew's expression changed—patience replaced by anxious concern as he took hold of his wife's hand and tried to calm her down.

Theo felt terrible. His mother's nervous vulnerability frightened him. She had been delicate for as long as he could remember. Her migraines had been a cloud over his childhood. But the illness she had suffered in New York the previous winter when she had come so close to death had changed her. Her brown eyes seemed larger than before. Their luminous brightness was a startling contrast to the pallor of her complexion. The pale, translucent skin was stretched tight over the bones of her face and her body seemed fragile, as if it were made of a thin glass that could break under the slightest pressure.

He wanted to reach out to her and make it all right, but he couldn't, not with his stepfather there. Besides, he knew that the two of them would take any apology to mean acquiescence in their decision to send him away to school, and he wasn't going to give them that satisfaction. So he resumed his moody silence instead, watching his mother out of the corner of his eye as she tried to compose herself, taking out the pretty gold compact her husband had given her and setting to work to repair her face so that she would look her best for the headmaster.

Then, just when it seemed that they weren't going to arrive before nightfall, the farm trucks turned off the road and Causier was able to open the throttle and get them to the school a minute before their five o'clock appointment.

They parked beside a flagpole in the center of a big asphalt quadrangle, enclosed on three sides with lines of tall gray buildings. The thick stone of the walls and the narrow lancet windows gave the school an oppressive, watchful feel, intensified by the overcast sky and the heavy atmosphere of the late afternoon. There was not a breath of wind in the air, and the Union Jack drooped disconsolately from its pole.

There were other cars parked here and there, and groups of boys passed between them, coming and going through scuffed doors that were set at regular intervals around the facade. A few stopped to point at the Rolls-Royce, and Theo shrank away, instinctively wishing to avoid association with his stepfather and his wealth.

On the other side of the car, a thin man with a pronounced limp had approached Sir Andrew and was ushering him and Elena toward a different door from the others, painted green and with a polished brass lion's head knocker at its center. He had the shortest hair that Theo had ever seen on a man, a semicircle of gray thatch above a white scalp, and large, protuberant ears. A toothbrush mustache, also gray, and an ill-fitting suit gave him an odd resemblance to Charlie Chaplin, except that there was no bend in his left leg as he walked, and Theo guessed that it was a prosthetic.

"Come on, Theo. Sergeant Raikes here is taking us to the headmaster," Sir Andrew called back to him, and Theo reluctantly followed, feeling sick to his stomach and wishing he was anywhere but where he was.

They passed into a hallway that surprised Theo with its lavish furnishings. A thick wool carpet covered the floor, and an elaborately arranged vase of blooming flowers sat on an antique mahogany table beneath a full-length portrait of a severe-looking monk, dressed in a pleated black habit and cowl that covered every inch of his body except his hands and the front of his face.

"'E's the founder, 'e is," said Raikes, nodding grimly. "'Anged, drawn, and quartered on Tyburn 'Ill by the Protestants back in fifteen hundred and ninety-one. A 'orrible, 'orrible way to die, but that's the way they did things in 'em days." Raikes finished his speech with several nods of lugubrious satisfaction and rubbed his hands together, which Theo later came to know was a characteristic gesture.

"Please don't frighten our guests, Sergeant," said a cultured voice behind them. "I'm sure that executions are the last thing they want to hear about after their long drive!"

The headmaster was a tall man with beady, watchful eyes that seemed to operate independently of his easy smile and warm handshake. He had been in the job for just over three years, moving back to Saint Gregory's from the order's house in London to take up his position following his predecessor's retirement, and perhaps it was his experience of the capital that gave him an unexpectedly worldly air. He wore his habit as if it was a suit, and a pair of expensive, well-polished Oxford brogues were visible below the hemline. His office, too, furnished with tufted leather armchairs and Persian rugs scattered across the floor, was anything but Spartan. Its main window faced out not onto the gray quadrangle but toward the wide front lawn of the school, with an attractive view of green hills in the distance, and shelves of carefully arranged leather-bound books lined one of the walls.

"I do apologize for Sergeant Raikes, Lady Campion-Bennett," he said, pouring her a cup of tea from a pretty Wedgwood pot that sat ready and waiting on a side table. "He has a regrettable habit of getting carried away when talking to visitors. He lost his leg on the Marne, and sometimes I think that the experience may have unsettled his mind as well, but I think we have an obligation to do our best for those who risked their lives for us on the field of battle, don't you?"

Sir Andrew and Elena nodded in agreement and the headmaster swept on. "I believe I read somewhere that you, too, fought in France, Sir Andrew, and were awarded the Military Cross for conspicuous valor. Is that right?"

"Yes," said Sir Andrew shortly. "It was a long time ago."

"Indeed, indeed. The war to end wars—let us hope that we never see its like again," said Father Philip gravely, putting the tips of his fingers together for a moment, as if in prayer.

"Now tell me about young Master Campion-Bennett?" he asked, glancing over at Theo, who had his eyes firmly fixed on the floor. "I'm sure he's going to be a most valuable addition to our student body."

"I'm not . . ." said Theo. He hadn't meant to speak, and the two words came blurting out of his mouth unexpectedly, leaving everyone in the room, including Theo, looking shocked.

"I mean I'm not Campion-Bennett," he went on after a moment. "I'm Theo Sterling. That's my name."

"Oh, I see," said Father Philip, looking as if he didn't see at all.

"Theo's my stepson," said Sir Andrew. "I'm sorry, Headmaster. I should've made that clear. His father was called Sterling."

"Perhaps it would be best if you were to discuss this issue amongst yourselves and then you can let me know your wishes," Father Philip suggested diplomatically. "And in the meantime, do you have any other questions?"

Elena had some—about such diverse issues as medical facilities and opportunities for confession, which Father Philip did his best to answer. But soon they were outside in the quadrangle again and Causier was getting Theo's trunk out of the back of the car.

"You embarrassed us," Elena broke out angrily, speaking in Spanish. "I asked you not to, but you did. I don't know what Father Philip must think of us."

"I don't care what he thinks," said Theo, digging his hands deep into his pockets. "I'm not his son"—he shot a vicious look over at his stepfather—"I'm Dad's, and I'm keeping his name whether you like it or not. Just because you want to pretend that Dad never existed doesn't mean I've got to too."

"You need to grow up and start showing some gratitude—" Elena began furiously, but her husband cut her off.

"No," he said, laying a hand on her arm. "The boy's right, Elena. It's his choice what he wants to be called. I'm going to go back in there right now and tell Father Philip, so there won't be any confusion."

Four and a half hours later, Theo lay in bed in Dormitory B of Cardinal Newman House, staring up through a high, narrow window at a scimitar moon. It was hanging in the black sky over the tower of the abbey church of which he could see only the topmost section due to his oblique angle of vision. He was lying very still, trying to empty his mind and forget what he had eaten for dinner—a piece of lukewarm greasy meat—called mutton, apparently—that had been almost impossible to cut as it slithered alarmingly across his plate, colliding with an equally inedible slab of half-mashed potato. Now the food felt as if it was sitting solid and horrible inside his gut, incapable of being digested. The pauper's rations that he and his mother had been subsisting on in New York the previous winter had not been as foul as this mutton, and yet his mother had spent the day assuring him that this was the most expensive Catholic school in England. It made no sense, but then, very little did anymore.

He closed his eyes, willing himself to fall asleep, but now he was distracted by the discomfort of his bed. The ancient springs had almost given way so that his body sagged, as if it was contained in a badly designed hammock with only the top of his trunk, stowed away underneath the bed, stopping him from sinking all the way down to the linoleum floor. He wondered if the other beds in the dormitory were as bad as his and decided that they probably were, judging from the sounds of tossing and turning all around. There was snoring, too, and occasional farts, and a low moaning coming from the next-door bed to Theo's, which abruptly ceased after an angry voice called out: "Put a sock in it, or I'll come over there and do it for you."

Theo sighed, trying to imagine what the noise would be like the following night after the rest of the boys had arrived. Currently, the dormitory was only about half occupied. It was a long room with two rows of identical iron beds divided one from the other by cheap pine chests of drawers labeled with their owners' names. CAMPION-BENNETT was on Theo's, and he wondered if it would be changed the next day. He hoped it would so he wouldn't have to protest again and draw attention to himself.

He thought of names and beneath them other names and other identities, peeling away like the insides of a Russian doll. He knew he was no Campion-Bennett, but was he a Sterling, when that name was just an invention of his father's, put on like a new suit to help him get ahead in a new country? Or was he a Stern, the star name of his Jewish grandfather, who had once tried to claim him for a tradition of which he knew next to nothing, and had never contacted him since? They were all exiles like his mother, running from far-off lands where houses burned and death cries went unanswered. Flotsam and jetsam, belonging nowhere and to no one.

Finally, Theo fell into a troubled sleep in which he dreamed he was searching for his father through the empty rooms of a cavernous house. He knew his father was alive because he could hear him talking to himself, like he did at night near the end in the apartment near Union Square. Up ahead, at the end of a windowless corridor, there was a door that was shut. He hurried forward. His father was inside. He knew he was, if only he could get to him in time. He put out his hand to turn the handle, but Frank was there beside him, pulling him back. "You don't want to see," he said. "It's for your own good." But Theo shook him off. He couldn't hear his father anymore and there was no time to lose and he pushed open the door. And he was falling hard, fast . . . screaming . . .

"Shut up, you sniveling little brat!" shouted the same voice that had let loose on Theo's neighbor earlier. "One more peep out of you and you'll pay for it in the morning. That's a promise."

Theo lay flat on his back, staring up at the moon. He felt wide awake, but as if in a dream, powerless to stop whatever was coming next.

He was woken by the ringing of an electric bell that made his body tremble with a responsive vibration, as if he was being wrung by the current too. He opened his eyes and found himself looking straight into those of his moaning neighbor, which were wide with anxiety and reddened from a night of silent crying. The boy looked far too young to be at a boarding school like Saint Gregory's. He ought to have got an exemption, Theo thought: "Not fit for frontline duty at this time."

"I'm sorry for screaming," Theo said, raising his voice so as to be heard over the noise of the bell. "I was having a nightmare. I'm Theo, by the way."

He stopped, expecting the other boy to introduce himself, but the boy just looked even more terrified than before and said nothing. Theo wondered if he could speak at all, but there was no time to test the hypothesis with further questions because Barker, the prefect on duty, was strutting up and down the central aisle of the dormitory like one of Mussolini's Blackshirts, rapping on each of the iron bedsteads with a swagger stick, and ordering everyone in a military parade-ground voice to get up, get washed, get dressed, and be ready for roll call in fifteen minutes. Theo recognized his voice as the same one that had shouted in the night.

Barker was dressed as if for dinner, with his black shoes polished so brightly that they shone and his school uniform clean and pressed, with the jacket unbuttoned to show an embroidered white silk waistcoat underneath. But his beautiful clothes only served to draw attention by way of contrast to his ravaged complexion. Each morning, Theo would learn, he woke earlier than anyone in the school and attempted to disguise the pimples and pustules and pockmarks with layers of dermatological creams, but their only effect was to make him look absurd as well as ugly. His mouth was set in a permanent grimace of pained self-awareness as his eyes darted from one boy to the next, searching for evidence that they were laughing at his disfigured face.

Theo's neighbor was already standing up, holding his toothbrush, by the time Barker got to his bed and stopped, staring at him like he was an insect he was debating whether or not to squash.

"Name?" he demanded.

"Cattermole," said the boy, proving he wasn't dumb after all. But his voice was little more than a squeak, and Barker glanced at the label on the chest by the bed to verify it.

"Cattermole! What kind of name is that?"

Cattermole didn't answer. He just trembled while Barker stared, tapping the silver head of his swagger stick rhythmically onto the open palm of his hand.

"You weren't so shy last night, were you, you little toad? Keeping us all awake with your carrying on." Barker reached out with the stick and placed it on Cattermole's stomach, adjusting it carefully until he had found the center of Cattermole's small solar plexus.

"You and me are going to be friends this term. Just you wait and see," he said and laughed, turning away, just as Theo was about to intervene. He was the one who'd screamed, and Cattermole shouldn't be taking the blame for that.

But he'd hesitated a moment too long and now he felt guilty and, worse than that, complicit in Barker's persecution, when he looked down and saw that Cattermole had peed in his pajama bottoms.

Somehow the boys got ready in time, standing beside their made-up beds, fumbling with their last buttons, and answering to their names as Barker read them out, making each one sound like an order by spitting out the syllables machine-gun style.

Over above the door, the thick black minute hand of the clock flicked onto half past seven and the electric bell began to ring again, summoning the boys to an unappetizing breakfast of watery porridge and burned toast.

The headmaster's beginning-of-term address delivered in the main hall at the end of the morning gave Theo a first sense of what the school was about. By now all the boys had arrived back, driven down by parents or met off the train by a fleet of yellow buses laid on for the occasion, and the hall was full. Row upon row of identically dressed boys sat on identical chairs, while Sergeant Raikes and a coterie of prefects in colored waistcoats patrolled the aisles to ensure that everyone sat up straight and listened.

The walls on either side were wood-paneled and covered from wainscot to ceiling with the names, in gold lettering, of scholars and athletes who had gone before and brought glory to the school. Some had a thin cross added after to denote that they had died in the Great War, making the ultimate sacrifice for King and Country. The rows of columns made the school seem as if it had been there forever, hallowing its teachings with the force of an ancient tradition.

On an elevated dais facing the boys sat the masters—a motley collection of old and young, fat and thin, monks and laymen, with the latter wearing gowns and mortarboards. And behind them on the back wall, Jesus hung on an oak cross, sending the message to the boys that Saint Gregory's was founded not just on tradition but on the word of God.

Father Philip came forward from the dais and stood behind a table on which a selection of highly polished silver cups and trophies were displayed on green baize. To Theo, he seemed a different man to the smooth-talking conversationalist of the day before. Gone was the urbane, ironic voice, replaced now by a commanding, almost military demeanor.

"Welcome back, boys!" he said. "Each year is a good year at Saint Gregory's, but I have a premonition that this is going to be a bumper year, an annus mirabilis. We will study hard and play hard, and with God's help we will receive our just rewards. Including the Challenge Cup . . ." He paused, looking down at an empty space in the center of the row of trophies. "For five years we have been beaten by our rivals despite our most valiant efforts, but I believe that this season will be different. However, for that to happen we must all come together and be as one. Not just those on the field of play but the rest of us, supporting them and willing them on to victory. And that is what we must aspire to in all our endeavors, academic and athletic. We must put school first. In these changing times, there are men in other schools who put themselves first, and that is the way to corruption of both the body and the spirit. But that is not how we do things here. That is not the Saint Gregory's way . . ."

At the end of the speech, the boys cheered long and hard, waving their hats in the air. One or two were even thrown, and Sergeant Raikes took care to take down the names of the offenders.

Back in the dormitory at the end of the day, Theo found he had been moved to a new bed at the other end of the room. He tested the springs and was pleased to find that they were an improvement on what he had had to contend with before, and saw to his satisfaction that the label on the adjacent chest of drawers read STERLING. It was as if Campion-Bennett had never existed. Except that his new neighbor to the right, a boy called Alwyn Thomas with carroty hair and a singsong Welsh accent, knew all about the change.

"How do you do it?" he asked, pointing at the label. And then without waiting for an answer, he started firing more questions: "Are you going to do it again tomorrow? Maybe call yourself Harry Houdini? Or Ramsay MacDonald?"

"I haven't decided," said Theo, looking undecided, and they both laughed. "How did you know I switched?"

"I know everything," said Alwyn mysteriously and then laughed again. "I'm curious, that's all. I like to know who everyone is, match names to faces, so that's what I was doing last night before lights-out. And I wasn't likely to forget a mouthful like Campion-Bennett in a hurry—it sounds more aristocratic than Queen Victoria. But now you're just plain old Sterling—about as interesting as me, except for you being American, of course. Don't get too many of them over here; more going the other way—seeking their fortunes in the Wild West. Might try it myself one day if I ever get out of this place. So go on—how did you do it?"

"Do what?" asked Theo, who'd forgotten Alwyn's original question as he tried to keep up with his scattergun chatter, bouncing along like a cork on a running stream.

"Change your name. How did you swing it?"

"I told the headmaster."

"Bloody hell—you're brave, aren't you?" said Alwyn, letting out a low whistle. "You don't want to get on the wrong side of the Old Man. I can tell you that."

"Old Man?"

"Yes, that's what we call him. That and *The Flogger*—he's got a whole rack of canes in his study. Sometimes he ties them together for extra punishment."

"I didn't see them."

"That's because he keeps them hidden when parents come. He's all sweetness and light then, like butter wouldn't melt in his mouth. But once they're gone, he doesn't have to pretend anymore. It's like that new film *Dr. Jekyll and Mr. Hyde.* I saw it in the holidays. You should too. It's scary." Alwyn's voice dropped and his eyes got bigger behind his thick glasses as though he were picturing the headmaster wrestling in his study with his schizophrenia, fingering his canes.

"How do you know all this?" asked Theo dubiously. "You're new, too, aren't you?"

"No, it's my second year, but I also like to keep my ear to the ground. It doesn't do not to know what's going on—not in a place like this. So come on—why did you want to change your name?"

"Campion-Bennett's my stepfather. I'm Sterling, like my father."

"And where's he, if he isn't married to your mater anymore? In America still? Will you go back to see him in the holidays?"

"No, he's dead."

"Oh, sorry to hear that." Alwyn sounded disappointed more than sympathetic. It was almost as if he'd been angling for an invitation. "How did that happen, then?" he asked, resuming his interrogation. He had no restraint, and with his carrot-topped head jutting forward with each new question, he reminded Theo of a demented woodpecker.

"He had an accident," said Theo and stopped, biting his lip. He'd had to either lie or say nothing. Telling a complete stranger that his father had put a gun in his mouth and pulled the trigger wasn't an option. Really, he should have told Alwyn to get lost—the boy had no right to ask him stupid personal questions before they'd even gotten to know each other, but he'd been feeling lonely with no one to talk to, and everything was so unlike anything he'd been used to.

Now he felt guilty, too, as if he'd denied his father in some essential way. "I don't want to talk about it," he said angrily. "It's none of your damn business what happened to my dad."

"All right, all right. Keep your hair on," said Alwyn, backing away a step and putting up his hands. "There's no reason to get sore—that's what they say in America, isn't it? Like in the movies? Or is it mad—don't get mad?"

Theo didn't respond. He started getting things out of his trunk to put in his drawers, hoping that Alwyn would go away and leave him alone.

But Alwyn didn't. He was clearly not one for taking a hint. "Do you want to know a secret?" he asked, coming closer and dropping his voice.

"What secret?"

"A secret about what's going to happen tonight. They're going to put you out. And it's okay if you don't look down. I know that from when they did it to me last year."

"Down! What are you talking about?"

"I can't say," said Alwyn mysteriously. "It's more than my life's worth if they found out that I told you. Just remember, though—eyes up, not down."

"Who's 'they'?"

"The prefects—the ones with the waistcoats. They do it at the start of every year to the new boys. It's like an initiation. You'll see."

"What is?"

But Alwyn wouldn't say any more, even when Theo threatened to hit him over the head with his pillow, which he would have done if lights-out hadn't intervened.

The prefects came at ten o'clock, waving flashlights and making all the new boys—or *brats*, as they called them—get up and follow them up the iron stairs to the corridor where the sixth formers had their studies. Some of these older boys were standing in their doorways, watching and laughing as the snaking line went past and halted in front of a door at the far end, where Lewis, the head of house, was standing with a list of names in his hand.

Theo was at the back of the group, standing beside the half-open door of a study in which a boy was sitting in an armchair reading a book laid open across his knees. Theo felt a jolt of envy, which startled him with its intensity. He would have given anything at that moment to trade places with the boy and leave behind the disgusting dormitory and whatever ghastly ordeal the idiots in the colored waistcoats had got planned beyond the closed door at the end of the corridor.

Theo was older than the other new boys, and it had been agreed that he would start school as a third-year fifth former, but that still meant he would have a year to wait before he became eligible for a study. It felt like an eternity as he stood outside, looking in.

He could see only half the room from where he was standing, and he couldn't resist taking a step forward into the doorway from where a disordered desk under the window and shelves overflowing with books came into view. On top of them, up near the ceiling, was a white plaster bust of a man with a vast beard that grew out of his chin instead of down over his chest. Theo recognized him straightaway. He'd seen the same face on statues for sale on the sidewalks in Union Square when the Communists had their meetings there and tried to sell copies of *The Daily Worker* to passersby and recruit them for the revolution.

He laughed. He couldn't help it. There was something just so wonderfully absurd about finding the father of atheistic Communism staring down at him from the top of a bookcase in the "best Catholic school in the country."

"Who the hell are you?" The boy's angry question shocked him. The books had made Theo think of him as a fellow spirit, but now he was staring up at Theo like he was a mortal enemy, his bright-blue eyes hard and unforgiving.

He had an arresting face. Fine and delicate and almost feminine, each feature drawn as if with a sculptor's scalpel, and all set within a mess of unbrushed blond hair that was so fair, it was almost white. He had an Elastoplast on his chin where he had obviously cut himself shaving, and was wearing an old, shapeless gray sweater over his uniform trousers. There were several small holes in the front and a paint stain on one of the shoulders.

"I'm Theo Sterling," Theo said, stammering over his name. "I'm sorry I laughed. I didn't mean to."

"Wait!" the boy commanded, stopping Theo in his tracks as he had begun to back away. "What were you laughing at?"

"The statue." Theo pointed weakly over at the bookshelf, not knowing how to explain himself. The boy intimidated him for some reason in a way that nobody else had up to now, not even the headmaster.

"Do you know who it is?" the boy asked.

"Karl Marx."

"And you think he's funny, do you?"

"No. It's just him being here in this place. I wasn't expecting it. That's all."

The boy continued to stare at Theo for a moment and then unexpectedly smiled. It lit up his face and made Theo want to laugh again, with relief this time, but he didn't, not wanting to risk giving further offense.

"Nobody here's got any idea who it is," the boy said. "They're all too stupid. You're the first one."

Theo nodded. He was happy that the boy didn't think he was stupid. It mattered to him for some reason.

"You're American?" the boy asked.

"Yes."

"Who do you want to win the election?"

"Roosevelt," Theo said without hesitating, and then winced.

"Having second thoughts?" the boy asked, noticing Theo's grimace.

"No, the election made me think of my father. That's all. He loved Hoover. He had a photograph of him on the wall, even used to talk to it sometimes. But I don't like him. I saw what happened."

"What? What did you see?"

"Sorry—I've got to go," Theo said, stumbling backward as someone pulled his arm. The door had opened at the end of the corridor.

"Now listen and listen good," called Lewis from the open door, "because I'm not going to say this again." The head of house seemed like he was seven feet tall, towering over them, lit by the wavering light of the prefects' flashlights, which threw moving shadows on the walls. "Up there behind me is the Folly. Some of you may have seen it from the ground. There are two towers and a ledge, and it's called a folly because there's no purpose to it, except that the man who built this place thought it would give it more class if he added on a couple of battlements at the end. And no one uses it except on one night of the year—this night, when boys who are joining the house walk the ledge. I did it, all the men in these studies behind you did it, and now it's your turn."

All around him in the darkness, Theo could hear the sharp intakes of breath and the start of whispering as fear spread through the group.

"Settle down," said Lewis, raising his voice. "You don't need to be scared. It's not like it used to be. The ledge is wide and there's a rope along the edge to hold on to, so you can't fall. It's only twenty-six and a half feet to the other tower, so it doesn't take long, and once you're done, that's it. You're one of us and no one can take that away from you."

"Who goes first?" someone asked in a squeaky voice.

"You'll go in alphabetical order. Barker here has got the list. He'll call out your names, and when he does, you go through this door and up the staircase, and I'll be waiting at the top with a flashlight. And be careful on the stairs. They're steep, but there's a rail to hold on to. It's the same on the other side."

Lewis turned and disappeared from view until after a few moments a beam of light appeared, illuminating the first steps of the winding gray stone staircase rising beyond the door.

"Addison, you're first," a new voice called out, and Theo immediately recognized it as belonging to the bullying prefect from the dormitory.

Up ahead a boy detached himself from the crowd and went up the stairs. Everyone was silent, standing utterly still. Theo's palms were clammy and he could feel sweat on his forehead, too, and it made him angry that he was frightened. He was sorely tempted to turn around and walk back down to the dormitory, and only stayed where he was because he did not want to be branded a coward.

After a minute, maybe two, they could hear Lewis's voice again, calling "Next," and everyone started moving again, exhaling their relief as the next boy was called forward.

And everything went like clockwork through the A's and B's, until they got to Cattermole, Theo's neighbor from the first night, who started crying hysterically as soon as he heard his name. Not the low moaning like before, but earsplitting cries that Theo wouldn't have expected someone so small to be capable of.

"Help!" he shouted at the top of his voice. "I can't. Please. No." Theo didn't understand why Cattermole didn't run like Theo had from the O'Donnell brothers all those years before in what seemed like another lifetime, but fear seemed to have paralyzed him.

And everyone else in the corridor seemed to be standing back, waiting to see what would happen next. Everyone except Barker, whose mouth had twisted into his version of a smile as he shone his flashlight at Cattermole, flattened like an X-ray of himself against the wall.

Barker put his list in his pocket and sauntered over, holding out his hand. "I'd be glad to help you, Cattermole," he said. "It'll be my pleasure."

Cattermole backed away, but he had left it too late to run and Barker's hand shot out, seizing him by the collar. Cattermole struggled but he was no match for Barker, who was four years his senior and almost twice his weight, and all he succeeded in doing was losing his balance and falling on the floor.

Slowly and methodically, Barker dragged Cattermole down the corridor toward the staircase, ignoring his pleas and cries. As they approached the doorway, one of Cattermole's slippers came off, and Theo saw that there was a small owl's face embroidered on it in brown wool. The sight of it triggered something in Theo's mind and started him moving, and afterward he didn't think he'd made a conscious decision to intervene but had just responded to the slipper.

He grabbed Cattermole from behind, just as Barker had lifted him up in preparation for pushing him up the stairs. Taken by surprise, Barker let go and Theo pulled Cattermole back, interposing his own body between Barker and his victim.

For a moment Barker was too shocked to respond, but then he exploded into rage, punching up toward Theo's face. But Theo was ready for him and grabbed Barker's wrist. It brought their faces together so close that they were almost touching, and Theo used all his strength to push Barker backward, where he stumbled and fell against the first step of the staircase.

"Leave him alone, you bully! Pick on someone your own size!" he yelled, hardly aware of what he was saying, just that he wanted to keep Barker back and yelling seemed the best way to do it.

But Barker was looking past him now, shouting to the other prefects in the corridor and, before he could turn around, Theo felt hands on his arms. Behind him, Cattermole was screaming again, and Barker was back on his feet and punched Theo hard in the stomach.

Theo staggered back. The pain was awful, exploding through his body and rising into nausea as he took a first shuddering breath. No one was holding him anymore, and he sensed that the other prefects' intention had been to stop him getting away, not to serve him up as a punching bag. He looked at Barker and saw the way he was watching him, enjoying his pain, and he wanted to punch Barker back, but he didn't have the strength.

"What the hell's going on here?" It was Lewis, who'd heard the noise and come down the stairs to find out what was happening.

"This brat attacked me," said Barker, pointing at Theo. "I was trying to get Cattermole up the stairs—he didn't want to go—and then this other one pushed me over. He could've broken my leg. He needs to be punished, Lewis. You can't let brats attack prefects. You know you can't."

"What's your name?" Lewis asked, turning to Theo.

"Theo Sterling."

"Sterling. We use last names here. Is this true, what Barker's said?"

"It's true I tried to stop him," said Theo, talking between panted breaths. "And I'd do it again. He was hurting that little kid, dragging him along the floor like he was a sack of potatoes. And then he punched me while they were holding my arms. He's not just a bully, he's a coward too."

Theo looked at Lewis, expecting the worst. Barker was a prefect and he was a brat. He didn't need Alwyn Thomas's inside knowledge to know how the situation was likely to play out. But then support arrived just when he least expected it.

"The American boy's telling the truth, Lewis," said a familiar voice from farther down the corridor. "I saw the whole thing from start to finish. Barker's a menace, and you need to do something about him before he really hurts someone."

The boy in the study with the Karl Marx statue emerged from the crowd and walked up to Lewis, looking him in the eye. He stood there fearless in his dirty, torn jersey, and Theo was struck by the irony that the boy still cut a much more impressive figure than the prefects gathered all around him, dressed in their silk waistcoats.

"It's unlike you to get involved, Lisle," said Lewis, sounding surprised. "I thought you were above all this schoolboy stuff."

"I am. But if I see something with my own eyes, I think I should tell you about it, don't you? There's enough injustice in Saint Gregory's already without me adding to it."

"All right. I've heard enough," said Lewis, making his decision. "Barker, Sterling, shake hands."

Reluctantly, Theo extended his hand, but Barker kept his by his side.

"Do it, Barker. Now, or you'll be sorry!" Lewis shouted, losing his temper, and Barker angrily slapped Theo's hand with his and turned away, but not before he'd hissed at Theo: "You're the one who's going to be sorry."

"All right, let's finish this so we can all go to bed," said Lewis. "Everyone's got to get across that ledge. And that includes Cattermole."

Behind Theo, Cattermole immediately started crying again. He was shaking, too, and Theo thought he was close to an attack of full-blown hysteria.

"I'll help him," said Theo without thinking. "I'll take him across."

"No," said Barker furiously. "It's against the rules. You know it is, Lewis. Each brat has to cross on his own."

"Says who?" said the boy in the torn jersey, intervening again.

"Shut up, Lisle," Barker shouted, turning on him with a vicious look on his face. "And stay out of it. You're not a prefect and this is none of your concern."

"Oh, but that's where you're wrong, Barker. It is my concern. I'm a member of this house, too, and I don't have to stand idly by while you try and bamboozle Lewis with lies about rules that don't exist. There's nothing written down anywhere about walking that ridiculous ledge. It's just a nasty initiation test invented years ago by Fascists like you who had nothing better to do than torment new boys."

"Bamboozle!" repeated Lewis before Barker could reply. "What the hell's that mean, Lisle?" Lewis was athletic as opposed to academic—Alwyn had told Theo that he'd just been made captain of the first eleven rugby team—but he clearly had a good sense of the absurd. Theo thought that if the situation had been different, he might have laughed.

"'Deceive by trickery' is the dictionary definition, I believe," said Lisle.

Barker, who had no sense of humor, shook with rage. "Are you going to let them get away with this, Lewis? Or are you going to uphold the traditions of this house? Because that's your job, isn't it?"

Instead of responding to Barker, Lewis looked hard at Theo. "Are you sure you want to do this?" he asked. "There's no risk if you're holding the rope, but if Cattermole goes nuts up there, it could be different."

"I'm sure," said Theo. "Just give me a moment with him. That's all. He'll be fine."

Theo picked up the slipper that had fallen off and went over to Cattermole and got him to put it on. Then he pushed his fingers around the heels and toes to make sure both slippers were on properly, like the shoe salesmen used to do in New York when he went shopping with his mother. Kneeling down, he smiled up at Cattermole, who smiled weakly back.

"They're nice slippers," he said, and Cattermole nodded. "You don't have to do this," he told him. "But I think you'll regret it if you don't. You need people to respect you, and if you back out, they won't. Not just Barker."

Cattermole looked hard at Theo, locking eyes like they had when they'd woken up that morning. But he didn't otherwise respond, and Theo didn't know what he was thinking.

"And I can make it safe for you. Lewis will shine his light, and you'll look down at my feet and do the same as I do with mine. One two, one two. Slow and even. And then, before you know it, it'll be over, finished, and no one will be able to say you're yellow anymore because you'll have proved to them that you're not."

Theo paused. Still Cattermole stared, and then, almost imperceptibly, he nodded. And Theo nodded, too, sealing their agreement.

At the top of the stairs, the air was cold and the sky was star-spangled, reminding Theo of the nights on the ship when he'd stood on deck with his head thrown back, gazing up awestruck at the glittering constellations. The height above the ground didn't frighten him; rather, it exhilarated him. He stepped out and took hold of the rope with his left hand. It was better than he expected: the ledge was easily wide enough to accommodate two people walking together if they were careful.

"Come out beside me," he said, beckoning to Cattermole, who was trembling beside Lewis at the top of the stairs. "The first step's the hardest, and after that each one gets easier. I promise you."

"He's right," said Lewis, and to their amazement, Cattermole stepped out, hugging the wall behind the ledge.

"Now walk beside me and copy my steps," said Theo. "One, two; one, two. Slow and even. Eyes forward. Not up, not down . . ."

It was as if they were performing a dance of an intensely elegant simplicity while time and space stood still all around them. And then they took a final step and were in the other tower, looking back across at Lewis, who was waving the beam of his flashlight across the sky in celebration.

Theo clapped Cattermole on the back, so that he almost fell down the stairs, and the two of them descended in a rush to join Addison and the other three boys who'd already made it over. Everyone was talking at once and nobody was listening to what anyone was saying, but they were united by a bond of at least temporary happiness now that their ordeal was over and their lives at the school could begin.

11

ESMOND

In the days that followed, Theo basked in his heroism. He'd earned Barker's hatred and Lewis's respect and the idolatry of Cattermole. Alwyn, meanwhile, interviewed everybody who'd been present in the corridor and pieced together an exaggerated account of events, which he repeated to any second or third year who was prepared to listen.

But for Theo, his success soon came to seem hollow. School life was demanding but drab. He had been out of education for over a year, and everything was taught differently to how it had been in America. In the summer he would be required to sit the school certificate, and the preparation work for these exams required an endless memorization of dates and conjugations and theorems, with facile mnemonics being provided by chuckling masters to help them stick in their pupils' wandering minds.

"All boys should come home please" gave the names of the six unfortunate wives of Henry the Eighth from Aragon to Parr, but told Theo nothing of what it had been like to be married to that terrible king. There was no point that he could see to any of the information he was cramming into his head as he hurried from one cold classroom to the next, sitting at ink-stained wooden desks carved with the initials of generations of similarly bored pupils who had passed through the gates of Saint Gregory's before him.

And when he was not in class, he was at the mercy of house prefects like Barker, who were entitled to shout "Brat!" whenever the mood took them. This call required all the junior boys to drop whatever they were doing and run to the summons. Whoever arrived last was obliged to carry out whatever menial duty the prefect had need of—carrying messages to friends in other houses or cleaning mud-encrusted football boots or making toast on an ancient toaster, kept in a small kitchen at the end of the study corridor, that was notorious for delivering nasty electric shocks to brats at periodic intervals.

This system of indentured servitude known as *fagging* had existed in English boarding schools for over two hundred years, but that didn't make it seem any less alien to Theo, for whom the customs and traditions of Saint Gregory's were a world removed from anything he'd experienced at school in America.

It was as he returned, thankless and greasy fingered, from delivering buttered toast to a prefects' tea party on a Saturday afternoon in early October that he almost collided with Esmond de Lisle coming out of his study.

He had thought often of the strange disheveled boy with the elaborate vocabulary and slow ironic drawl in the ten days since their first encounter. He felt grateful to him for taking his side against Barker when everyone else had kept quiet, and he had knocked on the door of his study several times with the intention of thanking him, but each time there had been no answer.

"Well, if it isn't the conquering hero himself!" said Esmond, stepping back and making a mock bow. "Are you still on top of the world, or has fagging dented your enthusiasm for Saint Gregory's?" he asked, glancing down at the smeared plates in Theo's hand.

"It has a bit," said Theo, telling the truth.

"I'm not surprised," said Esmond. "It's slavery by another name, you know. The oppression of the weak by the strong, except that here the weak go on to join the ranks of the strong and oppress those below them in their turn—Barker's career to date providing a perfect example. It's an endless recurring cycle of 'do as thou hast been done by,' with the children of the rich being trained up for a more general exploitation of workers and servants when they join the world outside!"

"Have you always been a Marxist?" asked Theo.

"As long as I can remember," said Esmond. "I read the Communist Manifesto before I got to Winnie-the-Pooh."

"Are you serious?"

"No, of course not." Esmond laughed. "Come on. Dump those things and we'll have tea, and don't worry, I'll make it. You've done enough fagging for one day."

Theo sat in the armchair while the kettle whistled hopefully in the corner, and Esmond searched for mugs and spoons and sugar amid the piles of books, newspapers, and magazines that seemed to cover every surface in the room including the bed. He had a bottle of milk perched on his windowsill but sniffed it and shook his head. "It'll have to be black, I'm afraid," he said.

"Isn't that how they drink it in Russia?" asked Theo, pointing up at a reproduction picture of the Kremlin hanging above his head, facing Karl Marx.

"Yes," said Esmond wistfully as he poured the tea. "One day I'm going to stand in Red Square and see it all for myself, maybe even catch a glimpse of Comrade Stalin on the wall if I'm lucky."

"It's a long way from Saint Gregory's," said Theo, accepting his mug as Esmond sat on the swivel chair at the desk under the window and swung it around to face his guest.

"Not as far as America," he said. "Which city are you from?"

"New York."

"I thought so."

"Why? You're not a mind reader, are you?" Theo laughed uneasily, looking down to take a sip of his tea. Esmond's penetrating blue eyes gazing into his made him nervous. He didn't know what Esmond was going to say or do next.

"You said you saw what happened," Esmond said, ignoring Theo's question and referring back to their first unfinished conversation as if no time had elapsed since then.

"Over there? In New York?"

"Yes. What was it you saw?"

Theo sighed, letting his mind go back. "I saw poor people when they had no jobs, lying on benches under newspaper or standing in breadlines going back as far as the eye could see with that cornered, hunted look in their eyes from where they'd lost their pride. Cold and hungry, stamping their feet by ash can fires with holes in their shoes from all that useless trudging, all that looking for work when there was no work, and the skyscrapers looking down on them night and day like they were ants, like they were nothing. And I saw them trying to fight back, too, and getting beaten for it and getting up again. Coming back for more, refusing to give in. They were brave—" Theo broke off, remembering what he'd seen from the desk in his father's office and not wanting to go there because of what happened after.

But Esmond wouldn't let him stop. "Who were brave?" he asked.

"The strikers." Theo didn't want to answer, but it was as if he had to, compelled by memory and the force of Esmond's questions.

"Striking against who?"

"My father. He had to cut their money because of the Depression, even though they were already on starvation wages. So they went on strike, and it destroyed the business, which was what he lived for. He'd built it up from nothing, and—"

Theo stopped, realizing to his horror that he was crying. He was furious with himself for losing control. Hated that he was shaming himself in front of this boy whom he liked but hardly knew. He pulled his jacket collar up over his face and fought against the tears, so he didn't see Esmond come over and squat down beside him on the floor, putting an arm around his shoulder. It was the first affectionate physical contact Theo had had since he arrived at the school, and he felt an intense gratitude to Esmond for his willingness to flout the unwritten law of boys and schools and express a genuine human sympathy.

"I'm sorry," said Esmond. "I shouldn't have asked. It's a fault of mine: I'm too curious, pushing into people's pain. Please forgive me."

Theo nodded, swallowing. "He killed himself. Put a bullet in his head. And that's why I'm here. My mother remarried—and she acts like he didn't exist," he said, needing to finish what he had begun and saying the words slowly so that he could get them out properly without losing his hard-won self-control. He felt instinctively that he needed to tell the truth after the lie about his father's death that he'd told to Alwyn on the first day.

Esmond got up and pulled out a big hardbound book with a metal clasp from the top shelf of the bookcase. *Holy Bible* was inscribed on the front in gold lettering. Theo was mystified. Was Esmond going to read a prayer? It didn't seem likely, if he was a Communist, but owning the book didn't fit either.

Esmond opened the Bible and solved the mystery. Half the pages had been neatly cut out to create a niche in which a thin silver hip flask was secreted.

"It'll help, I think. It does for me when Saint Gregory's gets me down," said Esmond. "I recommend it with the tea, but you can have it neat if you prefer."

Theo pointed at his tea and Esmond poured. And after he drank, Theo felt lightheaded and started to laugh, thinking of the Bible and the brandy and Esmond putting the two together, cutting purposefully away at Isaiah and Jeremiah with his blade. And then he felt he was being rude to laugh and tried to stop but couldn't, like with the tears before.

"Laughter's good," said Esmond, nodding sagely but not joining in.

"Communists aren't known for it," said Theo, wiping his eyes.

"Which is a pity, I think. I shall have to change that when I become an organizer. You'll notice I kept the Song of Solomon, even though that made it a tight fit," said Esmond, holding up the last pages of the mutilated Bible. "It's so beautiful and erotic and so utterly unlike the rest of awful holy writ. No chance of Father Philip reading us a passage anytime soon, though. Can you imagine him up there at the lectern in the abbey, solemnly intoning: 'Oh, may your breasts be like clusters of the vine, and the scent of your breath like apples, and your kisses like the best wine that goes down smoothly, gliding over lips and teeth.' Now that might make some of the boys sit up and pay attention on a Sunday morning!"

Esmond put the book down, smacking his lips. His mimicry of the headmaster was pitch-perfect, and Theo laughed even harder this time until the tears started running down his cheeks again, and he didn't think he'd ever felt like this before—happy and sad all at the same time. Perhaps it was the brandy—he'd certainly never drunk tea like this before.

"Someone gave me a drink like this a long time ago," he said. "Got out a silver flask when I was upset, but he had it in his pocket, not the Bible!"

"Did it help?"

"Yes. And he did too. He taught me to run. He was a Communist like you."

"You see!" said Esmond, smiling—it was his turn to be surprised. "We're the salt of the earth, us Communists."

"My parents didn't think so," said Theo, shaking his head. "They hated Reds—my mother still does—and when they found out, they used it as an excuse to take me out of school, and that was the end of my running. My coach left too. I don't know why."

"I expect they found out who he was. It happens a lot—that kind of persecution. Do you think your parents told the school?"

"No. We had an agreement and they said they wouldn't, but that doesn't mean the school didn't find out. He was called Eames—Coach Eames. I never knew his first name. I regret that now."

"Eames," repeated Esmond. "He sounds like he was a good man."

"Yes, he was," said Theo, nodding.

"You've lost a lot. I can see that," said Esmond, uncharacteristically hesitant now as he searched for the right words for what he wanted to say. "And your father . . . I can't imagine how you deal with something like that. There's grief, yes, but anger, too, about being left. A terrible sense of abandonment. Do you feel that?"

"Yes."

"You blame him. But perhaps in a way it wasn't his fault. It's capitalism's fault. Owners and workers are caught in its web. One must exploit the other—that is essential to their relationship—and so they become alienated not just from each other but from their own humanity. What Marx called the *Gattungswesen*—the species-essence."

Theo nodded because this made sense to him. It resonated with his experience. He remembered Frank telling him how his father had climbed from the Lower East Side to the Garment District by bleeding his workers dry. Forcing them to work day and night for practically nothing. Dog eat dog, Frank had called it. What had that done to his father and his humanity? Closing his eyes, Theo could see the sullen, angry faces of the factory workers glaring venomously at his father as he made his afternoon rounds, and he remembered how ashamed he'd felt to be associated with him. That was capitalism in action. Esmond was right—everyone had been dehumanized.

He looked up and saw that Esmond was watching him intently, as if gauging his reaction.

"Yes," he said. "That's exactly what happened."

"The exploitation and the suffering are at their worst now because this Depression we're in is the death knell of capitalism," said Esmond, leaning forward as he warmed to his theme. "It's like a rabid dog. It gets vicious and poisonous when it's dying, which is why it turns into Fascism. You can see that happening now all over the world. In Italy, in Japan, in Germany with Hitler, and here, too, I expect, before too long. But the workers like those in your father's factory have learned to be class conscious. They're ready to fight back, and they will prevail because a system built on the cruel oppression of the many by the few is doomed to fail. It's all as Marx predicted—history is on our side."

"You sound like a preacher," said Theo, startled by the change in Esmond. Gone was the humor and ironic drawl, replaced by an ideological fervor that made Theo instinctively pull away. He felt like he was being talked at instead of talked to.

"Sorry," said Esmond, smiling as he resumed his former tone. "I get excited sometimes because it's such extraordinary luck to be alive, just when the world is going through such a profound change. It's like Wordsworth said: 'Bliss was it in that dawn to be alive / But to be young was very heaven!'"

"Who was he?"

"A poet. He was talking about the French Revolution, which turned out to be a false dawn. But this isn't. I know it isn't. We're at the turning point of history, and I want to be a part of it and on the right side. Is that so much to ask?"

"No," said Theo, smiling too. "I guess it isn't."

The conversation with Esmond had a profound effect on Theo. In part, that was because it was unlike any he had ever had before. He had never met anyone who could explain Marx and quote poetry and make him laugh and cry all at the same time.

In the days that followed, he thought constantly about his new friend, while resisting the temptation to seek him out again too quickly. He did not want Esmond to think him an irritant.

But it wasn't just Esmond's personality that had affected him. It was also what they had talked about. Encouraged by Esmond, Theo had opened the door to memories of his father and of New York, which he had kept buried for so long behind a wall of numbness that only his troubled dreams could penetrate.

Now his past life came seeping back into his consciousness. He sat in class and was no longer there. Instead, he'd returned home across the ocean to the apartment off Fourteenth Street and could hear his father singing in the kitchen while his mother laughed. He reached out to open the door but, walking through, found he was not in the kitchen but in the office opposite the factory, and there was his father sitting with his shirtsleeves rolled up over his elbows and his fingers drumming on the desk as they used to do when he was impatient. He was talking on the telephone, but Theo couldn't hear what he was saying because beside him in the drawer was the gun, waiting to be taken out, to be inserted in the mouth, to be . . .

Theo imagined the moment of decision when his father's finger enclosed the trigger. He hadn't just pulled it. Theo knew he hadn't. He'd hesitated, splayed out and tottering between two worlds with his thoughts scattering through his mind, until he couldn't think anymore. Had he thought of his son? Before . . .

Bitterness and anger welled up inside Theo as he sat in the main hall on a gloomy Friday afternoon, looking down at three sheets of school-issue low-quality letter-writing paper, an envelope, and a pen that he had arranged in a precise geometrical pattern on the desk in front of him.

It was the weekly half hour when junior boys were required to write letters at least 150 words in length to their parents. Some found this task impossible, and there were various suggestions for possible subjects written on the blackboard, including *The weather has been wonderful* (a bald-faced lie, as it had been raining almost nonstop for the previous week) and Theo's favorite, *Yesterday I attended a very interesting lecture about South Africa.*

Once the letters were done, they had to be taken to the housemaster, Father Laurence, who vetted them for length and spelling and anything heretical or otherwise damaging to the school, before the envelopes were sealed and stamped, ready for mailing.

Theo didn't need suggestions for what to write. He wanted nothing more than to tell his mother what he felt about being sent away to school, but he knew it wouldn't pass the censor, and he was also deterred by the effect such a letter might have on her fragile state of health. And yet writing an anodyne letter reporting on the weather and his progress with construing Virgil would be to let her off the hook of any guilt she was feeling, which he was not prepared to do.

He sat and stared at the white paper and then suddenly pulled it toward him and began to write quickly, without stopping to think:

Dear Frank,

How are you? Earning a bit more money I hope—you deserve it!

Is the Babe still hitting it out of the park? I wish we'd gone once like I did with Dad, but I didn't know then how everything would turn out. I guess there's a lot of things I didn't know.

I'm at school now, boarding school, and a lot of it is just plain dumb. Most of the people here don't seem to know anything about real life. It's like they're just playing games. And they're different to me too. I mean, we speak the same language, but then we don't and they look at me like they don't understand what I'm talking about. It's hard to explain.

I miss you. I remember the dinners we had in the apartment when you came over and how you helped us through the bad times. If I had the time over, maybe I would have stayed in New York but I remember what you said about going being an opportunity, and hey, maybe it'll still turn out that way.

There's a boy here I like. He's called Esmond and he understands some of all this. I talked to him about Dad and it helped. I wish you were here so we could talk too. Well, not really—I think you'd find this place even more bedbug crazy than I do!

Your friend,

Theo

He sat back in his chair and sighed. He hadn't written to his mother and he'd insulted the school, so the only place his letter was headed was Father Laurence's wastepaper basket. But at least he'd expressed what he really thought, and he felt better for it.

He took the envelope and wrote out Frank's address, which he'd been careful to memorize before leaving New York, and then went down the hallway to Father Laurence's study. He was the last one with a letter, and after he knocked, he was called straight in.

Theo had had few dealings with Father Laurence up to now. He was a tall, thin man with an austere, scholarly face, and he had earned some renown in monastic circles for a monograph he had written on the subject of Saint Anselm's theory of atonement. He was an "abbey monk" who had had very little to do with the school until recently, when his predecessor as housemaster, Father Boniface, had upped and died in the middle of Sunday Mass. (Alwyn had provided a full description of this event to Theo, including the detail that Father Boniface's death rattle had occurred at the moment of consecration and so had been audible throughout the church, amplified by the building's excellent acoustics.) Father Laurence had been a stopgap choice as housemaster and was expected to be replaced as soon as a more suitable candidate could be found, and in the meantime he seemed content to follow school policy and leave the administration of the house as much as possible to Lewis and the prefects.

Theo stood in front of Father Laurence's desk while his housemaster read over his composition. When he'd finished, he looked up and pointed Theo to a chair.

"Who is Frank?" he asked.

"He's my friend," said Theo with a hint of defiance in his voice.

"But he's not related to you?"

"No."

"I see," said Father Laurence. "Well, we can't have everything, can we? He sounds like a man with many other qualities." He smiled and raised his steepled index fingers to stroke his chin in a gesture that reminded Theo of Father Juan in the presbytery of the church in Gramercy Park long years before.

"I can quite imagine that it's not easy for you coming here," he said. "You have clearly suffered, and your life experience is very different from many of the other boys, but I hope you will not rush to judgment. The school has much to offer, even if that's not immediately apparent."

"Yes," said Theo. He had not been prepared for kindness, and it left him temporarily tongue-tied.

"And Esmond de Lisle has much to offer too," Father Laurence continued thoughtfully. "He is a clever boy—one of the cleverest in the school—but I fear he *has* made his mind up, and that can be dangerous."

Father Laurence paused, looking at Theo, who saw for the first time that the monk's eyes were as penetrating as Esmond's. It was just that he kept them veiled most of the time.

Theo shifted in his chair. He sensed that he was expected to respond, but he felt that saying anything about Esmond would be disloyal, and so he remained silent.

"Well, I hope that Frank will enjoy his letter and send you a reply soon," said Father Laurence, handing the envelope to Theo to seal. "You will need some more stamps for America, I think."

At the door, he called Theo back. "I forgot to mention I had a telephone call about you today, from your stepfather."

"What did he want?"

"To see how you were getting on, and to increase your allowance. He said he felt he hadn't given you enough."

Hush money! thought Theo meanly, but he said nothing.

Father Laurence paused and then went on, as if having made a decision to continue: "It is never easy for a child when a parent dies and the other marries again. All sorts of emotions arise. But I think you are lucky to have Sir Andrew as your stepfather. He is a good man, and he has been a true friend to the Church in places where such friends are sorely needed, as I'm sure you know."

12

BARKER

Barker had no friends. In fact, he had never had any. At some point in the distant past, he may have wanted to reach out and form such a relationship, but no longer. Experience had taught him that boys were cruel, and he had yet to meet any girls. Indeed, he hoped that he would never have to, as their looks of disgust would be even harder to cope with than the daily aversion he experienced at school.

He had learned early on that life was a battle for survival. He bore the scars of a thousand torments that had begun at the age of eight when he was sent away to board at a preparatory school in the North. There he had been subjected to water tortures that came close to simulated drowning and an ordeal called roasting, in which he had been tied to a board and tilted backward and forward in front of a roaring fire with water being periodically thrown on his back by his persecutors as a form of basting.

There seemed no rhyme or reason why he should be singled out for this treatment while other boys his age sailed through unscathed. Perhaps it was a lack of self-confidence—a scent of fear that attracted the bullies like dogs.

Barker had always been anxious. His father, a colonel in the Horse Guards, had a military temper and ruled his family with a rod of iron. He dressed in full uniform for dinner and banged the table to make his points. It was therefore unsurprising that he took a stern line when his wife reported her son's misery.

"The boy needs to stop sniveling and learn to show some backbone," said the colonel. But it was easier said than done, particularly when his son developed acute acne and psoriasis in response to puberty and stress. The bullies rejoiced in Barker's disfigurements and refined and redoubled their cruelties, requiring everyone to keep an elaborate distance from him at all times on the basis that he was suffering from a highly contagious form of bubonic plague.

But Barker was a survivor. The acne didn't go away. In fact, it got worse, but he grew taller and stronger and able to defend himself. He fought back when he could and otherwise tried to ingratiate himself with his tormentors. At Saint Gregory's he had to start over, but the school wasn't as barbaric as where he had come from and he concentrated all his energies on the goal of becoming a prefect.

He volunteered for everything he could volunteer for. Dressed in a spotless white surplice, he carried the big brass cross in processions and held up the Bible in church for Father Philip to read the Gospel, and on Wednesdays and Saturdays he was the most dedicated member of the Officers' Training Corps. No cadet's boots shone like Barker's; no one's rifle bore was cleaner. He snapped to attention and stood ramrod straight on parade, proud to demonstrate that he had acquired the backbone that his father had demanded of him.

He received his corporal's stripe and his prefect's silk waistcoat on the same day—the best day of his life. His long years of struggle were over. He could no longer be hurt or humiliated. Now he was the one with the power to make or break the lives of others. He strutted the halls with his silver-handled swagger stick—a gift from his now-proud father—and enjoyed the cowering fear he could see in the juniors' eyes as they made way for him, scuttling away like rabbits in search of their holes. No more scorn, no more derision. Power changed everything. It was as if he had crossed the Jordan and reached the Promised Land.

Until the American boy attacked him.

Barker still could not quite credit what had happened that night. He had been deputed to get everyone up the stairs, and when Cattermole refused, he had had to force him. That was his duty, and for carrying it out he had been assaulted by this Yankee hick and had his authority undermined in front of all the brats by that prig, Lewis, who had chosen to believe a new boy and that dirty troublemaker, Lisle, over him.

Barker had always hated Esmond de Lisle. The boy had no respect for anyone or anything. He was an atheist and a Communist and probably a degenerate, and he wanted to tear down the system that had enabled Barker to succeed. But it was more personal than that. Barker sensed that Esmond saw through him and understood his weakness. Coming back from corps in the late afternoon, he would catch sight of Esmond imitating his marching steps, and sometimes in the study corridors he could hear his enemy mimicking his voice and people laughing. But there was nothing he could do. Prefects had power over brats but not sixth formers.

But with Lisle's protégé, it was different. Theo Sterling had defied him and was now being treated by the other brats as a hero for doing so. Barker had seen the way they gathered around him, hanging on his every word. That made him a threat to everything Barker had so painstakingly built. His authority was leaking away. Soon juniors would be laughing at him again. He needed to crush the mongrel boy before he lost any more respect, and after he'd finished licking his wounds, he set out to do so.

Fagging was Barker's chosen method of persecution, and Theo soon found himself spending every minute he wasn't in class running pointless errands for Barker or cleaning his uniform and spit-polishing his boots. It didn't matter that he got there first for the brat call when custom dictated that the last to arrive should do the work. Barker still always chose him for the task, and then watched while he performed it, sitting back in his armchair with his long legs stretched out, tapping his thighs with his swagger stick while he goaded Theo with well-chosen insults about his lack of class and breeding.

"I feel sorry for you, Sterling," he told Theo one afternoon as he was shining the brass buttons and badges on Barker's corps tunic for the second time that day (the first hadn't passed muster). "Everyone knows that the only thing Americans are good for is money, and you haven't even got any of that. No wonder you've been packed off here. I can't imagine your stepfather wanting you at one of his garden parties, letting the side down, and now of course he's got your pretty mother all for himself. I wonder what he's doing to her in that big four-poster bed of his. Have you thought of that?"

Theo stayed quiet. Alwyn had told him that Barker could beat him for insubordination, and he didn't intend to give Barker the excuse he was obviously looking for. But he couldn't stop his fists clenching as he imagined the satisfaction he would feel, knocking Barker to the floor.

Barker saw the movement, and it encouraged him to worse slanders. "Think about it," he said, pushing his swagger stick backward and forward along his knee in slow simulation of the sexual act.

It was too much. Theo got up and threw his rags and polish on the floor and walked out of the study.

Barker followed him, close behind. "Come back here," he ordered, making it sound like a parade-ground command. "I haven't released you."

Theo stopped, turning around to face Barker. He wasn't going to be seen running away. "No," he said. "Not until you apologize for what you said."

All along the corridor, doors were opening as prefects and sixth formers came out of their studies to see what the noise was about.

"Go to the bathroom," Barker said. "You're going to get the beating you deserve."

Theo could hear a breathlessness in Barker's voice and saw a drip of saliva forming at the edge of his mouth. He felt disgust as well as anger. He wasn't going to let Barker do this to him. Not willingly and not ever. All he had left was his dignity, ragged but intact, and that would be gone if he did as he was told and bent over a bath while Barker hit him with his swagger stick. Alwyn had told him that you had to shake hands afterward. Better to die than do that, thought Theo. He didn't care what happened. He stayed where he was in the middle of the corridor, digging his hands into his pockets.

"Damn you, Sterling," shouted Barker. "You do as I say."

"No," said Theo.

"Help me," said Barker, calling down the corridor to the other prefects. "This boy's been grossly impertinent. He's refusing to clean my tunic."

Nobody moved. "It's about you too," Barker told them. "If you let him get away with this, they'll all refuse . . ."

Theo felt hands taking hold of him, and he was being dragged backward. Past the closed door of Esmond's study. He was like Cattermole now and his struggles were useless. Up ahead was the swinging door of the bathroom. Someone was opening it and then they stopped.

"What are you doing?" asked a familiar voice, soft but commanding. Theo couldn't see him, but he knew it was Father Laurence.

"I'm going to punish Sterling," said Barker.

"Punish him for what?"

"For refusing to work. This isn't a matter for you, Father. You know it isn't."

"I'm afraid I don't agree," said the housemaster. "Let Sterling go, please, gentlemen. I'd like to hear what he has to say."

Theo almost fell back on the floor as the hands that had been gripping his arms and shoulders suddenly released him. He got unsteadily to his feet.

"Did you refuse?" asked Father Laurence.

"No, Father."

"He ran out of my study. Everyone here saw him," said Barker.

"And why did you do that?" asked Father Laurence, keeping his eyes on Theo.

"Because . . ." Theo stopped, tongue-tied. It wasn't his honor code, but nevertheless it held him back. He wouldn't have told the housemaster what had happened if it hadn't been for Barker, who had no such inhibitions, jumping in.

"He'd done a bad job cleaning my uniform. I pointed it out to him, and he threw it down and walked out," he lied.

It was intolerable. "I did no such thing," said Theo. "I left because of what he said about my mother and my stepfather."

"What did he say?" Father Laurence asked, continuing to focus his attention on Theo. He hadn't even looked at Barker when he was speaking.

"He talked about them together."

"Where?"

Theo searched for a euphemism and gave up. "In bed," he said flatly, feeling ashamed, as if he had betrayed his mother in some way.

Now, at last, Father Laurence turned to look at Barker. He didn't say anything. Just watched him and waited. To Theo, he seemed more like a trial lawyer than a scholarly monk in that moment.

"He's lying," Barker said, but he sounded uneasy now.

"Is he?"

"Yes. And besides, it doesn't matter what I said," Barker went on quickly. "Sterling refused to do the work. That's what matters. And for that I have every right to punish him."

"But you won't," said Father Laurence.

"Won't! Why not?"

"Because I forbid it. And not only that: you will have nothing more to do with Sterling. From now on, you will treat him like he doesn't exist. There are plenty of other juniors for you to call on to shine your boots if you feel unable to carry out that task yourself. Do you understand me, Barker?"

"No, Father, I don't," said Barker, who was now shaking with rage. "Prefects deal with brats, not masters. That's how it's always been."

"But not anymore," said Father Laurence evenly. "Not in my house. You can take it up with the headmaster, of course, Barker. But somehow I don't think you will."

Barker didn't. Instead, he followed Father Laurence's instruction to the letter, never addressing a word or a look to Theo. Even on the parade ground, he said nothing when Theo fumbled with his bayonet or failed to tie his puttees properly.

On rainy afternoons the cadets scrambled up and down the hills that surrounded the school, carrying out section rushes through the bracken, and then formed fours and trudged back through the drizzle, singing Great War songs of which Theo's favorite was "We're Here Because We're Here," sung to the tune of "Auld Lang Syne." It summed up his sense that there was no purpose to his life as he passed wearily through the days, circulating from classroom to refectory to dormitory in company with the other boys.

Only on Sunday afternoons was he able to be alone, when the juniors were sent on organized runs through the surrounding countryside, escorted by prefects riding bicycles and hectoring them through bullhorns. Theo ran with the others until he knew the route and then went up a gear and left them behind, settling into an easy pace as he filled his lungs with the clean air and absorbed the beauty of the landscape almost unconsciously through his senses. His experience up to now had been entirely urban, and he felt as if he had entered a new world. He saw the hills changing colors with the light as fleecy clouds chased the November sun across the wide-open sky, and he smelled the deep-green moss and the wetness in the fallen autumn leaves mixed up with the scent of woodsmoke rising from a group of thatched cottages he passed at a turn in the road.

Pausing on a stone bridge over a fast-flowing stream, he caught sight of his reflection in the dark-blue water, framed by overhanging willow trees, and smiled, realizing to his surprise that for the first time in as long as he could remember, he was happy. Acting on instinct, he clambered down the steep bank, using tufts of grass as handholds. At the bottom, he bent down and cupped his hands in the ice-cold water and splashed it up onto his face. Out of the corner of his eye he caught sight of the silver back of a fish as it jumped and twisted and fell, and he felt the moment as a sort of secret secular baptism—the ritual of a new beginning, which stayed with him even after he returned to the school and felt its twisting arms encircling him again.

"Yes, the countryside round here is beautiful. I like it too. But it's a deception like everything else," said Esmond, whom Theo had gone to see in his study, fresh from the pleasure of his run. The room with its overflowing bookshelves had become like a magnet to Theo, who had forgotten his earlier resolve to keep his distance. Not that Esmond ever treated him as an irritant. He always dropped whatever he was doing when Theo came, and made tea—black or white, depending on the state of the milk on his windowsill. His welcome and hospitality touched Theo, as he experienced it nowhere else at Saint Gregory's.

"What do you mean?" asked Theo, who often found himself asking this question when he was with Esmond. But without embarrassment, because Esmond never talked down to him; rather, he seemed to assume that Theo knew more than he actually did.

"I mean those pretty cottages you passed are hovels with no running water or sanitation, and the thatch you like so much is letting in the rain, dripping down onto dank earth floors. They're falling to pieces from neglect because the landlords won't repair them or update them. And yet we call them picturesque. It's a lie that goes back centuries, perpetrated by the ancestors of these landlords who hired landscape painters to make their estates look beautiful and then hung the pictures in their country houses while their tenants starved. It's obscene if you think about it."

"Yes," said Theo, shaking his head in amazement at the shamelessness of the behavior. "It's monstrous."

Esmond nodded. "Capitalism is founded on lies. Its supporters never stop telling them. Take the public schools, for example—they get charitable tax status because they say they're providing a public service, but in fact they're just serving the rich, perpetuating their power and keeping everyone else in wretched ignorance and poverty. It's a joke."

"So why are they called public schools if they're really private?" asked Theo, scratching his head. Listening to Esmond, he felt like he was in a hall of mirrors at a fairground where nothing made sense.

"Because hundreds of years ago they were founded to help the poor. And then the rich took them over and kicked the poor out. Public schools! You see—even the name's a lie!" Esmond laughed. "You have to admire the capitalists' effrontery, I suppose, and their success too. Ninety percent of the cabinet are public school men, and nearly ninety percent of bishops, too, and judges. And it's the same lower down the ladder: the old school tie will get an idiot a job, no questions asked, while a clever man with the wrong tie stands about as much chance of getting hired as a man without a shirt."

"It's not like that in America," said Theo, remembering Walter Chrysler's humble workman's tools in the case at the top of the skyscraper, and how far his father had gotten as a self-made man before the Depression ruined him.

"No, there it's just about money," said Esmond. "They haven't had the time to build a system like we have yet. But they will if they can. Capitalists aren't fools. They wouldn't be rich if they were, and they understand that they need to control education to keep power. Schools like Saint Gregory's are factories for the mass production of gentlemen trained up to maintain the status quo. Honor and tradition are their watchwords, but what they really mean is hanging on to what they've got."

"So how do you fit in here?" asked Theo. "You're the enemy of all that."

"Why don't they kick me out? Is that what you're asking?"

Theo nodded.

"Money talks. My father gives them extra for the Monks' Benevolent Fund, and they figure that one bad apple isn't going to upset the cart. And besides, I bear an ancient Catholic name. Father Philip doesn't want to be seen expelling a de Lisle from Saint Gregory's. It would be like blasphemy. Names and titles mean everything to him. That's why he went speechless when you said you didn't want to be called Campion-Bennett." Esmond opened and shut his mouth like a drowning fish to imitate Father Philip lost for words. "It's who you are, not what you are that matters here. And him a monk too—the old hypocrite! God knows what Christ would make of places like this!"

Theo felt awestruck by the vast edifice of deceit and hypocrisy that Esmond had conjured up in his mind. England seemed incomprehensible to him at that moment and he longed to be back in New York, where life made sense, even if it was going to hell in a handcart.

"How's Barker?" asked Esmond, changing the subject. "Is he still leaving you alone?"

"Yes. Treating me like I don't exist. It's wonderful," said Theo, smiling.

"I've noticed he's got Cattermole polishing his buttons now. Poor kid looks like a deer in the headlights every time he scuttles past me in the corridor. But I'd keep your eyes open if I was you, Theo. Barker's a nasty bit of work, and he's not one to forget a grudge. I don't think you've heard the last of him."

"I'm more worried about Cattermole, to be honest," said Theo. "He's more rabbit than deer, and he's not going to be able to cope with Barker terrorizing him. I think I'll talk to him, find out what's going on."

"Perhaps that's what Barker wants you to do."

"Maybe. But that doesn't mean I shouldn't do it. I feel responsible for him, somehow, after we got across that ledge together."

"Well, talk to him then. But be careful. There are some things I can't save you from."

Theo didn't approach the task of talking to Cattermole with any enthusiasm. The shared elation they'd felt after crossing the ledge had soon evaporated when Cattermole started following him around the school, as if he were auditioning for the role of a second shadow. Irritation had boiled up inside Theo, until one day he couldn't stand it anymore and ordered Cattermole to leave him alone.

"I can't protect you," he told him brutally. "I'm just a junior like you, and I've got my own problems. You've got to learn to stand on your own two feet."

Cattermole hadn't said anything. His eyes had just gotten very big, and his chapped lip had trembled like he was going to cry, which Theo couldn't cope with, so he had turned and practically run away.

Afterward, Theo had felt guilty, but he had also felt that he had had no choice. It was bad enough not to have any privacy because the school wouldn't allow it, but to have Cattermole attached to him like a limpet was more than he could stand. The boy's perpetual misery drove him crazy. Theo thought he had even more cause for wretchedness after losing everything in his life, but he didn't give in to his grief, so why should Cattermole feel entitled to carry on as he did?

Cattermole had left Theo alone since Theo had told him to stay away. They hadn't exchanged a word. But Theo had intercepted several bitter looks that left him in no doubt about how Cattermole felt, so he was surprised when Cattermole forestalled his own hesitant intention to seek him out by opening a conversation himself.

It was the middle of the afternoon, and Theo had had to go back to the dormitory because he had left a book by his bed that he needed for class. He turned around and Cattermole was standing right behind him. The boy's ability to creep up unexpectedly was unsettling and reminded Theo of how annoyed he'd become when Cattermole used to follow him around the school. But he swallowed his irritation and pasted a smile across his face instead, remembering his resolve to try to help Cattermole instead of hurt him.

"Are you looking for me?" he asked.

Cattermole nodded. He looked nervous, twisting his hands together and avoiding eye contact.

"Because it's funny. I was wanting to talk to you, too, but I guess you beat me to the punch."

Still, Cattermole said nothing. He opened his mouth several times to speak, but nothing came out and Theo was reminded of Esmond's drowning-fish impersonation of Father Philip.

"Is there something wrong?" he asked. "Is it Barker? That's what I wanted to ask you about, actually."

"No, it's not," said Cattermole, vehemently shaking his head. It was as if the mention of Barker's name had acted like a mini electric shock, jolting him into speech. "He's all right, really, when you get to know him."

"No, he's not," said Theo incredulously. "He's vile. Are we talking about the same person?"

Cattermole smiled nervously. "I wanted to thank you," he said, ignoring Theo's question and changing the subject.

"Thank me?"

"For getting me across. I couldn't have made it on my own."

"It's all right. You already did thank me," said Theo.

He could see the look of panic in Cattermole's eyes as if he was reliving his terror on the ledge, but then Cattermole swallowed and fought it down. "No, I mean thank you properly," he said. "I've got a cake from home. Do you want some?"

Theo didn't feel hungry, but he didn't feel he could say no. After all, he had been intending to talk to Cattermole, so it made no sense for him to turn down his offer now.

"Good," said Cattermole, smiling for the first time. "It's in my trunk. I'll go and get it."

Theo sat on his bed and waited until Cattermole returned with two large pieces of pumpkin cake in his outstretched hands.

"How is it?" Cattermole asked. He hadn't started on his slice, but was watching Theo eat with rapt attention, as if everything depended on his answer.

"It's delicious. Best food I've tasted since I got to this beastly place." It was true. The cake was rich and perfectly spiced. "Who made it?"

"My mother. Sometimes at home we make them together. We—" Cattermole stopped, realizing he'd broken the unwritten school law that boys should never under any circumstances talk about their mothers.

Theo, of course, didn't subscribe to any such law, and he had a momentary vision of the happy domestic life that Cattermole might have enjoyed if he hadn't been sent to Saint Gregory's. But just as he was about to ask who had been responsible for that decision, Cattermole changed the subject again.

"I got one before, two weeks ago, but someone took it out of my trunk. They must have had my key, because I'd locked it."

Theo looked at Cattermole with surprise. It was one of the longest sentences that Theo had ever heard him utter, and it had a prepared quality to it, as if he was reading off a script. Perhaps he was, Theo thought. He could see Cattermole working out what he was going to say before he said it. He'd heard that shy people did that sometimes.

"I'm sorry," he said. "Who do you think did it?"

"I don't know. I just don't want it to happen again, and I thought that if there was a good place to hide my key . . ." Again, he broke off, doing his drowning-fish impersonation.

"You're asking where I keep mine?"

Cattermole nodded and then swallowed several times. His eyes were roving around the dormitory, looking everywhere except at Theo. His nervousness over his cake was so extreme as to be comical, and Theo had to work hard to subdue an urge to laugh.

"I keep it hooked on a loose spring under my bed," said Theo. "At least there's some use to everything falling apart, and my key's the same color, so it's perfect camouflage."

Cattermole's face lit up. "That's so clever," he said. "I'll do that too. I mean, if I can find a loose spring. I'm sure I can. Thank you, Sterling."

"You're welcome," said Theo. "I'm happy to help. Now, about Barker . . ."

He stopped in mid-sentence because Cattermole had suddenly backed away, having the same negative reaction to the mention of Barker's name as he had had before.

"I don't want to talk about him," said Cattermole with panic in his voice. And then, reaching forward, he put the piece of cake in his hand down on Theo's bed, as if it was an offering, and fled.

Theo was left scratching his head. Cattermole's behavior didn't add up. One minute he was sharing cake and the next he was running away. It had to have something to do with Barker, given that just the mention of his name was enough to make Cattermole go to pieces. But what? Theo was curious now as well as concerned, but each time he saw him in the days that followed, Cattermole scuttled away, and Theo was no nearer to solving the enigma when Barker sprang his surprise.

One evening, just before lights-out, Barker and Lewis appeared in the doorway of the dormitory and announced an immediate spot search of the boys' trunks and lockers because someone had stolen Barker's silver-handled swagger stick.

The stick was part of Barker's identity. He tucked it under his arm as he gave orders on the parade ground, he tapped with it threateningly when he was watching a brat perform a task, and he beat with it when he had an excuse to administer corporal punishment. Stealing it was personal. It was what someone would do if they had a grudge against him. And it was valuable—whoever had committed such a theft could expect the most serious punishment.

"Here's the drill," said Lewis. "Pull your trunks out from under your beds and then stand beside them with your keys in your hands. No unlocking until I get to you. The sooner we get this over with, the sooner we can all get to sleep."

It took a long time, starting with Addison and going down the aisle as Lewis, with Barker beside him, watched each junior empty his trunk and locker item by item onto his bed. But long before they got to him, Theo knew what had happened and what was coming. He cursed his own stupidity for not seeing it before, because why else would Cattermole have wanted to know where he kept his key? He had trusted Cattermole because he had done him a good turn and expected the same in return, but he should have known that that counted for nothing if you were small and scared and being terrorized by a skilled sadist like Barker. He knew full well from his own experience what Barker was capable of, and he was made of much sterner stuff than Cattermole.

And he'd been a fool, too, to assume that Barker had forgotten him just because Father Laurence had told him to. Esmond had warned him, but he had taken no notice because he had wanted to believe that his life could improve, instead of remembering as he should have done that he was cursed with ill luck.

He looked down over the heads of the other boys toward Cattermole, but he had his eyes fixed on the ground.

Slowly they got nearer, and still Barker never even glanced in his direction. Theo almost had to admire him for it. He knew Barker must be counting down the minutes and the seconds, but he had the self-control to give no outward sign of his excitement.

Theo was tempted to put a stop to the charade but knew he couldn't. Owning up to having the swagger stick in his trunk would be tantamount to an admission of guilt, and so he and Barker and Cattermole remained locked together in silence, waiting for the final act of the drama that had been playing out between them since the term began.

Lewis's temper had become seriously frayed by the time he got to Theo. "Are you sure you haven't lost it, Barker?" he asked irritably.

"Quite sure," said Barker, looking at Theo for the first time and allowing himself a thin smile as Theo bent to open his trunk.

It was under a layer of clothing near the top, lying next to Theo's old running shoes that he had carried with him through the Lower East Side and across the ocean, from one school to another. It infuriated him beyond measure that Barker's vile swagger stick should be touching his most precious possession. Its very presence was a contamination.

As soon as the stick was visible, Barker darted forward and seized it, holding it up as if it were a trophy. "See," he shouted, waving it at Lewis. "Sterling stole it, and this time, by God, you're not going to let him off the hook."

"What do you have to say, Sterling? Did you take it?" Lewis asked. He seemed disappointed more than angry.

"No. And if I did, my trunk would be the last place I'd put it in. Is there anywhere more incriminating I could pick? Surely you can see that?" replied Theo angrily.

"What I see is that it's in your trunk," said Lewis grimly. "And that you've got the key."

"Cattermole took it and he gave it to Barker," said Theo. "I know because he asked me about where I kept it two days ago. If you don't believe me, ask him."

"This is ridiculous," said Barker. "How much more of this do we have to listen to? Sterling's been caught red-handed and he needs to be punished. It's got nothing to do with Cattermole."

Lewis looked hard at Barker and then back at Theo. "Cattermole," he shouted. "Come here!"

He came crying and shaking, and even though Theo had every reason to hate Cattermole in that moment, he felt sorry for him, too, realizing what horrors he must have been subjected to by Barker to get him to his present sorry state.

"Pull yourself together, man!" said Lewis angrily. "You should be ashamed of yourself, crying like a girl."

Cattermole swallowed hard, trying to hold back the tears, and then glanced over at Barker, who was staring at him fixedly while he tapped the side of his trousers with the swagger stick. The color had drained from Cattermole's face, and he was trembling worse than ever.

"Now, listen," Lewis told him. "Sterling says that you took the key to his trunk so either you or Barker could put Barker's stick in it. Is that true, or is he lying?"

Silence. Cattermole's eyes darted this way and that, as if in search of escape. From Lewis to Barker to Theo and back again.

Along from Theo, Alwyn looked like he was in the front row of a cinema on a Saturday night, wide-eyed and drinking in every minute of the action.

"Well?" insisted Lewis, leaning down close to Cattermole so that he could no longer see Barker. "I need an answer, Cattermole. You'll be beaten if you don't give me one. And worse, too, maybe."

Cattermole opened his mouth to speak, but nothing audible came out, and so Lewis leaned closer, almost putting his ear to Cattermole's mouth, and Cattermole tried again, this time with more success.

Slowly, Lewis resumed his full height and stepped back, turning to face Barker. "Cattermole says it's true and that you made him do it," he said. "I'm suspending you now as a prefect, and you and Cattermole will see Father Laurence with me in the morning. I expect he'll refer it to the headmaster. God knows, the offense is serious enough."

Barker stared at Lewis as if he couldn't believe what he was hearing. And then, without warning, he lunged at Cattermole with his stick and would have struck him if Lewis hadn't stepped in the way and taken the blow on his arm.

Immediately he grabbed the stick out of Barker's hand and looked for a moment as if he was going to strike him back with it before he dropped his hand. "Get out of here," he said. "And if I have anything to do with it, you won't be coming back."

"What about my stick?" said Barker, reaching for it.

"I'll keep that for now. We don't want any more tampering with the evidence."

A ripple of nervous laughter went around the dormitory. White with rage, Barker looked at the boys' faces, seeing his authority evaporating like water in the summer sun, and then he abruptly turned on his heel and walked out. Behind him, a few of the boys began to clap.

Next morning, Alwyn found Theo after class and told him that Lewis wanted to see him. Theo had never been in Lewis's study before. It was a larger room than the other studies and on a higher floor with a view down over the rooftops to the abbey garden, in which a black-hooded monk was at that moment walking the gravel paths in solitary reflection. There was a faint breeze in the air and autumn leaves were falling gently from the trees, floating down to settle in the mulched beds among the late-flowering asters and anemones. It was like looking through a window into another world, Theo thought. A vision of peace entirely at odds with the hubbub of the school.

The room was neat, unlike Esmond's, and there weren't many books, but the walls were covered with an array of framed photographs, all of different sportsmen. Among them, Theo recognized a picture of Eric Liddell, the great British sprinter of the previous decade. He was running with his head thrown back, his mouth open, and his hands clawing the air in an ungainly ecstasy.

Coach Eames had once shown Theo the same photograph. Theo remembered how he'd sat on a footlocker in the athletics hut and listened, enthralled, while Eames told him the story of the 1924 Paris Olympics, when Liddell, an evangelical Christian, had refused to run the 100 meters because the heats had been on the Sabbath. In the final, Liddell's great British rival, Harold Abrahams, had pipped Eames's hero, Jackson Scholz, the New York Thunderbolt, by a tenth of a second to win the gold medal. But then Liddell had won the 400 in a record time four days later.

Theo recalled how Eames had taken down a book from the shelf above his workbench and showed him Scholz's photograph—staring and severe—and then flipped back to the picture of Liddell. "Charlie Booker saw him run," Eames had said wistfully, a note of envy in his voice. "Said he was the ugliest runner at that distance he'd ever seen, but also the best."

The vivid memory of that summer afternoon in Manhattan, shortly before everything fell apart, enveloped Theo, and it was as if he could see his old coach's glowing face and hear his voice rising and falling as he described the rival athletes' glory and despair.

Theo winced—with the memory came a swamping feeling of loss as he thought of all that he had left behind.

"You're looking at Liddell," said Lewis, who'd observed Theo's intense reaction to seeing the photograph.

Theo nodded. "I guess he's the only runner," he said, looking around at the athletes in the other photographs, who all seemed to be rugby players and cricketers—games Theo did not begin to understand.

"Yes, but he was a rugby player too," said Lewis. "Played on the wing for Scotland before he gave it up to run. And then he gave that up too . . ."

"And went to China as a missionary," said Theo, finishing Lewis's sentence. They both smiled, amused by the unlikely coincidence of finding that they came from such different worlds and yet shared an interest in an athlete who no longer ran.

"Runners can make good rugby players," said Lewis. "In the middle, in the scrum where I play, it's a physical battle, but the point of the game is to get the ball out to the wings, and then it's how fast they can run and change direction, getting past their opposite numbers. That's how sides score tries. It's how they win."

"Tries?" Theo repeated.

"Like touchdowns in America," said Lewis. "The two games aren't that different. American football grew out of rugby. It wouldn't take you that long to get the hang of it."

"I'm sorry, I'm not following," said Theo, looking perplexed. He thought he'd been summoned to Lewis's study to talk about Barker and Cattermole, and instead Lewis was talking to him about rugby, of all things.

"I'm suggesting you should play," said Lewis. "On the wing, like Liddell. I saw those running shoes in your trunk last night. You're a runner, aren't you?"

"Not that kind of runner. When I ran, I ran distance."

"I know all about that," said Lewis. "Do you think I haven't noticed how you leave all the other juniors behind on those runs? What I want to know is if you can sprint too. I'm betting you can."

For the second time that morning, Theo could hear Coach Eames's voice in his head: *"Sprinters run on nerves; distance athletes run on heart and guts, and on brains too."* Perhaps it was time to test his nerves.

The forced unpacking of the shoes Coach Eames had given him seemed like a sign. Magic shoes from another time. Why had he kept them, dragged them across the ocean, if he didn't intend to run again?

"All right," he said. "I'll try."

13

CARBOROUGH

The running shoes that Coach Eames had given him no longer fit and the football boots he got from the school store felt tight and constraining, but Theo had not forgotten the art of running. Coach Eames's lessons were embedded in his unconscious, and he knew instinctively how to set himself to sprint for the line with his head still and upright (the opposite of Liddell's) and his shoulders dropped away from his ears and relaxed so as not to lock the hips. And he knew how to accelerate, too, with his arms working in tandem like pistons and his knees pushed up high for greater length of stride. Breath mattered less over a short distance, but the game of rugby required the same measurement against an opponent as he had needed for distance running. The feint and change in direction came naturally to him, just as it had when he sidestepped the O'Donnell brothers at Saint Peter's, evading their outstretched flailing arms as he ran past them and away.

It took him weeks to absorb all the rules of rugby, but his impact on the Colts' games was immediate, and when he got the ball, he scored tries almost at will.

Lewis, watching on the touchline, smiled with satisfaction at his own perspicacity.

"Who's that?" asked Father Philip, coming up to stand beside him. The headmaster took a close interest in school sports, especially rugby, and longed with a religious fervor for the restoration of the Inter-Schools Challenge Cup to the Saint Gregory's trophy cabinet. For the past five years, it had been residing at Saint Augustine's and then latterly at Saint Chad's, whose standing in the school tables had risen in inverse proportion to a fall in Saint Gregory's. For Father Philip's reign as headmaster to be considered a success, he needed the cup, and for that good players like Lewis were required, whereas they all now seemed to be headed to Saint Chad's.

"It's the American boy, isn't it? The peculiar one who doesn't want to be called Campion-Bennett," said the headmaster as Theo trotted back toward them, fresh from another scoring run.

"Yes," said Lewis. "The one who Barker tried to get into trouble."

"And did for himself instead," said Father Philip with a smirk. "No loss there. A transfer to the military academy was the best result for everyone, I think."

"It was nicely done, Father," said Lewis, who had been impressed, not for the first time, by the new headmaster's ruthlessness, as well as being overjoyed to see the back of Barker.

"So, is he good—the American boy?" asked Father Philip.

"Very," said Lewis. "He'll be in the first fifteen next year. I wish I could be here to see it."

"So do I," said Father Philip, thinking of the Challenge Cup. "So do I."

But Esmond was not impressed and accused Theo of selling out. "Lewis snaps his fingers and puts a shirt on your back, and lo and behold, you're eating out of their hands!"

"No, I'm not. I don't see why I'm under an obligation to have a bad time just because I'm stuck here, and if I can do something fun in the afternoons, I—"

"Fun!" Esmond interrupted, repeating the word like it was something obscene. "You think that's all it is, do you?"

Theo nodded.

"Don't you realize that games are the way these schools get inside your head and turn you into a fighter for their cause? They know that if they can get you to care about the rugby and cricket teams, then you're going to care about the school, and they've won the battle. That's why the Old Man has us all up on the touchlines every Saturday afternoon, screaming for our side to win. It's breeding a herd mentality, where no one thinks for themselves anymore but instead becomes a cog in the bourgeois machine. You're blind if you can't see it."

"Well, Communists don't think for themselves much either, do they?" Theo hit back. "Look at Russia—they do what they're told over there or they're on the first train to Siberia!"

Theo's unexpected attack infuriated Esmond. "You look at Russia," he shouted. "Stalin's trying to change centuries of exploitation in a few short years. Of course he has to force the peasants forward, when their lives have been so backward. They're illiterate and can't think for themselves, so he's got no choice. But the party is making a new world over there in which there will be justice and fairness for all, whereas here the poor are unemployed and starving, and no one does anything about it except play stupid ball games."

Esmond paused, out of breath. He'd gotten up from his chair and was looking down at Theo, who had shrunk back in the face of his friend's verbal assault. But then, as suddenly as he had become angry, Esmond was calm again. It was like a magic trick: he closed his eyes and breathed deeply, and when he opened them again, his characteristic ironic smile had returned, masking the fiery emotions that lay beneath his controlled exterior.

"You have to look behind the lies," he said quietly. "The public schools know the value of propaganda just as much as Hitler or Mussolini. 'Play up and play the game,' they say, but sport is not a game. Not here: it's how the ruling class wins hearts and minds. Do you know what they did on the first day of the Battle of the Somme when they sent those poor fools across no-man's-land?"

Theo shook his head.

"They gave them footballs to get them to run. Kicked them forward at zero hour and told the men to chase after them. Not that they got too far. Twenty thousand were dead by the afternoon, mown down by the German guns."

"What are you asking me to do?" Theo asked, stirring uneasily in his chair. He liked Esmond, but he didn't enjoy being lectured.

"Think for yourself."

"All right, I'll do that. But I'm going to play the rugby too. I need to do something I enjoy or I'll go crazy, sitting here."

Esmond nodded, saying nothing, and Theo got up to go.

"Where does that leave us?" he asked. "I hope we can still be friends."

"The trouble with you, Theo, is that you think you can have your cake and eat it. And maybe you can for now, but one day, sooner or later, you're going to have to choose. You're going to have to decide which side you're on." Esmond looked hard at Theo, as if measuring the effect of his words, and then turned away, picking up a book from his desk.

Theo hesitated in the doorway, not wanting to part on bad terms, but Esmond ignored him, and he left the room.

For the remaining few weeks of the term, Theo saw little of Esmond, who had an uncanny ability to disappear from sight when he wished to. Winter had arrived, and drifts of snow covered the cars parked in the quadrangle. Icicles like irregular white teeth hung from windowsills and from the high ledge that Theo had crossed with Cattermole, and he was grateful for the gloves and warm coat that his mother had sent him by priority mail.

There was no rugby or running, and the boys gathered, shivering, around inadequate classroom stoves, trying to keep warm. When the sun came out, they threw snowballs and dragged homemade toboggans to the top of the hill behind the school and came careening down the slope until one of them hit a tree and knocked himself out, and Father Philip put an end to their fun.

When school was over, Theo took the train to London, packed with boys in holiday mood, and was met at Waterloo Station by Causier, who raised his peaked cap an inch in welcome and drove Theo to Sir Andrew's opulent town house in Grosvenor Square, where his mother was waiting for him with open arms.

London was beautiful in the snow. In Hyde Park, there was ice on the Serpentine Lake, and he and his mother rented skates, hanging on to each other for dear life while Sir Andrew, wearing a Russian beaver hat, looked on and laughed, and the other skaters gave them a wide berth, thinking they were certain to fall, even though they never did.

They drank hot chocolate in the café afterward and the bells in all the churches rang and Elena was happy because it was Christmas and Christ was born again in Bethlehem.

The huge Christmas tree in the drawing room of Sir Andrew's house glittered with swans and trumpets and silver globes that shimmered in the reflected light of the ceiling chandelier, which lit Sir Andrew, too, as he accompanied his wife on the piano, while she sang Spanish carols and one in English called "In the Bleak Midwinter," which Theo was hearing for the first time. It began with the beauty and harshness of the snow magically connecting the song with the here and now of their own winter evening, and ended with a simple expression of a true believer's relationship to Christ:

If I were a Wise Man
I would do my part,
Yet what I can I give him,
Give my heart.

The last note hung on the air, and Theo was moved to tears that he turned away to hide. He loved his mother, but he could not share her faith. Not like his stepfather. Theo saw the perfect union between them expressed through the shared music, and he felt shut out and alone.

At the end of the evening, Sir Andrew called Theo into his study and gave him his present: a first edition of Lamb's *Tales from Shakespeare* illustrated by Arthur Rackham.

"I promised you this book a long time ago," he said. "And I'm sorry that it has taken me so long to give it to you, but it's not just for Christmas; it's also to congratulate you on your first term at Saint Gregory's. Your mother and I are delighted by your progress."

"Thank you," said Theo, picking the book up and slowly turning the pages. The pictures were magnificent, but the thought came unbidden into his mind that he must refuse the gift. He thought back to Sir Andrew's first present of *King Arthur and His Knights* and how agreeing to conceal it from his father had felt like a betrayal. He remembered how he had thought of giving the book back, but hadn't been able to because it had been so beautiful, opening doors to another world, and he remembered, too, how he had read it at night in his bedroom with the aid of a flashlight, turning the beautifully illustrated pages in wonder. He had been tempted and he had succumbed, and almost without knowing it, he had joined with his mother in a silent conspiracy to keep his father shut out from their Spanish-speaking world. Outside and alone. Perhaps if his father had felt less isolated, he would have been able to turn to them in his hour of need.

The ghost of Theo's father lay between the son and the mother, and between the son and the stepfather. Michael Sterling did not walk the halls of the Mayfair house like the ghost of Hamlet's father, but he was present in Theo's mind whenever Theo was there, telling his son to stand apart and not allow himself to be bought with expensive gifts.

"I'm sorry. I can't accept this," Theo said, putting the book down on Sir Andrew's desk and taking a step back.

"Why not?" asked Sir Andrew, surprised.

"I can't explain. I know you mean well, but—" Theo broke off, unable to translate into words the surge of competing emotions he felt battling for supremacy inside his head.

"Are you sure?" asked Sir Andrew, observing Theo closely as he offered him a second chance.

And now Theo wanted to accept. He tried to pull free of the past, but the words wouldn't come, and in a moment the chance was gone.

"I'm sorry you still feel this way," said Sir Andrew, pulling the book back to his side of the desk. "It's a pity, as I don't think you gain by it, but you must make your own decisions. However, you will understand that I can't allow them to upset your mother. She is easily distressed, particularly by you, and that can make her ill. She is better at the moment, but she could very quickly go downhill again. I have to protect her from that."

"Protect her from me, you mean?"

"Yes, if necessary."

A surge of hatred for his stepfather ran through Theo like an electric current. What right had this man got to come between him and his mother? Theo would have liked to tell Sir Andrew what he felt, but he wasn't going to give his stepfather the satisfaction of seeing him lose his temper. At least he hadn't taken the book—there was some consolation in that.

"Can I go?" he asked.

Sir Andrew nodded, and without another word Theo turned and left the room.

Next day, Theo took a walk on his own, hoping to clear his head with a change of scenery.

He wandered, taking turnings at random, until he reached the river and crossed Westminster Bridge, looking back across the gray lapping water to the Houses of Parliament dominating the north bank. Mother of Parliaments. Bastion of privilege and power, wrapped up in its own history. It was no Bastille waiting to fall, and Theo sensed at that moment the absurdity of Esmond's aspiration to tear down the social structure and start over, but at the same time he was moved by his friend's David-like commitment to his cause and his refusal to compromise his beliefs. He missed Esmond with a sudden intensity—his quicksilver talk, his unexpected humor, and his certainty.

He walked on into Lambeth, leaving the towers of Westminster behind, and entered a poor neighborhood where the air was full of soot from choked-up chimneys and the hungry, desperate faces of the inhabitants reminded him of what he had left behind in New York. The snow in the streets here had turned to black slush, and the melting ice dripped down the crumbling walls into doorways where hollow-eyed paupers shivered in the cold.

The snow was just another deception, Theo thought as he turned for home—a white cover to conceal the black rottenness of the city underneath. Esmond was right. Sir Andrew and his kind lived lives of luxury while the poor suffered unspeakable degradations only a mile or two away, and then drove to church on Sundays to be blessed for their participation in a system of vicious exploitation that went on uninterrupted from one generation to the next. Whatever the odds, something had to be done. Something had to change.

Theo vowed to himself that he would not forget and he would not sell out. He knew where his loyalties lay.

Back at school, Esmond was in a forgiving mood. He sought Theo out and invited him to tea, telling him he had something new and wonderful and bourgeois to show him.

It was a gramophone, complete with a small, eclectic collection of records, bought for Esmond for Christmas by his doting mother, who hoped that her only son's newfound interest in popular music might come to supplant his unfortunate obsession with Bolshevism.

Among the recordings were some of the Dixieland jazz hits that Theo remembered blaring out from the doorways of the Fourteenth Street dime stores in New York. The strutting rhythm of the trumpets and clarinets made Theo homesick, and he felt the connection to his childhood in the aching, time-jumping way that sound and smell can provide, but the remembering mind, laboring in the abstract, can never attain.

Perhaps it was Esmond's intention to create this effect, because he saved the song that he wanted Theo to listen to for last.

It was a fresh-off-the-press recording of Bing Crosby singing "Brother, Can You Spare a Dime?" and Theo's attention was captured immediately by the haunting, poetic lyrics that told the story of a hardworking man who lived the American dream and made a success of his life, but was then ruined by the Depression and reduced to begging for charity on the street corner.

Esmond wound the gramophone so Theo could listen to the song again and a third time, too, watching the effect on his friend. Theo was spellbound, straining to hear and understand every word.

"I thought of what you told me about your father when I heard it, and so I went straight out to buy the record because I wanted you to hear it too," said Esmond. Theo nodded, but his mind was far away, thinking of his father, who had dreamed the same dream, laboring to climb the ladder of success, only to see all that he had built come crashing to the ground. On and on, up and up, always believing, until he fell. The song told his story too.

Theo tried to imagine what his father must have felt when his dreams turned to dust. Disappointment, disillusionment, despair . . . *Why?* he must have thought. *Why?*—that must have been the last word in his father's mind when he pulled the trigger. No one's name, as Theo had once hoped or imagined, just *Why?*—the same question as the man with his hand held out was asking in the song.

"Thank you," he said, looking up at Esmond. "It helps that you understand."

"I do," said Esmond. "And I feel your pain. It's a terrible thing to lose your father the way you did, and your home too."

Looking back afterward, Theo was surprised that Esmond hadn't used the song to lecture him about the evils of capitalism. Instead, it had been a means—artificial but real—for him to convey a genuine sympathy for Theo's situation. The conversation stung Theo into realizing that Esmond was the only one who cared about what he felt, apart from Frank, who was too far away to make a difference. His mother acted like the past did not exist and was immersed in her new life in London with her new husband, but Esmond was his friend and that had a value beyond price.

It helped, too, that Esmond had become less combative. He spoke less about the evils of Saint Gregory's and its role in perpetuating class exploitation in Britain, and he refrained from any further criticism of Theo for playing rugby and trying to make the best of school life. Instead, he talked to him about the world outside and its dangers and iniquities, and here he found a willing listener, tapping into Theo's own belief, born of his experience in New York, that his contemporaries, with their selfish, petty concerns, were playing at life without any understanding of what it was really about.

As part of this change of approach, Esmond invited Theo to join him on his regular weekend visits to Carborough, the neighboring town, which was a half hour's bus ride from Saint Gregory's. This was technically permitted only to sixth formers, but Theo's popularity in the house and his sporting prowess meant that no one objected to him accompanying Esmond on non-match days.

Carborough was not a tourist destination. In fact, it was doubtful a tourist had ever set foot there, except by mistake. Its two most famous inhabitants were a Puritan fanatic who had signed Charles the First's death warrant and his great-great-grandson, who had founded an ironworks on the outskirts of the town during the Industrial Revolution.

The factory was still in business, but the Depression had severely curtailed its profitability and more and more of its employees were being laid off, adding to the long queues at the hideous chocolate-and-green Labor Exchange in the High Street. In the meantime, the coal smoke from the blast furnace continued to hang like a shroud over the town, poisoning the inhabitants, who suffered from one of the highest rates of lung disease in the nation. Misery was not hard to find in the narrow, cobbled streets of back-to-back houses smelling of damp and destitution, and misery was what Esmond was looking for.

Carborough possessed no cathedral and precious few theaters or public parks, but one amenity it did have in abundance was public houses. Practically every street had a Rose and Crown or Nag's Head at its end, catering to the local population's constant need to drown its sorrows in drink. And it was to the spit-and-sawdust taprooms of these pubs that Esmond went with Theo in tow to spread awareness of the class struggle and listen to the drinkers' tales of their wretched lives spent toiling on the breadline.

Theo couldn't help but admire Esmond's insatiable curiosity about what life was like for the poor. Not content to sit in his study, reading books and spinning theories, he pushed his way into the town's most blighted neighborhoods and asked questions, storing up all he was told for future analysis.

Theo was impressed, too, by his friend's fearlessness and candor. He didn't try to disguise his upper-class accent, and he told the men he met that he wanted to know what their lives were like, so he could find ways to change them for the better. He didn't lecture and he listened to the men's stories with care and respect, expressing sympathy at all the right moments. And yet, despite all this, Theo saw that Esmond remained detached. It was not that he was insincere but rather that he had a deficiency that he wasn't aware of and so could not overcome: he couldn't feel what these men felt and so he couldn't share their pain. Sometimes, this grated on Theo, who often found it unbearable to hear their stories, because it brought back his own experience of poverty in New York, when he, too, had felt the gnawing anxiety of not knowing where the next meal was coming from or how he and his mother were going to pay the rent. At such times he would look up and feel ashamed when he saw the avid eagerness of Esmond's expression as he probed for more detail. He looked like a collector of rare butterflies, Theo thought, viewing specimens through a microscope.

It was against school rules to even enter a pub, but Esmond had been able to overcome Theo's reluctance by pointing out that it was virtually impossible that they would meet anyone from Saint Gregory's in such down-at-heel locations. But the other side of the coin was that these small, out-of-the-way taverns on Carborough's dismal back streets were not the most fruitful venues for meeting interesting members of the working class. They were too wretched: inside the dilapidated bars there was an atmosphere of stupefying torpor, with the regulars staring morosely into the bottom of their pint glasses, measuring how much they had left before they would be forced back out into the cold. Like windup automatons, most of them stayed talkative for a minute or two after Esmond had bought them a refill of mild beer, but then relapsed back into dormancy, showing no interest in the copy of *The Daily Worker* that he had given them and answering his questions with grunted monosyllables.

"We need to go where the life is," said Esmond as they came out of a particularly dreary taproom and looked across the dirty cobbled street to where a group of ragged children were kicking a blown-up pig's bladder about on a piece of waste ground.

"And where's that?" asked Theo with a hollow laugh. "This is Carborough in February, for God's sake—there is no life. Let's go to the movies. At least we might have some fun there."

"No," said Esmond. "I haven't come all this way to go back empty-handed. We need a change of direction, that's all. Let's go up to the High Street."

Theo was too cold to argue, and fifteen minutes later he was happily gorging himself on a plowman's lunch washed down with a pint of best bitter beside a roaring fire in the public bar of the Eight Bells, while watching Esmond pit his billiard skills against a huge bald man with meaty hands, called Alf, who uncomfortably reminded Theo of Easey Goldstein in New York.

This pub was a going concern. Outside, there were red geraniums cascading down over the golden bells on the sign and across the tops of the etched glass windows. Inside, the brass fittings on the bar shone and the different-colored liquor bottles on the shelves behind sparkled in the bright light, reflected back in the ornate mirrors covering the walls.

Theo glanced up at the one facing the door and saw the reflection of Sergeant Raikes coming through.

"Get down!" he suddenly shouted, half knocking over his drink as he grabbed hold of Esmond and pulled him down onto the floor behind the billiards table.

"What the hell are you doing?" Esmond asked, looking at Theo like he'd lost his mind.

"Raikes," whispered Theo, putting his hand up to Esmond's mouth to keep him quiet. "He just walked in."

"Did he see us?"

"No, I don't think so. Look!" he said, pointing under the billiards table toward the bar, where they could see the bottom of the sergeant's wooden leg. He was waiting to buy a drink and had his back to them.

As they stared, their view of the leg was obscured by the appearance of a big eye and part of a head.

"Are you takin' the mickey?" Alf demanded, looking down at them belligerently. "Because I won't stand for it, you 'ear? You've forfeit the game goin' under there, and now you owe me that drink."

"Shhh!" said Esmond, putting his index finger desperately to his mouth as he passed up a shilling. Alf disappeared, and then his big legs joined the sergeant's wooden one in front of the bar.

Esmond turned back to Theo. "We can't stay here," he said. "He'll see us when he turns round."

Theo nodded.

"Okay," said Esmond. "On the count of three, run. One. Two. Three."

Keeping their heads down, they rushed for the door, knocking over a table and an ashtray on the way. Once outside, they ran up the street and turned the corner, catching their breath and peeping their heads back around to see if Sergeant Raikes was in pursuit.

But the sidewalk was empty and Esmond burst out laughing. Soon, he was doubled up, clutching his sides.

Theo looked down at him sourly and lost his temper. "I told you we shouldn't have come here, but you wouldn't listen," he shouted. "Oh, no, Esmond knows best. Like always."

"It doesn't matter. He didn't see us," said Esmond and started laughing again.

"It does matter," said Theo furiously. "I don't want to get expelled, even if you do."

"Because you've got so much to lose, haven't you?" said Esmond nastily. "Golden prospects: a prefect's waistcoat, captain of rugby, idol of the new boys. You've sold your soul for a few trinkets. I thought you were better than that. Really, I did."

"And you've got no soul to sell," Theo shot back. "You're a fake, Esmond. That's what you are. Making people think you care when all you want is information for your stupid notebooks."

He turned and ran away down the road, feeling his heart beating fast and already wishing he could take back what he'd said.

Theo stood alone at the bus station, stamping his feet and rubbing his hands to try to keep warm. A harsh wind was blowing across the concourse, whipping up empty cigarette packets and other rubbish and dropping them again as it changed direction. There were no trees. Everywhere was concrete and asphalt, and the whole place was deserted under a darkening sky. He peered again at the timetable fixed to the iron post beside which he was standing. Yes, the bus was due in five minutes, but that didn't mean it would come. He could be stranded here all night, he thought, and freeze to death without anyone being the wiser.

He wished he hadn't quarreled with Esmond. He'd gone in the pub of his own free will and the sergeant hadn't seen them, and the whole escapade *had* been funny. He could see that now. Raikes and his wooden leg and Big Alf's big eye. He wished he'd laughed instead of running off, but it was too late now.

It was Carborough's fault, he decided. If he ever got out of this hellhole, he wasn't coming back. Not for love or money . . .

Suddenly he went rigid. There were footsteps behind him, or rather a step and a clump, like the walking sound a man with a wooden leg might make.

"I got you now, Sterlin'," said Sergeant Raikes as he gripped Theo's collar. "'Eadmaster's goin' to beat you black and blue, you mark my words. You'll be regrettin' the day you was born by the time 'e's finished with yer."

Theo turned around and faced—not Sergeant Raikes but Esmond.

"You bastard!" he said, bursting out laughing. "I really thought it was him."

"You did, didn't you?" said Esmond, laughing too.

"How do you do it? You're like a parrot! It's unbelievable."

"I guess I'm a natural when it comes to sergeant-majors, and Raikes is a mimic's dream. He's come out with some great lines over the years. Not to be forgotten," said Esmond, tapping his forehead.

"Such as?"

"Well, it's hard to choose, but I suppose my all-time favorite is from this time last year when he was escorting me to the Old Man for a flogging—I'd done something blasphemous in church, I can't remember what—and he stopped outside the door, turned to me, leaning close, and told me: 'T'aint the agony, Lisle; yer know that, don't yer? It's the *disgrace*.'"

Again, the mimicry was perfect, combined, too, with the leaning close and a great deal of hand rubbing, so that Theo almost felt as if he could see the sergeant and feel his awful joy.

"Come on," said Esmond. "Here's our bus. I hope the driver's got the heater on."

Theo refused to go to any more pubs with Esmond after their narrow escape from the Eight Bells, but he did eventually agree to break his vow and return to Carborough, this time to go to the cinema. The Scala was showing *The Public Enemy*, and he wanted Esmond to see the movie and to experience again for himself that visceral feeling in his chest that had kept him going back to watch it in New York. But this time around, he felt nothing except a weary sense of treading old ground. He was disappointed but thought, too, that his lack of reaction was because he was starting to heal and no longer needed Jimmy Cagney to pierce the wall that he had built back then around his tortured emotions.

Esmond was unmoved too. His interest lay in what he could use. American gangsters meant nothing to him, and so he switched off, waiting for the Pathé newsreels that would follow the movie. And when they came, he was suddenly alert, sitting on the edge of his seat with his eyes glued to the screen as he watched the Reichstag burn and Hitler swoon over his microphone, brushing his hair back off his sweating face as he hammered out his hate. The camera panned down Berlin streets with *JUDE* scrawled across the shopfronts in white paint, and stopped to linger over a grainy shot of an old Jew being beaten by SA Brownshirts with swastikas emblazoned on their arms.

Theo was transfixed too. He remembered the photographs in his grandfather's book and the wooden house that had burned with his ancestors inside. The newsreel made the idea of pogrom real. It made him angry, and frightened too.

Later, as they walked back to the bus station, Esmond was energized, fired up by what they'd seen.

"It's just beginning," he said. "Hitler will stop at nothing and nor must we—"

"You need to know something," said Theo, interrupting. "My grandparents are Jewish. My father said that that doesn't make me a Jew and he didn't want to be one either. He changed his name, but it didn't change who he was or who I am. You are what you are. My grandfather told me that, and he was right."

"Where is he now?"

"I don't know. Dead, perhaps. I only met him once, and he was an old man then. But he said I would remember him, and I do, as if it was yesterday."

"He obviously made quite an impression."

"Yes, he did. He gave me a sense that I was part of something bigger than myself," Theo said thoughtfully. "That I belonged somewhere, and seeing that newsreel just now makes me feel that the Nazis are attacking me too."

"They are. You're mixed race as far as they're concerned, and soon they'll be calling you Jewish, too, because there can be no half measures with their hatred. Hitler needs someone to blame, and the Jew is his scapegoat. The persecution will get worse soon, much worse, and your blood will tell you that you cannot stand aside and do nothing."

"But what can I do?" asked Theo, opening his arms to express his impotence.

"I don't know," said Esmond. "But there will be something. That I am sure of."

A week later, Theo and Esmond were listening to a package of new jazz records that Esmond had just received in the mail from London when Theo caught sight of a black shoe out in the corridor, extended just beyond the half-open door of the study.

Putting his finger to his mouth, he got up silently from his chair and yanked open the door, jumping out to seize hold of the eavesdropper. He had expected it to be Alwyn or one of the other junior boys, and was shocked and dismayed to find himself with an arm around the waist of his housemaster.

He backed away, stammering out apologies, but Father Laurence didn't seem offended.

"No harm done," he said. "I stopped because of the beautiful music. When I was a boy, one of my ambitions was to play the trumpet, but it came to nothing, I am afraid. And perhaps it's for the best."

"Trumpets and monasteries don't go together, you mean?" asked Esmond, grinning.

"Perhaps," said Father Laurence, amused too.

"But you like Louis Armstrong?"

"Yes, very much. He's an extraordinary improviser. A natural genius."

"Well, come in and listen to some more," said Esmond warmly. "I can make you some of my horrible tea if you like."

Father Laurence hesitated. It wasn't normal for housemasters to keep company with boys in their studies. But then he smiled and sat down in the chair that Theo had vacated, opposite the statue of Karl Marx, while Theo moved to the bed. Theo wished he had a camera so he could take a photograph.

"You have quite a library," said the monk, running his eyes over the bookshelves crammed with Communist texts.

"I do, don't I?" said Esmond. "Marx and Engels are not really your line, though, I expect?" It had made his day to discover that Father Laurence was a fan of Dixieland jazz, but he thought it safe to assume that Marxism would be foreign territory.

He couldn't have been more wrong.

"I'm not an expert like you," said Father Laurence, "but I do try and keep up to date as much as I can. Renouncing the world does not mean that we monks have taken a vow to remain ignorant of what is happening in it."

"And what do you think is happening?" asked Esmond.

"I think that evil is spreading through Europe like a cancer. In Germany and Italy and in Russia too. I fear for the future—your future," said Father Laurence, glancing over at Theo.

"Russia too! Well, I suppose we can't expect a monk to like a state that says there is no God," said Esmond. There was a meanness about his smile now that Theo didn't like, and he also objected to Esmond's obvious attempt to rope him in on his side, but he said nothing, wondering what was coming next.

"It's not just their persecution of the priesthood that concerns me, although that is obviously an evil," said Father Laurence. "I was more thinking of the peasantry who have been forced into collectives that don't work, with those that refuse being shot or loaded into cattle trucks to take them to icy northern camps where they freeze to death or die of disease. My understanding is that millions have died, and that this horror is getting worse every day because the peasants that are left are starving, scrabbling for weeds and roots and even eating each other, while Comrade Stalin sells their grain to buy technology for his Five-Year Plan. The cruelty and suffering are unimaginable."

Theo noticed the expression of pain that briefly passed across Father Laurence's face as he finished speaking, before his features became composed again, and he sat sipping the lukewarm tea that Esmond had poured him from the pot.

Theo was impressed by the way that Father Laurence spoke so calmly and authoritatively and, despite his devotion to his friend, he couldn't help feeling that there was something refreshing about seeing Esmond so forcefully challenged after months of sitting at his feet, listening to him impart his pearls of Marxist wisdom.

Esmond, however, was feeling an equal mixture of surprise and fury. An unlikely enthusiasm for Louis Armstrong was one thing, but Father Laurence's entirely unexpected and knowledgeable attack on Stalin was quite another and had left him momentarily at a loss for words. "Those are all lies, filthy lies," he spluttered angrily.

"Yes, that's what Stalin says too," Father Laurence continued smoothly on. "'Lies, lies!' he sneers, but he is the one who is lying, and on a scale that no one before now could ever have imagined, because he's realized that the more colossal the lie, the more likely it is to be believed. No ruler could sell grain when his people are starving, and so they can't be starving. It's as simple as that. And so the peasants carry on dying without their deaths even being acknowledged. The shameless audacity of the performance is truly diabolical."

"I was wondering when you were going to get round to calling him the Devil," said Esmond. "Because these tales of yours are the worst kind of superstition. As I'm sure you know, they're the work of one disgruntled journalist and have been discredited by the entire press corps in Moscow, not to speak of George Bernard Shaw and H. G. Wells."

"Who see what they're paid to see. Malcolm Muggeridge got away from his minders. That's the difference."

"No, the difference is he hates Communism. That's why he wrote those articles. I'm not saying there aren't food shortages. Of course there are. Russia was fifty years behind the West, and it needs to catch up if it is going to survive. Otherwise, countries like ours will pick it apart just like they tried to do after the revolution. But there's been amazing progress. Investment in industry has quadrupled and the workforce has doubled, but those workers need to be fed, and the peasants hoard the grain or feed it to their livestock. They refuse to collectivize because they are stupid and selfish and so, yes, they must be forced, if necessary. Of course they must. They cannot be allowed to hold the whole country back."

"And that justifies murdering them?" asked Father Laurence, raising his eyebrows.

"No, of course not. That's not what I'm saying, and it's not what's happening. It's you who see what you want to see; not me. You have to discredit the Communists because you're frightened that they will do the same here and the ruling class will lose its land and money and privileges."

"But I am not the ruling class," said Father Laurence. "You seem to forget I have taken a vow of poverty!"

"You serve them, though, don't you? That's what the public schools are for, or would you deny that too?"

Father Laurence shook his head, the gesture conveying his sense that the argument had gotten out of control, and after a moment he got up to leave, carefully handing his half-drunk mug of tea to Theo.

"Thank you for the tea," he said. "I am sorry that we have become so antagonistic. It was not my intention, and I was enjoying the music."

"There won't be any schools like this, or monasteries, either, when the revolution comes," said Esmond, refusing to accept the olive branch. "And believe me, it is coming. The workers have woken up. Time is on our side, not yours."

Standing in the doorway, Father Laurence heard Esmond out and then inclined his head without making further response and left.

"Fool," said Esmond, spitting the word through his teeth.

"No, he's not," said Theo, speaking for the first time.

"What did you say?" asked Esmond, surprised by this new challenge.

"He's not a fool," said Theo. "It's just so blindingly obvious he isn't. If you can't see that, then you're a . . ."

"Fool?" growled Esmond, finishing Theo's sentence.

"Your word, not mine," said Theo, getting up to go. He'd had enough of Esmond suddenly and needed to get out into the air.

But as he was leaving, Esmond called him back. "Whose side are you on?" he demanded.

The old question.

"I don't know," said Theo.

Outside, as he walked out into the lightly falling rain, pushing back his head to let it wash over his face, he thought of Alvah Katz for the first time in a long time. Esmond's sardonic mocking smile when he attacked Father Laurence had been just like Alvah's, and there was the same wanton destructiveness underlying their embrace of the workers' cause.

Theo put his hands up to his temples, pushing his knuckles into the skin. He didn't want to think of Esmond that way. Alvah had destroyed his father, but Esmond was his friend who cared about him and made him laugh, and taught him to see the world in new ways.

Slowly, Theo succeeded in disentangling Esmond from Alvah, but as Esmond faded from his mind, Alvah became more vivid. He saw him as he had the first time in the cutter's room at his father's factory, with his clipped mustache and beard and curly black hair all oiled into place, and with the memory came an intuition that he hadn't finished with his father's old enemy. That Alvah was waiting for him out there somewhere, around some blind corner of his future. Waiting with malice in his heart.

14

CHOICES

Theo's flare-ups with Esmond didn't stop them being friends, but they were symptomatic of a tension between them that escalated when they returned to Saint Gregory's at the end of the summer.

Theo had passed the school certificate with distinction and now entered the sixth form, which meant that he was entitled to his own study. For the last week of the holidays, Elena took Theo on a round of the best London department stores, shopping for bedding and furnishings, to which was added a bespoke silk waistcoat rushed through by Sir Andrew's tailor in Savile Row after Sir Andrew received a letter from Father Laurence informing him that Theo had been selected to be a prefect, the youngest in the house. Success warmed relations between Theo and his stepfather, at least temporarily, although tensions still simmered underneath.

Away from Esmond's influence, Theo's attitude toward Saint Gregory's had undergone a change during the summer, and he was surprised to realize that he was looking forward to going back. Most of all, this was because the rugby season would be starting again, and his hopes were rewarded when he was selected for the first fifteen for their first match of the season away to Saint Chad's.

Five minutes from time with the scores level, he received the ball on the wing and put up the high kick that he had been practicing throughout the summer and ran through the opposition to catch it and touch down in the corner. Almost immediately afterward, the whistle blew and he was surrounded by his teammates, who practically carried him from the pitch, while the opposition looked on disconsolately, having tasted defeat in the fixture for the first time in three years. And then on the way back in the bus, they sang "Land of Hope and Glory" and "It's a Long Way to Tipperary," and Theo experienced again that same happiness he used to feel coming back from running meets on Coach Eames's battle bus—the happiness that comes from a sense of belonging to something bigger than oneself.

The story of his exploits on the pitch spread like wildfire through Saint Gregory's and led to a further surge in his popularity. Alwyn Thomas and Cattermole—transformed into a happy schoolboy since the departure of Barker—followed him about, bringing him tea and toast even when he didn't ask for it and competing with the other juniors for the honor of cleaning his football boots. His study was always full of people, and he had to throw them out when he needed to work.

Theo enjoyed his success, but it came with a feeling of dissatisfaction that he couldn't shake off because he could not share it with Esmond. Worse than that, he knew, without Esmond having to tell him, that his accomplishments were creating a barrier between them that he didn't know how to overcome.

He tried. He knocked on the door of Esmond's study and Esmond didn't turn him away, but nor did he make him tea like he used to before or talk to him about the cause. Esmond was polite, but it was as if he was waiting for Theo to leave so he could return to the thick Leninist tome that he had been reading before Theo came in. Theo would have preferred Esmond to attack him for selling out, like he used to before. That would at least have given him something to respond to, but Esmond's withdrawal left him in limbo.

He felt judged, and it rankled because he thought Esmond's silent reproach was unfair, but he couldn't dismiss it on that basis, because he had spent the previous year allowing Esmond to become his conscience. He noticed how Esmond wore his moth-eaten sweater with pride and looked askance at Theo's fancy waistcoat, and Theo began to feel ashamed of wearing it. All his accomplishments felt tarnished by Esmond's irony.

Beneath his resentment, Theo missed his friend. He missed his brilliance and unpredictability and his extraordinary humor, which no other boy in the school could even begin to rival, and above all he felt the loss of his sympathy. He forgot now how he had questioned Esmond's compassion for the poor and remembered instead how Esmond had been alone in consoling him for the death of his father and for all that he had lost and left behind.

But he would not give up the rugby. He remembered the despair he had felt when his parents took away the running. It didn't matter what Esmond said. He couldn't let that happen again.

In November, Saint Gregory's finally won the Challenge Cup, prevailing over Saint Augustine's in a hard-fought final played out in the driving rain. "Get it out to the wing, let Sterling have it!" Theo heard Father Philip shouting, and he loved the headmaster as he caught the ball cleanly and accelerated away toward the posts.

Late that night, he wrote to Lewis to thank him for all he'd done for him, but at midnight he was still wide awake and tiptoed down the corridor to Esmond's door so as not to wake anyone up. It was closed, but there was a crack of light between the bottom of the door and the floor and Theo could faintly hear Bing Crosby singing "Brother, Can You Spare a Dime?"

It was too much. He tapped softly and went in.

Esmond was sitting at his desk, looking out into the starlit night as the record played to its end, but he swung his chair around as Theo entered.

"The conquering hero honors me with a visit!" he said, the irony even heavier than usual—it was as if Esmond had himself grown tired of it. "What can I do for you?"

"Tea, maybe," said Theo, sitting down in the armchair under the picture of the Kremlin. He remembered how they had talked about it the first time he'd been in the study and how bowled over he had been by Esmond, and he wished that he could turn the clock back and that everything between them could return to the way it had been before.

Esmond looked at Theo for a moment as if he were a banker weighing up a decision that could go either way and then smiled. "All right," he said, leaning out of the window to get his milk. "I think I can stretch to that."

"You were playing the song you bought for me to listen to," said Theo.

"Yes. It's powerful, although Bing Crosby wouldn't have been my first choice as the singer. Not exactly a revolutionary, is he?" said Esmond.

"A bit like me?"

"You were more promising material. But now you seem to be rapidly turning into Father Philip's star pupil, so yes, I don't think you have much of a future on the barricades, either, do you?"

"It's not as easy for me as it is for you," said Theo. "I've lost more in my life, and so it's harder for me to stand alone."

"You need to belong, as do all collaborators. When the tribe calls, you come running," Esmond retorted harshly.

"Perhaps," said Theo. "But you are your own man because it's who you are. You are apart. You don't feel the pain of others. You care about their suffering, but you can't share it. It's why you can toss me aside as you have."

Esmond didn't respond straightaway. He handed Theo his tea and sat back in his chair, thinking.

"You've said this before about me," he said eventually. "And you may be right that I am more mind than heart. But it doesn't change what I believe in, or what I would give up for it. I know for a fact that you can't serve two masters. You have to choose."

"And you're angry with me because I won't?"

"Not angry," said Esmond. "Perhaps I was, briefly, but not anymore. And I think you have chosen. You just don't see it yet."

"Well, I'm asking you to keep an open mind," said Theo. "To remain my friend. To be patient. I need to find my way, that's all. I think it'll be easier when the rugby's over in the spring. There'll be more time then."

"Rugby or the class struggle? A choice for our times!" said Esmond, laughing at the absurdity of the dichotomy and breaking the serious spell of their conversation.

Theo laughed, too, and they drank their tea and forgot for a moment that they were at such loggerheads with each other.

Theo didn't know whether Esmond had decided to give him a second chance, because neither of them referred again to their nocturnal conversation. It was as if it stood outside their lives in a place to which they could not return. But Esmond did seem more friendly when Theo passed him in the halls, and he saw more of him after Christmas, when the upper sixth Latin teacher ran off with the assistant matron and the two sixth forms—upper and lower—were briefly taught the subject together, while Father Philip scoured the universities for a suitable replacement.

The lower sixth teacher was a thin, birdlike, shortsighted man called Bandy, who had had severe difficulty keeping control of one form and found the task impossible when he was handed responsibility for two. Years before, he had had pretensions to be a classical scholar, and he had never been able to get used to the daily dismemberment of the literature that he had once loved at the hands of boys bored to distraction by the poems of Virgil and Horace. It would have been better for Bandy if he had accepted failure and fallen back on a detached amusement at the hand fate had dealt him, but he couldn't. Instead, he got up each day hoping that everything would be different, only to collapse back into his chair in renewed despair when the first boy began to construe, making the same awful mistakes that Bandy had heard a thousand times before.

The boys laughed at Bandy's melodramatic groaning and mocked him behind his back, but he was not faced with outright rebellion until Esmond arrived in his class. From the outset, Esmond seemed determined to make trouble. He was clever and asked questions edged with sarcasm and ridicule, but then looked innocent and perplexed when Bandy lost his temper and began to shout and rant. But all this was no more than a softening-up process, and at the beginning of the second week, when news filtered down that a new classics master was on the way, Esmond moved in for the kill.

He was sitting next to Theo at a desk near the window at the back of the classroom, and when Bandy turned to write on the blackboard, Esmond opened the school bag that he had brought to class and produced two medium-size rocks. One he deposited on the floor under the window and the other he placed on Theo's desk.

"Throw it!" he said, pointing at the window. "Throw it and I'll know which side you're on."

He sat back down at his desk, watching Theo, not encouraging or discouraging him, but just waiting to see what he would do. All the other boys were in front of them, and no one seemed to be aware of what was going on.

Theo had no idea afterward why he threw the stone. Perhaps it was simply that he could not resist Esmond's challenge, but he did it straightaway without thinking, and the glass shattered.

Immediately, all hell broke loose. Bandy spun around, dropping his chalk, and rushed to join Esmond, who was standing at the window, holding up the second rock and pointing frantically toward the elm trees that dotted the green slope of the hill behind the classroom building.

"I can see him, sir!" he shouted. "It's one of the local boys. I think he's going to do it again."

"Where?" Bandy demanded, seeing nothing.

"I think he's gone behind that tree over there, sir," said Esmond. "Shall we go after him?"

"Yes," said Bandy and took off through the door and down the stairs with his gown billowing out behind him and his class following in hot pursuit.

And then for ten glorious minutes they ran from tree to tree with Esmond permanently at Bandy's shoulder, telling him that he'd just seen the stone thrower again.

It was cruel. Theo understood that, but it was side-achingly funny, too, and it was the dawning awareness that everyone except Esmond was laughing at him that finally brought Bandy to a halt.

He went over to the ground under the window and picked up and examined the stone that Theo had thrown, lying amid the shattered glass, and then climbed the stairs to the freezing classroom and examined the internal damage.

"This window was broken from the inside," he announced. "Whoever did this better own up now, or you'll all go to the headmaster. I mean what I say!"

Silence. Esmond had his eyes fixed expectantly on Theo, and then he smiled when Theo raised his hand and immediately did the same.

Bandy was shocked. Theo was one of the few pupils in the class who seemed to have any feel for the language, and there had been several times after lessons when he had come up to his desk and they had talked about Aeneas and the fall of Troy. But here he was now, revealed as the worst kind of vandal.

"Sterling, I'm disappointed in you," he said. "I know Lisle's a troublemaker, but what could have possessed you to do such a thing?"

"I don't know, sir," said Theo. He really didn't. Now that the craziness was over, he couldn't believe that he'd thrown the stone. It was as if he'd been possessed by a demon of some kind.

"You don't know! I see. Well, we'll have to find out what Father Philip thinks about it. I can't imagine he'll be best pleased."

The summons came less than an hour later.

"What do you think he'll do?" asked Theo as they crossed the quadrangle on their way to the headmaster's study. He felt sick with apprehension, whereas Esmond walked with a spring in his step, as if he didn't have a care in the world.

"Beat us, of course, and maybe write to our parents. But nothing more than that. You're his blue-eyed boy, and he wants to keep on the right side of my father."

They waited outside the headmaster's door, sitting on two hard-backed chairs. Theo looked up at the portrait of the founder and remembered Sergeant Raikes's lurid description of his execution. At least they weren't facing "'angin, drawin', and quarterin'," he thought, trying to find some silver lining in the black cloud hanging over their heads.

"Where's the sergeant?" he asked Esmond. "I thought it was his job to drag us over here."

"It's probably his day off," said Esmond. "But you know what he'd say if he was here, don't you?"

"T'aint the agony; it's the disgrace," said Theo, and they both started to laugh.

And it was just bad luck that Father Philip chose that precise moment to open his door to call them in.

Afterward, Theo thought that Raikes was right: the agony was entirely secondary to the disgrace. Father Philip hit hard, albeit not with the tied-together canes that turned out to be a figment of Alwyn Thomas's overactive imagination, but the pain was transient. What stayed with Theo was his self-disgust at his willingness to submit to the punishment. That was the disgrace.

He never forgot the instructions on where and how to bend over the ugly Victorian hard-backed chair in the corner of the room, whose purpose was now revealed, the tap of the cane on his upended buttocks as Father Philip set his mark, and, worst of all, the shaking of hands at the end that legitimized the assault. It was true that he'd been in a state of shock at what had just happened when he'd taken the headmaster's outstretched hand. But it was a poor excuse. He should have turned away, keeping his hands in his pockets like Esmond said he had. But instead he'd given in and then listened deferentially while Father Philip had told him that he hoped he'd learned his lesson and would go back to being the credit to Saint Gregory's that he'd been up to now.

He hated Father Philip and he hated Saint Gregory's and he hated himself, and he wished he'd ripped the stupid cane out of the headmaster's hands and broken it over his knee.

"He might have expelled you for that, although I'd say on balance it's unlikely," said Esmond, who'd been patiently listening to Theo rant for the previous ten minutes. "You won him the Challenge Cup, which is what he cares about more than the Second Coming, and he needs you to retain it next year. The old bastard knows which side his bread is buttered. I'll say that much for him."

"Why don't you care?" asked Theo, outraged by Esmond's lack of reaction to what had happened.

"I'm used to it. I've been beaten so many times and I suppose I welcome it in a way. It reminds me of what I'm up against—something which you seem to have been blissfully unaware of up to now."

"It feels like you set it all up," said Theo sourly.

"You didn't need to throw the stone."

"I knew what you'd do if I didn't."

"I wanted you to see what this place is really about. And I'm happy that the lesson does not seem to have been lost on you," said Esmond. "You asked me to keep an open mind, and that's what I'm doing. I think on the evidence of today that there's hope for you yet, Comrade Sterling."

Theo looked away, refusing to meet his friend's eye. He felt no hope at all at that moment, just a rage against everyone and everything boiling up inside him with no outlet for expression.

Father Laurence took Theo aside several days later and suggested that they should take a walk.

To Theo's surprise, they went up to the abbey, entering through the narthex and sitting on two chairs at the back. It was early evening and the building was cavernous and empty, except that far away on either side of the high altar, Theo could see a few monks in their black habits sitting in their stalls. Some had hoods over their heads, giving them an otherworldly appearance in the twilight coming in through the high windows of the clerestory. Silence hung like a presence in the air.

All at once, a bell rang somewhere out of sight, and the monks began to sing, or rather chant: a pure music that rose and fell with no apparent harmony or rhythm, but with a timeless beauty that felt like a balm to Theo, soothing away the agitation that had been gripping him for days. The notes seemed to have a life of their own, independent of those giving voice to them.

Across the aisle from where Theo was sitting, a single candle was burning in a votive stand at the entrance to a side chapel that was barely the size of an alcove. Above the empty altar, a dark baroque picture of a saint was barely visible in the gloom, eyes raised expectantly toward heaven. Theo wondered who the candle had been lit for as it flickered now toward extinction, dripping wax down onto the black iron of the stand. The small act of remembrance touched him and he thought all at once of his father, whose face appeared vivid in his mind's eye after months when it had become amorphous, dissolving with time. The physicality of the sensation jolted Theo, who felt for a moment as if his father was there beside him in the church.

And then as quickly as he had appeared, the ghost of his father was gone, and the chanting voices of the monks seeped back into Theo's consciousness like water washing away a picture from a slate. But the candle that had sparked the vision was still alight and, looking hard at its guttering flame, Theo adopted it as his own: a pledge against time to keep the past alive.

When vespers were over, Father Laurence took Theo to a side door in the north transept, and they walked out into the monastery garden that Theo had never entered before and sat on a bench beside a white marble statue of Mary set in a bed of Christmas roses. The moon had risen, illuminating the gravel walks and the snowdrops under the wintry trees, and, looking up, Theo was able to pick out the window of the room that had been Lewis's, high in the eaves of Cardinal Newman House.

He missed Lewis's plain-speaking benevolence. His obvious decency and natural enthusiasm had been a counterweight to Esmond's insistence on unraveling every aspect of school life and holding it up to adverse judgment. Without him, Theo was finding it hard to resist Esmond's gravitational pull on his heart and mind. Even when Esmond was not there, he was aware of it like a recurring whisper in his ear.

"Life can be very confusing sometimes," said Father Laurence, breaking the silence.

Theo drew in his breath. It was as if Father Laurence had been reading his mind. "Why did you bring me here, Father?" he asked.

"So you could see that there can be beauty and peace in the world if you choose to look for it. There are places where you can go to be quiet and to pray, and then in time the best way forward in your life becomes easier to perceive."

"I don't pray," said Theo. "I can't." There was something about the still silence of the evening that stimulated him to honesty.

"Then you can just be still. Esmond is never that. He is in a hurry to change the world, and perhaps he will. He is brilliant and magnetic. But he is selfish, too, and you should remember that, Theo, because he could take you to places you don't wish to go."

"He won't," said Theo. "I make my own decisions." It came out harshly, which was not what he intended, but his need to push back against Father Laurence's advice was instinctive. He denied Esmond's influence over him because he didn't want to think about whether it might be malign. Esmond was his friend. That was what mattered.

Father Laurence sighed. "I spoke to you before about this," he said. "But I fear that what I said was not enough, although perhaps stronger words would only have made matters worse. You were always going to be vulnerable to someone like Esmond."

"Why?"

"Because you have lost your father and are looking for a new leader, and because you have known the bigger world and have suffered in it. Such an experience can make school seem absurd, but you need education because you are still only sixteen. You are too young to be trying to change the world."

"That's not what I'm doing," said Theo, withdrawing into himself again. He recognized the truth of his housemaster's insights, but that just made them seem more threatening and invasive.

Father Laurence nodded. He looked weary as he gazed out across the twilit garden.

"Is that all, Father?" Theo asked.

"Yes, I'll show you the way out."

Theo had wanted to be gone, but now he felt a stab of sadness as Father Laurence let him through a door on the other side of the garden that led back to the school. It was as if he were leaving a magical kingdom behind, to which he would not be able to return.

He walked away but then stopped and turned, calling to Father Laurence by name.

The door opened again just as it had been about to close and Father Laurence reappeared, framed in its arch.

"Yes?" he said.

"I'm sorry, Father," said Theo. "I just wanted to thank you. That's all. I liked the singing and the garden. They are beautiful, like you said."

"And peaceful," said Father Laurence with a smile. "There's value in that."

"Yes," said Theo. "Good night, Father."

"Good night, and may God bless you."

Theo felt Father Laurence's eyes on his back and he longed with a sudden ache to turn again and ask to be readmitted to the twilit garden, but he knew that that moment had passed. A breeze had picked up, and he felt it cold on his face as he walked away down the path toward the school.

In May, Theo received a letter from Frank. In the almost two years since Theo left New York, his old friend had remained a faithful correspondent, and letters covered with heavily postmarked American stamps regularly arrived every couple of months, but they were always disappointingly short, consisting of a series of pithy remarks about the weather and the fact that Frank and his mother were keeping well, and sometimes a reference in baseball season to how the New York Yankees were performing in the race for the Major League pennant. Frank had many talents, but Theo had soon realized that letter writing was not among them.

But this letter was different. It was much longer, and Frank had compressed his handwriting to fit more words on the page. After thanking Theo for his last letter, he wrote that his mother had been in the Jewish hospital for two weeks after suffering a fall. It had been touch and go for a while, but he was pleased to say that she was now making a good recovery. God be thanked.

Then he went on:

> But while my mother was there, an old woman died in one of the other wards.
>
> Death happens all the time in these places, of course, but this one was different, because that evening, her husband didn't leave when visiting hours were over. He must have hidden somewhere—under the bed maybe—and in the morning, the nurses found the two of them lying side by side in the narrow bed. Both dead, and he was holding her hand.
>
> There was a lot of talk because something like that hadn't happened before in the hospital, and I suppose that was why the nurses mentioned their names—Yossif and Leah Stern. They're not uncommon names so I went to the Registry and found out their address because I wanted to make sure. They'd been living with another family in a tenement off Essex Street and the man there said that they had had a son, Micah, who'd married a gentile. So, I knew then that it was them—your grandparents—and I thought I ought to tell you because you've got a right to know.
>
> I'm sorry, Theo. More than I can say. They're buried in the same cemetery Michael is. I thought you'd be pleased about that. I can show you where when you come back.

There was more, but Theo couldn't bear to read it. He crunched up the letter in his hand and began to cry. Hard, wrenching sobs that racked his body. He had to get out, to walk, feel air on his face. He staggered blindly up from his chair, knocking over a coffee table that was in his way, pulled open the door of his study, and collided head-on with Esmond, who was coming the other way.

"What is it? What's happened?" Esmond asked.

"Nothing. I need to be alone. That's all," Theo muttered as he pushed past his friend, heading toward the staircase.

But after a moment, he heard running feet behind him and felt a hand on his arm, pulling him back. "What are you doing, Esmond?" he demanded angrily, turning around. "I told you I need to be alone."

"No, you don't," said Esmond, using his free hand to open the door of his study, before pushing Theo inside. "What you need right now is a friend, and that's why I'm here."

Theo was too surprised to resist. He stumbled into the room and collapsed heavily into the familiar armchair where he'd sat so many times before, and watched as Esmond pulled the mutilated Bible out of the bookcase and extracted the hip flask from inside, just as he had that first time when Theo had cried about his father.

He had been a frightened greenhorn brat back then, and now he was the most popular boy in the school. But how much had really changed? he wondered as the brandy hit the back of his throat, flooding him with a sudden softening warmth. It was still only Esmond who really knew him, still only Esmond who really cared. The news he'd just received would mean nothing to anyone else. Except his mother, who'd probably be dancing for joy when she found out that her hated father-in-law was gone from the world.

"My grandparents died," said Theo. His voice was flat, drained of emotion. "A month ago, I think. Maybe more. I don't know how long it takes an airmail letter to get here." He held up Frank's crumpled letter and began straightening it out. The date didn't matter. It was just a way not to have to think about what had happened.

"How?" Esmond asked.

"In the Jewish hospital in New York. Here, you can see for yourself," said Theo, holding out the letter.

Esmond read it twice before handing it back. "I'm so sorry," he said, putting his hand on Theo's arm. "Your grandfather must have been an extraordinary man. To be able to let go of life like that when so many cling to it for no reason. It's like the end of a great love story. The two of them together in the bed, hands entwined."

"You're right," said Theo, looking up. He felt unexpected comfort in Esmond's words. His grandfather *had* been extraordinary. The day he'd spent with him had been the most memorable of his childhood, and the things the old man had told him were still vivid in his mind.

One day! That was all he'd had, when there could have been so many more. It hurt Theo to the quick to know that his grandparents had been only a few streets away all that time he'd been living in the Lower East Side with his mother. If she'd only allowed him to carry on looking, then surely he or Frank would have found them. But instead she'd made him promise to forget them, just the same as his father had done in Washington Square. They were both selfish, thinking only of themselves. Not like Esmond, who was the only one who really cared about him. Apart from Frank, of course, who couldn't help him because he was on the other side of the world.

"What are you thinking?" Esmond asked, holding out the hip flask.

"That Father Laurence is wrong and that you are my one true friend," said Theo, raising the flask to his friend in salutation before drinking a deep draft to wash away his tears.

In the days that followed, Esmond spent every waking hour with Theo, going out of his way to be the best possible company. They played jazz records and drank beer, and Esmond even came up to the playing fields and watched a rugby match during which he stationed himself at an inaudible distance from Father Philip and delivered with perfect mimicry an exaggerated imitation of the headmaster's exhortations from the touchline. It wasn't one of Theo's best games, as his attention to the ball was frequently distracted by Esmond instructing him and his teammates to "kick the opposition where it hurts" and "beat the swine to a pulp," but laughter made him not care, and he felt a grim pleasure when Father Philip marched off enraged at the end after Saint Gregory's ended up losing by a heavy margin. Theo hated the headmaster now and would have liked nothing better than to kick him where it hurts if he'd had the chance.

He was grateful to Esmond for the distractions, knowing that his friend was trying to help him get through the first period of mourning when the news of his grandparents' deaths had left him raw with grief and anger. But by the end of the week, he was calmer and wanted to talk about them.

"My grandfather showed me a photograph album that day he took me to his apartment," he told Esmond. "There were pictures of my ancestors who died in the pogroms. He said that when he and my grandmother were gone, then I would be the only one left to know who they were and where they came from. He wanted me to honor them, I think."

"How?"

"I don't know," said Theo, shaking his head in frustration. "I don't even know their names. Just that they were Jewish and that they wouldn't give it up, even to save their lives."

"Perhaps it wasn't just about them that he was talking. Perhaps it was about all Jews," said Esmond thoughtfully. "Because the persecution is still going on, you know. In Germany, Hitler is taking away their rights, shipping them off to concentration camps. There's one near Munich called Dachau where they're worked and starved to death. The SS beat them with clubs and hang them from iron posts if they try to resist."

"But there's nothing I can do about any of that," said Theo. "This is England, not Germany."

"It's happening here too. Mosley's British Union of Fascists has got fifty thousand members already. Mussolini's filling its coffers, and the right-wing newspapers are telling their readers to join. Here—look at this!" said Esmond excitedly, pulling an old copy of *The Daily Mail* from a stack of newspapers on his desk and pointing to the banner headline: Hurrah for the Blackshirts!

"Mosley's as antisemitic as Hitler. I can promise you that. Once he's got power, there'll be Dachaus all over England, so we have to stop him before it's too late. That's how you can honor your ancestors."

"I don't understand," said Theo, shaking his head. "What can we do?"

"There's a BUF rally at the Kensington Olympia in London next month. They're expecting fifteen thousand to show up, which will make it the biggest one yet, and if we can get enough of our people there, then maybe we can halt them in their stride. But it's not just that. This is the best chance we've had to show the bastards up for what they really are. Most of them are vicious thugs like Hitler's Brownshirts, and if people here can see that, then they'll turn against them. The British aren't like the Germans—they don't like that kind of street violence. But we have to invite it to make it happen; we need to put demonstrators inside the hall, as well as outside."

"We—who's we?"

"The party's organizing the protest, but yes, I'm talking about us being a part of it. This is what we've been waiting for, Theo—an opportunity to do something that really matters. Not like handing out *The Daily Worker* to down-and-outs in Carborough."

"But we could get hurt?"

"Yes, but not too badly, I hope," said Esmond with a reassuring smile. "And afterward, if it all goes as we hope, then we'll be able to feel that we made a real difference in the world. What do you say?"

"I don't know," said Theo, overwhelmed by the enormity of the decision he was suddenly being asked to make. "When's the rally?"

"In two weeks' time—the seventh of June."

"That's a Thursday," said Theo, calculating the days.

"Yes."

"The weekend would have been better."

Esmond nodded. They both understood the significance of the day. If the rally had been at the weekend, then they might be able to find an excuse to get a leave of absence from the school and go to London. On a Thursday, they'd have to play truant and take the consequences.

"They'll probably let you back," Esmond said. "The Old Man won't want to lose his best rugby player, and you can blame it all on me for leading you astray, if that helps. I'm not coming back, so I won't need to defend myself."

"Not coming back! But I thought you were going to try for Oxford."

"That was my parents' idea, not mine, and I'm done with all that now. I'm not going to be any help to the cause, stuck inside an ivory tower."

"Jesus!" said Theo, feeling that everything had accelerated away from him suddenly. It was as if his whole relationship with Esmond had led up to this moment, which had crept up on him completely unawares.

"You don't have to do this, you know," said Esmond, opening his hands in a gesture of release. "I'll understand if you don't."

But he wouldn't. Theo knew that. And he couldn't bear the thought of losing Esmond again. His friendship and good opinion mattered more to Theo now than any other consideration. He felt that no one else cared about him, and the school had been poisoned for him by the beating he'd been subjected to by Father Philip. The soft words of Father Laurence in the garden couldn't change any of that.

He remembered what his grandfather had told him about his Jewish ancestors and the importance of being true to who you are. *"Because without that you are nothing, worse than nothing."* The Fascists wanted to hurt Jews and deny people their democratic rights, and this was a chance, perhaps the only chance he would ever have, to be true to himself and strike a blow for all that he believed in.

"I'll go," he told Esmond. "Count me in."

15

OLYMPIA

They left on the Thursday morning after answering the roll call at morning assembly. They crossed the playing fields and slipped away through a gate at the back of the school grounds into a copse, where they used the shelter of the trees to change out of their uniforms into the casual clothes that they had brought with them in their shoulder bags. Then they followed a track and cut back down to the bus stop on the main road, where they waited nervously, thinking that it would not be too long before one of the passing cars would screech to a halt and disgorge a schoolmaster or monk ready to drag them back to Father Philip.

Secretly, Theo would not have been unhappy with such an outcome, although he kept his cold feet to himself. He hadn't tried to get out of going because he knew that changing his mind would mean the loss not just of Esmond's respect but also of his own, which he valued more than his safety or his future. However, he couldn't be held responsible if fate now intervened and put a stop to their adventure before it had even begun. An attempted truancy would merit punishment but certainly not expulsion, whereas premeditated participation in a London riot could well lead to that end.

Looking back across the road to the tower of the abbey rising above the trees, he felt a stab of regret for what he was leaving behind, perhaps for the last time: his comfortable study and his friends. They were shallow perhaps and nothing like Esmond, but they liked him and he had shared his life with them for nearly two years. In that time he had become part of a tradition, captured in the photograph of the first fifteen taken at the end of the rugby season, now hanging on the wall of the main hall at the end of lines of similar framed pictures stretching back to the nineteenth century. In the photograph, he sat in the position of honor at the center of his team, holding the ball with which Saint Gregory's had won the Challenge Cup, and underneath, his name was recorded on the mount in black ink: THEODORE STERLING, LEADING TRY SCORER.

That tradition—that sense of being part of something bigger than himself, as his stepfather had once put it—called to him now as the bus appeared around the corner of the road. The summons was unexpectedly powerful and he closed his eyes for a moment, trying to push it from his mind.

"Come on. All aboard. We haven't got all day, sonny," the conductor called down to Theo, breaking into his introspection.

"Sorry," said Theo, stepping up. He could see Esmond with his back to him, taking his seat, and he didn't want his friend to be aware of his hesitation.

The die is cast, he thought, remembering Caesar at the Rubicon as he sat down beside Esmond, and then laughed at himself, thinking that boarding a bus was hardly analogous to taking a Roman army across a river. But the laugh sounded hollow in his ears and he breathed deeply, trying to prepare himself for what lay ahead.

They got to London early in the afternoon, and Esmond promptly led Theo down into the underground, where they took a series of subway trains, walking from one to another down long, cylindrical, white-tiled corridors echoing with the cacophonous noise of hundreds of hurrying footsteps. And then, just as it seemed to Theo that they would never see daylight again, he followed Esmond onto an escalator that took them up out of the troglodyte darkness into the afternoon sunshine.

They were in Acton, a run-down but not impoverished neighborhood in West London, with no trace of greenery anywhere in sight to relieve the ubiquitous concrete, except for a sickly sycamore tree on the other side of the road, under which a newspaper vendor was calling out the headline: MOSLEY RALLY TONIGHT—MPS TO ATTEND.

Theo had been lulled by the long train journey into feeling that their evening destination was far away, but now it seemed suddenly close and real, sending a shiver down his spine.

They walked down a road full of dusty shops until they came to the dustiest one of all—a bookshop with a bell that jangled as Esmond pushed open the door.

The window was so dirty that only a gray light entered the interior, so it was hard to make out the titles of the books crammed haphazardly into the shelves that lined the walls, but Theo recognized from Esmond's study some of the left-wing magazines that were spread out across the tables—*Student Vanguard*, *The Daily Worker*, and *Russia Today*. In a glass cabinet behind the counter were replicas of Esmond's white plaster statue of Karl Marx as well as representations of Engels, Lenin, and Stalin, whose iconic photograph in military uniform stared down at the customers from the wall above, inside a black frame.

Underneath, wedged in beside the cabinet, the owner of the bookshop sat on a high stool with a face that seemed to have been constructed as a caricature of the Soviet leader—the same thick walrus mustache and wide forehead with the hair brushed back above—but the overall effect spoiled by a pair of rimless glasses perched on the end of his nose.

"Hullo, Esmond," he said without moving. His stillness was unnerving. "Who's your friend?"

"Theo Sterling. I've told you about him before, Jacob. You remember?"

"Of course. I remember everything. You know that," said Jacob, tapping the big dome of his head with a smile that came and went in an instant. "But what I don't remember is agreeing to provide him with one of our valuable tickets for the show tonight."

"He'll do the job as well as me," said Esmond. "I wouldn't have brought him if I didn't think so."

"I'm sure you wouldn't," said Jacob evenly. "But what you think doesn't matter, does it? You're a foot soldier in this business. One of many, carrying out party orders, and you'd do well to remember it, instead of jeopardizing the security of the whole operation by bringing along boys who haven't been vetted and could rat us out to Mosley before we've even got started."

"I told you I'll vouch for him," said Esmond angrily.

"And I told you, you can't," Jacob shot back. "The party needs comrades who are disciplined, not schoolboys who think they know best. Now make yourself scarce while I have a chat with young Theo here."

Esmond opened his mouth to respond, but then thought better of it, and turned to Theo instead. "You'll be fine. He won't bite," he said, and then pulled open the door, which jangled again as he walked out.

Jacob didn't move and didn't speak. He just gazed at Theo, who shifted uncomfortably from one foot to the other, wishing there was somewhere to sit down.

He felt intimidated. He'd never seen anyone talk down to Esmond in the way this Jacob just had, and he was shocked at Esmond's submission to such treatment. But he was angry too. He'd risked everything to come, and now this old huckster was accusing him of being a rat.

"How old are you?" Jacob asked.

"Sixteen. I'll be seventeen in October."

"You're American," said Jacob, sounding surprised.

"Yes. Didn't he tell you that?"

"Maybe. So why are you here?"

"Because I don't like Fascists and bullies and people taking away other people's rights and because Esmond made it sound like we could wake England up to what's going on before it's too late."

"Are you a Communist?"

"I don't know. Maybe I am. There's something badly wrong with capitalism, and the Communists seem to be the only people who are trying to do something about it and about the Fascists. I know one thing I'm not, though, and that's a rat, so I'll thank you not to call me that again." Theo spoke without thinking, with the words tumbling out of him in a rush, but at least this had the merit of conveying sincerity.

Jacob looked at Theo quizzically for a moment and then got down off his stool and pulled back a curtain, disclosing a small pantry where a teapot was sitting atop an iron samovar. He poured tea into two small white cups and brought one over to a table near where Theo was standing and cleared a space for it among the magazines. Then he carefully transferred a tottering tower of books that was piled on an upright chair behind it down onto the floor and ushered Theo to sit.

"Do you believe me?" asked Theo. His mood had changed from the morning. He couldn't stand the idea of being excluded from the protest, now that there was a question mark hanging over his involvement.

"That you're not a rat? Yes, I think you've satisfied me on that point," said Jacob, smiling. "But I am concerned that you don't know what you're getting yourself into. You could get hurt. You know that?"

"Isn't that the point?" said Theo.

"Yes, in a way. Has Esmond told you what to do?"

"No."

"The disturbances are staged through the evening, beginning from when Mosley starts speaking, whenever that is. Every four minutes, in different parts of the hall, so the Fascists won't know where the trouble's going to come from next. You and Esmond will be nearer the front, and you'll have to wait for over an hour. Do you think you can do that?"

"Yes," said Theo with absolute conviction.

"I'd have put you in at the beginning if I'd known how young you are, but almost all the tickets have gone out now, so there's nothing to be done. It's Esmond's fault for not telling me you were coming."

"He's young too," said Theo. "But you trust him, don't you?"

"About the big things, yes. He's one of the best we've got."

Theo nodded. He thought the same. Esmond inspired him, and at that moment he would have followed his friend wherever he led, even through the gates of hell.

They went out for dinner at a workman's café next to the station. The menu chalked on a blackboard by the door offered an incomprehensible choice between bubble and squeak and toad in the hole. Ashamed to confess his ignorance, Theo chose the toad and was pleasantly surprised when the sausages-in-batter dish turned out to be delicious.

Esmond wanted to order beer, too, but Jacob stopped him. "You'll need to have all your wits about you tonight," he said.

He went over the instructions again, checked their watches, and gave Theo a small white card on which he'd written down the telephone number of the shop. "Call me if you need to," he said. "And good luck to both of you. This'll be the most important night of your lives. Make the party proud."

The words went to Theo's head even more strongly than beer would have done, and the aboveground train journey to Olympia passed in a haze of terraced houses and advertising hoardings and squat chimneys belching smoke. Once, the train stopped without explanation at the entrance to a tunnel and they looked out of the window at an ugly embankment of pale, churned-up soil in which a few brown weeds were clinging stubbornly to life. Theo gripped his armrests and willed the train to move, imagining what it would be like if they had to remain here imprisoned in the carriage as the sky got dark outside and history was made without them, a few miles down the line.

But the delay was short and they arrived at Olympia in good time. There were police everywhere, directing people coming up the escalators either to the left, where there was a big sign reading **TICKET HOLDERS ONLY**, or to the right, where a covered glass walkway led around to the road. Theo couldn't see the crowd that was out there, but he could hear it: a great baying, booming noise that unnerved him, even though he wasn't going to show it.

He started toward the left, taking the ticket that Jacob had given him out of his pocket, but Esmond pulled him back.

"We're early," he said. "There's no point going in yet. I want to see what it's like outside. Jacob said the party's got thousands here from all over the country. Come on."

The crowd dwarfed anything Theo had ever seen in New York. They were packed together in a seething mass being kept back from the entrance area by a squadron of mounted police. The protesters' faces under their flat caps were contorted with passion as they shouted anti-Fascist slogans and waved placards and clenched fists. Some were losing their balance but were prevented from falling by the tight press of bodies all around them.

Theo felt excited by their angry energy, but he was frightened too. His legs felt weak and he had to force himself to keep up with Esmond, who had found a way to get close to the front by edging along the side of the roadway nearest to the station, where the crowd was less concentrated.

Close up, the horses appeared huge and terrifying to Theo as they neighed and reared and clawed the concrete with their hooves, and the faces of their riders were taut with nervous concentration as they gripped the reins with one hand while holding their truncheons ready in the other. How much longer could they control the animals? Theo wondered.

Beyond the horses, Theo caught glimpses of men and women in evening dress getting out of Rolls-Royce and Daimler automobiles and hurrying into the hall through the monumental white-stone entrance archway, pursued by the jeering catcalls of the demonstrators.

Above their heads, newspaper photographers were leaning their cameras out of the upper windows in the hall's facade. At a distance, it was easy to mistake the lenses for the barrels of guns and the cigarette smoke of the cameramen for puffs of gunfire smoke. There was a palpable sense of danger in the air, as if an immense storm was about to break, even though there was not a cloud in the evening sky.

All at once the crowd surged forward, waving their placards and breaking into a deafening chant:

Hitler and Mosley, what are they for?

Lechery, treachery, hunger, and war!

Between a gap in the horses, Theo caught sight of a column of men in black led by a tall man whom even at a distance Theo recognized from the newspapers. Mosley! Seeing him shocked Theo. The enemy had always been an abstraction, but now he had taken physical form. It made their mission real, and he was glad that he'd come.

The Fascists were marching five abreast up the empty roadway beyond the police line and turned in tight formation as they approached the hall and went inside. They were singing, but their voices were drowned out by the crowd, who had now switched to a variation of the previous chant:

One, two, three, four—What are they for?

Thuggery, buggery, hunger, and war.

Theo wanted to laugh and he wanted to cry. His heart was pounding like a relentless hammer in his chest, and he thought he was going to be sick.

Esmond had hold of his arm. "It's time," he shouted, putting his mouth to Theo's ear to make himself heard. "Let's go."

They pushed their way back to the station, produced their tickets, and were waved through.

Inside Olympia, the noise of the crowd was muffled and soon disappeared as they walked down windowless corridors until they came to the metal stairway that matched their ticket number and walked up and out into the light.

Theo was overwhelmed. The vast size of the auditorium took his breath away as he craned his neck, looking up past tier upon tier of seats to high galleries under the great barrel-vaulted glass roof through which he could see a pale moon riding high in the twilit sky.

There must have been twice as many people inside the hall as outside, but their behavior couldn't have been more different. Instead of the deafening noise and chaos, there was an atmosphere of hushed expectation, and everything was rigidly ordered. There were no police, but the lines of stewards in black jerseys manning the aisles would not allow anyone to stand or mill around. They stood with their arms folded across their chests, exuding menace.

Soon every seat was taken, but still the minutes ticked by until the lights finally flickered and dimmed and invisible trumpets blew a fanfare. Four powerful searchlights that had been illuminating the empty speaker's platform at the front of the hall now turned their beams toward the back, where a phalanx of Blackshirts was entering, holding aloft Union Jacks and the black-and-yellow standards of the British Union of Fascists. And a few paces behind them came the leader, flanked by four young bodyguards. Mosley was unmistakable even at a distance because he was so much taller than everyone around him.

They came slowly down the wide central aisle as the audience on both sides got to their feet, shouting Mosley's name, and raised their outstretched right arms in salute, which Mosley acknowledged with a wave of his upturned hand. Theo noticed that a woman sitting next to him was crying, and she smudged her face with mascara as she reached up to wipe away her tears. He worried that sitting still amid the hysteria would draw attention to him and Esmond, but no one seemed to notice them. Everyone's focus was on the leader, who bounded up onto the stage and stood ramrod straight, facing his followers as the flag bearers arrayed themselves around the rostrum and the band played "God Save the King."

The din continued after the anthem was over, and Mosley let it flow over him for another minute or two before he raised his arm for silence and began to speak. Straightaway, Theo realized that this was a man in love with the sound of his own voice. It rose and fell, amplified to booming decibels by the loudspeakers, as Mosley switched from mourning the sacrifice of the soldiers who had fought in the Great War to unleashing his rage on the politicians who had betrayed them. He punched the air with his hand, and the floodlights picked out his rolling eyes and gleaming teeth and the flashing silver of his belt buckle against the black silk of his shirt. And then, as he paused for effect, the interruptions began.

The first was high up in a gallery near the back of the hall. It was indistinct to begin with, but then Theo caught it:

Hitler and Mosley, hunger and war.

It was the same chant as outside, but thin and ragged here in the great cavern of the auditorium. Mosley could have drowned them out if he chose, but instead he stopped his speech in mid-flow and the arc lights swung their beams up toward the disturbance, picking out a group of stewards who were attacking several protesters, while other Blackshirts were leaping across the chairs to join them. After a few moments the stewards manhandled the protesters to the nearest staircase exit and threw them out. There was a scream followed by a shocked silence, and Mosley began speaking again as if nothing had happened.

Four minutes later the protest was repeated, eliciting precisely the same response. And so the preplanned interruptions continued, erupting one after the other in different parts of the hall, and each time Mosley stopped, arms akimbo as he waited until his men had done their work under the blue-gray glare of the spotlights.

Now two young men and a girl rose up from their seats in the central stalls less than fifty yards from where Theo and Esmond were sitting. Theo could see the fear on their faces but the determination too. They had their arms around each other, supporting each other to stand, as they shouted, "Fascism is murder!" and "Down with Mosley!"

The girl was beautiful, with high cheeks and almond-shaped eyes and blond hair cascading down over her shoulders, and she was wearing an evening gown with blue flowers on a white background. Theo thought she must have dressed up to avoid suspicion, and his awareness of her planning made him feel connected to her, as if he knew her and they weren't strangers. She was so delicate and he wanted to reach out and push her back down out of sight before the stewards came, but he couldn't.

In a moment the girl and her two friends were surrounded and down on the floor, invisible as the Blackshirts pummeled them with their fists and kicked them with their boots. And then they were on the move again, carrying their victims away. Theo caught sight of the girl with her pretty dress half torn off and her head forced back by the pressure of the stewards' hands. It was appalling. He had to help her. He got up from his chair but immediately felt himself being pulled back down, and Esmond's mouth was at his ear again:

"Damn you, Theo! Stay in your seat! You agreed to wait. You can't back out now."

Theo closed his eyes and breathed. Esmond was right. He had to stay. But what was Esmond accusing him of? Trying to run because he was a coward, or trying to intervene to help the girl because he was brave? Which was it? He couldn't answer, but then he realized he wanted to do both, and so both were true.

He opened his eyes and the girl was gone, but he remembered her completely even though he'd seen her for less than a minute, and her eager face would remain imprinted on his memory for the rest of his life, not fading like his father's or others' that he loved and lost. He would remember her with an infinite sadness, as if he'd missed something that he knew he would never find again, and he honored her memory with a determination to stand up and be brave, whatever the cost.

There was pandemonium all around him. Chairs were flying through the air and people were screaming and heading for the exits and Mosley was shouting at them through the loudspeakers: "Keep your seats! Please keep your seats!"

His appeals had some effect, but it was the shift of the arc lights that really put a stop to the chaos. They were shining upward now, picking out a man who was clambering across the forest of iron girders that held up the great glazed roof one hundred and fifty feet above the audience down below. Five Blackshirts were up there, too, but they were hesitant in their pursuit, clearly frightened that they would fall. The man looked back at them contemptuously and shouted, "Down with Fascism!" and then pulled himself up acrobatically onto a higher platform out of sight, and the lights swung back to Mosley.

He was ranting about the Jews. "European ghettos are pouring their dregs into our great country. The dregs of humanity—you know who I am referring to!" he roared, and Esmond pulled Theo's arm and got to his feet.

"Down with Fascism!" he yelled, echoing the man in the roof, and Theo realized he was shouting too. At least he could hear a voice that sounded like his. And once he'd started, he couldn't stop. "Fascism is murder!" he cried. "They're murdering the Jews; they'll murder us all if we let them." He wasn't aware of his body or of Esmond, only his voice crying out in the wilderness, until he felt the blows coming and shrank into a ball, curling himself fetus-like on the hard floor as the stewards kicked him with their heavy boots. Then he felt their foul hands pulling him up and he couldn't resist as they twisted his arms behind his back, starting a new exquisite pain that he would have done anything to stop, but which was replaced with something new and even more terrible when they reached the top of the metal stairs and flung him down into the outer corridor, where more of them were waiting to administer a final crescendo of punishment before they finally threw him out into the street.

He lay on the ground where he'd landed. The pain was excruciating, but it was alleviated by his body's awareness that the blows that had caused the hurt had ceased. He moved his fingers and toes successfully but kept his eyes closed and didn't try to get up. He could hear the chanting of the demonstrators, but he paid it no attention: it was a background noise in his consciousness, irrelevant to his present situation.

"Can you stand? Can you walk?" This voice was close and he had to attend to it because whoever was speaking was lifting him, pulling his arm across broad shoulders. He began to move, tottering forward, and then he was sinking again and another voice was telling him to open his eyes. It was a young man with a beard and he was examining him, tapping and poking, and Theo cried out because it hurt, but the man said: "It's okay. You're lucky. They gave you one hell of a beating, but nothing's broken as far as I can tell."

Theo shook his head because he felt that he was the opposite of lucky, but it wasn't worth arguing, because it hurt to speak.

Theo couldn't see the other man—the one who'd lifted him up and helped him walk—because he was behind his head, but he heard him whistle in admiration and say: "You're a brave man, Comrade. A hero. Is there anything else I can do for you?"

"Where's Esmond?" Theo asked.

"No Esmond here," said the man. "Just you and me and Doctor Dan—well, he's more a medical student, actually."

"Second year at Saint Bart's," said Doctor Dan, handing Theo a bottle of water and a couple of pink pills, which he obediently swallowed without asking what they were.

"I need to go home," he said. "Can you help me?"

"Where's that?" asked the man who wasn't Dan. Theo could see him now—he looked like Frank Vogel. Solid and honest, someone you could depend on.

Theo could feel Jacob's card in his pocket, but he had no intention of going back to the bookshop. He wasn't going to get anywhere, living penniless in London. He knew he needed his stepfather's help if he was going to get back on his feet. "Mayfair," he said.

The man laughed. "You're joking, right? Are you some kind of toff?"

Theo shook his head, too battered and exhausted to try to explain. "No, I'm a hero," he said. "Remember?"

The man looked at him hard and then smiled. "So you are," he said, tipping his cap. "We'll have to walk a bit, but if you can do that, I'll get you in a cab."

The butler answered the door and had to half carry Theo inside, where he collapsed on a chair and closed his eyes. It had taken everything he had to get this far, and all he wanted to do now was sleep.

But he wasn't going to be allowed to do that. A scream punctured his stupor. His mother was shaking him and it hurt, so he screamed, too, to make her stop.

"Where have you been?" she shouted. "We've been so frightened since the school called us."

"I went to Olympia—to the Mosley rally," he said, too exhausted not to tell the truth.

"With this boy Esmond?"

"Yes."

"Father Laurence said he's a Communist. Is that true?"

Theo nodded.

"How could you?" she yelled. He thought she was going to shake him again, and he shrank away from her in the chair.

"How could I what?" he asked, playing for time. It was strange speaking in Spanish when he hadn't spoken it in months, and the raw immediacy of the language tore at him, cutting through his defenses.

"Take up with a Communist! After what happened to me—your own mother. They killed your grandparents. Doesn't that mean anything to you?"

"Not all Communists are the same," he said wearily, remembering the same argument they'd had in New York two years before. "Most of them are good men who want a just world, and are willing to sacrifice themselves for it too."

"A just world!" Elena repeated the phrase with contempt, practically spitting out the words. "It's a godless world that they want. All of them. Look at Russia now. It's just like my country. They're murdering the priests and the bishops, turning monasteries into prison camps. They've abolished Sunday and Christmas. Do you know that?"

"I know that religion is how rulers keep people subjugated when they have nothing," said Theo angrily, and he would have said more but the rush of emotion and the effort to speak were too much and he fell back in a half swoon, through which he was dimly conscious of his mother wringing her hands and talking, and then arms lifting him again like they had at Olympia and carrying him away.

He slept until the next afternoon, when Sir Andrew's doctor came and verified that Dan the medical student had been right and that nothing had been broken.

He gave Theo more painkillers and told him that his stepfather wanted to see him downstairs when he was ready.

All Theo wanted to do was swallow the painkillers and sink back into oblivion, but he knew he had to think. His mother and stepfather would want to talk about the future. They would make demands, and he needed to work out in advance how he was going to respond to them. He couldn't leave decisions that would affect his life to the whims of the moment.

Olympia—the name he forever afterward gave to his experience—had had a powerful effect on his psyche. He'd seen the enemy in the flesh and been attacked by them. The threat of Fascism had become real to him in a way in which it had never been before when he and Esmond had dissected the world order over endless cups of low-quality tea at Saint Gregory's. He was determined to fight them. That he knew. But he was far less certain about how to achieve his purpose.

One way certainly was to join the Communist Party. They were the only ones who appeared to be doing anything about the Fascist threat, while the Labor Party and the trade unions sat on their hands, and Theo agreed with the Communists wholeheartedly that the callous exploitation of the poor by the rich was intolerable on both sides of the Atlantic. He'd seen that, too, firsthand. He knew what it meant.

He'd been impressed, too, by the Communists' bravery and organization at Olympia, and he felt proud to have played a part in their attack on Mosley, but he remained less sure about the Socialist paradise that Marx had promised and the methods he'd proposed for achieving it. There was an embrace of violence and dictatorship in the doctrine that Theo distrusted.

The evils were there in Russia, however much Esmond tried to deny it. He vividly remembered the authoritative way in which Father Laurence had described Stalin's mass murder of the peasantry. Esmond had argued that Father Laurence was relying on a discredited source, but Theo had too high an opinion of his housemaster to dismiss what he said so easily. In recent months, Theo had kept his doubts about Esmond's arch-hero to himself as he'd worked to repair his relationship with his friend, but that didn't mean he didn't still harbor them.

So he was an anti-Fascist but not necessarily a Communist, and that was a good thing, he thought, because Communism was what his mother and stepfather hated above all else, with their rigid determination to see the world entirely through the prism of their religious faith. He'd seen that the night before with his mother: she'd become hysterical when she thought he had fallen under the spell of the Reds.

Maybe if he forswore Communism, he could earn their forgiveness, and then, with Sir Andrew's backing, he might be able to go back to Saint Gregory's and get a place at a good university. He wasn't going to change anything, living on bubble and squeak and trying to sell *The Daily Worker* on street corners. He needed to find a way to maneuver his boat back into the slipstream of life.

Theo closed his eyes, remembering Esmond leaning forward in his study chair and telling him: *"You can blame it all on me for leading you astray, if that helps. I'm not coming back, so I won't need to defend myself."* Not coming back! For the first time, Theo understood that Esmond had gone out of his life, and it made him feel that same sense of desolation he'd experienced in New York in the months after his father died. It brought tears to his eyes, but even as he cried, he realized that Esmond's parting gift had been a possible passport back into the world that Esmond despised.

He went downstairs slowly, hanging on to the banister of the staircase, feeling the pain of every step. He passed through the drawing room and into the library, where he was surprised to find a fire burning, even though it was summer. The crackling of the logs was the only sound in the somnolent house, and it was incredible to think that the great city was so close at hand on the other side of the high garden walls.

Above the hearth, a dark portrait in profile of a man in armor, some ancestor of Sir Andrew's, surveyed the room with a disdainful expression, and shelves of leather-bound books with well-tended golden spines bore witness to the present owner's literary tastes.

Everything from the crystal chandelier overhead to the thickness of the Turkish carpet under Theo's feet resonated wealth and privilege: appurtenances of the entitled world of the British ruling class that Theo, under Esmond's tutelage, had learned to set himself against. But he had to admit the room's beauty.

Its sense of history spoke to something in his soul—that same love of tradition that had kept him returning to the lines of old photographs in the hall at Saint Gregory's—and he felt a sudden longing for the school—his school—that had nothing to do with the calculations of advantage that he had been making before he came downstairs.

Theo advanced into the room, thinking it was empty, and then stopped abruptly when he caught sight of his stepfather sitting in one of two leather-backed armchairs by the fire. In profile, Sir Andrew's pale, aristocratic face bore an uncanny resemblance to the man in the portrait. He had a chain or something in his hands that he began to put away as he moved to get up, but then when he saw Theo's eyes on it, he held it up.

"It's my father's rosary," he said. "He gave it to me when I went to France in 1915, and I had it at the Somme. I believe it saved my life."

Theo did not know what to say. It was the first time he'd ever heard his stepfather refer to the war, other than his quick deflection of Father Philip's reference to it on that first day at Saint Gregory's.

"Was it bad? The war, I mean?" he asked, blurting out the first words that came into his head and immediately afterward wishing he could take them back because they were so inadequate to the question he'd wanted to ask.

"It was terrible," said Sir Andrew. "An abomination. And it must not be allowed to happen again." He nodded, as if he'd been talking to himself as well as to Theo, and gestured to his stepson to sit in the chair opposite.

"Your mother is very upset," he said. "And so I thought it best if I spoke to you alone."

Theo nodded, not objecting. Usually he was prepared to blame his stepfather for coming between him and his mother, but after what he had seen the night before, Theo thought he stood a better chance of a fair hearing without her present.

Sir Andrew said nothing for a minute and Theo waited watchfully, looking into the fire but keenly aware of his stepfather's knitted brow.

"Are you a Communist?" Sir Andrew asked eventually.

"No," said Theo, giving the answer he'd settled on before he came downstairs. The denial didn't feel like a lie as he said it, a fact that he filed away for later consideration.

"But you were with them last night," Sir Andrew pressed.

"Yes. They're the only ones who are trying to do something about Fascism."

"Mosley's a clown running a one-man circus," Sir Andrew said contemptuously. "He'll be forgotten by Christmas."

"Isn't that what they said about Hitler?" Theo hadn't come to argue, but he couldn't let his stepfather's casual dismissal of the Fascist threat pass without any response. Not after what he'd seen at Olympia.

"That's different. This country isn't Germany," said Sir Andrew. "And we're not here to talk about politics. It's you I'm concerned with. I need to know why you committed this act of lunacy."

"I wanted to make a difference," said Theo, falling back on the old phrase that he and Esmond had so often used as a basis for their aspirations.

"To what?"

"To the world. To make it a better place."

"Don't you think that's a bit of a tall order for someone your age?"

Theo opened his mouth to argue but then shut it again and nodded his head. He was convinced that he had made a difference at Olympia, but he knew he wasn't going to get anywhere with his stepfather if he wasn't prepared to swallow his pride and toe the line.

"Whose idea was it to go to London?" asked Sir Andrew, shifting tack.

"Esmond's."

"And do you regret it now?"

Again, Theo nodded, not trusting himself to speak. It hurt him to lie, even though he felt he had no choice.

Sir Andrew sighed, as if aware that Theo was not being sincere. "I don't understand you," he said. "You were doing exceptionally well at Saint Gregory's, and then you decide to throw it all away on an impulse. Which is the real you? I suppose you don't even know, yourself."

"I know I want to go back," Theo said. "Can you help me?"

It had been hard to say. It was the first time he'd ever asked his stepfather for anything.

"It depends on you," said Sir Andrew. "I've talked to Father Philip today, and they may be prepared to take you back if you write a letter expressing remorse and promising not to see or talk to this Esmond character. Saint Gregory's certainly seem to think that he led you astray and that there's some mitigation in that."

"Can I telephone Esmond and tell him?"

"No," said Sir Andrew, annoyed. "Aren't you listening? There's to be no more contact. You can write and tell him that, I suppose."

"But he may not get the letter, and then if he comes down to the school to see me, there'll be more trouble."

Sir Andrew tapped his foot with irritation and then gave way. "Oh, very well," he said. "Make the call before you write to the school, and then let that be the end of it."

Theo looked at his stepfather and felt a surge of gratitude. He needn't have helped, but he had. "Thank you," he said.

"You should thank your housemaster too. Father Philip told me that he had Father Laurence in his study, pleading your cause for twenty minutes this morning. It's a strange character trait you have, isn't it? You make your friends care for you, and then you let them down."

"I won't disappoint you this time."

"It's your mother you need not to disappoint. She's very highly strung, and self-inflicted trouble like this hurts her more than you can imagine. If you could turn over a new leaf and show her some love and kindness, then that would be all the thanks I need. Can you do that?"

"Yes, I think so," said Theo. It rankled with him still that his mother had stopped him finding his grandparents, but he knew there was nothing to be gained now by dwelling in the past and that what his stepfather was asking was hardly unreasonable.

"Good. Stay there," said Sir Andrew, getting up from his chair and laying a hand momentarily on Theo's shoulder as he went past him and out of the room.

He returned after a minute or two, holding Lamb's *Tales from Shakespeare* and put it in Theo's hand. "Better late than never," he said with a smile.

The next morning Theo used the telephone in the drawing room to call the number on the card Jacob had given him, and to his surprise it was Esmond who answered.

"Left Bookshop," he said. "Can I help you?"

"Esmond. It's me," said Theo, holding his hand around the mouthpiece to muffle his voice. He wouldn't have put it past his mother to be listening behind the door.

"Theo! Are you all right?"

"Yes. A bit sore."

"They gave us quite a beating, didn't they? But wasn't it worth it? Have you read the newspapers today?"

"No."

"Well, you should. Everyone's talking about how Mosley's Biff Boys behaved like a bunch of wild animals. The establishment's turning against them. And we did that, Theo. We showed them up for what they are. We changed the world!"

Theo was silent. He felt utterly happy for a moment, at a loss for words.

"Are you there?" asked Esmond.

"Yes."

"Look, I wanted to say sorry. I didn't mean for us to get separated. I went to look for you outside, but you'd gone."

"It's fine. I'm okay. I was just calling to tell you that they're letting me back . . ." Theo stumbled over his words, finding it hard to admit to the bargain he'd made with his stepfather.

"I told you they would."

"Yes, but there's more to it than that. I had to do what you said. I had to agree not to see or talk to you. Well, after this call. And I wanted to tell you myself."

"How long for?"

"I don't know. I've got to put it in writing."

"Who to?"

"The school."

"Well, if it's them you're promising, then it's only for as long as you're there. After that, you're a free man. It stands to reason."

"I suppose so."

"No, there's no supposing. It's definite. This is just a break for us. That's all. Okay?"

"Okay," said Theo, feeling better again. "What are you going to do?"

"Remember the picture in my room? Of Moscow? I think maybe it's time for me to take that trip. I'm going to work here until I've got the price of a ticket, and then I'll be on my way."

In the background Theo could hear the familiar sound of a jangling bell. "Look, I've got to go," said Esmond hurriedly. "It's a customer. Maybe I can sell him the complete works of Marx and Engels. Jacob's got a deluxe edition that's just come in. Commission on that would buy me a ticket tomorrow," he said, laughing as he hung up the phone.

But Theo didn't smile as he slowly replaced the receiver. He was filled instead with an aching sadness as he wondered how long it would be before he would see his friend again.

PART THREE

ANDALUSIA

1934–1936

But why are my thoughts in another country?

Why do I always return to the sunken road through corroded hills,

With the Moorish castle's shadow casting ruins over my shoulder

And the black-smocked girl approaching, her hands laden with grapes?

—*Edwin Rolfe, First Love, 1951*

16

THE VILLAGE

In July, they went to Spain. Sir Andrew said it was a new beginning for the three of them: living proof of the turning over of the new leaf that Theo had agreed to after the Olympia debacle. They could start being a family, just as Sir Andrew had always intended.

It was Elena's first visit to Spain as well as Theo's. Sir Andrew had close connections with the country. He had spent a significant part of his youth in Barcelona and Andalusia, where his family had business interests going back generations—something they had in common with many other English aristocratic families who had stayed loyal to the true faith through the Reformation and the persecutions of Queen Elizabeth. Like Theo, he had been bilingual for as long as he could remember.

He had wanted to take Elena to Spain as soon as they were established in London, but she had resisted, unable to cope with the prospect of another journey, albeit one much shorter than the crossing of the Atlantic. Now she agreed, and the voyage had been a success unmarred by Bay of Biscay storms that had been predicted but never materialized.

From Gibraltar they drove along the coast to Málaga, where they ate lunch on the terrace of an expensive restaurant overlooking the Mediterranean, shaded from the noonday sun by an arbor of magenta bougainvillea flowering in rich profusion.

They had been given the table with the finest view and Theo noticed how the waiters hovered obsequiously close to Sir Andrew, ready to respond whenever he signaled to them. He looked like he owned the place, Theo thought. A *señorito* among his lackeys.

At the end of the meal, the maître d' brought a dusty bottle to the table, showed it to Sir Andrew for his approval, and then carefully poured two-thirds measures into three tulip-shaped glasses.

"He's too young, Andrew," said Elena anxiously.

But Andrew brushed aside her concern. "Nonsense," he said. "I was drinking wine at my father's table when I was half Theo's age. It's time he learned about the good things in life."

"Smell it first," he told Theo. "Like this." He gently rolled the dark amber liquid from side to side as he bent over the glass, inhaling deeply.

Theo imitated him.

"Now what can you tell me?"

"Nuts," said Theo. "Hazelnuts. And salt, maybe. I'm not sure."

"Good," said Andrew, smiling. "And now drink slowly, savoring the taste on your palate."

It wasn't what Theo had expected. He had drunk wine a few times, but this was different: cold and dry and with a sharp, tangy flavor all its own, which he couldn't put into words. And then afterward there was a woody taste that he didn't know whether he liked or disliked.

Sir Andrew laughed, seeing the indecision on Theo's face.

"Do you know what it is?" Sir Andrew asked.

Theo shook his head.

"Sherry—it's an old amontillado fermented and fortified when I was not much older than you in my family's vineyards in Jerez, and then aged in oak casks in the vaulted cool of the bodegas. The aftertaste you were trying to understand is partly derived from the wood, which has to come from the Eastern United States. Quercus alba—the American white oak: no other tree will do. I was in New York buying casks when I met you and your mother, so in a way it is sherry that has brought us together."

"So this is yours?" asked Theo, pointing to his glass. He was impressed, in spite of himself. He'd always known his stepfather was rich, but he'd thought of his wealth as just money in a bank, not income derived from something real and romantic like a Mediterranean vineyard.

"Yes," said Sir Andrew, turning around the bottle to reveal the Campion name on the label as if it were a party trick. He pointed to the center, where there was a small picture of a woman in traditional Spanish dress with a rose in her hair and an enigmatic smile on her lips. "That's my grandmother," he said proudly. "My grandfather loved her, which is why he put her face on his bottles. She died before I was born, so I don't know how she felt about it, but I do remember my grandfather taking me down the stone stairs into the cool, dark vaults when I was a boy and telling me that his sherry was a homage to her beauty. There were tears in his eyes. It's my most vivid memory of him, one that I treasure."

"She was Spanish?"

"Yes, but her mother was from Mexico. Like yours. Perhaps I will buy another vineyard and put Elena's face on those bottles," said Sir Andrew, raising his glass to his wife, who blushed and laughed, drinking in the compliment. But Theo bridled, clenching his fists under the table. He had been fascinated by the sherry, but now he was angry again. He hated the way Sir Andrew acted the grand señor and paraded his marriage as if it were a Hollywood romance. It made Theo remember how his father had done the same, sitting over dinner at the family table in New York, describing his meeting with the young Elena in Penn Station. And now he was forgotten as if he'd never been, devoured by the Brooklyn worms, while Elena gazed starry-eyed at her second husband as if he were her first. At moments like these, Theo's gut ruled his brain, and no amount of rationalization could stop him hating his mother and stepfather.

He drank the rest of the sherry at a gulp, but Sir Andrew didn't notice, having eyes only for Elena.

After lunch, they drove into the center of the town and parked near the cathedral, standing in the square outside to admire the ornate stonework of the facade and the white tower soaring above it into the cloudless summer sky.

"There were meant to be two," said Sir Andrew with a smile.

"Two what?" Theo asked.

"Towers. They ran out of money to build the south one, which is why the Malagueños call the cathedral La Manquita—the one-armed lady."

Just at that moment, the bells in the tower began to ring: a joyous pealing—perhaps a wedding was being celebrated inside the church—and Theo looked across to his mother, who was craning her neck upward, past the belfry to the dome and cupola shining in the sunlight. The ecstatic expression on her face made him think of his father again, gazing up at the silver spire of the Chrysler Building on an equally beautiful summer's day four years before, and he was filled with a sudden sense of loss and vulnerability that pierced him like an arrow. Unexpected and razor-sharp.

Elena turned toward him, holding out her hand, but he instinctively drew back, seeing the tears in her eyes. His mother's uncontrolled emotion repelled him, just as it had when he was a small boy, but Sir Andrew had the opposite reaction, immediately going over to his wife and putting his arms around her.

"What is it?" he asked. "You can tell me, my love."

"It's just it's the first time . . ."

"The first time what?"

"The first time I have been in a country where the people speak my language and practice my religion. This beautiful church is the heart of this town. I can feel it beating—" Elena pressed her hand to her side as her voice broke. "Oh, I wish I had come here before," she went on, composing herself. "But I always feel so weak, as if I can't move or change anything. It's always been like that, but it's worse now, somehow. I don't know why."

Elena had her back to Theo, but he could hear what she was saying even though he didn't want to, and he could see his stepfather's face as he held her. Sir Andrew was frightened and Theo felt the fear, too, running through his veins like a contagion. He tried to suppress it but only half succeeded, knowing that the old terror of losing his mother was waiting in the wings, ready to spring out at him again like an evil genie released from its bottle.

Elena pulled away from her husband and took a handkerchief from her handbag, patting her cheeks and blowing her nose. She was smiling now and she turned to Theo, holding out her hand again, which this time he reluctantly took.

"I'm sorry," she said. "I know you hate it when I make a scene, but I can't help it. I'm crying because I'm happy. Because we are here, the three of us. In this place where God is too. Don't you ever feel that sometimes?"

Theo had his eyes on the ground, saying nothing. He wouldn't lift them because he felt sure that everyone in the square had come to a halt and was staring at them, even though he found that the opposite was true when he looked around a moment later, after Sir Andrew had provided the perfect answer.

"Like the sun shining in the rain," he said. "You are that because you feel everything—be it joy or sadness—without filter or translation. It's why I love you."

Elena nodded, and Theo could see in his mother's eyes that she felt understood. But by her husband, not her son. And Theo was on the outside, looking in, locked away with only bitter irony for company.

From Málaga they drove away from the coast across a rolling treeless plain the color of brick and yellow oxhide. The road was unsurfaced—little more than a wide track—and they stayed in third gear, bouncing through potholes and sweating profusely in the dry heat. The azure sea with its silver waves, lost to view behind them, seemed like a fading dream from which they had now awoken to the hard reality of a desert land. There was at most a trickle of water in the dried-out streambeds in which stunted pink and white oleander bushes clung to life alongside the ubiquitous gray-green agaves with their coarse, spiky leaves. Behind the car, a cloud of fine dust thrown up by the wheels hung in the still air like a curtain.

Sometimes they stopped to drink water and let a passing wagon drawn by a team of straining mules go by. Theo saw how the drivers shouted and cracked their whips and pitied the poor creatures anchored to their traces as they labored slowly on under the merciless hot sun. A lifetime of uncomplaining drudgery until they finally dropped dead, leaving their carcasses behind to be sold for leather and glue.

At a crossroads, a cart brightly painted with vines and flowers and laden with olives had been pulled to the side of the road under the shade of a grove of thick-leaved poplars. The driver was asleep in a hammock slung between the high front wheels, while his mule slept, too, standing up with only its tail twitching involuntarily against the attentions of the flies. A few yards farther on, a small wayside shrine made of peeling painted wood contained a chipped blue-and-white statue of the Virgin standing on a makeshift plinth. At Elena's insistence, they parked and went over. A small bunch of wildflowers was lying on the ground at the Virgin's feet, wilting now in the heat, and beside it, a handwritten notice weighed down with pebbles begged passersby to pray for the soul of a child, Maria Fuentes, killed here by a madman.

There was no date and no explanation. No answers to the obvious questions that sprang into Theo's mind—Why the killing? Why here? Just the hard, red plain stretching out on all sides baked dry by the sun. The child was dead. The madman had killed her. What was done was done. Elena crossed herself and prayed briefly before they returned to the car, leaving the driver and his mule still fast asleep under the trees.

Slowly, the road started to wind and climb toward the foothills of the distant snowcapped mountains. Men and women were working in the dusty fields, bent double as they hoed, and Theo was surprised to see teams of oxen pulling wooden plows. Nothing was mechanized except their car. It was as if they were driving backward, he thought, into a biblical world that had survived unchanged since the dawn of time.

They began to pass villages that appeared like splashes of white paint against the ocher-colored hills, with short columns of smoke rising into the still air above their crimson-tiled roofs. Outside one, they were stopped by a column of sheep moving slowly across the road like an eddying river. Below, a real stream defied the drought and trickled between the rocks where women with worn, leathery faces and hair tied up in kerchiefs were laundering sheets and shirts. They stopped their work and stood for a moment motionless, staring up at the car as if it were some alien visitor from another planet, and then as one went back to their washing.

"The peasant women are tough here," said Sir Andrew, looking down. "They give birth in the morning and are back washing their husbands' clothes in the afternoon. It's always been the same."

Theo saw his mother shudder.

There were more people on the road now as they drove on. Women with water jugs balanced on their heads as they walked and bent-over men coming down the paths from the hills with tied-up bundles of firewood and pine cones on their backs. Some were carrying such heavy burdens that Theo couldn't see their faces. They looked like some strange species of tree creature, he thought. Not human at all.

"What do they do with all that wood?" he asked. "It can't just be for themselves."

"The bakers need it to fire their ovens," said Sir Andrew. "They give the gatherers bread in exchange. It's not an easy life."

Such understatement! It was a terrible life, Theo thought. Not one worth living. He had never seen such work. The firewood gatherers endured worse than pack animals, who at least could stay upright under their loads. His mind reeled as he tried to imagine their wretchedness.

"Will we be there soon?" asked Elena, whose suffering in the heat made her oblivious to the misery of others.

"Yes. Very soon. These are my orange trees," said Sir Andrew, pointing proudly out of the window toward carefully tended groves running down the hillside as far as the eye could see in long, even lines. "We send them to Scotland for marmalade in the spring. It's a small business—not like the sherry—but profitable and guaranteed. The manufacturers in Dundee have to use these oranges because without them the taste changes. They tried switching to cheaper ones from Portugal in my father's time and lost half their customers, so I think they've learned their lesson. The British are connoisseurs when it comes to their marmalade." Sir Andrew laughed, and Theo wondered what else his stepfather owned. It was another version of Spain that he seemed to be projecting: a network of flourishing business interests flowing plentiful profits through the rural economy and into his capacious pockets, completely at odds with the vision of grinding poverty that Theo had been witnessing with growing disquiet outside the car window.

They passed a weathered stone calvary in a grove of silver-leafed olive trees and a sign announcing the name of the village as **LOS OLIVOS**.

"Half a village and half a town," said Sir Andrew with a wry smile. "Too big for one, too small for the other. The people have been arguing about it for years, but they can never come to a decision. So one day they are villagers and the next they are townsmen, and whatever you call them, they are insulted."

Ahead, the village-town climbed toward the silver-domed belfry and spire of the church rising above the tessellated roofs in the shimmering sunlight, and beyond and behind that in the haze, the pine-clad foothills skirting the mountains. Higher and higher, leaving the plain behind.

They drove slowly up through the narrow, winding lanes. Here, in the lower quarter, the single-story houses were no more than hovels with collapsing thatch for roofs and their once-whitewashed stucco walls fading to mottled gray, matching the faces of the inhabitants whom they passed here and there, leaning back against the crumbling masonry, staring into nothingness. Only the children were mobile, running barefoot after the car in their dirty smocks, with their hands outstretched and white dust streaking their tousled black hair. They were shouting, but Theo couldn't hear what they were saying through the closed windows of the car.

The confining walls on either side gave way as they entered a square with a small crumbling fountain in the center, dripping water into two galvanized tin troughs, where a donkey was drinking and a girl was filling an earthenware jug. Her face was turned away from Theo as she bent down, but she had a scarlet hibiscus flower in her hair—a stab of unexpected color amid the monochrome townscape.

Sir Andrew stopped the car, unable to go on because their way was blocked by an overturned cart that had lost a wheel. A sack or two of prickly pears had spilled out of the back onto the filthy cobblestones, and the children who had run after them into the square were busy picking the fruit up and dropping them as the thorns cut into their hands. The driver of the cart was yelling at them, but they paid him no attention.

Across the way, on the other side of the fountain, men in berets were drinking and playing cards at tables set up outside a small café, apparently indifferent to the commotion.

Sir Andrew wound down the window for a moment to shout at the driver to pull his cart out of the way, and Theo's senses were immediately overwhelmed by the acrid smells of the barrio—animal excreta and urine and rancid oil and smoke—and raucous sounds, too—a radio somewhere playing tinny flamenco, two invisible dogs carrying on a howling duet, and, closer at hand, the shrieks and cries of the children.

A few moments later the way was clear and they drove on, leaving behind the children and the girl whose face Theo had still not seen and now never would. As the car turned out of the square, he just had time to notice a line of red graffiti reading **VIVA LA ANARQUíA**, daubed on a wall that had previously been invisible behind the cart.

Looking back over his shoulder, Theo felt a secret excitement. The bent-over backs and the hollow stares of the peasantry were misleading. There was life here beneath the surface, and the same wish to change the world that Esmond had uncovered for him in England. *Anarquía*—he tasted the word silently on his lips, wondering who it was that had scrawled it so boldly on the wall with the trailing paint dripping down from the bottom of the letters like blood. He wanted to meet that person.

The car continued to climb and soon the village changed. The streets were wider now, and the houses were taller with tiled roofs and honeysuckle and bougainvillea trailing across their bright whitewashed walls, carefully pruned back from varnished oak doors and wrought iron grilles set over recessed windows. One door that they passed was open, and Theo caught a momentary glimpse of a shaded garden under fruit trees with a moss-covered fountain playing in the center, surrounded by ferns. A secret world hidden away from the burning sun.

Around a corner they came at last to a new square with the church at its center. Its architecture was entirely different from the rest of the village, built to last and to dominate. With its thick buttresses and iron-studded door, it seemed to Theo more like a fortress than a place of worship—a statement of intent in hard gray stone. The massive walls rose up above the surrounding houses to the open belfry that Theo had seen from below, with a heavy bronze bell hanging in its center. African swallows soared and swooped like tiny black airplanes around the dome, while the church's gleaming silver spire soared above them into the blue sky like a spear aimed at the sun.

Elena wanted to get out, but Sir Andrew insisted on driving on.

"We can go to Mass tomorrow," he said. "I will ask the priest. He is most accommodating. But now you're tired and we must get home. It's very close."

And so it was. A few more winding turns and they were there, driving in through a wrought iron gate between two rampant marble lions set on high pillars, and up past an ornamental garden to a long white house terraced into the steep hillside with a stone figure of the Virgin Mary in a niche above the door, her hand outstretched in a gesture of beckoning benediction.

"Welcome," said Sir Andrew. "Welcome to my childhood home." And going over to Elena, he picked her up in his arms as if she were weightless and carried her over the threshold into the cool, dark interior.

From the beginning Theo loved the house. It was built on three floors with its back to the hillside so that only the bedrooms on the top floor had views up toward the mountains.

On the ground level there were stables and storerooms with nets of fruit hanging down from the ceiling rafters—quinces and persimmons and Sir Andrew's own bitter oranges. There were hams, too, which kept through the summer if rubbed with salt, and jars of home-cured olives and dried apricots and figs stacked on shelves. A Shangri-La of food beyond the dreams of the emaciated peasants and children in the village below.

To the side, beyond the stables and the garage for the car, was the accommodation and office of Sir Andrew's steward, who watched over the house and the orange groves in his master's absence. He was a dour bachelor with hair tonsured like a monk's and a high, protruding forehead that Theo liked to think had expanded over time to retain the statistical information that he kept stored away inside. His mouth was thin, and he never smiled but bowed slightly whenever he encountered Theo in the hallways—his bows to Elena were deeper and to Sir Andrew a true bending of the back. He was called Señor Madera—Mr. Wood—and was always addressed as such. Theo thought the name entirely apposite to his character, and all the time he was in the house, Theo never found out if Señor Madera had a Christian name.

Above the ground floor were the main rooms of the house. At one end, with its own set of stairs going down to the storerooms and pantries, was the large kitchen presided over by the housekeeper, Señora Constanza, whom Theo liked from the beginning. She was as friendly as Señor Madera was distant and delighted in serving him exotic-tasting treats whenever he came visiting, just as she had done for Sir Andrew when he was a boy. She was also welcoming to Elena, who spent many happy hours in the kitchen learning about Spanish cooking, while reciprocating with recipes for Mexican dishes that she had once made for Theo's father on her Westinghouse electric range in New York. Such intimacy with a servant would have been unthinkable in Sir Andrew's house in London, but here it came naturally, adding to Elena's newfound happiness.

Beyond the kitchen was a large hall at the center of the house, suspended between staircases leading up to the bedrooms and down to the main entrance door. And from there, further paneled doors led into the dining room, where immensely heavy, elaborately carved chairs were assembled around a polished mahogany table that shone in the evening under the lights of a wrought iron chandelier, and then on into the salon with its red-tiled floor half covered with Moorish rugs, woven with geometric designs.

An oil painting of Sir Andrew's grandfather hung over the big stone fireplace in the salon—shades of black portraying the clothing and hair and necktie with only the flesh of the face, the narrow starched white of the shirtfront, and at the bottom of the picture, a glimpse of a pale hand holding a watch chain relieving the dark. He had been painted in middle age after the death of his beautiful wife, whose image he had placed on his sherry bottles in sunnier days, and Theo thought he could sense the suffering in the face behind the narrowed eyes and the slightly pursed, determined mouth, which reminded Theo of his stepfather when he was laying down the law.

There were other portraits, too, just like in London, and sometimes Sir Andrew pointed up to them as if they were old friends when he was reminded in conversation of some exploit or failure of his dead forebears. This connection back into a personal past and the associated sense that Sir Andrew conveyed of being part of a tradition with values and duties inherited from those who had gone before him irritated and attracted Theo in equal measure. Sitting in the salon in the evening with a glass of Campion sherry in his hand, he gazed into the dancing flames of the fire, listening to his stepfather talk, and thought of the contrast to his own history. Behind his mother and father lay nameless ancestors killed in pogroms and persecutions in distant unknown countries, leaving him now rootless and alone, washed up on another foreign shore.

Was his stepfather offering him a way to change his fortune? A way to belong? Had he been right to reject the offer of his name that Sir Andrew had held out and then courteously withdrawn on that first day at Saint Gregory's? Sir Andrew was the last of his line, with no son or heir. And yet, and yet . . . Theo heard the voice of Esmond telling him not to give in to temptation and join the ruling class, but instead to think for himself and not stand idly by while the few oppressed the many. The burning wood on the fire had been brought down from the hills by half-starved men bent double to the ground. The truth was hidden behind the dishonesty of the picturesque.

After dinner Theo liked to go up onto the *terrado*, the flat clay roof terrace above his bedroom, and sit in the summer twilight, gazing out at the immense panorama of the Andalusian landscape stretching away on all sides. Here, he was raised up in the sky facing the full moon as it rose lamp-like over the line of mountains to the east, while down below the roofs of the houses descended toward the vast plain in which the lights of other villages twinkled here and there in the gathering darkness. In a line of deeper blue on the edge of the horizon lit by the last rays of the sunset, Theo thought he could glimpse the sea.

He concentrated his mind on listening to the sounds of the evening: the desultory barking of dogs; the drip, drip, drip of the fountain in the garden; and the soft cooing of doves settling for the night. And if he listened hard enough, he could sometimes hear the faint magical twang of a guitar played by some lovelorn boy outside the window of the girl he was courting, or so Theo imagined. He yearned toward the music but without having any way to reach it. It hurt, laying bare the pain of his loneliness and isolation, but the ache excited him, too, because it made romance seem real and not just the stuff of books. He thought of the girl at the village water trough, with the hibiscus flower in her hair, whose face he hadn't seen.

And then the tolling of the church bell would wake him from his reverie and send him back down the cool stairs to his room, leaving the moon and the stars behind.

Theo loved the house, but he sensed, too, that it was coiled in upon itself, separated from the village and the land from which it was drawing its sustenance. It was like the other wealthy homes clustered around the hilltop, safe behind their iron gates with the church standing like a barrier between them and the barrio below.

He had seen how few people attended Mass when he reluctantly accompanied his mother and Sir Andrew to church on Sunday, two days after their arrival, and he instinctively understood that the church's thick walls and high tower were there not to welcome and unify but to dominate and divide. In this town it was the wealthy who were riding the highway to heaven, while the poor peered up at eternity through the eye of a needle.

Theo had spent the last two years in a bastion of privilege in the English countryside, and he wasn't slow to recognize that he had come to another rich man's citadel. He remembered the stench that he'd smelled when Sir Andrew rolled down the window of the car on the day of their arrival, and the daubed red scrawl on the wall of the tumbledown square in the village down below—*¡Viva la Anarquía!* There was another world out there, close but far removed from the expensive books and tapestries in Sir Andrew's salon and the musky scent of evening jasmine in his carefully tended garden. Esmond had taught Theo well, and he knew he must not remain on the *terrado*, looking down. Spain—the real Spain—was waiting for him, and he needed to go and find it for himself.

So, on that first Monday morning, he put an orange in his pocket and ventured out without telling anyone where he was going.

At first the way was clear as he retraced the route of their car journey from the church, which stood high above the houses like a beacon. But soon after that, he became lost in the twisting, narrow streets that all looked the same, with the sky no more than a strip of blue above his head. Downward, always downward, or so it seemed, but without ever coming to the end of the maze.

The smell of the real Spain became all too real now. The reek of rancid olive oil and garlic burning on invisible cooking fires kindled with rosemary and lavender brush was a pungent mixture of sour and sweet, but still not strong enough to overlay the universal stink of urine and excreta. The heat made Theo dizzy and increased his nausea, and he staggered over to the side of a broken-down house and regurgitated his breakfast into the gutter. On the other side of the street, an old woman with a face as wrinkled as a dried prune watched him with beady eyes, saying nothing. Flies buzzed around his spinning head and crawled in the vomit.

He called out an apology and then hurried on, ashamed and directionless, turning corners at random until he came out into another square even more rundown than the one through which he'd passed in the car on the first day. Two uniformed men wearing strange, shiny three-cornered hats sat on a bench in the far corner beside an open door, but Theo took no notice of them. He had eyes only for the gray fountain at the center, which he stumbled toward, desperate to drink. He swallowed greedily and pushed his face down into the trough as if he were a donkey. It was cool and he felt momentarily better, but now someone behind him had hold of his sleeve, pulling him back.

He looked around and there was no one. Down, and there was an old man with no legs, just stumps, pointing at them with one hand while he tugged at Theo with the other and began his ritual wail:

"Por el amor de Dios y de Maria Santisima, una limosna, caballero, una limosna . . ."

Alms, alms . . . Seized with an unreasoning panic, Theo twisted out of the beggar's grip and walked quickly away, leaving the crying, angry voice behind as he turned onto the first street he came to, hoping that it would take him back up to the church instead of down, farther into the labyrinthine heart of the barrio.

Behind him he could hear footsteps, accelerating as his grew faster.

He wanted to run, but his legs wouldn't obey his brain's command. He was too weak and exhausted and so he just stopped and turned around, taking his pursuer by surprise so that they almost collided with each other.

The man started talking straightaway, with his feverish dark eyes jumping from side to side. Theo could barely understand what he was saying. He was on the brink of hysteria, and his heavily accented Spanish was almost like another language. It seemed to lack half the normal consonants, so that it sounded as if his mouth was full of pebbles. The unexpected language barrier increased Theo's sense of alarm.

But slowly he began to make sense of often-repeated words—Señor Madera and Don Andrés, oranges, money—too little money and no money—and hungry—everyone hungry: he, his wife, his children. Each outburst was accompanied by a crazed nodding of the man's head and repeated rubbing of his emaciated stomach.

Theo was frightened but also appalled. The man's meaning was clear now: he had been paid so little by his stepfather's steward that he and his family had been reduced to starvation and semimadness. But how did he know who Theo was? How long had he been following him? And what was he going to do next if Theo couldn't give him what he wanted?

Theo never found out the answers to his questions, although he guessed later that the man must have seen him with his mother and stepfather outside the church when they went to Mass the previous Sunday and then recognized him when he was drinking at the fountain.

Behind the man's back, the two Civil Guardsmen whom Theo had seen in the square were quickly approaching. Abruptly, one of them took hold of the man and pulled him back, and, when he began to protest, slapped him hard across the face with the back of his glove. As the man reeled away, the guardsman seized him by the collar as if he were an animal and began frog-marching him back down the street. The quick brutality—over in a moment—astonished Theo, leaving him rooted to the spot, at a loss for words.

The second guardsman was asking him for his name. "Theodore Sterling," he whispered, but then added, "Campion-Bennett," because he was lost and wanted desperately to go home. The name worked like a magic spell. The guardsman bowed and offered with elaborate courtesy to show him the way, and in a ridiculously short space of time, Theo found himself back in front of Sir Andrew's house, feeling infinitely relieved and utterly ashamed.

17

ANTONIO

The rest of that day and half the next, Theo wrestled with whether to tell his stepfather about what had happened. He was nervous of appearing to interfere in Sir Andrew's business. But the man who'd accosted him had been starving—Theo had never met anyone so skeletal. Surely, he thought, Sir Andrew needed to know about that. Theo had resentments aplenty against his stepfather, but he didn't think he was cruel. Perhaps Señor Madera was deceiving his master about what was happening in the orange groves.

And Theo also needed his stepfather's help. He felt like a complete fool for getting lost and frightened, but wouldn't that just happen again the next time he went out if he didn't understand the lay of the land?

So, plucking up his courage, he made an announcement at the start of lunch the next day that he had something to say and then launched into the story of all that had happened, omitting only the one detail of how he had vomited in the street. It wasn't necessary to his narrative, and he was trying hard to erase that particular humiliating memory from his mind.

When he got to the part about the beggar, Elena, who had already shown signs of increasing agitation, couldn't contain herself any longer. "You should never have gone out alone, Theo. What were you thinking?" she demanded angrily.

Sir Andrew raised his hand before Theo could answer. "Let him finish," he told Elena, but she ignored him. "Anything could have happened!" she cried.

"But it didn't," said Sir Andrew, stopping her in mid-flow with the same authority in his voice that Theo remembered from when he had seen him commanding the attention of the congregation in the church in Gramercy Park. "Something happened to the boy, something specific. And I for one would like to know what it was. Carry on, Theo."

Elena was silenced and Theo finished his story.

Sir Andrew listened carefully, keeping his eyes fixed on Theo, and at the end he stroked his chin with his forefinger, reflecting on what he'd heard.

"This man who came after you—did he threaten you?" he asked.

"No. I was frightened because he was so agitated and I couldn't understand what he was saying, at least to begin with. But then I felt sorry for him," said Theo. "I've never seen anyone as hungry as that. It was like he could die of it."

Elena was wide-eyed, her attention distracted from Theo's disobedience by the shock of this new revelation. "Do you think this man does work for you?" she asked her husband.

"I don't know. Perhaps he did during the harvest and the sowing, when we take on extra hands," said Sir Andrew.

"But not now?"

"No. We only keep on a few regulars in the summer for irrigation and maintenance. It's always been the way."

"But surely you have an obligation not to let the others starve for the rest of the year? Isn't that your Christian duty?"

"No business could afford that," said Sir Andrew, sounding irritated. "You can't pay someone for nothing."

"But what are they supposed to do if they can't eat?" asked Elena.

"I don't know," he said. "It's not my responsibility. These matters are not your province, my dear. I think you know that."

"I know that as Christians we should help those who are hungry," said Elena, refusing to back down. "Isn't there something you can do, Andrew? Even if it's only a little? I feel so much that I could be happy here, but not if the people who work for you are starving."

Theo felt a surge of affection toward his mother. Her intervention had been the last thing he expected. She had never involved herself with Michael's business and, as far as Theo knew, she had followed the same policy in her second marriage. Up until now.

Sir Andrew looked equally surprised, and Theo thought for a moment that he was going to lose his temper. But then he shook his head instead, as if to rid himself of the emotion, and smiled. "You are my better angel, Elena," he said, bowing his head as if in submission. "You see the truth plain as a pikestaff when I can only see the obstacles in the way. I'll talk to Madera and see what we can do."

Elena's face lit up as he rose from his chair and bent to kiss her.

"And thank you for telling me about what happened, Theo," he said, turning to his stepson. "The village has clearly changed since I was last here, and your mother is right that you should avoid the barrio. But I can see it is no fun for you to be a prisoner of the house. That was not my intention when I brought you here. Let me see what I can do to solve the problem and, in the meantime, stay home. Agreed?"

Theo nodded, feeling better disposed to his mother and stepfather than he had in a long time. He admired the way his mother had stood up to Sir Andrew for what she believed in, when he was so strong and she was so weak, and he liked the way his stepfather had been prepared to listen. He would never have admitted it to himself, but at that moment it was almost as if he felt part of a family.

A solution to Theo's confinement in the house arrived quicker than he had anticipated.

The next day, the village priest, Don Vincente, came to lunch. He was a fat, hairless man in his sixties with a broad smile on his full lips and pale, watery eyes that darted this way and that.

He shook Theo's hand for longer than was necessary, holding it in his clammy palm, and complimented him on his Spanish.

"You speak the mother tongue, young man, like they do in Madrid," he said approvingly. "It's nothing like the half-Moorish babble they talk here. I was there last year for the wedding of the marquis's son," he went on, switching his attention to Sir Andrew. "The marquis did me the honor of sending an invitation, and it was a source of great satisfaction to me that I was able to assist with the celebration of the wedding Mass in the cathedral. I wish you could have been there to see it. It was truly a splendid occasion. The marquis is a man of God. Like you, Don Andrés."

Sir Andrew inclined his head, and looking down, Theo noticed the gleaming silver buckles on Father Vincente's shoes, with a glimpse of violet silk stockings showing beneath the hem of his cassock.

"The Church is so grateful for your generous donations," the priest went on. "I am sure Señor Madera has told you that just this last year, we have been able to rebuild our beautiful chapel. I made sure to give you a special mention at the service of rededication."

"What chapel?" asked Elena, curious as always about all things religious.

"It's on the hilltop, dedicated to Santa Leticia, our patron saint," said the priest. "The Moors dragged her up there to cast her from the cliff, but the Archangel Michael took hold of her as she fell and bore her gently to the ground so that she could continue God's work. It is a most holy place. You must see it while you are here."

"I should like to," said Elena eagerly. "Why did it need to be rebuilt?"

"It was burnt and desecrated by the Anarchists," said Father Vincente, crossing himself. "A terrible thing. But it will not happen again. The Guardia will see to that."

Elena drew in her breath as if she had received a blow, and her hands began to shake. Sir Andrew immediately reached out and put his hand on her arm. "It's all right, my love," he said softly. "It's not like you think. Yes, there were two bad years at the beginning of the republic when the Left was in power, but the Catholic Party won the election last year, and they have got everything back under control. And as Father Vincente says, there are Guardia here to protect us. You remember how they came to Theo's rescue the other day.

"My wife is from Mexico, so she has had firsthand experience of such outrages," Sir Andrew explained, turning back to Father Vincente.

"I am sorry to hear that. It is terrible what God's people have had to endure in that benighted country at the hands of the Red Antichrist," said the priest, his voice brimming with emotion as he crossed himself again. "I know of the great work you have done to help the Church in those parts, Don Andrés. Word of your goodness and bravery reaches us even from afar. Please be sure to tell me if I can provide any spiritual comfort to Doña Elena while she is here. I will be sure to include you both in my prayers."

"Thank you," said Sir Andrew and Elena, speaking at the same time. Watching them both, Theo had the sense that his mother's gratitude was more fervent than his stepfather's. He knew that his mother believed that priests were Christ's ministers who could do no wrong, but Sir Andrew was different. He was more cerebral than emotional, more English than Spanish, and Theo wondered if he shared his own instinctive aversion to the priest's flowery language and flattering words. All his talk of the marquis and Madrid jarred when men were starving a stone's throw from Father Vincente's church, and it hadn't escaped Theo's attention that the priest was eating second helpings of every course that was served.

"There is something you may be able to assist us with, Father," said Sir Andrew, reopening the conversation after the plates had been cleared. "My stepson got lost in the barrio the other day and was harassed several times. Fortunately, as I was reminding my wife, the Guardia were there to help."

"I am most sorry to hear that," said the priest, switching his look of compassionate concern from Elena to Theo, although he refrained from crossing himself this time. "It's not sensible for people of quality to go there alone. There have been attacks."

"I have told Theo that and he understands," said Sir Andrew. "However, I equally don't consider it fair to the boy to keep him immured inside this house all summer. I was hoping that you might be able to suggest a suitable companion and guide for Theo so that he can explore our countryside. It's beautiful at this time of year. I would see to it that whoever you recommend was properly remunerated, of course."

Father Vincente scratched his perspiring bald pate, looking doubtful, and then suddenly brightened. "I know the very person," he said. "Bernardo Alvarez, the café owner, has a son, and I am sure he would be happy to help. They are good Catholics. Shall I talk to him for you?"

"No, I'll do it myself. But thank you, Father Vincente. You have been most kind."

Sir Andrew summoned Theo as soon as lunch was over and the priest had gone, and they set out on foot, heading down the hill. He had put on a panama hat and was carrying a walking stick with which he beat a rhythmic tattoo on the cobblestones.

"Father Vincente always puts me in a bad mood," he told Theo. "He's a good man, of course, but all that scraping and bowing and crossing—ugh! It makes me want to scream. So I drink too much to try and keep my temper while he's there, and then I'm left with a sore head and am no good for the rest of the day. But maybe a brisk walk will help, and if his recommendation of old Alvarez's son works out, then it'll all have been worth it."

They walked across the square in front of the church through which Theo had passed on the day he got lost and approached the half-open door out of which a powerful smell of incense was emanating from the interior gloom—a world away from the bright afternoon outside.

But then, just as Theo thought they were going to go inside, Sir Andrew veered away around the side of the building and walked on through an archway into a much larger square with a tall fountain in the center, surmounted by a weathered stone statue of the Madonna. Women and girls were standing at its spouts, filling water jugs, while others were hard at work, washing clothes in the surrounding basin. On either side of them, two lines of pollarded plane trees raised their decapitated limbs fist-like to the sky.

A stone arcade ran down one side of the square with peasant women underneath, squatted down beside small piles of produce—onions and peppers and dried tomatoes laid out on burlap sacking. Beyond, opposite the archway through which they had entered, was an imposing building constructed of the same gray stone as the church that, as Sir Andrew explained, housed the ayuntamiento, the town hall and center of power in the village. The red-, gold-, and purple-striped flag of the Spanish Republic hung limply down over its closed entrance doors.

Opposite the arcade, on the west side of the square, shaded from the afternoon sun, groups of men in every kind of headwear, from broad-brimmed Seville hats to cloth berets, were sitting or standing at tables, set up outside a bustling café. Some were playing cards but most were talking all at the same time, shouting and gesticulating at each other and only stopping to toss off tiny glasses of some sort of clear spirit, washed down with tumblers of water. A radio loudspeaker set on the wall was blaring out a political speech, but no one was paying it any attention.

Without hesitating, Sir Andrew advanced on the café. As he approached, some of the noise died down as the men outside eyed him curiously, but he ignored them, striding in through the open door with Theo in tow.

Inside, there was a crowded bar behind which a big, burly man in a dress shirt, clearly the proprietor, was holding forth to his customers in a booming voice. All around, the walls were covered with bullfighting pictures and memorabilia—gaudy posters advertising long-gone corridas and photographs of matadors with their red capes held out at precise angles as bulls charged toward them across dusty arenas.

The proprietor stopped talking as soon as he saw Sir Andrew, pulled his necktie into place, and came out from behind the bar to greet his visitor. He walked with a pronounced limp, and Theo deduced from the lack of bend in his right leg that he was wearing a prosthetic, like Sergeant Raikes at Saint Gregory's. As if at a signal, everyone else in the room had become quiet, too, and Theo felt suddenly as if he were standing in the middle of a brightly lit stage, just as the curtain had risen.

"Don Andrés, you honor me with this visit," said the big man, bowing low. "May I offer you some refreshment?"

"No thank you, Señor Alvarez," said Sir Andrew. "Is there somewhere we can talk?"

"Of course, follow me," said the proprietor, leading the way through a door and down a long corridor to a room at the end that was completely unlike the raucous bar they'd just left behind. Everything was neat and orderly. An expensive walnut desk was positioned under the window with a swivel chair behind it and two upright chairs lined up on the other side, and several filing cabinets and a safe were arrayed along the far wall under two framed photographs of soldiers in military uniform, hanging side by side. It was the kind of office that Theo might have expected the mayor to be occupying in the ayuntamiento on the other side of the square, but not the proprietor of the village café.

If Sir Andrew was experiencing the same sense of surprise, he showed no sign of it. "This is my stepson, Theo," he said.

Señor Alvarez got up from his chair and made a short bow to Theo before turning his attention back to Sir Andrew.

"I heard you were married, Don Andrés," he said. "May I offer my congratulations."

"Thank you," said Sir Andrew. "But I am here on Theo's account. He is new to the village and would benefit from having a guide when he goes out, a friend of his own age who can show him the district and take him up into the mountains, perhaps. Don Vincente mentioned that you have a son who might fit the bill."

"Antonio? Why yes! It's an excellent idea," said Señor Alvarez, clapping his stubby hands. "Let me send for him now." He pressed a button on his desk and spoke rapidly into a speaker.

"I will pay him for his time, of course," said Sir Andrew. "Shall we say . . ."

"No, I would not hear of it," said Señor Alvarez, shaking his head vigorously. "You will be helping me by taking Antonio off my hands, and he will learn from your boy just as much as your boy will learn from him. About England and Buckingham Palace and important places he has never seen."

"Theo is American," said Sir Andrew.

"Even better. The White House and the Empire State Building. Antonio will be broadening his horizons. That's the point. Because what I can give my son is very limited, Don Andrés. I am just a simple soldier, you see. Not a man of culture and education like you. I lost my parents when I was young, and when I joined the Legion, I had nothing and knew nothing. My officers were my family and my teachers," he said, pointing up at the photographs on the wall. "I owe them everything. That's why I keep them here beside me—so I don't forget."

Theo turned around to look at the pictures. He had never seen anyone like the man on the right. Standing ramrod straight in a cocked hat, he had an eye-patch over his right eye, a bright-white glove on his right hand, and an empty sleeve over what had been his left arm. He looked quite terrifying.

"That's General Millán-Astray, Theo—the best and bravest man I've ever known," said Señor Alvarez, enjoying Theo's shocked reaction to the photograph. "He was my first commander in Morocco. We came to him as boys your age, and he made us into men. He told us that we were already dead, so we had nothing to fear, and we believed him. We became *novios de la muerte*, bridegrooms of death, and we cried *'¡Viva la muerte!'* when we rode behind him into battle, because we knew that to die in combat is the greatest honor, just as to live as a coward is the worst disgrace."

Señor Alvarez paused for a moment with a distant look in his eye, as if he was reliving one of his cavalry charges, before continuing:

"We were strong because we were together and because we believed in Spain and in ourselves and feared nobody. When the general came to see me in hospital after I lost my leg, he laughed and said we were a pair now, him and I—eye, arm, leg. And I laughed, too, even though the pain was terrible, and we sang the 'Hymn of the Legion' and all the other wounded soldiers on the ward joined in. It was the proudest day of my life."

Theo opened his mouth to speak, but nothing came out because he didn't know what to say. He felt amazed and appalled in equal measure by Señor Alvarez's incredible harangue. The world that he was describing was alien to anything Theo had ever known. But before he could repeat his impersonation of a dying fish, Sir Andrew came to his rescue.

"General Franco seems to have been more fortunate with his injuries," he said, pointing at the second picture with a hint of irony in his voice that was entirely lost on the grandiloquent café proprietor.

"Fortunate, yes, but that is because he is invulnerable," he replied with a wave of his hand. "The Holy Mother protects him. When we attacked, he was always out there in front, riding a white horse so that we could see him and follow him, but the enemy's bullets flew all around and never touched him. I saw it with my own eyes, and each time it was a miracle. I tell you, Don Andrés, that with more leaders like these, Spain would never have lost its empire and its honor."

Theo looked over at the man in the second picture, who could not have been a greater contrast to his mutilated colleague. Franco was short, with the beginnings of a potbelly jutting out from his uniform. His face seemed pale and soft, effeminate even, and it was hard for Theo to reconcile it with the intrepid warrior that Señor Alvarez was describing. Where Astray was fanatical, Franco was composed, but there was something distant and opaque about his eyes, which unnerved Theo.

There was a knock at the door, and a young man of Theo's age came into the room.

"Ah, Antonio," said his father. "Come and meet Don Andrés and his stepson, Theo. Don Andrés is giving you the opportunity to do something useful for a change. You are to be Theo's guide. He wants to see the mountains."

"Would this be something you'd be willing to do?" asked Sir Andrew, who had stood up to shake Antonio's hand.

"Of course he's willing," said Señor Alvarez before his son could answer. "He is if I say he is."

"I'd still prefer to hear it from Antonio direct," said Sir Andrew, who had kept his eyes on the boy while his father was speaking. Behind his stepfather's back, Theo could see a look of angry annoyance pass across the café proprietor's face. He was clearly not someone who liked to be crossed or have his authority questioned.

But Antonio grinned and the smile lit up his face, making Theo like him before he had even spoken. He looked nothing like his father, and the contrast between them was as marked as between the two generals on the wall. He was slightly built with curly hair and hazel eyes that sparkled with amusement and good humor. It was a candid, truth-telling face with no trace of the calculating craftiness that lurked under his father's thick-set brows.

"I'd be honored to guide," he said enthusiastically. "When can we start?"

"Why not now?" said Señor Alvarez brightly—all trace of irritation wiped from his face. "Give Theo something to eat, Antonio. I'm sure he's hungry, and you can discuss your plans. There are a couple of other matters I want to talk about with Don Andrés."

Theo looked at his stepfather, who nodded his approval, and five minutes later he and Antonio were seated outside the café, watching the world go by.

"Your father certainly likes bullfighting," said Theo, looking back through the door at the pictures on the walls.

"Oh, yes. Anything with blood in it," said Antonio, smiling. "Did he tell you about the Legion and being a bridegroom of death?"

Theo nodded.

"He always does that when he meets people for the first time."

"Why?"

"He wants everyone to know the kind of man he is. Or was, before the Moors shot his leg off and sent him back here to lick his wounds."

"He told us about the general with the eyepatch coming to the hospital."

"And singing the hymn. Yes, he's scary, isn't he? Did Dad tell you about the heads?"

"Heads? No."

"I'm surprised. He usually does. One time when the dictator Primo de Rivera went to Morocco to inspect the troops, Astray had one of his battalions line up with Moors' heads stuck on their bayonets!"

"What?" gasped Theo. "You're joking?"

"No, I'm not. It was his way of saying 'This is who we are!' It's one of Dad's favorite stories. Used to give me nightmares when I was a kid. 'Millán-Astray's coming,' he'd whisper in my ear if I got into trouble. 'I'll tell him what you did.' It worked every time! I'd run screaming to my mother. Not that she was much help. She was terrified too. I take after her and not him. That's the problem. Lack of backbone, he calls it, but it's nothing the army can't sort out, or so he says. We'll see."

"Do you want to be a soldier?" Theo asked, trying to keep up with this flood of personal information. Self-revelation was not something he'd been used to at Saint Gregory's, where the boys would suffer tortures rather than reveal details of their home life.

"No, of course not," said Antonio. "But I haven't got any choice, have I? So there's no point crying about it."

Theo was about to disagree but then remembered his own inability to stand up to his father over leaving school and going to work in the factory. For a moment he was back in the apartment off Union Square with his father's hand on his chin, forcing him to look up and give in. He understood about having no choice.

"When do you have to go?" he asked.

"In eighteen months. I could go to military school, but my father wants me to start from the bottom and work my way up. Like father, like son, he says. Except that we're not alike. It's my sister, Maria, who takes after him. She's strong-willed and has her own opinions about politics and the Church and pretty much everything else, but that's unacceptable, of course, because she's a girl, and so she's been packed off to Málaga to be straightened out by my grandmother, who's nearly as scary as old Millán-Astray. The problem for Dad is he's got his kids the wrong way round and it sends him crazy. 'Where's the justice?' he shouts and clips me around the ear because I've been daydreaming. So you arriving today is about as good news as I've had in a long time. I can't wait to get out of here."

"Me too," said Theo. Antonio's friendly chatter made him realize how lonely he'd been, and he felt a surge of excitement about this strange new country that he was now going to have the chance to explore.

It had become cooler as the sun sank down over the roofs, and the evening paseo had begun. The girls of the village were parading in a slow circuit around the square, either with each other or with their *novios*. They wore lace mantillas draped over high combs set in their lustrous dark hair, and walked with their heads and torsos held back, as if their upper bodies had no relationship to the swinging movement of their legs below. Their thin flowered cotton dresses clung to their full figures, and the polished tin jewelry around their necks shone like Cartier diamonds in the evening light.

Theo caught their scent on the air as they passed and the side glances of their velvety eyes, and he imagined what it would be like to touch the hand of one of them and feel the brush of her fingers on his wrist.

"It's not what you think," said Antonio, looking at Theo with wry amusement.

"What do you mean?"

"The girls look at you to collect your admiration like it's a coin to put away in their purses. But it's nothing more. They are as untouchable as the angels. Unless you want to marry one, of course, and I think you're a little young for that."

"I'm not doing anything," said Theo, annoyed by Antonio's ability to read his mind.

"Oh, yes, you are. You're falling in love, just like I do every night. Dreaming impossible dreams. The wine helps. Here, drink some more," said Antonio, laughing as he filled Theo's glass and his own.

Suddenly the parade stopped as three men rode up on tall gray horses with thick manes and massive chests, and dismounted at the café. One of them was much older than the others. He was grossly overweight and waddled as he walked, and his thick waxed mustache ended in spiny black points that seemed like twins to the small black pupils of his eyes, which peered out watchfully from the fleshy folds of his face. Beside him, a young man not much older than Theo was dressed from head to foot in white, set off only by a black hat and tie. The effect was so contrived as to be absurd and needed a devil-may-care flamboyance to carry it off, but a weakness in the young man's chin and a petulance about his mouth achieved the opposite effect, making him appear ridiculous instead of impressive. The third man, walking behind with a rifle over his shoulder, was clearly a servant to the others.

Straightaway, before they had even gotten to the café, Antonio's father appeared at the door to greet the new arrivals with a show of even greater fawning humility than he had laid on for Sir Andrew, and ushered them to the best table, laid with a lace cloth and gleaming silver cutlery.

"Who's that?" asked Theo.

"The cacique, Don Fadrique. He runs everything around here. Nothing happens without his say-so. Tomorrow at dawn his foreman will be out in this square, picking people for work, and if you're a troublemaker or in one of the unions, then you're going to be left behind. And if you protest, then you'll end up on the wrong end of a beating or worse from one of his men—like Calvo over there. He went too far and killed one of Don Fadrique's tenants a couple of years ago when he'd been sent to collect the rent, but he wasn't even charged. Don Fadrique's got everyone on his payroll—except the Guardia, of course, but they're on his side anyway."

"And the boy in white?"

"That's his son. Pedrito—Little Peter, we call him, because he hasn't got the brains or the balls to be a full Pedro." Antonio laughed. "You never see him before the afternoon because he's too busy powdering his face in front of the mirror and trying on his fancy clothes. My father wants him to marry my sister, and he might well ask her if he gets the chance."

"Why?"

"Because she's the most beautiful girl in the village, although that may not be enough to persuade Don Fadrique to give his consent. He values everything in pesetas, and beauty isn't worth as much as a title or a dowry to a dried-up old devil like him."

"What does your sister say?"

"She's an Anarchist. She doesn't believe in marriage. To anyone, and definitely not to a dumbass like Pedrito. That's why Dad's sent her off to my grandmother, so that the old battle-ax can knock some sense into her. Two high Masses a day and twenty rosaries in between, backed up with a solid program of good works with the Little Sisters of the Poor. I pity her. I really do. Because Dad's not going to give up. With Don Fadrique as his father-in-law, he can join the ayuntamiento and really throw his weight around. He'll be Don Bernardo instead of plain old Señor Alvarez. Respect is what he craves, and he'll do anything to get it. I tell you, he'll be on at your stepfather to help him, too, now that I'm guiding you and he can ask a favor in return. That'll have been what he wanted to talk to him about in the office after we left. I know how his mind works."

"Does your sister have other admirers?" Theo wasn't going to admit it to Antonio, but the absent Maria had captured his imagination as he tried in vain to conjure up the image of a girl who could be more attractive than all the goddesses he'd been watching in the square.

"Yes, of course she does," said Antonio. "Every boy would like to be her *novio*, but they know they've got no chance. Except Primitivo over there, who won't take no for an answer." Antonio pointed over at a swarthy, thick-set boy sitting on a wall on the other side of the café, dressed in dirty workman's clothes with a red kerchief tied around his neck. "He thinks she's his *novia* just because she's talked to him about politics a few times. But I reckon he's just playing at being an Anarchist so he can get her attention. He really wants to be a bullfighter, but he's not quick enough. Sometimes he falls over his own cape and everyone laughs at him when he practices, but not so he can see. He's vicious when he's crossed. Like Calvo."

Looking over, Theo saw that the boy had a gang of friends with him, packed in close together but giving him room at the center of their group. His mean, thin-lipped mouth was set in a permanent scowl, and even at a distance he gave off an air of restless menace. Theo quickly looked away so that the boy wouldn't see him staring.

"Why is everyone here?" asked Theo. The square had filled up as they had been talking, and it seemed as if the whole village was present.

"For the movies!" said Antonio excitedly. "I was wondering when you were going to ask. Look, they're putting up the screen now."

He pointed and Theo could see that men were climbing like monkeys in the plane trees, pulling up what looked like an enormous sheet that they set about tying at the corners to the branches.

All at once, a projector somewhere began to whir and the word **DRÁCULA** appeared, grainy and white on the sheet screen, accompanied by a burst of cheering.

It was extraordinary. Theo had seen the same film in New York when he haunted the cinemas in search of distraction from his demons in the spring of 1932. Not once but three times, and he vividly remembered how Bela Lugosi had joined his dead father in the nightmares that he endured in the airless tenement apartment that he and his mother had been forced to move to after his father's suicide.

He recognized the same sets in this movie, but the actors were different and spoke in Spanish. However, it wasn't just the strange mirroring of past experience that affected Theo so profoundly; it was also the sudden unexpected transformation of the square. Its essential characteristics of sunshine and noise had given way to a deep darkness and quiet in which the sinister voice of the count echoed back off the walls of the arcade. As if by a magic trick, Andalusia had become Transylvania.

All around Theo, the villagers gazed up, enthralled, at the actors and actresses who were there but not there. He could see their wondering faces lit up in the glow of their cigarettes: the movie was a miracle, just like the archangel-assisted parachute landing of the town's patron saint, eight hundred years earlier. A cinematic wonder sent down to them from a Hollywood heaven.

And as Dracula and his acolytes crossed the stormy sea to England, dispatching the ship's terrified sailors one by one, Theo became absorbed in the drama too. The heroine was beautiful, and he imagined her as Antonio's sister and felt a shameful rising in his body as the count leaned over her while she slept, the long fingers of his hand stretched out over her breast and his teeth white and sharp as he bent to her neck. Several of the girls in the audience screamed at this moment of crisis but were quickly silenced by their neighbors.

At the end, the audience erupted into cheers when Van Helsing impaled Dracula through the heart in the catacombs and rescued the girl, but Theo wondered whether this was to exorcise the guilt that they felt at having acted as the count's vicarious accomplices as he sucked her blood before.

The whir of the projector slowed to a final rattle, and the magic spell was broken. Paraffin lamps were lit and everyone was talking and getting to their feet as the screen sheet was lowered from the trees.

"Thank you," Theo told Antonio, holding out his hand. The evening had been one of the best of his life, and he felt the inadequacy of his words.

Antonio kept his hands in his pockets and shook his head. "I'll walk you home," he said. "Remember, I'm your guide now. I don't want to be blamed if you get lost in the dark."

"I won't," said Theo, but then remembered what had happened before and smiled sheepishly. "All right," he acknowledged. "Maybe I would."

They walked through the archway and past the looming buttressed wall of the church.

"I reckon Don Vincente would make a good Dracula," said Antonio with a chuckle.

"Why?" asked Theo.

"Because he sucks our blood and likes pretty girls. I've heard tell he had a niece living with him years ago who wasn't his niece, and there's a rumor that he has children in Seville. I don't know if it's true. Don't look surprised! All the priests in Andalusia used to have nieces for housekeepers and everyone would call them Father except their children, who would call them Uncle."

Antonio roared with laughter, enjoying his joke. Theo felt a little shocked by his friend's open contempt for the Church and didn't know at first what to make of it. He thought of his mother's enthusiastic reception of Don Vincente and wondered what she would say if she heard about his niece who wasn't his niece. And then, quite unexpectedly, he remembered Esmond's Bible hollowed out to accommodate the silver flask and his perfect mimicry of Father Philip as he recited the Song of Solomon, and he wanted to laugh with Antonio, but to cry, too, for the loss of his irreverent friend. He felt it as a stabbing pain in his heart and wished he could bring Esmond back from wherever he was to share this new adventure on which he was now embarked.

"What are you thinking about?" asked Antonio curiously.

"The past," said Theo. "And the future. When can we go to the mountains?"

"As soon as you like."

And they both laughed, feeling as only the young can that anything was possible in the world.

It was late. Theo crossed the hall softly and began to climb the stairs, which creaked under his weight. But as he turned to go up the next flight, Sir Andrew called to him from the salon.

"How was your evening?" he asked.

"It was wonderful," said Theo enthusiastically. "There was a film in the square, and then I walked back with Antonio."

"You like him?"

"Yes, very much. Thank you for finding him for me. I want to see everything, but it's impossible without a guide. I realize that now."

"It's a hard country to get to know," said Sir Andrew. "I've been coming here all my life, and I feel I understand it less now than when I was a boy like you. Perhaps it's changing, or maybe I'm seeing things for the first time." He spoke meditatively, and Theo had the sense that his stepfather was continuing a train of thought that he had been immersed in long before they'd begun their conversation.

"I liked the look of Antonio too," Sir Andrew went on after a moment. "I can usually get the measure of a person by looking him in the eye, and I'd say he's cut from a different cloth from his father."

"He certainly thinks he is."

"Does he?" said Sir Andrew with a chuckle. "I'm not surprised."

He got up and went over to a curved table by the wall and poured two glasses of sherry from a decanter and then handed one to Theo, ushering him to sit.

"From your vineyard?" Theo asked, and Sir Andrew nodded but was otherwise silent. Theo stared into the dying embers of the fire, quiet but with all his senses alert, still tingling with that hair-trigger excitement that had possessed him in the square.

"Alvarez is a brute," said Sir Andrew. "Of course he is, but his violent talk resonates with the people here at some deep level. That's why his café's so successful. It's because he's telling his customers what they want to hear. They're obsessed with death. All of them, even if they don't want to admit it. Do you know what they call a cemetery in Andalusia?"

Theo shook his head.

"*La tierra de la verdad*—the land of truth, because as far as they're concerned, everything else is an illusion. Death is what matters. Look at the bleeding, broken Christ in the church here—caked blood, broken tendons, crying agony on his poor, tortured face. He isn't a representation of violent dying, he *is* it. The artist made it real because that's what the people wanted. It's what they still want."

"To be bridegrooms of death," Theo said, remembering Señor Alvarez's bizarre phrase.

"Yes, exactly. *Novios de la muerte.* It's why they love bullfighting. Because it's about man pitting himself against death, staking everything on that one final moment that everything else has led up to. The matador twitches his cape, flicking it away like the edge of a dancer's skirt, and the bull is deceived—or not. Usually, he dies, but not always. Sometimes it's the man, gored like Joselito in Talavera. I was there that day. I will never forget it. The greatest matador in Spain coughing up his lifeblood. I felt the crowd's pain but their ecstasy too. It was monstrous. Awful."

"But you didn't feel it? The ecstasy, I mean?" asked Theo, sensing how his stepfather spoke like a witness and not a participant. Looking in at Spain from the outside.

"No," said Sir Andrew. And it seemed to Theo that there was a note of sadness in his voice. "I have spent nearly half my life in this country, but I am not Spanish. If I am at home anywhere, it is in the North, where there's mist and fog and nothing is certain, not here in the glare of the sun, where everything is exposed and there's no room for doubt or mercy. This is a land of inquisition," he said and laughed softly.

"And yet I am Catholic," he went on thoughtfully. "I'm nothing if I'm not that, so my allegiance should be to Spain, which has spread the faith through the centuries and fought for it on all four continents. Not to England, which has been the sworn enemy of the true Church. But which side would I have been on when the armada sailed? England or Spain; Elizabeth or Philip? Francis Drake was an admiral of the English fleet that defeated the Spaniards in the Channel in 1588, but he was also the pirate who stole three thousand barrels of sherry from Cádiz the previous year and brought the drink to England and made it popular. In that sense, he is the father of my business. So is he my true ancestor? I don't know."

Theo looked down into his sherry glass and understood Sir Andrew's ambiguity. In that moment, he felt a sense of kinship with him that he had never experienced before. It had never occurred to Theo that his self-assured stepfather, embedded in a historical tradition dating back through centuries, should suffer, too, from that sense of not belonging that Theo had endured all his life.

He wanted to express this connection to Sir Andrew but found himself tongue-tied because he needed the right words and they wouldn't come. Perhaps it was a reluctance to expose his own weakness to a man whom he had become too easily accustomed to think of as his enemy.

He remained silent and Sir Andrew got up to rake the fire, and the moment of opportunity passed.

"Good night, Theo," said Sir Andrew as they parted at the top of the stairs. "I'm pleased about Antonio."

"Yes. Thank you for helping me. It means a lot," said Theo. It was the best he could do. Better than nothing at all.

18

THE MOUNTAINS

Theo and Antonio set off for the mountains at the beginning of the following week.

They left in the early morning, riding two gray mules. Theo stroked his burro's high ears and soft coat, looked into his big trusting eyes, and laughed as the mule wrinkled up his wet papery nostrils, exposing a set of enormous teeth that looked like a pair of miniature picket fences stacked one on top of the other. He had red tassels hanging from his bridle and a garland of leaves around his neck to keep off the flies.

"What's his name?" asked Theo, sitting uneasily in the saddle.

"Hers, you mean. Yours is Isabella. And mine's Ferdinand. The king and queen of mules! What's wrong? You look nervous."

"I haven't ridden before."

Antonio looked dumbfounded and then burst out laughing, but stopped when Theo didn't join in.

"I come from New York. Remember?" said Theo. "They ride buses and trains over there."

"A land without mules. I can't imagine that," said Antonio, shaking his head. "I'm sorry I laughed. Riding's easy, though—just use your feet a little and pull the reins to stop. The mules know the paths, and yours will follow mine. There's no need to push them."

It was as Antonio said and Theo slowly relaxed as they rode up out of the village. Behind them, cocks were crowing in their wooden cages on the flat roofs of the housetops, their sharp, thin cries challenging and answering each other across the cold morning air.

Then, just as it seemed that they had left all the houses behind, they rounded a bend and saw in front of them a tumbledown cottage hemmed in by weeds and thornbushes. It was a desolate place, but a thin plume of smoke rising from its crooked chimney showed that it was still inhabited. As they approached, Antonio moved over to the other side of the track and urged his mule forward with Theo's following behind. And once they'd passed the cabin, he crossed himself several times.

"Why are you doing that?" asked Theo curiously as he drew level.

"Because a witch lives in there," said Antonio nervously. "She won't harm us if we leave her alone, but it does not pay to get too close and attract her attention."

It was Theo's turn to look incredulous. "Witches don't exist," he said. "They're just in fairy stories."

"Of course they exist," said Antonio. "I've seen them flying on All Hallows' Night. They steal babies from their mothers so they can inject their veins with the infants' blood and become young again, and rich old men pay them for it, too, so they can continue their villainies."

"Nonsense," said Theo, shaking his head. "These are all just crazy superstitions. And people can't fly. It's physically impossible. Everyone knows that."

"Who are you to say?" demanded Antonio angrily. "You don't live here. You know nothing."

Theo was silenced. It was as if a chasm had unexpectedly opened up between him and his new friend, and he realized in that moment that a great deal more divided them than horse-riding skills. When they had talked in the square, Antonio had seemed almost sophisticated and even cynical in his description of the conflicts in his family and in the village, but here he was talking of flying witches as if they were an established fact of life.

But Theo also understood that he had seriously offended Antonio, who had generously offered to act as his guide and had clearly gone to a great deal of trouble to organize the present expedition. "I'm sorry," he said. "You're right. I don't know anything about this country. Please forgive me."

Antonio, who had been looking thunderous, smiled and clapped Theo on the back. His forgiveness was immediate and complete, and they rode on into the foothills, leaving the witch's cottage behind.

The ground on either side of the track was elaborately terraced and planted with olive trees and wheat, which blue-shirted peasants were already out reaping. Their curved sickles flashed silver in the early sunlight, matching the glow on the leaves of the trees. Between the terraces, irrigation channels running down from streams higher up the slopes were bordered by blue periwinkle and purple-and-white iris, and skylarks hovered above their heads, singing. It was a beautiful day and not yet hot enough to make the riders sweat.

Soon they reached the chapel that Don Vincente had spoken of. Theo remembered that the priest had made possible his introduction to Antonio and so was inclined to think well of him, notwithstanding his general unctuousness and Antonio's allegation that he had kept a concubine in days gone by. He wondered, too, whether he should take Antonio's stories with a pinch of salt henceforward in the light of his supernatural beliefs.

No expense had been spared on the rebuilding of the chapel, and the stone had not yet weathered and so was almost white. Theo tried the door, but it was locked. He walked around to the side window and looked in, meeting the glass eyes of a statue. It was so lifelike that he thought it was a real woman for a moment. She had a pale rosebud face with crystal teardrops sculpted onto her waxy cheeks and black human hair cascading down over her gown of rich brocade. Her lip appeared to tremble as if she was about to speak. Theo wondered whether this was Santa Leticia or just another Madonna, and he began to understand how witches and ghosts could seem real in a land where statues became saints and answered people's prayers.

Behind the chapel was the cliff from which the saint had been thrown. Theo looked for a moment over the edge and glimpsed a deep ravine filled with rubbish, and then he stepped back quickly as he felt a surging vertigo pulling him forward toward self-destruction. He knew for a fact that there would be no saint or Virgin to save him if he fell, but, looking over at Antonio, he thought that his friend would certainly not be ruling out the possibility of a divine intervention.

A little way farther on was the village cemetery, surrounded by a low wall. It was an arresting sight: the busy lines of gravestones, many with photographs of the dead preserved behind glass, overlooked by effigies of angels. Flowers wilted in vases of brackish water, unable to last even a day in the harsh summer heat.

Through a small gate at the back, Theo could see a farther enclosure with just a few crudely fashioned wooden crosses sticking up out of the rough, uneven ground. Weeds grew in abundance, whereas there were none inside the main graveyard.

"*La olla*—the stewpot!" said Antonio, seeing where Theo was looking. "Where the poor go. Don Vincente says a prayer or two if they're lucky, closes the gate, and then they're forgotten. Thrown away like garbage!" He laughed hollowly as he turned away.

Looking at *la olla*, Theo remembered the anonymous cemetery in Brooklyn where his father lay, also without a headstone, forgotten by everyone except him and Frank. *La tierra de la verdad*—the land of truth: that was what Sir Andrew had told him the people here called their cemeteries, and looking out at the pathetic makeshift crosses against the background of the vast landscape spread out below and the hard-rearing mountains behind, Theo understood the perfect aptness of the term. He felt as if his illusions were being stripped away so that he could see death unobscured by life and fully understand its universality and finality. It was here in this place: utterly real, waiting and brooding, not to be cheated.

He turned away with a shudder and got on his mule, following Antonio up the path as they climbed steadily into the higher country.

The sun rose in the sky and it felt to Theo as if it was seeking him out, burning every inch of his flesh that he had left exposed—neck, face, hands, even his wrists. The heat hung before them in a shimmering haze, and the poppies growing in profusion across the rocky outcrops appeared to Theo like streams of crimson blood oozing across the parched land.

Relief came with the pine trees that began to appear here and there and then quickly developed into small woods. They passed through shaded corridors between the tall, thin trunks with the sunlight dappling down through the needled branches. The cicadas, invisible in the trees, maintained a ceaseless clicking song that reminded Theo of the whirring noise of the film projector in the square, while on the ground emerald-green lizards slithered away into the undergrowth as the mules approached.

It was a land untouched by man, and they met no one until a peasant in a broad-brimmed hat appeared as if out of nowhere, riding a mule with his wife sitting behind him with her stout arms circled about his waist. Her legs were splayed out wide to accommodate bulging saddlebags, creating a comic effect of which she seemed completely unaware.

The peasant stopped, regarding Antonio and Theo with frank curiosity. "Good day," he said. "I am going to Parauta because my brother is sick. Perhaps he will die. I do not know. I have all my family there. Where do you come from?"

Antonio named his village and said that Theo was from America.

"America. Popeye the Sailor," said the peasant, putting a hand over his right eye and bursting into uproarious laughter. Theo laughed too. It seemed the polite thing to do.

"In America you have much to eat?" he asked.

Theo nodded, surprised by the unexpected question.

"Good," he said. "Much is good. In my village we have little, but in Parauta they eat well." He gestured with his fingers to his mouth. "But it is as God sends. He giveth and he taketh away. Blessed be his name." The peasant made the sign of the cross and his wife did the same, making her first movement since they had stopped.

And then abruptly he decided it was time to move on.

"Vaya con Dios," he said and rode on with his wife swaying gently from side to side behind him.

"Is everything about food?" Theo asked Antonio, smiling at the unreal quality of the conversation they had just had.

"Yes. For most people," said Antonio, speaking seriously. "If they don't work, they don't eat. And if they don't eat, they die. *La olla* is stuffed full of their bones."

Theo nodded, remembering the emaciated man who had confronted him in the barrio. He felt ashamed of his flippancy and hoped that his stepfather had found some way to help the workers whom Señor Madera had laid off in the spring.

But his shame didn't diminish his appetite when they stopped for lunch soon afterward, sitting with their backs to the tree trunks as they ate ham sandwiches and sardines. And afterward they slept, stretched out on the thick pine needle carpet with saddlebags for pillows.

In his dream, Theo was running in the magic shoes that Coach Eames had given him. His stride was easy and fluid, and it was as if he was floating effortlessly above the track. And as he ran, he passed the people he'd known in his life, each of their faces distinct as if they were in a picture gallery. All of them—his grandfather and his grandmother and the whores on Rivington Street and Father Laurence and Jacob from the bookshop with his walrus mustache and Cattermole and Alwyn Thomas. And they were all cheering him on, their faces radiant with warmth and love. On and on he ran, through and past his life.

Until everything abruptly stopped. He stumbled and fell and the faces dissolved, crumbling in upon themselves as if all the time, they'd been puppets made of papier-mâché, and he was looking up at Antonio, who was shaking him awake. He didn't understand. He wanted to push Antonio away and go back, but he couldn't. The sense of loss was for a moment almost unbearable and then like gossamer it was gone, leaving only a dull ache for something he could no longer remember.

"Come on," said Antonio. "We've slept too long. We've a way to go yet. And we need to get there before sunset or we'll end up out in the open, and you don't want that."

"Get where?" asked Theo.

"Where we're going," said Antonio, smiling enigmatically. "It's beautiful. You'll see. But it's better if it's a surprise."

They came out of the pines, and the ascending path led them through a wilderness of gray rocks and low brush. Bees buzzed greedily around the blue blossoms on the rosemary bushes that filled the air with an aromatic woody scent, even though they had left the trees behind.

A tinkling of tiny bells announced a line of thin sheep with ribs like radiators, followed by a shepherd in a ragged cloak walking behind them, holding a crook. He raised a stiff, grave hand as he walked by and bid them "go with God," and that was the last human being that they met that day. The world was empty except for the hawks and eagles circling overhead in search of prey. Theo wondered what they fed on, given the barrenness of the landscape that provided scant cover for field mice and voles amid the scree and shaley slopes.

Above their heads, the cliffs rose to great heights, fretted with holes.

"Some of them are caves," said Antonio. "Gangs of brigands used to live in them. They would ride down into the village at siesta time and seize a rich man and hold him for ransom, turning the screws on his family by sending an ear or a finger or both until they got their money."

"And if they didn't?"

"They'd throw him off the cliffs like Santa Leticia," said Antonio, drawing a finger across his throat.

"Are they still doing it?" asked Theo, feeling a shot of anxiety that they were being observed themselves and assessed for what price they might bring.

"No, the Guardia have cleared them all out. But I can remember when they brought the last capo in. I was six or seven, and they rode with him through the main square with ropes around his waist and neck. They stopped for water and he opened his mouth to drink and all his teeth were gold, so you couldn't see any white at all."

"What happened to him?" asked Theo.

"He was garroted in Málaga. They say the spike missed his spinal column and he died a terrible slow death, pierced and strangled by the iron collar."

Theo shivered, remembering his stepfather talking of the Spaniards' fascination with killing. In this lonely, empty place, he could picture the condemned man's terror and agony as if on a screen, and he struggled to erase the image from his mind.

"Come, we must walk now and lead the mules," said Antonio, dismounting. "The way up from here is steep and narrow."

He untied his saddlebag, producing a pair of well-sewn jute-soled sandals. "Give me your boots," he said. "With these alpargatas you are less likely to slip. But you must still be careful. If you fall, you die, and the birds will peck out your eyes." He laughed but Theo couldn't tell if he was really joking, and it didn't help that he fancied he could hear a raven croaking ominously somewhere nearby.

The path twisted and turned through a wilderness of immense boulders lying at haphazard angles to each other, as if they had been tossed about as playthings by a vanished species of giants. Theo kept his eyes fixed on the ground, measuring every step, but felt encouraged by the sure-footedness of Isabella, who picked her way forward unerringly beside him.

And then suddenly they were at the summit—a misty plateau covered with a fine turf in which the green grasses were intermixed with azure-blue gentians and white star-of-Bethlehem flowers. At the back a series of cave mouths ran along the base of the rearing cliffs that receded as the ground widened to accommodate a small lake of still, silvery water. Below, a panoramic view opened up of the foothills and the plain leading away to the distant sea.

"You're right. It's magnificent," said Theo, gazing around with admiration.

"Worth the walk," said Antonio. "See, I'm a guide who delivers on his promises. Perhaps there's a future for me here after all."

"Doing this?"

"No, of course not. I was joking," said Antonio, laughing. "Los Olivos is the end of the world. You don't need me to tell you that. No one comes to visit, and so no one needs guiding."

"Except me."

"Yes, except you. Look, there's our village," he said, pointing down to the right, where distant red-tiled roofs and whitewashed houses clustered around a hilltop with the familiar tower and spire of the church rising up above.

Below, Theo could just about make out his stepfather's orange groves and the gray line of the road. Small farmsteads were dotted here and there outside the village, surrounded by a patchwork of fields and fruit trees.

"We look at this landscape and we say it's beautiful," said Antonio thoughtfully. "And we're right, of course. But my father sees it and thinks something else entirely. He sees opportunities. He calls it a checkerboard because it's divided up into tiny squares which he wants to own. Some of them he does already, and if he has his way, he'll end up claiming them all."

"I don't understand," said Theo. "His business is the café, isn't it?"

"That's just a part of it. The café gives him the money to play his game."

"What game?"

"Checkers. He lends money to the peasants when they can't pay their taxes. He's all smiles then, couldn't be friendlier, except there's the small detail that he needs a mortgage as security. 'Just a precaution,' he says and he walks them over to the ayuntamiento, where they sign or put their thumbmark on the dotted line and the clerk seals the deed with red wax and files it away in the registry up on the third floor. And then afterward, my father waits patiently like a spider, for years if he has to, until they can't pay the interest because there's a bad harvest or some other piece of bad luck, and then, quick as lightning, he forecloses." Antonio darted his head forward like a lizard, opening and shutting his mouth with a snap. "But then comes the masterstroke: he doesn't take their land. Oh no, he's much too generous for that. He leaves them to farm it as sharecroppers."

"What does that mean?"

"They work the land—fields that their grandfathers tamed and tilled—and then they have to bring him a half share of everything. You've seen that office he has at the back of the café. That's where he counts and weighs the produce, and he has a big warehouse next door for storage. He watches the poor bastards like one of those hawks up there," said Antonio, pointing up at the great birds still circling the sky above their heads. "And in the afternoons when the café's closed for siesta, he goes on tours of inspection and checks that they aren't cheating him. 'There are ten grapefruit missing!' he'll shout because he's counted every one of the grapefruit on his previous visit, and the peasants tremble, knowing he can evict them whenever he feels like it. But later, in the café, he acts like he's their friend, doing them all a favor, allowing them to stay on the land. He's the life and soul of the party then!"

Antonio shook his head bitterly. "Money talks," he said and spat on the ground. "I shall be glad when I'm out of here, marching with the soldiers."

"You don't mean that," said Theo.

"No? Maybe I don't," said Antonio with a smile. "To hell with my father! I won't let him spoil our day."

The sun was sinking now toward the sea, dropping fast like a golden stone, and they watched, riveted, as it was swallowed up, leaving on the horizon line a green glow that was gone in a moment, as if it had never been. In the violet twilight, the shape of everything seemed distinct before it began to fade.

"Come on," said Antonio, getting up. "We need to find some brushwood for a fire while we can still see. I know the best cave for the night."

Antonio squashed the rosemary and lavender and broom into cushions that he called *piornos*, and the air was pungent with their smell as they caught alight, flaring into flame. The fine white ash blew up and settled on the boys' hair and eyelashes and they laughed, looking at their shadows dancing on the walls of the cave in the firelight.

Out in the gathering darkness, the stars were glittering low in the sky, seeming to Theo to be so close that he could reach out his hand to touch them, even though they were light-years away.

Antonio produced a frying pan and eggs and more ham and oil from his saddlebag like a conjurer and cooked omelets that they ate with a loaf of bread. There was also a goatskin *bolsa* of red wine that Antonio tried but failed to teach Theo how to drink from in the Spanish way. He demonstrated, moving the spout of the pouch to his lips and then up and away as far as his arm could reach, from where he released a purplish-red stream that arced gracefully into his open mouth. But Theo made a complete mess of his attempt at imitation and had to drink directly from the *bolsa* with half the wine spilling down over his shirt, at which they laughed even more, and their happy voices echoed off the cave walls, until they lay back exhausted and fell suddenly fast asleep, watched over by their faithful mules.

Antonio woke Theo just before dawn, shaking him out of another deep sleep. "I want to show you something," he said.

Over at the top of the path, they stood looking down. The sky was the palest of blues, and the stars, so vivid in the night, were still faintly visible. There was a cool breeze in the air.

"See?" said Antonio, pointing, and Theo, following his finger, caught sight of groups of people on the hillside, where there had been none when they had passed that way the previous afternoon.

"They're threshing the grain," said Antonio. "Each spot they're at is a floor. See how the mules pull the carts over the sheaves going round and round in tight circles and look, over there, they're winnowing the crop now. They've been waiting for the wind and the light. It's perfect weather."

Theo stared, transfixed by the unexpected beauty of the scene, as the threshers used wooden forks to toss up the ears, letting the chaff stream away in a white cloud while the grain fell in drifts of gold to the floor.

Afterward, they walked to the tarn to wash and renew their supply of water. The breeze was eddying the surface, sending lines of silver ripples running in all directions.

"You must not swim," said Antonio, who had hung back, leaving Theo to fill the water bottles. "There's an enchantress in the deep who lures men out from the shore with her song and then leaves them to drown."

"Of course there is," Theo was about to say, but then bit back the words, remembering the enchanted lake in *King Arthur*, the beautiful book Sir Andrew had given him in New York that he had held on to through thick and thin ever since, taking it with him across the Atlantic and to Saint Gregory's. He prized it so highly because it was magical and allowed him to dream of worlds beyond the hard, narrow one in which he'd lived. And he was beginning to understand that Spain was a land where the dividing line between the imagined and the real blurred and disappeared so that the two became one. Looking at the lake, it was as if he could see the arm clothed in samite rising from the water holding aloft the sword, Excalibur, gleaming in the golden light of the rising sun.

In the weeks that followed, Sir Andrew was away on business, first in Jerez and then in Barcelona, and Elena was every day at the church, where Don Vincente had gratefully accepted her offers of assistance with flower arranging both there and in the chapel up on the hill. Blossoms didn't last long in the incense-laden half darkness where the deep reds and blues of the stained-glass windows filtered out the sunlight, and the flowers needed constant replacing.

She was warmly welcomed into this new world by a group of similarly devout well-to-do ladies in black lace mantillas who spent as much time on their knees as on their feet. In only a short time, the church became a second home to her, just as it had once been in Gramercy Park and Little Italy, except that here it provided a greater fulfillment because the faith was the beating heart of Spain, or so she believed, in the same way it had been when she was a girl in Mexico before the revolution. It was as if she had paradoxically crossed the ocean to come home out of her exile, and had at last found happiness at the end of the journey.

Left to his own devices, Theo accompanied Antonio on further expeditions into the wild country that lay in the foothills of the Sierra Nevada above and on either side of the village.

Soon he grew to love this new world, where each experience seemed crystallized, as if it were a picture: a pony turning a waterwheel under poplar trees with the dappled sunlight playing on its brindled coat or a herd of little black goats drinking at a white-pebbled stream watched over by their shepherd. Every such moment and encounter felt separated in its own present from the before and after.

But Theo also came to understand that this impression of permanence and immutability was superficial and deceptive. In the village and in the surrounding countryside, many of the people were stirred up and angry, eager for a change that would come not slowly over time but all at once in a day, ushering in an earthly Utopia in which they believed as fervently as they had once believed in the God that had gone from their lives.

Theo had seen signs when he first arrived in the village: the scrawled red graffiti on the wall, his encounter with the starving man, the priest's passing reference to the desecration of the chapel by the Anarchists. But he had turned away, following his stepfather's instruction not to return to the barrio, and instead had followed Antonio up into the mountains, leaving the village behind.

However, the Anarchists were there, too, and a chance encounter in a wayside inn at which they stopped one August night lifted the scales from Theo's eyes.

He and Antonio had been wandering in the foothills all day, descending in the evening to a wide track that led them to a single-story, barnlike building with big double doors standing open. Outside, in the cobblestoned courtyard, a man was washing a child in a tin horse trough, lathering and scrubbing and singing lustily as the child screamed. He was stripped to the waist, and his feet were stained blue from a lifetime of treading grapes.

Antonio dismounted to ask about food and accommodation, and the man broke off from his song, holding the dripping child suspended in midair as he bid the newcomers welcome and directed them to enter with an expansive wave of his other hand.

They led the burros inside and stood blinking for a moment, adjusting their eyes to the sudden change of light. They were in a long, whitewashed hall without partitions. Outside the pool of sunlit illumination in which they were standing, the farther reaches of the interior were dark and shadowy, lit only by a fire that was burning beneath a hooded chimney at one end.

There was a simple rough-hewn table and chairs, but otherwise no furniture, and blackened pots and pans, harnesses, and farming tools were hanging from nails on the walls. At the other end of the hall from the fire, a donkey was eating at a manger. Swallows swooped and darted between the roof rafters and a pig was fast asleep on a bed of straw, snorting and snuffling in its dreams.

Three women in musty black dresses overlaid with lace shawls were seated on low stools in front of the hearth, and as they turned their heads toward the new arrivals, their gaunt, skin-stretched faces reminded Theo of Rackham's picture of the witches in *Macbeth*, one of his favorites in the book of Shakespeare's tales his stepfather had given him earlier in the summer. He assumed that one of the women had to be the innkeeper's wife and another his mother, but he could not tell the generations apart. The bloom of youth and beauty was fleeting in the sierras, burned quickly away by the ravages of sun and wind and hardship.

One of the women brought straw and barley for the mules, which Antonio and Theo tethered beside the donkey, and the other two busied themselves around the fire, beginning to cook the evening meal. An iron pan sputtered, and the hall was filled with the smell of sizzling oil and garlic.

Theo and Antonio washed, taking it in turns to use a tin dipper to pour icy cold water from a ewer over their heads and hands, and then sat at the table, drinking coarse red wine that scraped their tongues while they waited to eat.

Soon the innkeeper came in carrying the child, whom he deposited on the straw beside the pig, where it promptly went to sleep. He went around lighting smoky oil lamps, ignored by and ignoring the women at the fire.

Outside there was the sound of hooves, and through the open door Theo saw two riders dismounting in the twilight. Without reason, he felt a sense of foreboding, wondering who these late-arriving strangers might be as they came into the hall, leading their mules.

They couldn't have been more dissimilar in appearance. One was short and rotund with an easy smile, whereas the other was tall and thin with a pale ascetic face in which his eyes burned like two live coals. Theo couldn't help staring: the second man was an El Greco portrait brought to life, complete with the dagger-like features beloved of the artist—the long, straight nose and the narrow chin ending in a pointed black beard.

The landlord pushed the doors closed, sliding a bolt across, and the men joined Antonio and Theo at the table. The shorter of the two introduced himself as Pablo and helped himself liberally to the wine, but his companion drank only water. Pablo was as talkative as the other was taciturn.

"I can tell this is a good inn," he said, rubbing his hands. "A bright fire, strong wine, an openhanded welcome. Where we stayed last night, they demanded money in advance and stood over us while we ate, and then they snatched our plates away before we had finished eating, gobbling down what was left." He imitated the gobbling with his mouth and banged the table and laughed, but his friend didn't even smile.

And so they continued, verbose and closemouthed, throughout the dinner of rice and salt cod served on a wide pan from which the guests each ate a quarter section, except for Pablo's companion, who barely touched his food, leaving it to Pablo to finish it for him, as if by prearranged custom.

Only when the pan had been removed did the tall man break his silence, addressing himself to Theo.

"You don't speak like us," he said. "Where are you from?"

"America," said Theo. "I grew up in New York."

"The land of the free, where the people are slaves to their money," said the man, and Theo could hear the scorn in his voice, grating like his harsh Andalusian accent.

"Oh, come on, Carlos," said Pablo. "There's no need to pick a quarrel. We're all friends here."

There was an uneasy lull in the conversation, but the tall man's intervention had made Theo curious. Carlos was rude and intimidating, but there was a power about him that made Theo want to find out who he was.

"You don't like money?" he asked.

"It is the root of all evil," said Carlos. The phrase was a cliché, but spoken by Carlos, it seemed newly minted, full of pith and force.

"So you agree with Saint Paul about that?" asked Theo, remembering his Bible lessons at Saint Gregory's.

"About money, yes, but about his faith in God, no. That is a lie, used by the Church to deceive the poor and keep them in submission and ignorance. But no longer. In America, perhaps, but not here. Our work is almost done. Men far better than me have been walking these tracks for sixty years, bringing the truth to the people, and their eyes have been opened. Many can read now, and those that can't, listen to those that can. They understand that they have the right to be free and to enjoy the fruits of their labor. No one is entitled to control them or starve them or exploit them, as the landlords and priests have done for centuries. They are idle parasites living off the sweat of the poor, grown fat on it because they say the land is theirs to do with as they like. But it is not. There is no property. The land belongs to the people. It always has and it always will. There is more than enough for everyone if it is farmed together."

"From each according to his ability, to each according to his needs. Is that what you mean?" asked Theo.

"Marx!" said Carlos, spitting out the name as if it was a profanity. "Another liar like Paul, who knew how to use the truth for his own ends. The Communists say the state can make people equal. But there can be no freedom or justice when one man has power over another. In Russia, the Bolsheviks are the new parasites. They have betrayed the revolution, so it might as well never have happened."

"It's the truth," said Pablo, refilling his glass with wine and lighting a fat cigarette that he had rolled while his companion was speaking. "Carlos here is like old Fanelli. He can explain the Idea so everyone can understand. One in a thousand he is."

Theo nodded. Pablo's easy jocularity was a world removed from Carlos's harsh rhetoric, but he was right about his friend. At first Carlos's certainty and fierce intelligence had reminded Theo of Esmond, but the resemblance was misleading. Carlos had none of Esmond's humor or detachment or intellectual prowess. Instead, he possessed the unique gift of translating the fire burning inside him into simple words. He was what he said.

"But how then do people achieve liberty? Can you tell me that?" asked Theo, leaning forward eagerly. It was the question he had often asked himself without ever finding a satisfactory answer, the one that had kept him ideologically separated from Esmond, even when they had papered over the cracks to fight Mosley's Fascism together.

Carlos didn't respond at first, keeping his dark eyes fixed on Theo's. And then, as if making the final move in a game of chess, he said simply: "They take it. And they do not rest until the last marquis has been strangled with the guts of the last priest."

For the first and last time, he smiled, and then, getting up from the table, he walked over to where sacks of straw were laid in a corner, took off his boots, pulled a rug from a pile over his body, and lay still.

Theo sat on for a while, lost in thought, while Antonio and Pablo talked and smoked. Carlos's certainties had made him think once more of Esmond, and his heart ached as he wondered where Esmond was and whether they would meet again. There were so many friends he had left behind. He tried to picture Coach Eames and Frank so unimaginably far away across the great ocean. New York had been everything to him, but now it hardly seemed real, with his mind unable to form a connection between the skyscrapers of Fifth Avenue and this ancient rural world, where men farmed the land with oxen and wooden plows.

Shadows flickered across the whitewashed walls in the guttering lamplight and in the corner the child still slept on its bed of straw, reminding Theo of the boy in his grandfather's apartment asleep on the pile of cloth. Another path that had led nowhere except to loss. Would Spain be like that too? Where would his wandering end?

And beneath the night sounds—the stamping and neighing of the mules and the snoring of the innkeeper and his family—Theo sensed the far-off approach of a coming storm. Thunder in the mountains, the crackle of gunfire, and the beating of drums; blood of beasts and men staining the earth.

19

STRIFE

After the long day and the red wine, Theo slept deeply on his sack of straw, and when he awoke, Carlos and Pablo were gone, vanished into the cold pink of the early morning outside the opened doors, as if they had never been.

He and Antonio ate a breakfast of maize polenta and sardines fried over the fire, paid the innkeeper handsomely, harnessed their mules, and set off down the treeless track.

Around the corner, they came upon one of the women from the night before, bringing water from the well in an earthenware jug balanced upon her head. She was singing a malaguena—a quavering lament of drawn-out notes and trills—and as they stopped to listen, Theo felt a return of the trepidation he'd experienced in the night. A nameless sorrow for events that had not yet occurred. And in the weeks that followed, he could never quite banish the song from his mind; it lingered on the edge of his consciousness, adding to his sense of unease.

Perhaps the song was an augury of trouble, and if so, it was correct. The expedition to the inn was the last Theo made with Antonio, as a series of events in the following few days brought a premature end to their time together.

The first came soon after their return. Theo was sitting in the morning sunshine on the *terrado* at the top of the house with a book of F. Scott Fitzgerald forgotten in his lap when voices below cut into his daydreams. Going to the parapet, he was surprised to see the cacique, Don Fadrique, walking up the path to the front door with that same waddling gait that Theo remembered from the night of the film show. Just as before, he was followed by the same lean youth with the rifle over his shoulder, who kept an exact six feet behind his employer, while turning his head in all directions as if scouting for potential assassins or measuring shots he would take with his gun if he got the chance. Looking up, he caught sight of Theo, who instinctively ducked back and went over to the stairs, descending past his bedroom and stopping on the half landing above the hallway leading to the salon, where he leaned back against the wall, waiting.

It felt wrong to be listening like an eavesdropper, but he sensed that Don Fadrique would not be visiting the house unless it was for something important, and he wanted to know what that something was. From where he was standing, he would be able to hear what was being said in the salon as long as the door remained open, and he thought it unlikely that he would be seen. His mother was at church, and Sir Andrew was in his study down below.

Theo listened as Señora Constanza opened the door and then came back up the stairs to report to Sir Andrew, whose steps Theo could soon hear crossing the hall just below where he was standing.

"Not your man, if you don't mind, Don Fadrique," said Sir Andrew. "I don't like guns in the house."

Theo didn't hear Don Fadrique respond, just his puffing and wheezing as he mounted the stairs and followed Sir Andrew into the salon.

At first, there was nothing. Perhaps Sir Andrew was serving his guest sherry. But then Theo heard him asking the cacique to what he owed the honor of his visit.

"The municipal councillors asked me to come," said Don Fadrique. His voice was unexpectedly soft, so that Theo had to strain to hear. "They are concerned that your decision to pay your braceros for not working is causing others to make similar demands, which we as employers simply cannot afford to meet. They say that work should be paid for, not idleness, which makes sense, does it not?"

"The braceros are not idle," said Sir Andrew, brushing aside the question. "They are starving. That's something as Christians we should be striving to prevent."

"And so we do, Don Andrés. So we do," said Don Fadrique in a soothing tone. "We make generous donations to Don Vincente, who provides charity to the deserving."

"Tiny amounts, and only if the deserving confess their sins and attend Mass on Sundays. The rest he spends on beautifying the church and taking trips to see the marquis in Madrid, which I'm sure you know about, given you are in charge of His Excellency's affairs here."

"I do have that honor," said Don Fadrique. "And I think that you do Don Vincente an injustice, if you don't mind me saying so. The marquis was kind enough to invite him to his son's wedding. It would have caused offense not to go."

"The marquis's kindness does not extend to the poor, though, does it?" said Sir Andrew, returning to the attack. "He—or should I say you—keeps half his land fallow so he can raise fighting bulls and shoot pheasants. Good land that could be rented out and worked. And why? So that you can keep unemployment high and wages low. But that isn't enough, is it? At harvesttime, you bring in migrant labor to drive the pay down even further. Three or four pesetas a day—no man can support his family on that. And once the harvest is over, nothing. There were laws to stop all this, of course, but since the election they've all been repealed. It's a disgrace."

"It's democracy," said Don Fadrique mildly. "Something which I would have assumed a liberal like yourself would support, Don Andrés." His voice was just as soft and unperturbed as before, and Theo couldn't help being impressed by the cacique's equanimity, knowing from his own experience how intimidating his stepfather could be.

"It's nothing of the kind." Sir Andrew was almost shouting now. "The elections are fixed and you know it. Cognac and cigars on Election Day for the compliant and threats and coercion for the rest. If you vote Socialist, then you won't work or worse. There are some villages, from what I've heard, where councils have sent in the results even before the people have voted."

"Are you saying that is what has happened here?"

"I'm saying I won't be a part of starving these poor people. I shall do my best for them, whatever you and the others say, and I've given my steward instructions accordingly. I'm sorry this has been a wasted visit, Don Fadrique."

"Nothing is wasted, Don Andrés, I assure you. Indeed, our conversation has been most instructive. Please don't trouble yourself. I will show myself out."

Theo listened to more wheezing as Don Fadrique went down the stairs and closed the door, and then a moment later he jumped at the sound of his stepfather's glass smashing against the back of the fireplace and narrowly avoided falling down the stairs.

Theo would have liked to talk to Sir Andrew about the cacique's visit, but couldn't without admitting that he had been eavesdropping.

He felt grateful to his stepfather for having acted on what he had told him about his encounter with the poor man in the barrio, and he was impressed by his willingness to stand up for what he thought was right. Following on from their conversation about bullfighting, Theo was surprised to realize that he had started to feel an affection for Sir Andrew that he wouldn't have believed possible a few months earlier, when he had him firmly cast as the enemy interloper who had stolen away his mother.

However, Theo remembered all that Antonio had told him about the cacique's power in the village and he felt certain that Don Fadrique would take steps to try to bring Sir Andrew to heel, now that his attempt at persuasion had been rebuffed. What Theo didn't anticipate was that the first move would be made against him personally.

Early the next day Theo received a call of his own at the house. Antonio stood awkwardly outside the door, twisting his hat in his hands as he explained that his father needed him in the café, so there could therefore be no more guiding. He refused Theo's invitation to come in, but didn't go, either, and it seemed to Theo that his friend had something else to say but couldn't think of a way to say it.

"What is it?" he asked.

"This isn't what I want," said Antonio.

"Nor I," said Theo warmly. "I don't think I've ever been happier than these last few weeks. I've loved what you've shown me. All of it. I—" He broke off, inhibited by his natural reserve from expressing the depth of his feeling.

"Have you?" said Antonio, looking amazed. "But you've seen so much of the world. London, New York. This is nothing compared to them."

"No, you're wrong. It's everything," said Theo passionately. "The country here is so raw. It's real. Not like anywhere else I've ever been. The people too. But now . . ." He bit his lip, unable to hide his disappointment.

"Now you can't see it anymore. Because of me," said Antonio miserably, finishing Theo's sentence.

"No, not because of you," said Theo. "That's not what I meant at all. You have to do what your father says. I know that."

"It's something to do with your stepfather. My father wouldn't say what, just that I'm not to see you anymore. I can't stand up to him. I wish I could, but I can't. I'm not like my sister. I haven't got it in me." Antonio had his eyes fixed on the ground, ashamed of his weakness, and then abruptly turned on his heel and walked away.

Passing between the lions at the entrance gate, he looked back for a moment and half raised his hand, and was gone.

Sir Andrew's mood worsened as the days passed. It wasn't just the rebuff by Bernardo Alvarez that Theo had felt obliged to report to his stepfather. A more general ostracism was occurring, and he had a stand-up row with Señor Madera when the steward urged him to reconsider his policy of out-of-season payments. Theo didn't need to eavesdrop to hear his stepfather shouting at the steward, accusing him of being an agent of the cacique, and Señor Madera's usual dour expression had become funereally grim when Theo passed him in the corridor later that morning.

The taut, oppressive atmosphere in the house affected all its occupants except Elena, whose single-minded focus on the church and its elaborate furnishings and rituals made her unaware of everything else that was going on. It was as if she and her son had both fallen in love, but with two different sides of the same country. One light and one dark, one poor and one rich. Not that she saw it that way.

Theo couldn't understand his mother. He was repelled by the lifelike statues in the church with their brushed hair and dainty shoes and eyes of glass, clothed in damask and velvet, with rings on their fingers and diadems in their hair. They had nothing in common with the Joseph and Mary who had slept with the animals in the Bethlehem stable and laid their baby in a manger.

It made it worse that that simple world of the Nativity that his mother professed to love did exist here in Spain, in a way that had vanished elsewhere in the world. He had seen it in the inn when he breathed the night air with the pig and the mules. There had been nothing in that long room that wasn't essential for life. It was just as it had been in the time of Christ. But the Spanish Church had no interest in such simplicity. Their houses of worship were furnished with gold and silver and precious stones, glittering in the incense-filled gloom. A storehouse of worldly things.

To Theo, they were places of death, not life, and the waxlike statues suggested a netherworld of decay and corruption. He hadn't forgotten Antonio's image of fat Don Vincente sucking the blood of the village while his parishioners starved. But for Elena, the opposite was true. As she passed the rosary beads through her fingers, she felt the church's womb-like, candlelit darkness holding and protecting her as if she were gently rocking in the arms of her Savior.

But her bliss was brittle. Like ecstasy, it ran skin deep. Because she knew that outside, the forces of darkness were gathering, ready to attack. She had seen it happen before. In Mexico, the Reds had killed and burned her parents, and she had fled across the fields, lucky to escape with her life. They were still murdering the faithful there and in Russia, too, and they wanted to do the same here in Spain. Don Vincente had told her what the Anarchists had done in the chapel. The statue of the Virgin had been stripped and decapitated and her breast daubed with their red graffiti. *PUTA* they had written. Whore!

At night, Elena dreamed of fire. At first, just a gleam on the horizon and a whiff of smoke in the air, but then leaping into orange flames in the crackling trees with the smell of sulfur pressing down on her lungs until she could hardly breathe. She woke screaming when she felt the heat on her flesh and Andrew held her, trembling like a wounded bird in his hands.

So, she was a receptive audience when Don Vincente and his black-laced ladies began to whisper in her ear that her husband was putting money in the Anarchists' pockets with his out-of-season payments to his braceros. Money they would use to finance another outrage or to recruit more members into their Red ranks.

At Mass on Sunday, Don Vincente preached that Spain was the spiritual home of the true Church, not Rome. Spain had brought Christ to the heathen. She had driven out the Jews and the Moors and had fought the Protestant heretics all over Europe. But now she was facing a new and more deadly foe, an enemy within that was determined to destroy religion and property and marriage and everything that was holy. This was the time of trial that had been prophesied when Catholics must stand together and fight to the last for Christ and Spain.

Elena took Don Vincente's instruction literally. She had been quiet on the way home and through lunch, steeling herself for the ordeal ahead, although she glanced over at her husband several times and inwardly trembled, seeing his creased brow as he pondered his troubles. But when Señora Constanza had finished serving the coffee, she launched herself into battle:

"Andrew, I want you to stop making these payments."

"What payments?" he asked.

"To the men when they are not working. I want you to stop them."

"Why? It was your idea in the first place," said Sir Andrew, looking incredulous. "What on earth has made you change your mind?"

"Don Vincente says that the money's going to the Anarchists."

"Don Vincente knows which side his bread is buttered," said Sir Andrew, his voice laced with sarcasm. "The cacique's put him up to this. That's what's happened. And I won't tolerate it, I tell you. They have no right trying to get at me through you."

"I have a right to my opinion," said Elena, getting to her feet.

"Even when it's the opposite of your opinion a few weeks ago? Your Christian opinion that led me to start paying the money?"

"Yes."

Theo was appalled by his mother's about-face. Couldn't she see the injustice of what she was asking? The men were starving: Did that mean nothing to her? But just as he was about to weigh in on the side of his stepfather, he stopped, anger turning to fear as he noticed how deathly pale his mother had become and how she was gripping the chairback with both hands for support.

"Andrew, please . . ." he began, but his stepfather ignored him. He had been on the verge of losing his temper for days and now it spilled over.

"How dare you interfere!" he shouted at Elena. "I decide what to pay my workers. Not you and not that good-for-nothing priest or his fat paymaster. Me. No one else. Do you hear me?"

"No," she yelled back, refusing to back down. "I won't allow you to make us outcasts. Not here. Michael did it in New York when he—" She stopped, swallowing hard and then went on, pushing out her words between labored breaths. "Don Vincente is right. We Catholics have to stand together, because if we don't, they'll . . ."

She swayed and would have fallen if Theo hadn't jumped forward to hold her. Her eyes were closed, and Theo thought she had fainted. But then she opened them again and smiled wanly, looking up at her son. Her fury had disappeared, replaced by a quiet calm that frightened him even more.

"I'm sorry," she said. "I can't get it out of my head. What happened to them. I can't get past it. I try, but I don't know how."

Theo knew who *they* were. She'd said the same about her murdered parents that day in New York when they'd been honest with each other, but she'd had hope then of overcoming her past, whereas now she sounded defeated. His heart lurched as if something inside him was giving way. It was as if their roles had been reversed. She was supposed to be the parent, showing him the way, but instead she had become like a lost child, begging for guidance, which he couldn't give her because he was too young.

"Help me," he said, turning to his stepfather, and together they moved Elena to the sofa in the salon, where she lay down and closed her eyes, while Andrew, overcome with remorse, sat beside her, holding her hand.

Sir Andrew summoned the village doctor, who prescribed sedatives and told him what he already knew: that his wife needed expert care. And the next day, once Elena had awoken and eaten a little breakfast, Sir Andrew told Theo to pack, because they would be leaving at noon.

"I'm sorry," he said, bowing his head. "I shouldn't have shouted. I feel I've let you down as well as your mother. It won't happen again."

"It's all right," said Theo. "I was angry with her too. She gets into a state and she can't see anymore. Right from wrong, I mean."

Sir Andrew nodded. "It's this place, I think. She wants to believe she's gone home to Mexico. But wanting something doesn't make it true. The Church is different here. It has power and wealth and it's fighting to keep them, and if people get hurt in the process, then that's a price Don Vincente and his friends are willing to pay. But as you say, she's blind to all that. Leaving will help, I hope. Part of me wishes we'd never come."

"I don't," said Theo, and Sir Andrew looked at him curiously, picking up on the vehemence in his stepson's voice.

"Will you still pay the men?" Theo asked.

"I don't know."

"I think you should. They'll starve if you don't."

Sir Andrew thought for a moment and then nodded, making up his mind. "I'll tell Madera," he said.

It didn't take Theo long to get his things together, and then, going up onto the *terrado*, he gazed out one last time at the landscape he'd come to love. He remembered how he had felt shut in and isolated here until Antonio had opened up this new world to him in all its infinite variety. Sights and sounds and scents came crowding into his mind: the dark-eyed glances from the girls in the square, the smell and feel of pine needles in the dappled morning light, the cold water of the tarn icy on his skin, the snorting breath of the mules. And Antonio always beside him, pointing, explaining, laughing, and finally leaving with his head cast down, past the gate down below through which Theo would soon be departing himself, perhaps never to return.

He felt a surge of gratitude toward his friend. He owed him so much, but he had never thanked him properly, and he realized suddenly that he couldn't bear to leave without saying goodbye.

There was just time if he went now. He ran down the stairs, taking them two at a time and almost knocking over Señora Constanza, who was coming up the other way, and then hurtled through the door and down the road past the church, only pausing for breath when he got to the square.

He'd forgotten about Antonio's father, who was standing outside his café with his hands on his hips, holding forth to a group of customers drinking at the nearby tables. He caught sight of Theo, and his expression changed as he moved to station himself in the doorway. If Antonio was inside, Theo knew he was wasting his time. But he wasn't. Out of the corner of his eye, he caught sight of his friend coming up through the stone arcade on the other side of the square, where the peasant women sold their wares on market day. He had a girl with him, but Theo took off running anyway, dodging past the women at the fountain. He had no time to lose if he was to get back to the house by twelve.

"My mother's sick and I've got to leave," he burst out as soon as he got to Antonio. "And I didn't thank you properly when you came over because I wasn't expecting—"

"This is my sister, Maria," said Antonio, interrupting. He was smiling and looked transformed from the picture of misery he'd been a week earlier.

Theo turned to the girl and stopped, stricken to silence by her loveliness. Her hair, the color of golden-brown amber, fell in waves around her shoulders, framing the perfect oval of her face in which her blue eyes shone, sapphire-tinted like the sea at evening. She had a queen's head, Theo thought—full of decision and command, taking for granted its own beauty.

She was dressed simply, in a black dress with a red scarf around her neck tied in a loose knot—Anarchist colors—and her body was lithe, as if she could, if she chose, run faster than the wind.

But for now she was still, looking Theo up and down with an unashamed curiosity. He sensed at once her confidence, her devil-may-care attitude to everyone and everything, and he knew that he couldn't stand there gawping a moment longer without losing her good opinion before he had even begun.

"Hullo," he said weakly. "I'm Theo."

"I know who you are. Antonio has told me all about you," she said, and her voice was not what he had expected. There was the Andalusian harshness of pronunciation, but also a faint lilt that was all her own and a power, too, that felt almost masculine.

"Good things, I hope?" asked Theo and then immediately regretted his question. It made him sound like a supplicant—an approach he felt sure would earn her contempt.

But she didn't respond that way. "Yes, good," she said. "What's happened to your mother?"

"She got upset with my stepfather and had some kind of nervous attack. She's fragile, and it feels like she could break. I don't know what will happen." There was something about Maria that made him want to tell the truth, even though he didn't know her at all. He'd never experienced anything like it before.

"I'm sorry," said Antonio, putting his hand on Theo's arm. "That's terrible. And I'm sorry, too, about what I did. I shouldn't have given in to my father. Maria's made me see that. Will you forgive me?"

"Of course," said Theo, feeling stupid. He'd come to thank Antonio, not accept his apology.

"He's a bastard," said Maria simply, looking across the square toward the café, where her father was still standing guard over the entrance, his arms folded across his barrel chest. "A stupid, ignorant peasant greedy for land, just like his mother. He's our enemy. That's what he is. Yes?"

"Yes," said Theo, while Antonio simply nodded. It felt like he was signing up to something without knowing exactly what it was. But he hadn't hesitated. At that moment he thought he would have followed her off a cliff.

"Good. I'm glad we agree," she said and smiled, and he took it as a gift that she was bestowing directly on him. A spark of connection between them.

"Will you come back?" asked Antonio, and the question restored Theo to himself. Behind him, the church bell was tolling the hour.

"Yes," he said. "I'll find a way. And thank you. You showed me so much. I won't forget."

He stepped forward and Antonio put out his arms and hugged him hard and Theo realized he was crying. And Maria was watching him. And he wanted to reach out to her too. But he couldn't. He mustn't. He had to go.

20

MARIA

Theo did find a way to come back, but it was not of his making. He returned to the village the following summer because his mother insisted on going back, overriding the advice of her doctors and her husband. And when the opportunity came, he rode on her coattails, supporting her desperate desire to return to Spain because he longed to go back too.

He thought he was in love, although he admitted it to no one, realizing that his school friends would find the idea absurd when he had met the girl for less than five minutes! So instead he nursed his desire in secret, taking it out when he was alone to examine, as if it was a jewel that he had found by accident, lying in his path.

Although that, of course, was untrue. It was Andalusia that had enraptured him: wild and primitive and so utterly foreign, separated from all he had ever known by a barrier not of language but of experience. A city boy in a new world, he had been filled with an amorphous longing from the day of his arrival, when he sat on the roof terrace of his stepfather's house under the glittering stars and listened to the faint sound of guitars. All summer long he had watched the village girls in the square, walking the paseo arm in arm in the evening twilight, throwing sidelong glances that felt like arrows from under their black eyelashes, until that last day when he met Maria, the most beautiful of them all. And in that brief moment she crystallized his yearning, focusing it in one place, and captured his heart.

Elena sank into a dangerous lethargy after she got back to London, eating almost nothing and paying no heed to Andrew's pleas to preserve her strength, while he sat distraught at her bedside, powerless to arrest her slow but steady decline. Theo was given special leave to come home on alternate weekends from Saint Gregory's, but she was unresponsive to him, too, and he began to make excuses to stay away, throwing his energies into running and rugby and schoolwork as a way of distracting himself from his gnawing anxiety.

In March, a crisis was reached, and Theo was summoned home by telegram. Sitting alone in the night train as the sleeping towns rolled slowly by, he shut his eyes to force back the tears, sure that he would not arrive in time to say goodbye. But then when he got to the house, he was astonished to find his mother sitting up in an armchair, sipping tea.

"I need to go back," she said. She didn't need to say where. "God is waiting for me there. I know it."

She looked at her husband, but he dropped his eyes, and so she turned to Theo, who took her outstretched hand and answered her look of appeal without hesitation. "Yes," he said. "That's what we must do."

Now it was Andrew's turn to stand on the outside, looking in. He felt an immense gratitude to God that Elena had rallied, but he was unsure of whether the divine command to return to Spain should be obeyed. The religious fervor and hatred of the godless Reds whipped up by Don Vincente and his acolytes had precipitated his wife's illness, and wouldn't the same occur if she went back? But how could he stop her if she was so determined? Wouldn't that have the same effect, or worse?

Elena recovered just as she had in New York three years earlier. It was as if she had reached the crossing point, looked over the Styx, and decided to turn back. She possessed a fierce will to survive when she wanted to exercise it, the same fire that fueled her faith. But it consumed her, too, and she returned to the land of the living more spirit than flesh. Her skin was so pale now as to be almost translucent, stretched tight across the delicate bones of her face, and her eyes shone with an unnatural brightness. She was like an old star, Andrew thought, burning up from within.

She was weaker in body but stronger in will, and he could not oppose her, and in June they returned to the village.

Andrew lost no time in going to visit Don Vincente. Within an hour of their arrival, he was knocking on the priest's door with a bottle of the finest Campion sherry in his hand. He held Don Vincente personally responsible for Elena's illness, and he would have been happy to receive news that the meddlesome priest had been pushed off Santa Leticia's cliff by the Anarchists, but he knew that he had to make his peace with his enemy without delay, given that he was not prepared to do the deed himself.

He had remained true to his word and was still paying his workers subsistence out-of-season wages without telling Elena, and he ran the risk that, unbribed, the priest would inflame her against him just as he had before, and with the same disastrous result.

Andrew was not naive, and he knew that it would take considerably more than a bottle of vintage sherry to buy Don Vincente's compliance, but a handsome check, made out to the chapel restoration fund and slid across the priest's lacquered coffee table, had more than the desired effect.

"My wife has been very sick," he said, "and she needs calm. Nothing must agitate her. Nothing. I hope you understand me."

"Perfectly. I have prayed for Donna Elena's safe recovery every day since she left, and I give thanks that the Lord has answered my prayers and returned her to us," said Don Vincente, joining his hands together and looking piously up at the ceiling. "The Church will offer her the peace of God, which passeth all understanding. You can rely on me for that, Don Andrés," he added, glancing down at the check.

"Thank you," said Andrew, getting up to leave and just about maintaining a rictus smile of goodwill until he was outside, when he took aim and hit the metal footscraper a terrific blow with his walking stick as a vent for his bottled-up frustration.

Don Vincente was true to his word, but he couldn't deliver the "peace that passeth all understanding." Spain had changed while Elena had been away. In October, the Left had risen in rebellion, inflamed by the new government's lurch to the right. Risings in Barcelona and Madrid had been quickly suppressed, but in the northern province of Asturias the fighting had been brutal on both sides, and General Franco had brought in the Moors and the Foreign Legion to defeat the rebels. Now, nearly a year later, the events in Asturias were still the main topic of conversation on both sides of the political divide, and Elena couldn't help but hear about them from the devout ladies who looked after the church, with whom she had become fast friends the previous summer.

They relished the opportunity to whisper the worst atrocity stories to a fresh audience, and hardly a day passed without Elena coming home from Mass trembling with outrage.

"I can't bear it," she cried. "I can't bear what they did. They hung the naked body of the priest of Sama upside down in a butcher's shop window with a placard advertising pig meat for sale. Pig meat!" She began to weep—great, heaving sobs, and Andrew took her hand to try to comfort her.

"It's not true," he said. "The newspapers made it up. There was an investigation that proved they did. It was just propaganda. Both sides do it. You know that."

But his attempt to calm Elena down had the opposite effect.

"Whose side are you on?" she shouted, pulling away from him. "In New York you brought us Father Miguel Pro's blood. You gave me a photograph of his martyrdom. You made me weep. But now, when I show you pictures of the De La Salle Brothers and their priest, whom the Reds shot in Turón, you turn away. You don't want to know. You've changed. You're not the man I married."

"It's not true, Elena. I'm still that man. I promise you I am," said Andrew, putting his hand over his heart. "But Spain isn't Mexico. You have to understand that. The rebels are in prison, and the government is on your side. They have everything under control." He was making every effort to keep his voice calm and level, but Theo could see that he was frightened, and he felt the same fear, too, remembering what had happened to his mother when she became hysterical in this same room the previous year.

"We don't need to stay here, you know," Andrew went on. "We can go back to London anytime if you don't feel safe."

"No!" she shouted, banging her glass down on the table so hard that the wine in it spilled out over the cloth. "I know that's what you want, but I won't leave. This is where my home is now. This is where God wants me to be."

"Of course. It's your decision," said Andrew, putting up his hands.

Elena was calmer now, but she was staring fixedly at her husband with an icy look that Theo had not seen on her face before. He tensed, unsure of what was coming next.

"You're paying them, aren't you?" she said, and her voice was quiet, hard with accusation.

"Who?"

"The Reds. Your workers. They're all the same."

Andrew met her eyes and shook his head. "I'm not paying any Reds," he said.

Elena held her gaze and then laughed contemptuously, swiveling her head to look at her son. "And you too!" she said. "Don't think I've forgotten what you did."

"What? What did I do?" asked Theo, taken aback by his mother's sudden hostility.

"Went with them to that demonstration and fought the police. Almost got yourself expelled from school. You said you've turned over a new leaf. But have you? Who are these friends you spend your time with in the village? You think I don't notice, but I do. I see you sneaking out."

"I'm not sneaking," said Theo defensively. "And it's just Antonio. There's nothing wrong with him."

Elena continued to glare at him, and he looked away. He was lying, and he hated doing it, but he had no choice. Maria was an Anarchist through and through, and he had spent every hour that he could with her since his return.

She was always with the same group of friends: Antonio and Primitivo, whom Antonio despised, and Primitivo's friend, Jesús, who was thin and nervous, worried that his given name undermined his Anarchist credentials. Theo made a fifth after Maria had made short work of Primitivo's objections, telling him that he could find himself some new friends if he didn't like it.

There were no girls except Maria, but the constant presence of her brother kept this from being a scandal. Not that Maria cared about scandals, having escaped from her grandmother's clutches in Málaga by a systematic campaign of outrageous behavior, culminating in the proudest moment of her life, as she referred to it, when she had stood up in the middle of High Mass in the cathedral and begun singing "The Internationale" at the top of her voice. That had been the final straw for the old lady as she stared social ostracism in the eye, and Maria had been dispatched home on the morning train.

The group spent most of their time in the café and shop that Jesús's father ran in the square that Theo had passed through with Andrew and his mother on the day of his first arrival in the village. All the previous summer, he had never been back, and it seemed to him strange but symmetrical that he should be returning there now at the start of a new one. He remembered how he had felt that he was glimpsing the real Spain that day in the car, and here he was now, entered in behind the facade.

The bloodred Anarchist graffiti on the wall had been painted over, but the square was otherwise the same, with the dilapidated fountain dripping slow gray water down into the tin troughs and the hot summer sun beating down on the dirty cobblestones.

The café was a much poorer version of the thriving business that Bernardo Alvarez was running in the main square up above. Here there were never more than a few drinkers at the rickety tables outside, and Jesús's father kept a small shop in the front room of his house around the corner to help make ends meet. It was dark and cool inside, with ancient tinned goods lining the shelves, gathering dust, and the friends often met there, with Jesús waiting on the occasional customer that came in.

They could talk freely in the shop, except when Jesús's mother passed through on her way to church, crossing herself with fluttering hands to ward off the Anarchist contagion that she was powerless to prevent her son's friends from bringing into the house. Maria mocked her behind her back, perfectly imitating her reedy, querulous voice: "Oh, Jesús," she wailed. "That Jezebel has ensnared you with her honeyed words and darting looks. Come back to Jesús, Jesús. Come back and save your soul before it's too late."

Jesús laughed with the others, not because he found the parody of his mother funny, but because he had to if he was to avoid becoming the butt of the joke too. Mockery came easily to Maria, and she had a sharp tongue.

But not for Theo. From the outset, she seemed fascinated by him, asking endless questions about his life and comparing its glamour and variety to her own meager experience. And in response, he made it a rule to always tell her the truth. It was a way to give himself to her without declaring himself, while it also helped him to remain grounded when the effect that she had on him was so unsettling.

He told her about his father's suicide and the slum tenement where his mother almost died, and she cried in sympathy, but then a minute later she was asking him about the skyscrapers and the Statue of Liberty and the great boat in which he had crossed the ocean and whether it was like the *Titanic*. He told her everything, far more than he had told Antonio, who watched and listened with a half smile on his face, saying nothing, while Primitivo glowered in the corner, enraged at being so eclipsed by this scrawny newcomer with whom he could not hope to verbally compete.

When Theo got to the part about Olympia, Maria slowed him down and made him tell everything twice, and the rapt attention in her beautiful eyes fastened on his own inspired Theo to a vivid description of the events worthy of a journalist.

"Were you scared?" she asked.

"Yes, I was," he said. "Terrified really, because I'd seen the beating the Blackshirts gave to the others who stood up, and we had to wait until it was our time. I don't know how long it was, but it felt like forever. And I was scared of backing out too. I didn't want to have to look in the mirror the next day and know that I'd failed."

"But you didn't. You made people see those Fascists for who they really are. Oh, I wish I could have been there."

"I don't. There was a girl there . . ." He stopped, closing his eyes to shut out his recollection of the girl in the blue-flowered dress being attacked by Mosley's louts. Her torn dress, her head forced back. "I couldn't bear to see you hurt like that."

For a moment she was silent, and it was as if there was no one else in the shop. He felt the connection between them, running tense like an electrical current. He could see how her lip trembled and he wanted to put out his hand to touch her, to allow her to be still. But then she turned away, as if from danger, and the moment was gone, as quickly as it had come.

"See!" she said, rounding on Primitivo. "Theo's done something that matters. He had the guts to stand up and take a beating for what he believed in, and it made a real difference to the world."

"No, it didn't," said Primitivo angrily. "England doesn't matter. It has nothing to do with us. And, anyway, I've done things too."

"Like what? Written slogans on walls and statues when no one's looking? That's brave." Maria laughed and Antonio joined in. Behind the counter, Jesús looked more than usually nervous, shooting fretful glances at Primitivo, wondering what was coming next.

Theo could see Primitivo clench his fists, although it was unclear whom he was going to hit. Theo hoped that he wouldn't be the target, but feared the worst. Primitivo had openly declared that he loved Maria and claimed to be her *novio* when she wasn't present to correct him, and he was always going to hate any boy whom she showed any interest in, particularly one who was richer and cleverer than him and came from New York.

Theo didn't want to admit it to himself, but he was frightened of Primitivo. He could feel the coiled-up animal rage inside him, straining to get out. He'd sensed it when he first saw him from a distance in the square the previous year, and now, up close, it was as if he could smell it too. It crossed his mind that Primitivo's violence was the price he was going to have to pay for getting close to Maria. He really would have to earn her love.

Glancing over at her, Theo was surprised to see that she was flushed and excited, and he realized that she'd provoked Primitivo deliberately, as if for her own entertainment. But then, just as Primitivo was about to lose control, she used her power to stop what she had started. "Don't be a fool," she told him. "I swear I'll never speak to you again if you start anything."

He looked at her defiantly, keeping his fists clenched, and then abruptly dropped his eyes, turning to Jesús. "I'm hot," he said. "Give me a beer."

Jesús hesitated—he was under strict instructions from his father not to take anything out of the shop—and Primitivo pushed him hard on the shoulder, causing him to lose his balance. He laughed as Jesús got to his feet, then helped himself to the beer.

Now there was an ugly atmosphere in the shop. Theo felt a pressure in the air, rendering him tongue-tied when before he had been speaking freely, telling his life story to Maria. He edged to the door, muttered a goodbye, and began to walk home.

Halfway across the square, he heard pounding feet behind him and panicked, thinking it was Primitivo, come to exact revenge. His legs were weak and he felt a shrinking at the base of his spine and in his shoulders, which stopped him running away. He turned and almost collapsed with relief when he saw it was Antonio.

"Damn you!" he said. "You did that deliberately."

"No, I didn't," said Antonio, laughing.

"Liar!"

"All right, I'm sorry," said Antonio, falling into step beside his friend. "Primitivo's nuts, isn't he? All that anger he's got locked up inside. It can't be good for him."

"He looks like he could kill somebody."

"Yes, I'd say it's only a matter of time, if he hasn't done it already."

"Well, I don't want it to be me, that's all."

"Then I suggest you stop making eyes at my sister," said Antonio. "Primitivo's a jealous bastard, and he's crazy about Maria."

"But she's not crazy about him, is she?"

"No, he's too stupid. She despises fools. She always has."

"So why does she keep him around?"

"Because she enjoys the power that she has over him, turning it on and off like a tap. You saw what she just did."

"Yes, but it's more than that," said Theo thoughtfully. "I was watching her. She likes his violence. It excites her."

Antonio turned to look at his friend and nodded. "Yes, you're right," he said. "I didn't know you'd seen that. It's the Anarchist in her, I suppose. She's a true believer."

"And you're not?"

"No. And you neither. You haven't got it in you."

"I've got other things," said Theo defensively.

"That my sister will like, you mean?" asked Antonio, smiling.

"Maybe."

They passed through the square where the Guardia had rescued Theo from the starving man. Theo walked slightly ahead with his eyes on the ground, lost in his turbulent thoughts.

Antonio laughed. "You know your way now," he said. "So I suppose you think you don't need guiding anymore."

"I guess not," said Theo distractedly. He was thinking about Maria.

"But I think maybe you do," said Antonio, taking hold of Theo's arm so that he had to stop. "At least listen to a little advice. See my sister if you like, but don't fall in love with her. It'll bring you nothing but grief. She doesn't want love; she wants freedom. Freedom and power, although she won't admit that last part."

"I think it's a bit late for advice," said Theo, smiling sadly.

Antonio looked hard at his friend and then shook his head. "I'm sorry to hear that," he said. "But if it's true, don't tell her. She likes you now, but she'll get tired of you very quickly if you play the lovelorn boy and ask to be her *novio*. You'll be like Primitivo, but without even his crazy violence to commend you. I'm saying this for your own good. Do you understand me?"

"Yes," said Theo. "I understand. But I'm not a fool. I know it already."

"Well, at least that's something," said Antonio, looking relieved. "And now maybe we can forget about my sister and think of something more rewarding. Like lunch, for instance? I'm famished."

"All right." Theo nodded. But they'd walked on only a few yards when he returned to the subject of Maria. "How do you know she likes me?" he asked.

"Because she told me so. A breath of fresh air is what she called you, I seem to remember."

Antonio blew air out of his mouth and smiled, but Theo ignored his attempt at comedy. "Anything else?" he pressed.

"She said she's never met anyone like you before. But whether that's good or bad, I don't know. Traveling the world isn't part of the Anarchist training book, the last time I looked. And now, enough! I've told you what will happen if you carry on with this obsession, and I've had my fill of talking about my sister for one day."

"Okay," said Theo, raising his hands in mock surrender and this time staying true to his word.

But that didn't stop him thinking about all that had happened, puzzling over everything Maria had said, and Antonio too. He knew his friend was right when he'd said that his sister liked power. He could see how she'd used him to inflame Primitivo, but there was more to the way she looked at him than that. He could feel her interest in him, her attention. It was real. He knew it was. Perhaps riling up Primitivo was her way of not having to face what she felt.

He longed to reach out to her and reveal himself, but he sensed that Antonio was right that this could lead her to withdraw. She was quicksilver, acting on the instinct of the moment. It was enough that a seed had been planted; if he didn't force it, then maybe it would grow.

Primitivo was away sometimes in the weeks that followed, laboring with his father in the fields when work was available, and with only her brother present as a chaperone, Maria became freer, flirting with Theo and confiding in him and sometimes touching his hand to emphasize a point, apparently unaware of the charge she was sending through his body.

He could never get used to the flash of her eyes or the sweep of her hair, the sense that she was in perpetual movement, searching for new experience, just as he had dreamed of adventure as a boy in New York. He recognized that they were alike in this, and he felt a kinship with her that was as real as the longing that gave him no rest, pulsing in his brain day and night. The miasma of feelings that he called love.

"Everything in this village is so narrow," she told him, tapping her foot on the ground to vent her frustration. "Nothing happens; nothing changes. People become their parents. They're born, they get married, they die. On and on, round and round, like mice on a wheel. It's unbearable."

They were sitting on the low wall inside the stone arcade where Theo had met Maria the previous summer: a moment that had remained as vivid in his mind as if it had occurred just the day before. Antonio had left them alone for a moment while he went to speak to an acquaintance out in the square.

"But you changed," said Theo. "You weren't born an Anarchist, were you? It's the opposite of what your father would've wanted you to be. Something must have happened to cause that, surely?"

Maria was silent and Theo was worried for a moment that he had offended her, but then she smiled. "You're right," she said. "Something did happen here, and I spoke as if it didn't. I shouldn't have done that. I'm sorry."

It wasn't the answer Theo had been expecting. Maria was always so quick and confident. She wasn't one to criticize herself.

"What was it?" As he asked the question, he realized how badly he wanted to know the answer. He had told Maria so much about himself, and yet he still knew next to nothing about her. It was as if she'd wanted it that way, or maybe it was just that she wouldn't talk about herself when others were present.

"I'll show you if you like," she said, surprising him again as she got up and set off along the arcade with Theo following in her wake.

At the end she turned sharp left, crossing quickly to the open door of the ayuntamiento, and they went inside. It was siesta time and the place was empty.

"Shouldn't we get Antonio?" Theo asked. He was an outsider in the village, but he knew enough of its ways by now to know that it would cause a scandal if he and Maria were found together.

"Do you want to?" she asked, turning the question around.

Theo hesitated and then shook his head and Maria smiled, beckoning him forward into a large room to the right of the entrance hall. A line of chairs was stacked against the far wall, but there was otherwise no furniture, and sheer lace curtains that had seen better days hung down over the tall windows, diffusing the incoming sunlight. Theo guessed that the room was used for meetings and that these were infrequent, judging from the fine layer of dust covering the tiled floor. He breathed easier, thinking there was a good chance that no one would come in, but at the same time he could feel his heart beating hard. It was the first time he and Maria had been alone together, and she was the one who had brought that about.

"This is where I met Nicolás. Two years ago next month," she said, breaking the pressing silence that had enveloped them after she'd closed the door. "I was standing over there, looking at a painting"—she pointed to the blank stretch of wall behind the stacked-up chairs—"and he came up to me and we talked about it. I think it was the most important conversation of my life."

"Who's Nicolás?" asked Theo, feeling confused. It wasn't a name he'd ever heard Maria refer to before.

"He was a missionary. Don't worry—not a religious one," said Maria, laughing when she saw Theo's look of bewilderment. "Educational missions were an idea of the new liberal government after they got rid of the king—they sent teachers out into the countryside to show the peasants that there was more to life than working in the fields. There were four of them that came here—three young men and a woman. They drove up the hill in a clapped-out truck with a gramophone and books and six big paintings packed in the back, belching out so much exhaust smoke that we didn't think it would make it to the top. But it did, and that afternoon they hung the pictures up in here with a sign outside saying **Museum of the People**. There were flowers on tables and a colored carpet on the floor and violins playing on the gramophone. You wouldn't have recognized the place. It was beautiful . . ." Maria broke off with a distant look in her eye, as if she were seeing the room not as it was now but as it had been two years before.

"What kind of paintings were they?" Theo asked, impressed by the vivid strangeness of the scene Maria was describing.

"Copies of Spanish masterpieces in the Prado. The idea was that we had a right to see them because they belonged to all of Spain, not just the rich people in Madrid. There were religious pictures, of course, and portraits, and then there was the Goya. The painting was called *The Third of May 1808*. I couldn't take my eyes off it. I'd never seen anything like it before."

"Why? What's it a picture of?" asked Theo, angry with himself that he had never heard of the painting and knew nothing of the artist.

"An execution. One that's about to happen, and the kneeling man with his hands up in the middle of the picture knows that there's no escape. You can tell from the look in his eyes. He's terrified, outraged that his life is going to end, but the point is it doesn't matter. All around him are peasants that have already been shot and behind him are those that are going to be next, and the soldiers in the firing squad don't care. They're pitiless. Nothing will stop them. The man's not a martyr or a hero, he's just a target—a sunburnt laborer in a white smock who they're going to kill. There's no hope, no justice, no God—that's what the picture is saying."

"But you don't believe that," said Theo, taken aback. "About the hope, I mean. I know you don't."

"No, you're right, but you have to start with what Goya says. That's what Nicolás told me. He said no one had painted like that before. Before him, it was always how things should be, not how they are. But Goya told the truth. That the rich are pitiless and cruel and will always starve and kill the poor to keep what they have, because that's their nature. So we have to end all the things that subjugate—money, capitalism, the state, the Church. It's the only way to—"

"Nicolás was an Anarchist?" Theo interrupted. He knew what Maria believed; what he wanted to know was why.

"Yes," she said. "I met him again the next day and he gave me books, and we walked through the village, and he made me see it in a way I never had before.

He showed me the houses of the rich and the hovels of the poor. He ran his hands over the crumbling walls and he told me that the poor starved because they were ignorant, and he pointed up to the church and said that it kept them that way with its lies, but that a change was coming and that we had to help make it happen, that we could—" Maria stopped suddenly, the rising tide of her recollection cut off as she turned away, putting her hand up to her face, as if to ward off an attack.

"Could what?" Theo asked.

She shook her head, and he could see that there were tears glistening in her eyes and that her small hands were balled into fists.

"What happened, Maria?" he pressed, putting his hand on her arm for a moment. "Please tell me."

"Nothing."

"What do you mean, nothing? Something must have." The deflation with which she pronounced the single word, *nada*, was like a death, a sudden plunge into void that he instinctively rebelled against.

"Someone saw us together and told my father. In this village, there are eyes in every window, whispers behind every door."

"What did he do?"

"Shut me up and locked the door, and kept it locked until the mission left. They never came back."

"Why?"

"The Right won the election." Maria shrugged. It was as if the energy had drained from her as her vision of the past slipped away. The dreary, empty room in which they were standing had replaced the art gallery it had once been.

"What about Nicolás?" Theo asked. "What happened to him?"

"I don't know. I wrote a letter to the ministry in Madrid but I never got a reply. And if he wrote to me, my father would have intercepted it."

"I'm sorry," said Theo, catching the sadness in her voice. "I know what it's like to lose a teacher."

Maria nodded. "You remind me of him," she said, looking closely at Theo now as if she was measuring him, trying to get a sense of who he really was. "You know things, you've seen the world, and you've tried to change it too. I admire that. New York, London—when you talk, it's as if I can see the buildings and the crowds and the traffic and the noise. Life: I can feel its pull. Here!" She clasped her hand to her chest. "It's everything that this place is not. And I think it has to mean something that you found me here, because it's so unlikely. No one comes to a village like this, but Nicolás did, and now you too. But then I lie awake at night and think that you are devils sent to taunt me." She laughed bitterly. "You will leave just like he did, because you are free, while I am in chains and can't escape. You can't see them, but they're as real as the curtains on those windows over there. My father holds me in his fat fist and wants to sell me to the highest bidder like I'm one of his prize pigs fattened for the slaughter, and he laughs when I protest. Laughs! Do you know that?"

"I won't let it happen," said Theo, even though he had no idea what he could do to stop it.

"Nor will I," she said with renewed passion. "Because I believe that the day is coming when we will all be free. Not just me, everyone. And for that we will have to draw blood. Are you prepared for that, Theo? To join me?"

"I don't know," he said. It would have been easier to lie, except that he had promised himself to always tell her the truth.

"Why? Why can't you believe?"

It was the same question he'd so often asked himself. From the day he broke his mother's Christ statue in the apartment in New York through his dogged refusal to embrace Esmond's Marxism at Saint Gregory's. He remembered Carlos's answer at the inn when he'd asked how the Anarchists would achieve liberation: when *"the last marquis has been strangled with the guts of the last priest."* He couldn't fight for that.

"It's who I am, always on the outside looking in," he said sadly. "But I promise I'll fight for you. Isn't that enough?"

"I don't know. Maybe," she said, and it was as if the words had been dragged from her against her will. "I haven't met anyone like you before."

"Nor me you," he replied. He was filled with a sudden elation, knowing with certainty for the first time that Maria cared for him. She'd said as much to Antonio, but it was different to hear it from her directly. He wanted to take her soft hands in his and draw her to him and tell her what he felt. Put an end to the waiting and the longing, regardless of the consequences and Antonio's warnings.

But perhaps she sensed this, because she moved away just as he was about to speak. "I've got to go," she said without explaining why. "Wait a minute before you come out. I don't want my father to see us."

But then no sooner had she left than she put her head back around the door. "I'm glad I told you about Nicolás," she said. "I didn't know I was going to, but then I did. It'll be our secret."

And before he could think of a reply, she was gone.

Theo couldn't sleep that night or the next. He paced his room or the moonlit *terrado*, waiting for the dawn to bring another day when he could see Maria again. His love was an addiction, eating him up from the inside.

He longed to kneel down beside her and make his confession and put an end to the uncertainty between them. The way she touched him and watched him seemed to invite that, as if that was what she wanted too. But each time he was tempted, he drew back, remembering Antonio's advice.

He couldn't deceive himself. He was sure he would lose her if he told her, and the way she spoke of love was like a warning.

"These girls are such fools," she said as they sat with Antonio in the main square one evening a few days later, watching the paseo. It was twilight and Theo had been filled with that same electric sense of possibility that he had felt in the same place a year before, until Maria's icy contempt brought him crashing down to earth. "Look at them! They're like animals in a zoo," she jeered, spitting out her words. "All they care about is finding a *novio* and then hanging on to him for dear life until they've got him to the altar."

"And what's wrong with that?" asked Antonio, smiling.

"Because there should be more to life than that," she said passionately. "Women should be free. They're as good as men, and they should have the same rights to study and get good jobs, but instead they're just cleaners and child rearers. That's all they have to look forward to—stuck in their miserable houses with screaming babies, while their husbands drink away the family's money at bars like this. Old before their time."

"But that's what they want, isn't it? To get married and have houses and children?" asked Antonio, who seemed to be enjoying playing devil's advocate.

"Only because they don't know any better," said Maria. "And because they're frightened of idiots like you laughing at them because they're spinsters. *Solterona*—that's the dirtiest word in our language, but it should be the proudest."

"Maria la Solterona!" said Antonio, laughing. "It certainly has a ring to it."

"You can laugh at me all you like, but it won't change the fact that you're a weak-willed coward who jumps when Dad snaps his fingers. You don't want to join the army, but you're going because he tells you to. It's pathetic, and I won't let that happen to me. Not now, not ever. I'd rather die than marry that pig Pedrito!"

"Maybe you'll have to, when the time comes," said Antonio, who seemed to have lost his sense of humor in the face of Maria's attack.

They were silent, with Antonio turned away in his chair, watching the girls in the square, and Maria breathing hard, trying to control her anger. Theo could see how it was only her brother who met her on equal terms and told her what he thought, and how sometimes she hated him for it, even if she loved him too.

"Antonio doesn't understand because he's Spanish and so he thinks that women are men's property," she said, laying her hand on Theo's wrist. "But you're not like that, are you? In America it's different."

Theo wanted to agree with both statements, so he didn't know whether to nod or shake his head, and ended up doing a bit of both. Anything to keep her hand where it was.

"It's all going to change," she went on after a moment with a faraway look in her eye, and it seemed to Theo as if they were back in the ayuntamiento and she was testing him again. "There's no going back now, not after the rebellion in the North. Soon it won't just be Asturias, it will be the whole country up in flames. Freedom is coming. It's so close I can feel it. Can't you?"

"Yes," said Theo. And he wasn't lying. Something was coming. He was sure of that much. What it was he didn't know, but he could smell it in the air, thick and heavy.

21

AYUNTAMIENTO

The days passed and everything remained the same. Stagnant and inert like the summer heat. It was as if they were all balanced equally against each other, requiring some outside force to precipitate a change in their relationships.

And when it came, it was from an unexpected source.

Theo arrived at the shop one morning, pulled the blanket back from the door, and stopped, rooted to the threshold, as he came face-to-face with Carlos, the Anarchist whom he and Antonio had met in the mountains the summer before.

Carlos looked the same. Black hair and beard and eyes smoldering in a thin, pale face, hollowed behind high cheekbones that exaggerated its length. And just like at the inn, he dominated the room with a natural charisma that kept everyone's eyes fixed upon him, even though he was sitting in a low chair in front of the counter while everyone else, including Maria, was standing. He reminded Theo of Mosley on the rostrum at Olympia, waiting to speak.

But something was missing.

"Where's Pablo?" Theo asked, the question coming out of his mouth rude and unbidden, before he'd spoken any words of greeting. Because it struck him as so strange to see Carlos alone. He and his friend had seemed such a pair in the mountains, united by the utter contrast of their appearance and temperament.

"He's dead," said Carlos, staring Theo in the eye, as if daring him to look away.

Theo was shocked. He hadn't met Pablo for long, but he remembered how he had seemed so alive: joking and laughing and drinking, filling the big barnlike inn with his noise. It didn't seem possible that he was dead.

"How?" he asked. "How did it happen?"

"We were prisoners in Asturias," said Carlos, looking around the room now to capture everyone's attention. "We went there to help the miners. They were brave and fought with all they had—sticks of dynamite they use in the mines when there were no more bullets—but it was hopeless. Franco sent in the Moors and they went through the villages, raping and looting and murdering. They hacked the workers to death like they were animals, which is what Franco thinks we are, of course. Those of us that were left were rounded up and sent to detention centers run by the Guardia Civil. The one we were in was a converted convent, and they tortured everyone. With rods, with water, with electricity. They were quite ingenious. And they made no exceptions. I think they went through the prisoners alphabetically, and when they got to *Z*, they started again. They wanted to know where we had hidden our arms and the money stolen from the Bank of Oviedo, but that was just an excuse. They tortured us because they wanted to, because that is their nature. Until one day they got careless and we escaped. They came after us, firing their guns. Pablo was hit, I wasn't."

The matter-of-fact voice in which Carlos had been speaking made what he was saying even more horrifying, and after he'd finished, everyone was silent, except Primitivo, who slammed his hand down on the counter. "We have to do something," he shouted. "We have to fight back."

"Yes," said Carlos evenly. "We do. And that's why I'm here. Tell me this, friends—what is wrong with our country? What is the root of the evil?"

"Capitalism," said Primitivo straightaway. "The latifundistas treating the braceros like slaves."

"Yes," said Carlos. "But how do they do it?"

"They own the land, they set the wages . . ." said Primitivo, tailing off uncertainly. He was like a kid in school, Theo thought. Wanting to give the right answer to a favorite teacher, but anxious that he'd got it wrong.

But he needn't have worried. Carlos had got exactly the answer he was looking for. "That's right!" he said, snapping his fingers. "*They own.* Or they say they do. And their false claim to property is what the whole rotten edifice of money exploitation and suffering is built upon, and so we must destroy it. In this village and in all the villages."

"You mean, burn the property records? In the ayuntamiento?" said Maria excitedly. Theo looked over at her and saw that she was gazing at Carlos with rapt admiration, as if he were some kind of higher being. It struck fear into his heart to see how with just a few sentences, this cold-blooded fanatic could hold her in the palm of his hand.

"Yes," said Carlos. "I do mean that. But it's not enough to break a window and throw in an esparto torch and hope for the best. You need to find the records where they're locked away and destroy them, every last one of them, because you'll only have one chance. You have to get inside the building. Your mother works there as a cleaner, doesn't she?" he asked, turning unexpectedly to Jesús, who had been standing behind the counter, saying nothing up to now.

Jesús nodded, surprised to be the sudden focus of attention.

"So, she must have keys?"

Jesús swallowed. "Yes," he stammered.

"Will you get them for us?"

Jesús took a deep breath and then committed himself. "Yes," he said. "And I'll go inside, too, and do the burning. You can rely on me, sir."

"Good boy," said Carlos. "Now, who else? Jesús can't do it on his own."

"I'll do it," said Primitivo and Theo both at the same time and then stopped, glowering at each other across the room.

Theo was surprised at himself. He'd spoken without thinking, without knowing what he was going to say before he said it. Why? Because he believed, like the Anarchists, that property should be abolished and everything should be owned in common? No, he didn't believe that, or at least he didn't think he did.

Maria was the reason he had volunteered. Because he'd understood in that moment that all that had passed between them—the conversations and half declarations, the seeds from which he'd promised himself that love would grow—would become an irrelevance, swallowed up and forgotten in Carlos's call to action. Unless he followed her down the path that she had chosen. But was that a good enough reason to risk everything to commit such a crime, when he had everything to lose and she had nothing?

He felt confused, but there was no time to think because Primitivo was attacking him. "He's never worked," he told Carlos furiously, jabbing his finger in Theo's direction. "He's not one of us. He's not to be trusted."

"Yes, I am," said Theo, stung by the accusation. "Just because I'm not stupid and ask questions doesn't mean I'm not—" He broke off, seeing the doubt written on Maria's face.

"Not what?" said Carlos. "An Anarchist?"

Theo nodded.

"Show me your hands," said Carlos.

Theo thought of refusing, but then held them out reluctantly, hating how soft they were, hating Primitivo's contemptuous laugh. As if hands proved anything.

But Carlos didn't laugh. "Now look at mine," he said.

Theo went closer. The backs were beautiful—artist's hands, with long, thin fingers tapering to their ends, but turned over, they were red and raw, with the palms crisscrossed with multiple tiny lesions. Theo recoiled, sensing how painful they must be, and wondered why he hadn't noticed them in the mountains, but then recalled how Carlos had hardly eaten, leaving Pablo to finish his share of the food. Pablo, the life of the party, now lying dead in some unmarked grave in the North.

"Is it a disease?" Theo asked.

"It's life," said Carlos. "My life. When I was a boy, I lived in a village like this one, but closer to the sea. And every day except Sunday I got up with my father in the middle of the night, and we walked the road to the beach to buy cod from the fishermen when they returned with their catch in the dawn. Others, too, were there, standing ready with their coins. We had baskets on our back held in place with halters on our heads like we were oxen, and once we had the fish, we ran. Racing up the hills to get back to the village because if we got there first, we could sell all we had on the street corner in a few minutes, but if we were last, we were lucky to sell half, and that for next to nothing. Sometimes the baskets broke open as we ran and the brine seeped onto our backs and down our arms to our hands, poisoning the skin. But we still ran. On and on until the blood came out of our eyes. And then one day my father crested a hill and fell down dead. After that I didn't run anymore. I just starved."

Carlos looked down at his hands and then at Theo's and smiled. "The boy's right. You're not one of us," he said. "You should go home. This is not your fight."

Theo wanted to argue, but no words came. He felt like a man who had been sentenced and had no right of appeal. All that was left was to leave.

"So it's settled then," said Carlos, looking around the room. "Jesús and Primitivo will go in, and all you need is someone to stand lookout outside. Can you do that?" he asked, turning to Antonio, who'd been standing at the back up to now, watching but saying nothing.

"No," said Antonio. "I want no part of it."

"Very well, but will you keep silent?"

"Yes."

Carlos stared at Antonio for a moment and then nodded and looked at Maria. "You then," he said. "Agree on a flashlight signal with the others for if there's trouble."

"What about him?" asked Primitivo, pointing at Theo. "Do you trust him? Like you said, he's not one of us."

"He won't talk," said Carlos, getting up.

It was as if Carlos knew him better than he knew himself, thought Theo as he trudged away up the hill. Once again, he felt that sense of not belonging that had haunted him throughout his life. He could shake it off for a while—at school or here—but sooner or later it seemed to always come back to find him, leaving him standing in the same place: on the outside, looking in.

Volunteering wasn't enough. He could deny it all he wanted, but the truth was he did ask too many questions. Why? Because he was too clever for his own good. Carlos had known from the beginning, up in the mountains, that he was no true believer, and so had rightly pushed him away, preferring to use a vicious thug like Primitivo and a yes-man like Jesús to carry out his plans.

But what mattered to Theo now was that Maria had witnessed this rejection and would adopt it as her own. He had seen how she'd hung on Carlos's every word. He was a born leader, and she was as committed to her faith as Theo's mother was to hers. All his tall tales of Broadway and the Bowery couldn't save him now. Maria would throw in her lot with Primitivo and leave him behind without a backward glance.

Theo stopped to catch his breath. He had been walking fast to keep pace with his thoughts and now, at the entrance to the main square, he caught sight of Maria's father standing proprietorially in his white apron outside his café. Theo was tempted to go over and tell him what his daughter had got herself into. That would put an end to Carlos's plans once and for all. But in the next moment, he knew he couldn't. Carlos had been right about that too. Whatever Theo was, he was no rat.

In frustration, he smacked his hand against the wall beside which he'd been standing and immediately remembered that Primitivo had done the same thing half an hour before. He felt like an idiot, and that made him hate Carlos even more. But there was nothing he could do and so he turned around and went home, just as Carlos had told him to.

The next morning Antonio came to the house, and they talked outside in the garden.

"We need to do something," Antonio said. "Before it's too late."

"About what?" asked Theo morosely. He'd hardly slept and was in no mood for visitors.

"About my sister, of course. She's going to be ruined if she goes through with this."

"What can I do? She won't listen to me."

"Maybe she will. She thinks a lot of you. I know that."

"Not anymore!" said Theo bitterly. "Our friend Carlos has seen to that. And you seem to forget that I volunteered to do the burning, so I don't see how I can start telling her that it's all a bad idea now that I'm not needed. Can you?"

"You volunteered because you wanted to impress her, not because you thought it was right. You need to admit that and start thinking about her and what she needs. Not everything is about you, you know."

"Do you think I don't know that?" said Theo peevishly.

"For Christ's sake, stop feeling sorry for yourself, Theo," Antonio shouted in exasperation. "It's too bad if my sister doesn't love you. I told you not to go down that road, but you wouldn't listen."

He stopped, breathing heavily as he fought to bring his temper under control. And then, once he was calm, he turned to go. "If you really cared about Maria, you'd try and help me," he said, shaking his head sadly. "But it seems like the only person you're interested in is yourself."

Theo watched his friend walk away through the gate, anchored in place by pride and indecision. He knew that Antonio was right, but he didn't want to lose what he had left of Maria's good opinion by telling her to desert the cause. And yet doing nothing was worse. Standing alone on the outside was what he couldn't bear and Antonio had offered him a way back in, at least to talk to Maria and try to save her from herself. He had to take it and so, without further thought, he set off at a run and caught up with Antonio in the shadow of the church.

They didn't speak. Antonio just nodded, and they walked quickly on through the narrow twisting streets, side by side.

As they approached Jesús's father's shop, Theo wondered whether their march across town would turn out to be in vain. Perhaps the conspirators had already laid their plans and were waiting somewhere else for night to fall so that they could carry out Carlos's orders.

But they were inside. All three of them, looking up in surprise as Antonio came purposefully through the door, followed by Theo, who hung back, feeling much less sure of himself.

"What do you want?" demanded Primitivo, his voice brimming with hostility.

"To talk with my sister," said Antonio defiantly.

"Whatever you want to say, you can say in front of them," said Maria. She seemed as angry as Primitivo and almost spat out her words.

But then, just as Antonio was about to speak, she cut him off. "If you two have come here to try and get me to pull out, then you're wasting your time. Is that why you're here, Theo?" she demanded, rounding on him.

Theo hesitated, faced with an impossible choice. If he said yes, she'd hate him; if he said no, then he'd be letting her down.

She laughed, and he fancied that for the first time he could see contempt in her eyes when she looked at him. It took the wind out of him, wounding him with a new pain that he had not felt before.

"You heard your sister. You're wasting your time. And ours," said Primitivo, taking a step toward Antonio. "Now why don't you just fuck off?"

Behind Primitivo, Jesús joined in. "Get out of my store!" he told Theo and Antonio. "You're not welcome here."

"Your father's store, you mean?" Antonio shot back. "It's you who'll need to get out, Jesús, when he finds out that you've burnt his title deeds."

"If you tell him, I'll . . ." Primitivo had his fists clenched now.

"Kill me?" asked Antonio.

"Yeah," said Primitivo, lowering his voice so that it was icy now. "You can count on it."

"Good to know," said Antonio. "But fortunately you can save yourself the trouble and the garotte, because I've got no intention of telling anyone. I already told your fisherman friend that."

"Maybe you did," said Primitivo. "But I still don't trust you. You're going to join the army. That makes you the enemy in my book."

"Your book!" said Antonio, laughing. "You haven't read a book in your life. And you never will. You're too stupid. And you're not even a real Anarchist. You don't want freedom; you want power—the power to own my sister and tell people what to do."

Primitivo had heard enough. Jumping forward, he hit Antonio with a sucker punch to the stomach, following it up with a quick, vicious uppercut to the chin that sent him crashing to the floor.

Theo didn't think. Just as before on that first day at Saint Gregory's, he hurled himself forward and threw the bully to the ground. He was bigger now and had developed tackling skills on the rugby field, but Primitivo was a stronger adversary than Barker, and it might have gone badly for Theo if Maria hadn't intervened.

"Stop!" She screamed the word at the top of her voice and with an unexpected authority that caused everyone to freeze.

Slowly, they got up from the floor. Primitivo and Theo dusting themselves off, and Antonio still crouched over with both hands holding his stomach.

"Are you all right?" Maria asked him, and he nodded, even though his face was a rictus of pain.

"Okay," she said, and turned her attention to Primitivo, looking him hard in the eye. "Don't do that again!" she told him. "Not to either of them. Not ever. Do you hear me?" Her voice was like a whip, lashing against him.

Primitivo looked defiant for a moment, as if he was going to argue, but then he dropped his eyes and nodded.

But that wasn't enough. "Promise!" she ordered, taking his arm.

And again, he obeyed. "I promise," he said, and then turned away and spat on the ground.

"Now get out," she told her brother. "And don't come back."

"Maria—" he began, but she cut him off.

"Go!" she said. "It's my life, not yours."

Theo watched Antonio as he reluctantly went out. Grief had replaced pain on his already swollen face.

Theo looked back at Maria. "You too," she told him, but softly this time. And then, just as he was passing through the door, she spoke his name, causing him to turn around.

"Thank you for stopping him," she said.

And he smiled for the first time in a long time. "You're welcome," he said, speaking softly, too, and dropped the blanket.

"Idiot!" said Antonio furiously.

"Who? Me?" asked Theo.

"No. Not you. Me." Antonio was standing, bent over the trickling fountain in the middle of the square, splashing water on his face, although whether to ease his physical pain or to try to wake up from his nightmare experience inside the shop wasn't clear.

"Why? What did you do?"

"I allowed myself to get distracted by that oaf. I lost my temper with him when I should have been talking to my sister, trying to make her see sense."

"But you seemed in control," said Theo, surprised. "I thought you were brave, the way you talked back to him. You showed him up for who he is. An oaf, like you said."

"I wasn't brave. I was scared. That's why I said those things. They were just what came into my head to keep me going."

"Well, I'm glad you did say them," said Theo. "Somebody needed to, and maybe Maria will think about it now."

"Think about what? Primitivo? Well, I can see how that might help you. But it's not going to stop her burning down the ayuntamiento, is it? That's Carlos's idea, and as far as she's concerned, he walks on water."

"She's not burning it," said Theo. "She's just the lookout."

"It doesn't matter," said Antonio. "She's part of it, and if the Guardia get one of them, they'll get them all."

Theo didn't respond. He had no basis to disagree with Antonio's reasoning, but at that moment he was in no mood to share his friend's pessimism. He remembered the way Maria's attitude to him had changed from contempt to gratitude during their encounter, and he replayed in his mind the promise she'd extracted from Primitivo to leave not just Antonio alone, but him too. Surely she wouldn't have done that if she didn't care about him.

In contrast to his companion, Theo walked back up the hilly streets with a spring in his step. He was glad he'd gone to the shop. A few hours earlier, he'd woken in despair, but now he felt something very like hope bubbling up again in his overworked heart.

But his mood didn't last. At home he wandered the house, unable to settle to anything, waiting for news. It was hardest to cope at night because he knew that that was when the attack would come. He stood motionless on the *terrado* for hour after hour, staring down toward the square, looking for the sudden leap of flames in the darkness, while the moon traveled serenely through the glittering constellations above his head. His nose twitched like a hunting hound's as he sniffed for the smell of smoke, but there was nothing. The air stayed still and hot without a breath of wind, and the silent village spread out below seemed suspended in time, waiting.

It made it worse that he could do nothing and tell no one. He sought distraction in company, but then withdrew when his mother peered into his tired eyes and asked him suspiciously what was wrong. She had become calmer as the weeks had passed since her outburst at lunch, and even laughed sometimes in the kitchen with Señora Constanza as they cooked paella together, arguing good-naturedly over the ingredients. Theo liked to be there then, running out to the garden to cut sprigs of oregano and thyme and coming back to stand close to his mother as she used the sharp knife in her petite hand to cut and chop and peel with extraordinary precision and rapidity. Sometimes she would notice him watching and would run her fingers through his hair like she used to do, and for a moment it was as if they were back together in the apartment in New York before their troubles began.

But such moments didn't last. The laughter would subside and the look of stretched fragility would return to her pale face and he became frightened that her health would collapse again, just as it had before. On the day after Maria had turned him away, he went into the salon in the evening and found his mother lying on the sofa with a cushion under her head. Out of the blue, the thought came to him that she was dead.

She was so still, and in the fading light he could not see her breathing. But instead of going forward to find out the truth, he hung back in the doorway, clinging to the remnants of his uncertainty. It was as if he could glimpse the desolation that awaited him when she was gone and wanted to keep it at bay for as long as possible. If he didn't go close, she could still be alive, and he couldn't give up on that chance.

He stood without moving, almost without breathing, matching her immobility, holding on to the moment. And she opened her eyes.

"Why are you standing there like that?" she asked, smiling. "You look like a ghost."

"I didn't want to wake you," he said. "You looked so peaceful."

"I was," she said with her brow creased, puzzled for a moment, as if she was trying to remember a vanishing dream. "But I'm happy to see you, too, my son."

She looked at Theo quizzically and beckoned him over and took his hand, and he knelt down beside her because he couldn't stay towering above her. It was too awkward.

"Are you all right?" she asked, looking into his eyes. "I'm your mother. You know you can tell me if something's wrong."

He wanted to. He would have liked to pour his heart out to her, but he couldn't. She wouldn't understand, and it would make her sick to know the secrets that he was keeping from her. He felt desolate as he surveyed the chasm, years in the making, that now lay between them.

"Nothing's wrong," he said, getting to his feet and crossing over to the window where he stood, looking down past the church toward the wide tiled roof of the ayuntamiento.

Another night passed, and Theo's nerves were stretched to the breaking point. He couldn't stand the suspense. He had to see Maria and ask her what was happening, even if it meant a return of her anger and contempt.

But then, just as he had formed the resolution and was about to act on it, she came to him.

He was at lunch in the dining room with his stepfather when Constanza came in to announce that there was a visitor waiting at the door. Elena had woken with a migraine and was lying down upstairs.

"Who is it?" asked Andrew.

"A girl," said Constanza. "She didn't give her name."

"Tell her to come back tomorrow," said Andrew irritably. "I haven't got time today. I've got to go out again after lunch."

"But she wasn't asking for you, sir," said the housekeeper uncomfortably. "It's Master Theo she wants. She said he'd know what it's about, even though I told her that it was irregular."

"Irregular?" repeated Andrew.

"She's on her own, sir," said Constanza, looking distressed.

"Oh, I see," said Andrew, turning to Theo, who had already gotten to his feet. "Do you know who this young lady is?"

"Yes, I do," said Theo, moving toward the door. "And it's all right. I'll be back soon."

He went out without waiting for an answer and ran down the stairs and opened the door.

Maria was standing on the threshold. He'd been thinking of her constantly, picturing her face in his mind, and now here she was where he had never expected to see her, turning dream into reality. He wanted to take her in his arms and kiss her and hold her and stroke her hair, and perhaps he would have done if she hadn't started talking straightaway. In a flurry, with her words tumbling out in a cascade of staccato half-whispered sentences, as if she couldn't hold them in a moment longer. He had never seen her so agitated.

"I had to come. Jesús has chickened out and Antonio won't help. Says he's washed his hands of me. And there's no one else I can trust except you . . ."

Theo pulled the door shut behind him and took hold of Maria's arm. "Not here," he said urgently. "Go to the top of the hill. I'll follow you. We can talk about it up there."

She looked for a moment as if she was going to keep talking, but then she nodded and walked quickly away.

Theo went to the gate and stood waiting for several minutes, looking back nervously toward the house to see if his stepfather was coming out. But the door remained closed, and he set off up the hill.

He realized he hadn't gone this way since the previous summer, when Antonio and he had ridden their mules up into the mountains. It seemed like a lifetime ago now, and he felt a stab of regret for those days when Andalusia had seemed so vast and timeless and beautiful. Before Antonio's father took the mules away and his daughter captured Theo's heart, narrowing his life away from the sierras and the pine forests toward the drab interior of Jesús's father's shop down in the barrio.

He found Maria sitting on a stone at the turning in the track that led to the old tumbledown cottage where Antonio had said the witch lived. On any other day, Theo couldn't have imagined anything he would have wanted more than to be alone with her in the countryside, lying hidden together in the sun-bleached wheat fields, but now he wished fervently that Antonio was here, too, to back him up. His old friend might believe in witches and flying broomsticks, but he also possessed a healthy endowment of common sense, unlike his sister, and Theo had had enough time now to realize that burning down the ayuntamiento was a truly terrible idea. It wouldn't achieve anything except an incitement to rage and chaos and some awful punishment for the perpetrators, which was what Carlos wanted, of course. More martyrs for the cause meant more recruits.

Carlos was a fanatic who cared nothing for individual suffering, not even his own. He'd have forgotten Maria by the time he arrived at the next town.

Theo knew that he needed to try to make her understand this, even if Antonio had failed. This time he couldn't hesitate like he did before. But she didn't give him a chance to speak. As soon as she saw him, she took his hand and began to talk, rushing on from where she had left off in front of the house.

"It has to be tonight," she said. "It's the old woman's day off, and if we wait until tomorrow, she's going to notice her keys are missing and tell someone. Jesús only got them today, and then straightaway he said he was scared. He started sniveling and wailing, and Primitivo was going to force him, which he could've done easily—he's scary when he wants to be—but I told him no. I know I'm going to do a whole lot better in there, finding the records, than that crybaby. Carlos should have chosen me in the first place, but he didn't because I'm a girl, which is stupid. A lot of the Anarchists are like that. They're all for liberty and equality until they get home to their wives and daughters and start telling them what to do . . ."

She stopped, having lost her thread, and Theo took his chance to jump in:

"You shouldn't do this, Maria. Your brother's right. It won't do any good, and if they catch you—"

"They won't," she said, cutting him off. "Not if we have someone watching outside. And it can't be Jesús. I don't trust him. He'll cut and run the first chance he gets."

She let go of Theo's hand and got to her feet, breathing heavily. "Will you help us?" she asked, staring down at him. "Yes or no?"

"It's not as simple as that," he said, playing for time. There had to be some way to make her see how crazy all this was.

But she was already turning away. "I shouldn't have come," she said furiously, stamping her foot. "I should've known what you'd say. We'll do it on our own. We don't need anyone's help."

She began to walk away down the hill. Quickly, without looking back. Soon she was at the turn in the track, and then he couldn't see her anymore. He was alone with the incessant trilling of the invisible cicadas making a mockery of his hopes and the heat and dust of summer stifling his breath.

He ran. Without thinking, he ran. He had to. Thought could come later. She heard him and turned, and the sun was on her face so that it glowed golden, framed by the burnished cloud of her hair—a hundred shades of brown.

"I'll do it," he said breathlessly as he caught up to her. "Not because I agree, because I don't, but because I don't want you to get caught. Because I—"

"Because, because," she said, laughing, and reached out toward him, laying her hands on his shoulders, where they had never been before, silencing him. And kissed him. Once.

Taken by surprise, he didn't respond. Just reeled, feeling as if he would fall, even though he was standing on solid ground. And when he recovered, she had already stepped back and was talking, as if nothing had happened. As if everything was the same as before, which perhaps it was, for her. He didn't know what she had meant by the kiss, and he didn't have the words to ask her to explain.

"We'll meet by the church at two o'clock," she told him. "You'll stay by the arch when we go in, and if you see anything, you shine this three times," she said, reaching into her shoulder bag and handing Theo a square green Bakelite box with a magnifying glass lens set in the center. "Look, it's easy," she said, showing him. "You just hold it up and press the switch backward and forward. One of us will be watching all the time."

"How will you get out?"

"There's a back door in the lane behind the square. That's how we're going in too."

Theo gulped. He felt like he had a hundred questions to ask, but he couldn't think what they were. Maria reached out and took his hand. "Thank you," she said. "Carlos was wrong. I knew I could count on you."

He didn't understand. She'd said the opposite two minutes before. But she'd brought the flashlight, so maybe she did know. Understood him better than he understood himself, while she remained a mystery to him, continuously throwing him off-balance every time they were together.

Where they were standing, they were in sight of the houses at the top of the village and she moved away now, taking a path that led off to the left. "I'll go down this way," she said. "You're right. It's best if we're not seen together."

A moment later she was gone, but he remained where he was, as if rooted to the spot: a bizarre, effigy-like figure holding a flashlight up toward the sun.

He took the flashlight home and sat looking at it on the *terrado*. Everything about the day felt unreal. How had he got to this point when he had intended the opposite? It made no sense. He felt like he was in a fairground hall of mirrors in which everything was an illusion.

Everything except the flashlight. Square and squat and solid, sitting on the top of the wall with its tiny bulb in the big reflector bowl, looking back at him like an eye floating in silver water.

He looked at the eye and knew he would go. He had no choice. He had given his word. For better or worse.

He dressed in black and would have rubbed charcoal on his face if he had any. He felt like a character in one of the boys' adventure books he had read voraciously in his first year at Saint Gregory's to distract himself from his loneliness, and he kept the thought in his mind, remembering how those stories always had happy endings.

Outside, his nostrils filled with the rich scent of evening jasmine as he crossed the garden to the gate. The full moon enabled him to see his way, but also filled him with foreboding, because if he could see, then he could be seen too. He was alert to every sound. The unexpected creak of the gate as he pulled it open had him looking back fearfully toward the black windows of the house, and in the road a soft repeated hooting made him look up sharply into the staring yellow eyes of an eagle owl, perched utterly still on the long branch of a cypress tree.

He pulled his soft hat down over his ears and hurried on toward the church, walking around it once before he took up a position under the overhang above the entrance door, figuring this at least kept him out of the moonlight.

He pulled back his glove to look at his watch, counting the seconds down as he prepared himself for the noise of the church bell striking the hour. But when it came, the clang was louder than he expected and he shuddered, feeling each tolling as a knell.

Maria didn't come, and he worried that he had missed her. She hadn't said where to stand, but surely this was the logical place?

Or perhaps she had had second thoughts. Maybe Antonio had talked to her again and gotten her to see sense. And he would be able to go home whistling a tune, because he would have done nothing wrong. Out for a walk in the night because he couldn't sleep.

He stepped outside the doorway to look around. The archway leading to the main square was only a few yards away and beyond, in the shadowy distance, he could just about make out the long, flat outline of the facade of the ayuntamiento. Where Maria's journey had begun in the improvised art gallery two years before and where perhaps now it was going to end. A dog barked somewhere, and then everything was still.

Overhead, the church bell struck the quarter hour. How much longer should he wait? Another five minutes. Surely that was enough? He was wide awake and desperately tired, all at the same time, and his heart was beating too fast, thumping inside his chest. Even though it was a warm night, he felt cold sweat forming on his forehead. Just a moment to close his eyes was all he needed. Just one moment of rest . . .

Suddenly he was aware of someone coming up behind him. He went to turn but he couldn't, because there was a gloved hand over his mouth and another on his arm, holding him in a viselike grip.

"Keep your mouth shut!" said a voice that he recognized as Primitivo's. Through his shock, Theo could feel Primitivo reveling in his superior strength, communicating through his hands that he could do with him as he liked. Release him or hold him or squeeze the life out of him if he chose.

"Fuck off," said Theo, rounding on Primitivo as soon as he'd taken his hands away, so that their faces were only inches apart. He was furiously angry but retained enough presence of mind to whisper the profanity, hissing it through his teeth.

Primitivo laughed. "You were asleep," he said accusingly. "Fat lot of good you're going to do us like that. You might as well have stayed home with your sugar daddy."

"At least I turned up, unlike your friend," Theo shot back. "You should show some gratitude."

"Shut up!" said Maria. "Shut up, both of you! We need to work together to do this. Theo's going to be fine, aren't you?" She had her hand on Theo's arm and reached up and touched his cheek for a moment, resting the tips of her fingers on his skin as she looked into his eyes.

He trembled. Her touch compelled him. "You can count on me," he said. "You know that."

"Yes," said Maria softly. "I do. Now let's go. I'll show you where to stand."

They went through the archway and Maria stopped, pointing back to a small recess where the wall met the rounded column of the arch. He could see at once that it was a good position, facing the ayuntamiento, but commanding a wide view of the square with the café on one side and the stone arcade on the other.

"What do I do?" he asked.

"If you see anyone, wait and see what *they* do. There's no point drawing attention to yourself unnecessarily. But if it looks like they could be trouble, shine the light. Three times, like I said. One of us will be watching all the time. And when you see burning, then you run."

Burning! The word unnerved him and he longed to make one final last-ditch attempt to make her see reason and walk away, but he knew that it was hopeless. They were here now and there was no going back.

"Good luck!" he said, putting out his hand.

It felt like a quaint gesture, belonging to his school in England but out of place among Anarchists, and Theo felt like even more of a fool when Primitivo sneered at his outstretched hand as if it was an object of ridicule.

But Maria took it and held it, looking into his eyes as if sealing a compact, before she turned away and followed Primitivo down the stone arcade and into the darkness.

He watched, gazing out into the square that he had come to know so well in its many different guises. He thought of the girls walking the paseo in the evening, slow and loose and seductive, and he remembered the white sheet screen stretched between the plane trees, transporting the villagers as if on a magic carpet to Dracula's castle. In his mind's eye, he could see the patient, sun-worn faces of the peasant women squatted down by their wares beneath the arcade, and Maria's face when he first saw her there with Antonio: she was so beautiful that he didn't understand why everyone didn't stop what they were doing just to look.

And now, enveloped in the darkness, the square had another character: sinister, deserted, but alive with expectation, as if it could spring to life in a moment.

Up ahead, Theo saw a beam of light in the ground floor window of the ayuntamiento. They were inside.

And immediately, over to his left in front of the café, he sensed an alien presence. The moon had disappeared behind a bank of clouds, so he couldn't be sure, but he thought there were shapes moving beside the stacked tables and chairs.

Were his eyes tricking him? Was fear making his brain conjure up mirages in the night? He darted into the arcade and hid behind a stone pillar from where he had a better angle of view, looking straight across the square. He was sure he could see them now: shadowy figures creeping forward with rifles in their hands. Momentarily, the moon peeped out from behind the clouds, and he caught a glimpse of a Civil Guard's three-cornered hat. They were close to the door of the ayuntamiento.

Up above, Theo could see lights wavering in the windows of the third floor. He had to act now. A minute more and they would be trapped. But if he flashed the light, would Maria see him? She'd told him they'd be watching, but would they, now that they'd reached their goal and got inside the registry? And even if they did see, would they act on the warning? All he knew for certain was that the guards would notice, and then he'd have to run, and after that there would be nothing more he could do.

He had to make Maria understand she had to get out. Immediately. And there was only one way to do that. Running forward past the fountain, he took aim and hurled the flashlight up toward the window on the third floor, in which he could still see the lights.

He launched it like a discus, and as he stumbled to regain his balance, he heard the sound of glass smashing and an outbreak of confused shouting up ahead.

This time there was no paralysis. He pirouetted on his right foot and ran back toward the arch. He needed light now to see his way and, as if in answer to his thought, the moon was out again, breaking free of the clouds, and he was sprinting up into the streets above the church, just as if he was making for the try line at school.

After a minute he stopped, ducking into a doorway. Lights were coming on in several of the houses, and a man in a white tasseled nightcap leaned his head out of a window, looking for the cause of the commotion.

Theo knew he needed to be quiet. He was desperate to get home, but he forced himself to wait until the houses were dark again before he began to pick his way softly and slowly through the winding streets until at last, after what seemed like hours, he slipped in through the iron gate of his stepfather's house.

22

REPERCUSSIONS

Upstairs, he collapsed on his bed and woke up fully dressed and sweating with the morning sun pouring through the window.

How could he have slept like that? His hands shook as he tried to untie the laces of his shoes. He turned the bows into hard knots and ended up dragging the shoes off his feet and throwing them away into a corner.

And he was still trembling as his mind raced, forming a stream of questions to which he had no answers.

Had he been seen? He thought not, but he couldn't be sure. And even if he hadn't, might he still be named as an accomplice? By whoever had tipped off the Guardia, or by Maria or Primitivo if they had been arrested and interrogated?

Would they do that? Yes, of course, if they were pushed hard enough. Everyone had a breaking point. Theo remembered Carlos's description of the detention center in the North, where he and Pablo had been tortured. Spain was not like England or America. The Guardia treated the Anarchists like animals and would stop at nothing to extract the information they needed.

He thought of Maria being tortured. And himself too. Rods and water and electricity. How could he have got himself into this? How could he have been so stupid?

It made him nauseated to think of what they might do, and he ran to the bathroom and vomited, kneeling by the toilet bowl as he tried to calm down.

Maybe Maria and Primitivo had gotten away. He had thrown the flashlight with amazing precision. But had he thrown it too late? He remembered how close the Guardia had been to the door. The flash of the three-cornered hat in the moonlight.

Up on the *terrado*, he kept craning his head over the parapet, expecting to see men in uniform coming up the road.

But nothing happened. No one came, and at lunch Andrew and his mother talked about Don Vincente's elaborate plans for the celebration of the feast of Santa Leticia at the end of the summer, seemingly oblivious to Theo's agitation and loss of appetite.

By late afternoon he couldn't stand the suspense any longer and went out, retracing his steps from the night before until he got to the square, which was alive with the normal noise and bustle of a weekday afternoon. Women were washing clothes at the fountain, tousle-haired children and stray dogs were running this way and that, and the men at the café were drinking and arguing and playing cards and dominoes, shouting to make themselves heard above the sound of the radio loudspeaker on the wall. It was incredible to Theo that he was standing on the same ground where he had risked everything less than twelve hours earlier. Up on the third floor of the ayuntamiento, a piece of opaque plastic covered the window he had broken, but there was otherwise no sign that anything unusual had occurred.

Theo wasn't reassured. Out of sight, anything could be happening. He needed answers to his questions, and he stared over at the café, willing Antonio to appear. But there was no sign of him. Only his father, who came outside in his apron after a few minutes and stood looking up at the ayuntamiento with a thunderous expression on his fleshy face.

Theo retreated behind one of the stone pillars in the arcade and was just about to give up and go home when he heard someone calling his name, and turned around to find Antonio beckoning to him from the archway where he had parted from Maria the night before.

"I can't stay long," said Antonio as he led the way, walking quickly up the street behind the church. "My father's angry as a bull."

"Where's Maria?" asked Theo.

"At home, for now."

"So she got away!" said Theo ecstatically. "Thank God!" His relief was overpowering, passing like a wave through his body, releasing breath that had been trapped inside his diaphragm since the night before.

"Yes, thanks to you," said Antonio. "I heard what you did. It made me ashamed that I wasn't there, too, to help her, but I'd gotten so angry at her that I couldn't think straight. She won't listen to anyone, except that bastard, Carlos, of course. She can't see him for what—"

"Stop," said Theo, taking Antonio's arm and pulling him to a halt. "You've got to tell me what happened. Please."

Antonio looked at Theo and took in his distraught expression. "I'm sorry," he said. "Where do you want me to start?"

"Do you know who tipped off the Guardia? They were waiting when we got there."

"Don Vincente. At least, that's what my father says. It turns out Jesús's mother has been listening to everything we said in that shop for the last month, and after Carlos's visit, she got down on her knees in the confessional and spilled the full story to the padre. He gave her a few Ave Marias to say as a penance, walked down the road to the garrison, and repeated the whole thing to the Guardia, who then went round and put the screws on Jesús. They made him give Primitivo the keys because they wanted to catch Primitivo and Maria red-handed. But you put paid to that, and now Jesús and the old lady have fled the coop, worried that Primitivo will be coming after them, I expect."

"Where is he?" asked Theo.

"Primitivo? Released from custody, like my sister. The Guardia questioned them this morning, but they both denied it, and the Guardia can't prove they were inside the building or that anything happened, for that matter. There was no damage except to the window, and that was from the outside."

"So is that the end of it?" asked Theo hopefully.

"For them, yes. At least for now. But the Guardia are still looking for the person who broke the window."

"How do you know?"

"Because they've already been to talk to me about it, and they may pay you a visit, too, so you best be prepared."

"Me! Why me?" asked Theo. His anxiety had been slowly receding during the conversation, but now it returned with a redoubled intensity, bordering on outright panic.

"Because Jesús and his mother told them who was in the shop," said Antonio. "Look, I'm sure you'll be fine if you just deny it. That's what I did. Unless anyone saw you, of course?"

Theo shook his head. "I was careful," he said. But had he been careful enough? He felt a lot less confident now than he had in the morning.

"I have to go," he said. Driven by alternating compulsions, he couldn't wait to be alone now to think, when less than an hour earlier he'd been desperate to find Antonio and get answers to his questions.

"Me too. My father will be looking for me," said Antonio. "But listen, there's one other thing you need to know. He doesn't believe my sister. Not a word. The Guardia lieutenant talked to him, and he thinks that everything Jesús and his mother told the Guardia is the gospel truth. So he's sending Maria to a special convent in the North—somewhere up near Burgos—to learn obedience."

"What do you mean: *special*?"

"It's like a prison. They have locks on the doors and guards outside to stop the novices running away. And hair shirts, I expect, for if they try. It's my grandmother's idea. My father called her on the telephone this morning. She's been itching to teach my sister a lesson ever since Maria humiliated her in the cathedral, singing that song at the top of her voice."

"He can't do this," said Theo, aghast. "He's got no right. He's—"

"He's got every right," said Antonio harshly. "He's her father. He can beat her black and blue if he wants to. You just don't understand this country, do you, Theo?"

Theo shook his head, feeling suddenly defeated. Antonio was right. How could he understand? Spanish women were treated no better than slaves, and he came from a country where a war had been fought to abolish slavery long before he was born.

"Novices!" he said, repeating the word Antonio had used. "Is your father going to make Maria a nun? Is that what he's planning now?"

"No, she's going to marry Pedrito, just like I told you before."

"You said the cacique might not agree," said Theo, clutching at straws.

"Now he will. My father has gotten richer since last year, so he can afford a bigger dowry for his daughter, and money speaks with Don Fadrique. You know that. And besides, Pedrito's got his heart set on the idea, apparently."

"'Apparently'!" Theo repeated the word bitterly. "How do you know all this?"

"Because my father told her it today. Or shouted it rather, bellowing it in her ears. He broke the door open when she tried to lock herself in her room."

"That's terrible," said Theo, feeling sick. "Isn't there something we can do?"

"I can try and stop him hitting her before she goes away, although I don't think there's much chance of that, because he won't want to spoil her looks for Pedrito. But you—you can do nothing. My father didn't like you much before, but now he won't let you near my sister. He thinks you're the one who broke the window, so you're as bad as Primitivo in his book. My advice to you is to forget about her. Get on with your own life."

"Didn't she say anything? About me?" asked Theo. He couldn't bear that everything should end this way, without even the chance to say goodbye.

"She told me to thank you," said Antonio. He hesitated and then reached into his pocket and handed Theo a small envelope. "I don't know what's in it," he said. "But whatever it is, don't let it give you hope. Because you'll be wasting your time. That's the best advice I can give you."

Theo nodded. "What about you?" he asked. "Will you still see me? Or will your father stop that too?"

"No, you're my friend. I got it wrong last summer, but I won't again. I promise." He spoke slowly, solemnly, as if he was taking an oath, and then abruptly reached out and put his arms around Theo, hugging him close for a moment, before he turned and walked quickly away.

Theo hurried home. He'd thought of opening the envelope straightaway, but he wanted to be alone when he read what was inside, away from any possibility of prying eyes.

He opened the door and climbed the stairs, and was about to go on up to his bedroom when he heard his stepfather calling to him from the salon.

Something was wrong. He could tell from Andrew's insistent tone of voice, shorn of its usual courtesy. He thought of pretending he hadn't heard and creeping back down the stairs, but he dismissed the idea, knowing it would just make things worse.

He cursed his stupidity. Antonio had warned him to expect trouble, but instead of preparing for what lay ahead, he'd run home like a schoolboy, clutching his letter. He pushed it deeper into his pocket and breathed slowly, trying to summon up his depleted reserves of courage before he went in to face the music.

His worst fears were confirmed when he saw a young man in a handsome blue uniform sitting on the edge of a chair opposite his stepfather. His back was straight, his expression severe, and he was holding his three-cornered hat in his hands. The sight of the hat reminded Theo of his close encounter the night before and unnerved him even more than the fat pistol resting in a shiny black holster on the man's hip.

"Sit down, Theo," said Andrew, pointing to an empty chair beside him. "This is Lieutenant Robledo of the Guardia Civil. He has some questions for you about an event that occurred in the main square last night."

Theo's mind raced. Deny everything! That had been Antonio's advice. Antonio had denied involvement and escaped arrest, and if Antonio could do it, then surely he could too. But Antonio had been innocent, he remembered. Whereas he, of course, was guilty.

"Do you know Maria Alvarez?" asked the lieutenant. He fired the question like a bullet, staring hard at Theo as he answered to assess his veracity.

"Yes," said Theo. There was clearly no point in denying a known fact.

"Primitivo Moreno?"

"Yes."

"Do you know that they are Anarchists?"

"Yes."

"Are you an Anarchist?"

"No."

"Do you know that they were plotting to burn the ayuntamiento?"

"No."

Theo shifted uncomfortably in his seat, unable to meet the lieutenant's gaze. He felt hot and was sure his cheeks had flushed red.

"Were you involved in their plot, acting as a lookout while they went inside?" The lieutenant's voice was savage, demanding the truth.

"Really, Lieutenant, this is absurd," said Andrew. "My stepson has already said he did not know of the plot, so how could he be involved in it? And knowing an Anarchist may be unwise, but it's not a crime as far as I know, is it?"

"You will please let me ask my questions," said the lieutenant, turning sharply to Andrew.

"Very well," said Andrew, undaunted. "But please make them sensible."

The lieutenant paused, and Theo felt grateful to his stepfather. His interruption had eased the pressure, at least for a moment, and the lieutenant seemed a little less sure of himself than he had been before.

"Did you throw a flashlight through the window of the ayuntamiento at half past two last night?" the lieutenant asked, turning back to Theo.

"No," said Theo, looking the lieutenant in the eye this time. *If you're going to lie, lie well,* he heard an inner voice in his head telling him.

"I should think not," said Andrew, stirring in his chair again. "The boy was in his bed asleep."

"Can you vouch for that?" the lieutenant shot back.

"Of course not," said Andrew, sounding exasperated. "I was asleep too. Really, Lieutenant, I think you had better tell us if you have any evidence against my stepson. Coming here and making baseless allegations seems like harassment to me, and I shan't hesitate to make a complaint to your captain if the circumstances warrant it."

Now it was the lieutenant's turn to look nervous. He began to speak but thought better of it, getting up instead and putting on his hat. "This matter is under continuing investigation," he said officiously. "We will let you know if we have further questions."

"Of course," said Andrew, getting up too. "And my stepson stands ready to answer them, don't you, Theo?"

"Yes," said Theo faintly. He wished he could have made his voice sound more resolute, but the lieutenant had rattled him, and now he was reduced to counting down the seconds until he was gone, like a battered boxer waiting on the bell.

"I will show myself out," said the lieutenant, clicking his heels together and bowing slightly to Andrew. He shot a last look of dislike and disdain at Theo and was gone.

As if by mutual agreement, Andrew and Theo remained where they were, standing and sitting, saying nothing, until they heard the sound of the front door closing down below, whereupon Theo sighed heavily. Looking down, he saw that his hands were shaking again, and he felt a terrible stiffness in his neck.

"Thank you," he said, looking up at his stepfather. "I was all over the place and you saved me."

"From your own foolishness," said Andrew harshly. "I assume you did throw that flashlight?"

Theo nodded. It didn't occur to him to lie. He needed his stepfather and instinctively realized that Andrew wouldn't be able to help him if he didn't know the truth.

"So why did you do it?" Andrew demanded icily. "Because you're an Anarchist now? Is that it?"

"No."

"No? So you told the lieutenant the truth about that, even though the rest of what you said was lies?"

"I understand why they're so angry about the exploitation and the injustice, but I don't agree with what they want to do about it." Theo spoke slowly, trying to get his words right, refusing to be provoked by his stepfather's angry sarcasm into a reflex response.

"The burning and the violence, you mean?" asked Andrew. "Is that what you don't agree with?"

Theo nodded.

"So why did you try to help them burn down the town hall?"

"That wasn't why I was there. I tried to stop Maria, but she wouldn't listen. And then I went with them because I didn't want her to get caught. I threw the light because that was the only way. The soldiers were so close . . ." Theo stopped, remembering the terror of that moment.

"How do you know this Maria?"

"She's Antonio's sister."

"Do you love her?"

"Yes."

"And does she love you back?"

"I don't know. Maybe not," said Theo. He'd found this answer harder to give than all the others. He was admitting that Maria might not love him not just to his stepfather but to himself. He dropped his head, feeling the knowledge as a darkening of all that was bright inside him. It hurt, almost more than he could bear.

"Was she the girl that came here yesterday?" Andrew's voice was softer now, as if he sensed Theo's pain.

Theo nodded.

Andrew stood, thinking for a moment, and then went over to the side of the mantelpiece and pressed the bell that connected the salon to the kitchen.

"What are you doing?" Theo asked nervously.

"Wait!" said Andrew, holding up his hand.

A minute later the housekeeper appeared in the doorway.

"Constanza, you remember the young lady that visited the house yesterday asking to speak to Master Theo?"

"Yes, sir."

"Well, she didn't. Do you understand me?"

"Yes, sir," the housekeeper answered evenly, without any change of expression.

"Have you spoken of it to my wife?"

"No, sir."

"Good. Let's keep it that way. As if it never happened."

"Yes, sir. Will there be anything else?"

"No, thank you, Constanza," said Andrew, smiling. "I appreciate your understanding." But his smile was fleeting, put on for the benefit of the housekeeper, and it vanished as soon as she had gone.

He went over to the cocktail cabinet and poured himself a double measure of whiskey and then sat back down in his chair with a sigh, nursing his drink as he gazed into the firelight.

"We've been here before, Theo," he said at last, and there was a pained weariness in his stepfather's voice that Theo had not heard before. "In London, remember? And I really thought you'd learned your lesson. But it seems I was wrong. There's a recklessness inside you that I just don't understand. You don't show it to me, but I think it's there all the time, driving you to make bad choices. People impress you with their personality or their beauty or their arguments, and you follow them blindly over the cliff. Communists before, Anarchists now. You have to start thinking for yourself before it's too late."

Andrew looked at Theo, expecting a response, but Theo didn't know what to say. It was all true. Life pulled and pushed him in different directions, as if he was forever walking in a buffeting wind, and he'd ended up the night before a hairbreadth from being arrested. It scared him how easily it had happened, and how quickly too. "I want to be in control," he said. "It's just hard sometimes."

"Yes, I can see it's not easy," said Andrew. "Everywhere you go you are new, and so you try to fit in. But you must grow up and learn to be your own man. I'm not going to pretend to you that this is a good situation you've got yourself into. I was bluffing the lieutenant about making a complaint. I don't have the influence here that I have in England, and what little I had has gone by the wayside since I fell out with the cacique. The Guardia captain will have no sympathy if he decides you're an Anarchist, and he could well call you in for further questioning. I think you need to get out of here now while you've still got the chance."

"But isn't that like admitting I did it if I run away?" asked Theo nervously. He was frightened of the Guardia, but he also found it hard to accept the idea of leaving if it meant he would never be able to return.

However, on this point, his stepfather was more reassuring. "I don't think so," he said. "Nobody has told you not to leave. At least, not yet. And by next year it should all have blown over. But for now you must concentrate on your schoolwork. Your reports from Saint Gregory's have been excellent, and you have a great opportunity to get into Oxford if you work hard next term. That is how you will be able to make a difference in the world, as you say you want to. Not by fighting the Guardia Civil."

"What about you and Mama?" asked Theo. "Will you be going back?"

"No. Your mother is determined to stay here. She says it's her home now, and she refuses to go to England. Not even for a short visit. She worries about the traveling and thinks that if she leaves, she'll never come back." He sighed. "It isn't what I had planned at all. I've explained to her that London is my base and that staying here all the time causes me serious difficulties, but then she says that she's happy for me to go there on my own. But I can't do that. I can't leave her. Not after what happened before. So we go round and round, getting nowhere. It's a mess."

"She thinks God is here," said Theo. "That's why it's home for her."

"God and the Devil!" said Andrew bitterly. "This country is breaking apart. I tell you, I can feel the tide running out beneath my feet."

"But surely the government can do something to stop it," said Theo hopefully. "That's what they're there for, aren't they?"

"In England yes, but not here. The problem is that Spaniards aren't political. They're religious. The Left just as much as the Right. They all think they've got God on their side. Or Marx or Bakunin or history. It doesn't matter. What does is that they believe the people on the other side are the Antichrist or the class enemy, not human beings but rabid dogs. And you don't talk to diseased animals. You shoot them, particularly if you have a taste for violence like the people here do. Violence is where all this will end. Asturias was just the beginning."

"If you think that, you should leave. It doesn't matter what my mother says," said Theo, alarmed by the picture his stepfather had painted.

"I can't," said Andrew. "Your mother is fragile. You of all people ought to know that. She mustn't be upset or crossed. It's another reason why you should leave now, so that she doesn't get to hear about your escapade."

"Won't Don Vincente tell her? He's the one who warned the Guardia. Not about me, maybe, but about the plan."

"How did he find out?" asked Andrew, looking surprised.

"The mother of Primitivo's friend went to confession and . . ."

"And Don Vincente waltzed down the road to the Guardia and violated the sacramental seal without so much as a backward glance," said Andrew, laughing grimly as he finished Theo's sentence. "Dear God, he's a terrible priest, but his immorality also makes him susceptible to bribery, which is a blessing. Don't worry. I can keep him quiet."

In spite of the awfulness of everything his stepfather had been saying, Theo smiled.

"Don Vincente's ridiculous, but this situation's not funny," said Andrew sharply. "You need to take this seriously, Theo."

"I am. It's just the irony I was thinking of. About us, I mean."

"What irony?"

"It used to be me on the outside looking in, hating you for taking my mother away from me, and now we're the ones working together to try and keep her safe. And not just that—you're the one who seems to be looking out for me. I wouldn't have expected that either," said Theo, finishing his thought.

"Well, I guess stepfathers aren't all bad," said Andrew. He got up and held out his hand. "Make us proud," he said as Theo took it.

"And now go and pack and leave me to my whiskey. Things will look better in the morning."

Upstairs in his bedroom, Theo took out the envelope Antonio had given him, crinkled now from having been pushed down in his pocket.

Inside there was a note folded over a lock of Maria's hair. "Please don't forget me," it said. Just that. Not even her name.

He held the hair to his face, brushing it across his cheek, imagining, before he replaced it carefully in the envelope.

He couldn't forget Maria, but he had to live without her. She was going where he could not follow, and he had to start thinking for himself. What had happened in the square had been a warning. His stepfather was right. He had to learn to be his own man.

He went over to the open window. The shadows were lengthening across the roofs and everything was still, but from somewhere in the distance he could hear the faint sound of a woman singing. A lament like the one he'd heard on the morning he left the inn the previous summer. *Malaguena,* Antonio had called it. A song of loss, falling through the octaves and filling him with that same tinseled melancholy he'd felt with his father on Coney Island years before.

And he felt in that moment as if the song had always been there, playing on the edge of his consciousness like an underground river running through his life.

He closed the window and pulled his suitcase out from under his bed and began to pack.

23

SAINT GREGORY'S

Back at Saint Gregory's, Theo's resolution held firm. He worked hard in the classroom and played hard on the rugby pitch, and time passed in a blur. In November he went to Oxford on the train and stayed in a cold, gloomy room dominated by a full-length portrait of a severe nineteenth-century ecclesiastic who bore an uncanny resemblance to Herbert Hoover. The gray water pipes gurgled malevolently through the night as he lay shivering in his overcoat under clammy sheets, but sleep deprivation had no effect on his exam performance as he raced through the papers, filling the pages with fluent argument.

On the last day, he had two hours before the train left and wandered through the city streets, gazing up at the towers and spires and dreaming of the life he would have if he got in. Intoxicated by books and history and new beginnings. And three weeks later to the day, he received a letter from Trinity College informing him that he had been awarded an exhibition to study Spanish and modern history, starting in September of the following year.

Theo's name in gold letters was added to the honor roll engraved on the wall of the main hall, and at the award-giving ceremony on the last day of term, he received so many prizes for his academic and athletic achievements that he needed help from Cattermole to carry them back to his room.

Cattermole was unrecognizable as the terrified weakling that Barker had terrorized three years earlier. He had grown up and filled out and now played rugby for the Colts, but he still worshipped Theo, although now from a respectful distance.

Outside, in the quadrangle, Cattermole suddenly stopped, looking as if he wanted to say something but couldn't get it out.

"What is it?" asked Theo impatiently.

"I just wanted you to meet my parents," said Cattermole timidly.

"Of course. I'd like to," said Theo, putting his books down on the ground, and as if they'd been waiting for a cue to enter, two rotund adults with red faces appeared from behind the flagpole on which the Union Jack was fluttering cheerfully in the breeze.

Mr. Cattermole was wearing an ill-fitting black suit with a lurid green tie and his wife was in a pink dress with a bow, but they still somehow succeeded in looking like identical twins.

"We've heard so much about you," they said, bobbing up and down in synchrony.

"Good things, I hope?" asked Theo, resisting the temptation to bob up and down too.

"Oh, yes," Cattermole's mother said. "Jason thinks you're the cat's whiskers."

"Mother!" Cattermole protested in agonized embarrassment. And Theo had to breathe hard so as not to laugh.

"We wanted to thank you because you've done so much for Jason, particularly when he was starting out and finding his feet," said Cattermole's father, sounding like he was delivering a prepared speech.

"No, you've got it the wrong way round," said Theo. "Your son—Jason—he saved me when I was starting out. There was an older boy who wanted to hurt me with a lie and Jason told the truth, even though he was frightened. No, worse than frightened—terrified. I don't think I've ever seen anyone show more courage than your son did then."

Mr. and Mrs. Cattermole looked uncertain. It wasn't the answer they'd been expecting.

"You should be very proud of him," Theo said insistently. He was surprised by how much it mattered to him at that moment that these strangers should understand what he was trying to tell them.

But he needn't have worried. "Oh, we are proud," they said, bobbing in unison again.

Theo shook their hands, and they disappeared back into the milling crowd that was still spilling out from the hall.

Theo could sense people's attention on him and set off across the quadrangle at a quick pace, not wanting to be delayed or distracted by meaningless small talk.

"Thank you, Sterling," said Cattermole, half running to catch up. "You didn't need to say that."

"Yes, I did. It was important your parents should know what happened. I'm glad you introduced me to them."

"Are your people here?" asked Cattermole. "They should be proud of you, too, with all these prizes." He laughed, looking down at the armful of books he was carrying.

"No. No one's here," said Theo, feeling suddenly sad. It was strange to be so alone when all the other boys were surrounded by their families.

They climbed the stairs to Theo's study—the room high in the eaves that had once been Lewis's and that he had inherited as head of house, and Cattermole carefully placed the book prizes he'd been carrying in a pile on the floor.

"I'm going home with my parents now. I wish you all the best," he said, holding out his hand.

But Theo didn't take it.

"My father's dead. That's why he's not here. He blew his brains out in New York four years ago. I should have told you before," he said in a rush.

Cattermole looked thunderstruck. "I'm sorry," he said. "I didn't mean . . ."

"No, it's me who's sorry. I wish I'd told you. You're my friend and you deserved to know. But better late than never. Good luck to you, too, Cattermole—Jason, I mean," he said, smiling, as he shook Cattermole's still-outstretched hand.

Theo had already done most of his packing, and the study looked forlorn. Reaching up, he took down the framed picture of Eric Liddell that Lewis had given him when he left, and held it in his hands.

"He was a rugby player too." Theo's recollection of Lewis's voice was so clear that it almost felt as if Lewis was standing there in the room beside him. Back on that autumn day three years earlier, when he had suggested the new sport that had changed Theo's life at Saint Gregory's and given him purpose.

And set him against Esmond.

"Whose side are you on?" He could hear Esmond's voice, too, reaching out to him from the past, entwining him in memories.

Dropping the picture into his suitcase, he went down the stairs to the corridor where he had had his study the year before and stopped halfway along it, facing the door that had been Esmond's. It was slightly ajar, but he could not see inside.

He remembered that first evening when he and the other brats had stood in line to go up on the ledge and he had seen Esmond for the first time, reading a book in his armchair, oblivious to the crowd outside. The unbrushed blond hair falling about his ears, the gray sweater with the holes, the sculpted face when he looked up.

Theo remembered the room too. Every detail of it. The cheap bust of Marx on top of the bookcase, the mess of books and papers hiding the tea and sugar, and the gramophone in the corner playing "Brother, Can You Spare a Dime?" And he remembered himself in the room in the same armchair, crying over his dead father with Esmond's arm around his shoulder. No one had ever comforted him like that. No one.

Theo pushed open the door and found nothing. The most recent occupant had already left for the holidays, and all that was left was the iron bedstead, a set of dusty vacant shelves, and the dirty white walls.

He closed his eyes because the pain of loss was almost too much to bear, and a moment later heard a familiar voice calling his name. Was this one real or remembered? He turned and saw Father Laurence coming toward him down the corridor.

"I was looking for you and now I've found you," he said happily, but then stopped in his tracks as he took in Theo's pale, drawn face. "You look as if you've seen a ghost," he said. And then, glancing through the door into the empty room, he understood. "Ah, Esmond!" he said. "I should have guessed. He's been thinking of you too."

"What do you mean?" asked Theo, surprised. It was the last thing he'd expected his housemaster to say.

"A postcard. It arrived this morning," said Father Laurence. "Come downstairs to my study, and I'll give it to you."

Theo sat in the chair where he had spent so many happy hours, particularly since he had been made head of house—a job that required him to work closely with his housemaster, whom he had come to regard more highly with each passing term. Quiet but firm, religious but open-minded, perceptive and sympathetic—the monk possessed a combination of qualities that Theo had never known in anyone else.

He looked around at the familiar objects in the room, while Father Laurence searched for the postcard among the jumble of papers on his desk. An overcoat with a fur collar hanging from a hook on the door, the old whistling kettle that Father Laurence had set to boil when they came in, a small brass calendar with little inset wheels that turned the days and dates, and on the back wall a reproduction of El Greco's portrait of Christ, *Salvator Mundi*, which had made Theo think of Spain even before he went there for the first time.

He realized with a jolt that all day he had been collecting his memories of the school—people and objects—as if to put them in a bag to take with him when he left. To the extent that he belonged anywhere, he belonged here where he had succeeded, even while constantly questioning the school's validity and looking beyond its walls to the wide world, which had called to him ceaselessly to take sides, take a stand, take action, make a difference.

"Here," said Father Laurence, passing over the postcard. "I'm sorry for the wait."

On one side was his name and the school's address and a single word, *Congratulations*, and on the other the same picture of the Kremlin that had once hung on Esmond's wall upstairs. The postcard bore a British stamp and had been posted several days previously.

"I assume he is referring to your admission to Oxford and not your departure from Saint Gregory's," said Father Laurence dryly.

Theo nodded. It was hard to take in. He'd assumed Esmond was far away, gone from his life. But here he was, somewhere in England, monitoring his academic progress.

"I didn't tell him," he said, looking up. "I've kept my word."

"Yes, I don't doubt you," said Father Laurence. "But when you leave here, your promise expires, and Esmond may come back into your life."

"He's my friend," said Theo. "I miss him. But that doesn't mean I'll do what he tells me. I've grown up since he left. Become my own man."

Father Laurence looked hard at Theo and smiled. "You have grown. More than I could have hoped," he said. "But you're not finished, which is just as it should be. It's why you're going to Oxford."

The kettle whistled and Father Laurence got up and made the tea, placing a steaming mug in front of Theo, adorned with a poorly executed picture of the abbey church, so bad that it was almost a caricature.

"You're right that we must try to become ourselves," he went on thoughtfully. "That is the challenge God sets us. But our best selves and not our worst, and not something average and mundane, which is the lot of so many, drowning in unfulfilled mediocrity. We have to be patient to find fulfillment. We have to learn to walk before we run. And for some of us with the greatest potential, that is hard, because running comes naturally. Especially to you, Theo!"

"What are you saying, Father?"

"I'm saying you shouldn't get ahead of yourself. Enjoy Oxford for its own sake. Use your time there to read and to listen and to think—and to grow. That's the way to become your own man."

"It's what I intend to do, Father."

He was speaking the truth, but sitting there on that winter's day in Father Laurence's study, he had no idea how difficult it was going to be to carry out his good intentions.

24

THE ELECTION

Andrew had written to Theo before the end of term telling him that he now judged it safe to return to Spain:

> The authorities' focus is on the upcoming elections, which they expect to win handsomely with support from landowners like me. Past quarrels are forgotten and the cacique and the captain and I are now firm friends, which delights your mother, who really seems to have turned a corner . . .

And two weeks later, he and Elena and Señora Constanza gave Theo a hero's welcome as he was driven up through the wrought iron gates to where they were standing on the front step of the house under a handwritten sign reading **BIENVENIDO A CASA, THEO**.

As Theo dutifully ate his way through the huge feast that Constanza had prepared, Elena kept up a constant flow of questions about Trinity College, focusing particularly on its dress code, and told him that they would have to go shopping for a new wardrobe now that he was going to university. "You must look the best. The best of all the clever students with their grand titles!" she said, clapping her hands. "Mustn't he, Andrew?"

"Definitely," said Andrew with equal enthusiasm. "And then perhaps we can pay Theo a visit and see him in his magnificent rooms, dressed up in his new clothes."

Theo remembered his last conversation with his stepfather and understood that he was trying to use the news from Oxford as a way to coax his wife to leave Spain for England, at least for a visit, and he smiled, feeling like a coconspirator.

Andrew opened a bottle of champagne and they drank to Theo's health, and two round pink spots appeared in Elena's pale cheeks, which made Theo laugh. And while he was laughing, Andrew disappeared into his study and came back with a present in silver paper tied up with a red bow—"Wrapped by your mother," he said.

Theo opened it and took out a beautiful watch in its own special box.

"It's a Rolex," said Andrew. "They're a Swiss company, and they make the best watches in the world. The case is white gold and so is the dial. It's worth a good deal, so you must take care of it."

"I will," said Theo as he put it on his wrist. He loved the watch, with its strange, unexpected design of six larger black numbers at the top and bottom and six smaller ones on the sides, all enclosing the Rolex name at the center in tiny gold letters above a separate miniature dial for the seconds.

"Thank you," he said, shaking his stepfather's hand and leaning down to kiss his mother.

She took hold of both his hands and looked up into his eyes. "To think of how far we have come since New York," she said wonderingly. "Who would have thought it? You and me."

It was the first time in as long as Theo could remember that his mother had referred to their previous life or spoken of them as a pair, and he felt a surge of gratitude and hope for the future.

In the new spirit of reconciliation, he went to church with his mother the next morning and sat through a fire-and-brimstone sermon by Don Vincente in which he attacked the Popular Front as the Antichrist and urged the congregation to put their hands in their pockets one last time and give generously to the National Front, whose mission was to save Spain and the Church from the godless Marxists, Freemasons, and Jews.

"We will win the election," he shouted, thumping the pulpit with his pudgy fists. "Because God wills it. *Viva Cristo Rey!*"

And next to Theo, Elena crossed herself fervently, looking up with the rest of the congregation past Don Vincente to Christ bleeding on his cross above the altar, imploring him to answer their prayers for victory.

After Mass, Elena insisted on Theo waiting with her for Don Vincente to emerge from the vestry.

"Many congratulations, young man! I have heard from your dear mother about your splendid success," said the priest, keeping hold of Theo's hand even though he knew Theo wanted to let go, just as he had when they first met. Don Vincente's Spanish seemed to have become even more flowery than he remembered, Theo thought, as he mumbled an acknowledgment. Just as his stomach had grown rounder.

"You are fortunate to have your mother to guide you in your progress. I have always thought that the commandment to honor thy father and mother is among the most important of the ten," said the priest, looking hard at Theo.

"My father is dead," said Theo, unable to resist the obvious response.

But Don Vincente was ready for him. "All the more reason to honor thy mother," he said.

Theo knew what the priest was telling him. If Don Vincente hadn't known before about Theo's suspected involvement in the abortive attack on the ayuntamiento, then he was certainly aware of it now, and he was using the commandment to warn him to stay on the straight and narrow.

The old fraud! Theo thought with disgust. Lecturing him about the commandments when he had broken the sanctity of the confessional without a second thought, as well as sundry other priestly vows, if Antonio was to be believed. But Theo knew better than to rock the boat when his mother was happy, and so he swallowed his irritation and bowed his head respectfully to Don Vincente.

In the afternoon, Antonio came to the house. They embraced warmly, and Theo felt happy and relieved that Antonio had kept his promise not to allow his father to come between them.

Theo fetched his coat, and they began walking up the hill toward Santa Leticia's chapel.

"Nothing's changed, if that's what you're wondering," said Antonio, glancing over at Theo and answering the question that he could see Theo was burning to ask. "Maria's still locked up in Burgos, learning how to be a good Catholic."

"Have you heard from her?"

"No, but I didn't expect to. If Mother Superior is under instructions not to let her out, then she's hardly likely to furnish her with writing materials. My father's intending to bring her back to marry Pedrito once the election's over and he's finished bargaining over the dowry with Don Fadrique."

"You're making it sound like she's a lump of merchandise. Something to be auctioned off to the highest bidder!" Theo protested, feeling outraged by Antonio's matter-of-fact tone.

"No, I'm not," Antonio shot back. "Maria's my sister and I love her. But she's also my father's daughter, even though she likes to pretend she isn't. And as I've told you before, this country's not like America: girls do what their fathers tell them to do. That's how it's always been and how it always will be."

"Not if the Anarchists have their way!"

"If they have their way, we'll all be dead," said Antonio, slicing his finger across his throat. "I thought you'd learned your lesson about them last time you were here."

Theo had no answer to that. Antonio was right. He had learned his lesson, which was why he was trying to make a new start. And to do that, he needed to stop thinking about Maria, even though that was far harder now that he was back in the village and walking past the exact spot where she had kissed him only a few months before.

"Everyone's talking about the election," he said, changing the subject. "I went to church this morning to make my mother happy, and Don Vincente's sermon was like a political fundraiser. You should have seen him: banging his fists on the pulpit and demanding more money for the cause, while one of the altar boys went round with a special collection plate."

"Did you give?"

"No, of course not. What do you take me for? I kept my hands in my pockets, even when my mother gave me a dirty look. I hate that the Church is so political and takes the side of the rich against the poor."

"Yes, God help the priests of Spain if Christ comes back and sees what they've got up to while he's been away," said Antonio, grinning. "But, in the meantime, they're having quite an effect with their sermons, particularly on women. Last time, most of them voted for the CEDA, the Catholic Party, because the Church told them to. And the Right is hoping for a repeat. Maybe the republic made a mistake giving them the vote."

"Surely you don't mean that?"

"No, I'm a democrat like you. But I wish they would think for themselves, that's all."

"Who do you think is going to win?" asked Theo. He felt nervous asking the question, because it made him realize how much he cared about the outcome.

"People say the Right," said Antonio. "They've spent ten times as much as the Left, and they haven't just got the priests working for them. They've got caciques all over Spain fixing the vote as well."

"But you're not so sure," said Theo, picking up on the underlying doubt in his friend's voice.

"No," said Antonio, shaking his head. "I'm not."

"Why?"

"Because of the Anarchists. They didn't vote last time because they don't believe in elections, but this time they're putting their principles in their back pockets and turning out in force."

"Why?" Theo asked, impatiently this time. He wished that Antonio would just explain everything, instead of speaking in riddles.

"Because the Popular Front has promised an amnesty for the thousands of Anarchist prisoners that the government has kept locked up since the rebellion two years ago. But it's not just that. The working class as a whole are angrier than they were before, angry enough to defy the caciques and the priests. The few concessions they were given at the beginning of the republic have been taken away since the Right won in thirty-three, and they've had enough of starving while parasites like Don Vincente and my father live off their labor."

"I hope you're right," said Theo.

"I hope I'm right too. But it could go either way. The only thing I know for sure is that it's going to be ugly, whoever wins. Largo, the Socialist leader, spouts Marx and calls himself the Spanish Lenin, and Franco and the generals are itching to carry on where they left off in Asturias, with the Church and the landowners cheering them on. And you know from Carlos what the Anarchists have in mind."

Theo shivered. It was the same forecast of disaster that he had heard from his stepfather when they had talked in the salon before he left for England. *"Violence is where all this will end,"* he'd said. *"I can feel the tide running out beneath my feet."* And now Antonio was telling him the same thing.

"Look, even the heavens agree with me. The Day of Judgment is coming," said Antonio with a smile, pointing up to where a flotilla of black clouds had suddenly appeared, rushing over the mountains toward them. It was extraordinary. One moment the sun had been shining on a beautiful afternoon; the next, it was being swallowed up in a vast darkness stretching out like a grasping hand over the village. The birds fell silent and gusts of wind blew this way and that through the trees, bending and contorting their branches.

Ahead of them, lightning flashes lit up the peaks, followed by rolls of reverberating thunder. The air turned cold and rain began to fall. To Theo's surprise, the drops were solid and white—hailstones bouncing up off the ground like miniature ping-pong balls. They hurt with a sting when they hit his hands and face, and he felt disorientated. He'd never been in Spain in winter, and this kind of rain was a novelty to him.

But he remembered the electric storms in New York when he was a boy. Standing at the window with his father's arm around his shoulder, watching the lightning drawing jagged white lines between the skyscrapers.

"When thunder roars, get indoors," his father had told him. He'd loved mottos, particularly ones that rhymed. *"And don't go near trees. If lightning hits one, it'll explode the trunk and spread through the roots in the ground. That's how a lot of people get killed, because they don't know that."*

Clearly Antonio didn't, because he'd taken shelter under a big oak with a canopy of thick branches. Theo told him to move, bellowing to make himself heard above the noise of the thunder, and when that didn't work, he took hold of his friend's arm, pulling him into the open.

The hail was coming down harder now, pounding the beaten-earth track and breaking the surface into rivulets of running water, and the lightning had moved overhead as they came under the eye of the storm. Theo looked frantically around, searching for shelter. The houses of the village were hundreds of yards behind, but the old woman's cottage was only a stone's throw away up ahead. He knew it was there because a lamp was burning in the window—a solitary gleam flickering in the gloom.

"Come on. We have to get inside," he shouted to Antonio, pointing toward the light. He tried pulling him again, but Antonio wouldn't move. It was as if he was anchored to the ground.

"No," he said. "I won't. Not there."

Going up close, Theo saw panic in his friend's eyes. He took hold of his collar with both hands and shook him hard. "You've got to. We can't stay here," he yelled. And when that had no effect, he reached up and smacked the side of Antonio's face.

He was prepared for Antonio to hit him back, but the blow had the opposite effect. Antonio stroked his cheek and nodded and began to walk. Theo ran on ahead and knocked on the door, just as a flash of lightning lit up the overgrown weeds and bushes surrounding the cottage.

"Is anyone there?" he shouted. "We need to get out of the rain."

He knocked again, harder this time, the noise in synchrony with the hail that was hammering the ground, and then stumbled involuntarily over the threshold when the door suddenly opened. Picking himself up, he found himself staring into the small, hooded eyes of the oldest human being he had ever seen. The skin of her face was like an ancient brown parchment covered with a myriad of thin lines grooved by time and stretched tight across her sunken cheeks. Her hair and ears were concealed under a black cowl, and she was smoking a short white clay pipe that poked out from the thin line of her mouth.

Antonio was in the room too. Like Theo, water was dripping down from his clothes and soaking down into the rushes covering the earthen floor. The old woman closed the door and walked across to a rocking chair beside a fire burning on a small hearth, and sat down. A paraffin lamp stood on a low table beside her: a counterpart to the one flickering behind the window that they had seen from outside.

There was a bed on the far side of the room and several cupboards, but the only other piece of furniture was a high-backed settle facing the fire, and Antonio and Theo sat on it after taking off their coats, shivering as they held their hands out to the flames. Steam rose from their sodden clothes.

Theo remembered the cottage from the times he and Antonio had passed it on their way up into the hills. A tumbledown ruin, he'd thought it, so he was surprised to see that the roof was holding firm without a leak, in spite of the storm, which was reaching a crescendo of fury outside.

Inside, everything was clean and swept, but he could see no sign of a broomstick. The old woman looked like she was over a hundred, but that didn't make her a witch.

She sat and rocked gently in her chair, smoking her pipe and looking into the fire, saying nothing. It was as if she was unaware that they were there.

"I'm sorry," Theo said, feeling he needed to say something. "The rain came on so quickly and there was nowhere else to go, so thank you. You really saved us . . ." He stumbled to a halt, not knowing what else to say in the face of the old woman's silence.

"Have you money?" she asked, turning to look at Theo. Her voice was a harsh whisper, grating on the ear, and she spoke without taking the pipe out of her mouth.

"I don't know," said Theo, rummaging in his waterlogged pockets. "Yes, two pesetas," he said, holding out the silver coins that he had withheld from Don Vincente's collection plate in the morning. "I'd be happy for you to have them."

But instead of taking the coins, the old woman held out her hand and Theo, leaning forward, placed the coins on her outstretched palm.

"One," she said, holding up a finger, and put the top coin on her table, while placing the other somewhere inside her black dress.

Theo was about to sit back in his seat, but the old woman's hand shot out and seized his wrist in a surprisingly strong grip, bringing his palm under her eyes.

"The other too," she said, beckoning, and when Theo complied, she looked intently from one to the other, while he squatted down awkwardly beside her.

After a few moments, she let go of his right hand and began to trace the lines on his left. The unexpectedly delicate touch of her fingers had an extraordinary effect on Theo, making him feel as if she was looking inside him and that he was powerless to stop her seeing what was secreted there.

And when she began to speak, he believed utterly in what she was saying, even though it made little sense. It was only afterward as he was walking home that his natural skepticism returned, and he laughed at her contradictions and decided they were absurd.

"You will be lucky in love, and you will be unlucky in love. You will save your friend, and you will betray your friend," she said as she traced a line crossing his palm at the base of his fingers.

"You are clever, but you are a fool," she told him, shifting her finger to a line that seemed to rise from his wrist to above his thumb. "You run forward faster, faster, but you will go back to where you began."

Without warning, she let go of Theo's hand, severing the connection between them, and he felt an intense disappointment, as if he had lost something of immense importance that he would never now get back.

She pointed at Antonio and picked up the coin from the table and held it out to him, while extending the open palm of her other hand, just as she had done with Theo.

To Theo's surprise, Antonio did what she was asking him to do. It was as if he was under some kind of spell that he had to obey. Crossing her palm with silver.

Again, she pocketed the coin and held his hands. But this time she didn't read the lines. She stared down at Antonio's palms for half a minute or less, and then abruptly dropped them as if they were live coals.

"What did you see?" asked Theo.

But she wouldn't answer, resuming her rocking as she gazed into the fire, acting as if they weren't there.

"Tell me!" he demanded, raising his voice and getting to his feet. He was surprised by the force of his own anger. It wasn't his fortune that she was concealing, and Antonio wasn't protesting. But he couldn't stand the unspoken implication of disaster. If the old witch wouldn't say what she saw, then how could they deny it?

"He has a right to know," he insisted, leaning down over the old woman. "We paid."

Reluctantly, she looked up and met his eye, and then reached inside her dress and dropped one of the coins on the floor at Theo's feet. "Go," she said, pointing at the door.

Theo would have stood his ground, continuing to demand the truth, if Antonio hadn't intervened. He bent down and picked up the coin, gave it to

Theo, and opened the door, standing aside for Theo to pass through. Outside, the rain had slackened and the sun was peeping out from behind the retreating clouds.

Theo hesitated and then walked out, and Antonio closed the door behind them. And the falling of the latch acted on Theo as more than a physical separation. It was as if an electrical current connecting him to the old woman had been turned off, and now he could not remember why it had been so important to force her to speak.

They walked back down the hill in silence, picking their way through the puddles and mud. The rain had stopped and the air was cold and fresh, filling Theo with a sense of new beginning, which made it hard for him to hold on to his experience inside the cottage. It was like the storm, which had so quickly come and gone. It felt like it had happened to someone else.

And what the old woman had said made no sense. "Save a friend, betray a friend; lucky in love, unlucky in love!" Fortune-telling was easy if you told it both ways. Which was how to do it, of course. Because no one could predict the future. He laughed at himself for believing in such a stage-managed fraud. If he wasn't careful, he'd end up like Antonio, who saw witches flying over the village on All Hallows' Night.

Theo glanced over at his friend. He was walking with his head down and his shoulders slumped. A picture of misery.

"You can't let her upset you," he said as they approached the gate to his house. "She didn't see anything. It's all hocus-pocus."

Antonio looked at Theo and smiled sadly. "It's fate. You can't change what is written," he said, holding up his palms in resignation. "I would prefer not to have known, but I think that she was always there waiting for me. I sensed it every time I went past her cottage."

"But she didn't say what she saw," Theo insisted. "I asked her, but she wouldn't. Because there was nothing there. That's why. She saw nothing." Antonio's stoic acceptance of his fate infuriated Theo because he didn't believe in destiny. He refused to. Human beings' ability to change their lives was the foundation of what made the world bearable. There was no meaning to life without it.

But Antonio was unmoved. "I know you care," he said. "Because you are my friend, and I love you for it. But you have to understand that it doesn't matter. There is nothing I can do to change what will happen. Nothing."

"Yes, there is," said Theo passionately. "Don't join the army. Tell your father to go to hell. It's not who you are. You know that."

"But it is who I am," said Antonio. "It's my duty."

Reaching out, he embraced Theo and then walked away down the path.

The rains continued through the weeks that followed. The streets and squares turned to mud. Carts got stuck and drivers beat their steaming mules in vain efforts to get them to move. The air was full of oaths and imprecations, and everyone spoke darkly of the effect that the storms would have on the saturated crops.

Another year of unemployment and hunger loomed for the landless laborers shivering in the barrio as the thatched roofs of their hovels leaked and collapsed under the weight of the relentless rain. Unless there was change. Their hopes crystallized around the election. This time it would be different. It had to be.

On the day of the vote, they climbed the hill in droves, headed for the wide door of the ayuntamiento, where the cacique and his underlings were waiting with their threats and inducements, backed up by a squadron of Civil Guardsmen in their tricorn hats.

"If you vote for the CEDA, you will work; if you vote for the Socialists, you will starve. Or worse, if we have occasion to pay you a visit in the middle of the night. Have a cigar, have a drink. Think of your family. They are depending on you. Be wise in your choice."

All day the braceros and their wives came and went, passing under the dripping, drooping flag of the republic until the polls closed at dusk and the counting began.

Four days later, the results were announced. The Popular Front had received 4,654,116 votes, the National Front 4,503,505. A difference of 1 percent, but in the Cortes, it meant 130 more seats. The Left had won.

Alone on the *terrado* the next morning, Theo looked out over the village and the plain lit by golden sunshine and felt a euphoric sense of expectation and excitement. Everything would change now, and this long-suffering, ancient people that he had come to love would at last be free of their chains. Free to lead the lives of dignity and fulfillment that they deserved.

A memory of Esmond floated into his mind. In his room at Saint Gregory's quoting poetry: *"Bliss it was in that dawn to be alive / But to be young was very heaven."* Yes, that was it exactly. Heaven.

Theo took a deep breath and composed his features into an expression of deep concern, just as if he was an actor entering the stage in the final act of a tragedy, and went down the stairs. In the salon, he could hear his mother's voice raised in lamentation.

"They will murder us in our beds," she cried. "Just like they did in my country. And in Russia. Hammers to break down our doors; sickles not for wheat but to cut off our heads and parade them through the town."

"No, they won't," said Andrew. "They can't. There are laws, and the Guardia will enforce them. There will be changes. Yes. But some change is needed. People can't be left to starve for half the year and be paid next to nothing when there is work."

"You're on their side," Elena shouted, losing her temper. "You always have been. I expect you voted for them."

She got up from the sofa, pulling away from Andrew, who had been trying unsuccessfully to comfort her, and went over to the window. She looked out and then drew quickly back, beckoning to her husband.

"They're coming," she said—her voice a fearful whisper. "I told you."

Standing beside his stepfather, Theo could see the marchers several streets below. Wearing blue shirts and scarlet ties—the Socialist colors, although there were some wearing Anarchist black and red too. Their arms raised in clenched-fist salute were like the pollarded branches of the plane trees in the square, and even through the glass he could hear them singing "The Internationale."

Spanish words, but the same song that Theo had heard years before in New York, sung by the athletes in the City College stadium and the strikers outside his father's factory. Sung the world over by brave men and women refusing to give in to exploitation and injustice. His heart leaped.

The marchers didn't come any higher. They turned back to the main square, and the sound of their singing faded away.

"They were celebrating. That was all. And they've gone now, so there's nothing more to worry about," said Andrew, kneeling down beside Elena, who had curled up into a fetal ball on the sofa as she relived the horrors of that day when she'd heard her parents die and fled across the fields from her burning house.

Slowly, he coaxed her back up to a sitting position, and Constanza brought tea and the green and blue and orange-and-white-striped pills that had replaced the yellow ones that Theo used to get for his mother from the pharmacy on MacDougal Street in the Village when he was a boy.

The medicines had changed with the years, becoming more powerful and varied and expensive, but Theo understood that the underlying cause of his mother's trouble had not. She was seared by the experience of her youth. It had sapped her capacity for reason, twisting her naturally loving character to support a ruthless regime that her Savior would have abominated.

Looking at her now, Theo felt a gulf between them that he did not know how to bridge. He feared for her health, knowing that another nervous attack would weaken her still further, loosening her grasp on the side of the cliff down which she was slowly falling, slipping from one handhold to the next. But he did not know how to haul her back to the top. Andrew had a better chance with his unending store of patience and understanding, and Theo no longer felt excluded by his stepfather's love for his mother. He was glad instead that Andrew could give her comfort, because he did not know how to provide it himself.

He needed to get out. Away from the doom-laden atmosphere in the house. He got his coat and went looking for the marchers, hoping to hear more of their song.

But they were gone, and instead he found Antonio when he got to the square, sitting alone outside his father's shuttered café with a half-drunk bottle of wine on the table beside him.

"Theo! Just the man I wanted to see! Sit down and have a drink!" said Antonio, patting the empty seat beside him. "Celebrating can be a lonely business when you're on your own. And there's no need to worry about my father," he told Theo when he saw him hesitate. "He's down on his knees in the office in front of his Franco photograph, praying for a coup. We've got the whole place to ourselves."

It was true. It wasn't just the café; the whole square was empty, and Theo sensed a false note in Antonio's enthusiasm, as if he was trying to defy the surrounding desolation.

National Front posters lay trampled in the dirt. A slight breeze caught one where it lay and blew it up into the air where it fluttered for a moment before falling into one of the fountain troughs, where its inky headlines dissolved in the gray water.

"Where are the marchers?" Theo asked. "They were up near my house, but now it's like they've vanished into thin air. Something's wrong, isn't it?"

Instead of replying, Antonio poured himself another glass of wine, and Theo could see that his hand was shaking.

"Tell me, Antonio," he insisted.

"They've gone to occupy the marquis's untilled land that he leaves fallow for raising his fighting bulls," Antonio said quietly. "They're going to plow it and claim it for their own. But I don't know how it's going to turn out. My father says the cacique's got men waiting for them and the Guardia's there too. I told you this would turn ugly, didn't I?"

All morning, they waited for news, listening for the sound of the marchers returning. But when news came, it was not from below but from the café behind them. The door suddenly opened and Señor Bernardo appeared, wreathed in smiles that didn't disappear, even when he saw Theo.

"They drove them off and killed one of them, too, so they won't be back," he boomed. "Order is restored. And we can open again, praise be to God. Antonio, lay the tables. It's business as usual!"

25

EASTER

It wasn't quite business as usual in the days that followed, but nor did anyone get murdered in their beds. The Guardia enforced the law with their usual brutality, and in Madrid, the new government dithered. The Agrarian Reform Institute that it set up was a talking shop that didn't stop the landowners cutting wages and refusing work to union members. Braceros starved under the rule of the new government just as much as they had under the old.

The newspapers were full of stories of brawls and assassinations on the streets of the great cities, where left- and right-wing militias mounted machine guns on their motor cars and terrorized each other's neighborhoods, and there were constant rumors of guns and grenades packed in wine barrels or stacked up chimneys or stored in buckets hanging in underground wells, ready to be used by the Socialists or the Anarchists or the right-wing Falange to seize power. But nothing happened. The rumors remained rumors, the violence was far away, and life in the village went on as before, strained but essentially unchanged.

Elena recovered and resumed her daily attendance at the church, where Don Vincente and his ladies were making preparations for the great Easter feria—the most important day in the village's calendar. There were repairs to be made to the costumes of the Virgin and the saints, and a magnificent new canopy was being embroidered for the Virgin's throne. The vestry had become like a miniature textile factory as the ladies sat in a semicircle under the skylight, plying their needles in honor of the Lord.

And Antonio was getting ready to leave for the army. On his last evening, he sat with Theo in the square and watched the girls walking the paseo with their *novios*, just as they had done on their first night together nearly two years earlier.

It was cooler and the sunset had come earlier, but otherwise it felt as if nothing had changed. Just as before, Maria was absent, with only the location of her banishment having switched from South to North, and Don Fadrique and his dandified son were sitting at the same table of honor at the front of the café, with Antonio's father dancing attendance on them and catering to their every whim.

Pedrito was even dressed in the same all-white costume he had worn on that first night, and it looked just as absurd now as it had then. Even more, perhaps, because the cacique's tailor had had to let the trousers out several inches to accommodate Pedrito's expanding stomach, although the young man still had a long way to go before he could rival his father's gigantic waist. Now he sat back in his chair with his legs splayed out, looking like he owned the place—which was not far from the truth, as Don Fadrique had negotiated a share in the café's thriving profits as part of Maria's dowry.

Antonio's father frowned, as he always did when he saw his son sitting with Theo, and called him over to the cacique's table. Theo could hear their conversation from where he was sitting.

"Shake the hand of your brother-in-law and your father-in-law," Señor Bernardo ordered Antonio.

"Maria's not married yet, Papa," Antonio protested mildly, and his father's scowl returned for a moment, until Don Fadrique intervened in that soft, soothing tone that Theo remembered from when he had eavesdropped on his visit to Andrew two summers before. "But they will be," he said, smiling. "I can assure you of that." And he reached across the table to clasp Antonio's hand in his pudgy fist, as if he were a king claiming power over a new subject. His son's marriage to Maria would unite the two families, and he wanted to leave no doubt in Antonio's mind about who was going to be the head of the clan.

"I hear you are leaving tomorrow for Barcelona," he said.

Antonio nodded.

"I wish you good fortune and hope you will follow in your father's footsteps and make Spain proud of you," said the cacique, raising his glass.

Señor Bernardo beamed. "He will, Don Fadrique, but I hope he can keep both his legs while he's doing it and not just one like his papa." He laughed uproariously at his own joke and then snapped his finger to a waiter to bring more wine.

"A toast," he boomed, handing around glasses. "To Spain. *¡Arriba España!*"

The cacique rose to his feet, and Pedrito reluctantly followed him. He resented the way Antonio had usurped his father's attention and he jostled him as he got up, hoping that Antonio would make a fool of himself by spilling his wine. But his action had the opposite of its intended effect. Antonio held his glass still and it was Pedrito who upturned his, staining his white jacket crimson as the deep Rioja red soaked into the cloth.

He was furious and immediately began to abuse Antonio, blaming him for the accident, but the cacique stopped his son in mid-flow. "It was your fault. Now fill your glass," he ordered him, and then turned back to Antonio and Bernardo, raising his own. "To Pedro and Maria," he said and drained his wine in a single gulp.

Theo shuddered. He had tried hard every day to keep to his resolution and forget about Maria, but that hadn't stopped him from unconsciously keeping alive a hope that something would happen to stop her marriage to the horrible Pedrito. The overheard conversation extinguished that hope, and in despair he gazed up at the stars, wishing he was anywhere but where he was.

When he looked back down, a familiar face caught his eye, illuminated by a streetlight. Primitivo was standing by the same wall where Theo had first seen him two summers before. He had grown a beard and wore a cheap hat pulled down over his eyes, but Theo was sure it was him. And then in the next moment he moved out of the light and was gone.

Antonio came to the house the next day, wearing his new olive-wool uniform, looking like he'd already become someone else.

"Come and see me in Barcelona," he said. "It's a beautiful city, and I can get a weekend's leave to show you the sights. They say it's where dreams come true. There's certainly more chance of it happening there than in this place, where nothing's changed since the Moors were driven out."

He laughed and they embraced, and then after Antonio had gone, Theo experienced the same sadness that he'd felt when he parted from Esmond. His life seemed to be a succession of separations from those he loved, leaving him lonelier each time than he'd been before.

Antonio was right. He was suffocating in the village with no friends and nothing to do. He made up his mind to ask his stepfather for money to go traveling to Barcelona, and perhaps across the frontier into France, and was about to make his request when his mother forestalled him by announcing at lunch early in April that the banns for Maria's marriage to Don Fadrique's son had been read in church that morning.

"I thought she was away in the North. Has she come back?" asked Theo, trying to make his voice sound unconcerned and neutral.

"Yes. Don Vincente is going to marry them in the church on the Sunday after Easter. It's going to be quite an occasion, with no expense spared, and the church will be beautiful with the spring flowers. I'm looking forward to it," said Elena happily.

Theo breathed hard, fighting to keep control of his emotions. He'd resolved to live without Maria, but how could he do that when she was now only a few hundred yards away, locked up in her father's house, about to be sacrificed on the altar of his financial and social ambitions? It felt like condoning a murder.

He could feel his stepfather's eyes on him as his mother chattered on about the wedding, oblivious to the pain she was causing her son.

"It's a good match for the girl," she said. "And her father. He's going up in the world."

"I'm sorry," Theo said, unable to bear any more. He pushed his plate away and stood up. "I'm not feeling well."

Elena looked alarmed. "What's the matter, Theo? You're never unwell. Is it something you've eaten?" she asked anxiously.

But he was already at the door. "It's nothing. I just need some air. That's all," he said. "I won't be long."

Outside, he ran down the winding streets past the church to Maria's house. It was just below the main square, a stone's throw from the café. Despite his long friendship with Antonio, he had never been inside, and he had no idea which room was Maria's. At the front, the windows were shuttered against the noonday sun, so he walked around to the street behind and gazed up over the white wall of the garden to where a chestnut tree obscured his view of the back of the house. Halfway along was a black wrought iron gate with a silver mesh across the bars to stop people looking in. He tried the handle, but it was locked.

She was here. He knew it. Perhaps she could see him if he stood back from the wall. Or hear him if he called. It was hard to shout when everything all around was silent, but he forced himself.

"Maria! Maria! It's me: Theo. Can you hear me? Open your window if you can."

His words felt like stones dropped into a black well with no bottom, and there was no reply, until suddenly, magically, the gate opened.

Theo's heart leaped. It was her. It had to be. But instead he found himself face-to-face with Bernardo Alvarez, red with fury.

"Come here," he shouted, taking hold of Theo's sleeve. "I'll teach you to come barking round here like a dog after a bitch."

But Theo twisted away and ran. Behind him, he could hear Maria's father's booming voice: "Stay away from my daughter! Next time I'll take my whip to you, you hear me?"

Theo fully expected Señor Alvarez to complain to his stepfather, but nothing happened, and he sensed that this was because the café owner had decided that he posed no threat to the forthcoming nuptials.

He didn't know how Alvarez was going to make his daughter say yes at the necessary moment, but no doubt he and the cacique had a plan. Months of merciless confinement might well have broken her spirit.

And Theo was powerless to rescue her. The knowledge was a hard emptiness inside his chest and he took to running so as not to think, pounding up and down the hills as lizards slithered out of his way. He met no one. The town had turned inward, waiting in a taut, curled-up silence for the coming of Easter.

On Maundy Thursday night, he went with his mother and stepfather to church. Andrew had insisted. "You have to see the procession," he told Theo in the voice he reserved for requests that brooked no denial. "When I was a boy here, I would long for it and fear it in equal measure, and then dream about it for weeks afterward. And the Mass is a part of the whole: the one without the other is like a story without its beginning. You'll see."

Theo was amazed. The church, usually half empty, was now full to overflowing. It was as if the population had taken a collective decision to suspend its disbelief for this one day.

In the square outside, latecomers kneeled under the stars on the stony ground and joined the long queue to receive the host from Don Vincente, who was dressed in a gleaming white chasuble trimmed with gold.

Afterward, the servers stripped the altars bare and draped the statues and the pulpit in black cloth, while chosen men stepped forward and lowered the crucified Christ from above the empty tabernacle and walked slowly out of the church and into the night.

Behind them, a small group of white-robed figures stepped forward out of the shadows and took their place at the head of the procession. They must have been at the back of the church, because Theo had not seen them before. They wore high conical cloth hats that entirely covered their faces except for eye slits and looked exactly like the American Klansmen that Theo had seen in newsreels in New York when he was a boy, except that these men were barefoot and several wore chains around their ankles. Two more walked bent forward and with their arms outstretched, tied to the horizontal beams of crude wooden crosses carried on their backs, making them look like strange white birds of prey.

Astonished, Theo turned to his stepfather, who smiled and put his finger to his lips. "I'll tell you afterward," he said. "For now, walk and watch. And stay silent."

No one was speaking, and the only sound was the rhythmic funereal beating of a single drum, except for bursts of sudden wailing song offered up by people kneeling in the gutters as the crucified Christ went swaying past, lit by tall candles and esparto torches. The air was thick with the smell of incense and burning wax.

They had entered the barrio. There was no moon, but in the starlight, Theo recognized the shadowy outlines of the square with Jesús's father's shop, where he had spent so much of the previous summer. Down farther, they left the last hovel houses behind them and halted in front of the stone calvary that stood in the grove of olive trees at the entrance to the village.

The bearers carefully set the cross on the ground and the villagers gathered around in a semicircle, bowed their heads, and prayed. In the dancing lights, the village was Palestine and the olive grove where they were standing was the Garden of Gethsemane.

Theo looked at his mother and saw tears streaming down her face as she knelt on the hard ground with the other women, and in that moment he did not share her faith, but he understood it. He leaned down and took her small hand to help her to her feet, and in years afterward, when he wanted to recall her to his memory, it was to this moment that he often returned.

Andrew kept his promise to explain the men in white. In the salon the next day, he took down old leather-bound books from the shelves and laid them open on the low table in front of the fire.

"It began with the Inquisition and the autos-da-fé," he told Theo, pointing to a picture of a crowded medieval square and men wearing tall conical hats being paraded in front of a platform on which two robed men sat on thrones with a cross set up behind them. "The hats are *capirotes*. The prisoners wore them as a humiliation when they were taken out from the dungeons to hear their sentences being read. Their crimes were written on them and on the yellow sack shirts they wore underneath. If there were red flames drawn, it meant they might be burnt."

"What crimes were they accused of?" Theo asked.

"Sorcery and heresy sometimes, but usually it was apostasy. Jews were expelled from Spain in 1492 unless they converted to Christianity, and if they carried on practicing their faith in secret, then they were handed over to the Inquisition, who tortured and burnt them because the Church and the Crown required Spain to be pure. *Limpieza*—cleaning—they called it. See," Andrew said, pointing to pictures of torments in the other books, from which Theo recoiled. "As I told you before, this is a cruel country."

He paused, shaking his head, before he went on: "Later, after the Inquisition was disbanded, penitents—or *nazarenos*, as they called themselves—wore the *capirotes* but extended them into hoods to cover their faces so as to hide their shame. But then they raise them on Easter Sunday when all is forgiven, and you can see who they really are." Andrew laughed.

On Sunday morning they returned to the church, waiting outside until the doors opened on the stroke of eight o'clock. Six men in black suits emerged, carrying a golden throne at shoulder height, on which a life-size alabaster statue of the Virgin was seated under the newly finished embroidered silk canopy. No expense had been spared. The Virgin was wearing a silver crown and a shimmering green gown with a long train that flowed over the back of the float to where it was being held up by two other men, also dressed in black. One of them was Pedrito. Theo hadn't recognized him at first without his white suit, and he laughed at the way he had been given the lightest load to carry. But Pedrito didn't see the joke. He walked carefully with his head held high. Carrying the Virgin and her train was the greatest honor the village could bestow on its men, and he basked in his moment of glory.

Behind Pedrito, the *nazarenos* fell into step, although this time without their crosses and chains, followed by the doñas in black, who included Elena, wearing a long lace veil, and the villagers bringing up the rear. They all walked in silence but with a suppressed joy that made this daylight procession entirely different from the one on Thursday night. Theo could see that some people were carrying trumpets and drums, and several had rifles over their shoulders.

At the head of the procession, the statue of Mary bobbed her crowned head. She had found the tomb empty, and now she was out seeking her son.

When they got to the calvary, a different Christ was waiting for them. The dead man on the cross had been replaced by a beatific, standing Savior dressed in a green robe like his mother and holding a sheaf of barley in his right hand and a bunch of flowers in his left. The land, too, had been redeemed from the death of winter and brought back to life.

Slowly the Virgin was lowered from her throne and made to curtsy to Jesus. Three times up and down, and on the third his arms reached out on strings toward her, and everyone erupted into cheering. *"¡Viva la Purisima! ¡Viva El Señor!"* they shouted, and beat their drums and blew their trumpets and fired their rifles into the air. Above them in the village the church bells, silent since Thursday, answered the cacophony with peals of celebration, and the *nazarenos* pulled back their hoods, blinking and smiling in the morning sunshine.

After a few minutes, the bearers raised up the statues and began to climb the hill, but one of their number was missing. Behind them, voices were crying out in alarm as they gathered around a figure lying on the ground. Face up, glassy-eyed, covered with the rose petals that everyone had thrown at the moment of the statues' embrace, Pedrito lay motionless with a crimson stain spreading out over his white shirtfront. In just the same place where the wine had spilled on him a few days before.

Theo took off running. Past the crowd and the olive trees where he saw a *nazareno*'s robe and hood hanging tangled in the branches, and up through the empty streets. Faster and faster until he got to Maria's house. There was no sign of movement at the front, but at the back he almost fell over a bicycle that was lying on its side, discarded on the ground. And up ahead, by the open garden gate, he could see two figures on horseback.

"Wait!" he shouted, running after them. "Wait!"

They turned. Primitivo had blood on his hands, and Maria was more beautiful than he had ever seen her, with her golden-brown hair blown up around her face and her blue eyes wild with excitement.

"We can't," she said.

"Do you know what he did?" Theo asked breathlessly, pointing at Primitivo.

"Yes," she said. And there was ecstasy in her voice, as if she had been enraptured by the unexpected absoluteness of the deed.

Primitivo sat up in his saddle, breathing in her admiration.

"Where are you going?" Theo asked.

"Barcelona," she said. "Once we're through the hills."

"Why are you telling him?" Primitivo demanded angrily. He looked like he wanted to knife Theo too.

"Because he's one of us," she said. "He saved us. Remember?"

"Have you any money?" Theo asked.

"Just a little," she said, shaking her head.

He looked down at his wrist and took off his watch, handing it up to her. "It's worth a lot," he said. "The case and the dial are gold."

"Thank you," she said, and leaning down, she kissed him and ran her finger over his face down from his forehead to his chin, sealing him like an envelope.

"Don't forget me!" she said. And turning her horse, she rode away.

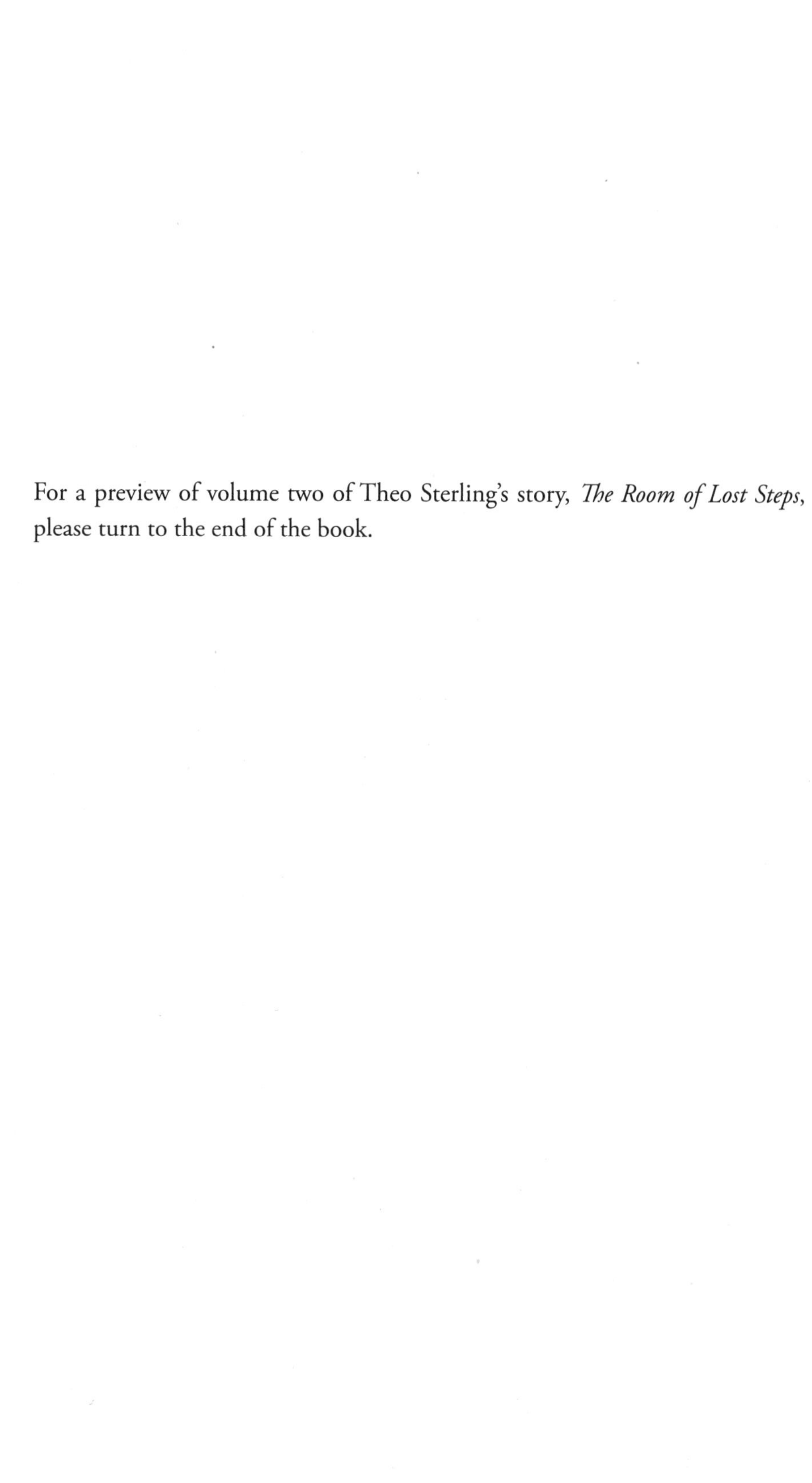

For a preview of volume two of Theo Sterling's story, *The Room of Lost Steps,* please turn to the end of the book.

AUTHOR'S NOTE

A long time ago, I came across an article about the Abraham Lincoln Brigade—American workers and students who volunteered in the last years of the 1930s to fight for the democratically elected Spanish Republic, which was under attack from the Spanish army supported by Hitler and Mussolini. Thousands of them crossed the ocean without any previous experience of soldiering and risked their lives to fight for their ideals; many never came back. I was astonished by their courage and thought that their story would make a wonderful subject for a novel, particularly as no one seemed to have ever written one before.

Years went by and in 2016 I finished *No Man's Land*, set before and during the First World War, and began to cast around for a subject for my next book. I had emigrated to the States eight years before and knew that I wanted to honor my adopted country by writing for the first time from an American perspective, trying to bring some part of its history to dramatic life. I remembered the Lincolns.

I soon discovered that more than thirty of the volunteers had written accounts of their experiences after they returned home defeated. The books were now long out of print, but I was able to order them through the mail and I read them all avidly, hoping to find out who these young men were and what made them tick. I learned that most but not all were Communists, that many were Jews determined to try to stop Hitler, and that some were African Americans who fought in Spain because they couldn't fight in Ethiopia, where Mussolini had committed the most appalling atrocities during his unprovoked invasion a year earlier, bombing peasants with canisters of poison gas. The Lincoln Brigade was the first racially integrated battalion in American history and the first to be commanded by a Black man.

The volunteers came from all walks of American life—university graduates and mill hands, teachers and truck drivers, even a governor's son—but they were all united by a burning desire for justice. Not an abstract notion but a visceral outrage that the Fascists were trying to take away the democratic rights of the Spanish people who had voted to escape from under the yoke of centuries-old poverty and ignorance. The volunteers' idealism and suffering moved me, and I wanted them to no longer be forgotten on the dusty shelves of book depositories, but instead to try to use my skills as a novelist to make their extraordinary experience come alive for readers today.

So I began a journey that lasted more than eight years—far longer than I had anticipated when I first set out! But necessary because I soon came to realize that I could not tell the story of the Lincolns without painting the wider canvas of the thirties—a decade of idealism and cynicism, hope and defeat, illusion and disillusion, that ended in the horrors of the Second World War. I knew that I needed to portray both the divided American society that the Lincolns came from, savaged by conflict between the haves and the have-nots suffering through the Great Depression, and the world of rural Spain, unchanged since medieval times, where beneath its beautiful surface and ancient customs, the landless braceros suffered from the most terrible poverty and degradation.

Most challenging of all, I set myself to bring to life the Spanish Civil War—a cruel conflict of competing ideologies in which no quarter was given and the great hope of the Spanish Republicans, and the volunteers who crossed the ocean to fight beside them, was finally extinguished in a tragic defeat that left Spain marooned in a Fascist darkness that lasted for thirty-six long years until Franco died in 1975. Novelists since Hemingway have steered clear of the tangled complexities of the war and have left its history to the dry pens of the historians, but I think this has been a great mistake. The war was a dramatic, multifaceted conflict with immense human interest that formed the gateway to the Second World War. Understanding the one is key to understanding the other, and I hope that my two novels will appeal to the many readers who continue to be fascinated by that extraordinary period of our shared history.

I have tried throughout to tell a fast-paced, panoramic story, rich in character, that brings the vanished worlds of America, England, and Spain in the 1930s to life—an era that has multiple resonances with the troubled world we live in today, where there is the same extreme wealth inequality, the same longing for social justice, and the same rise of totalitarianism abroad. Now, once again, the Western democracies face the challenge of a Fascist power launching a barbaric war of aggression and must decide whether to go down the road of appeasement or resistance. Now, more than ever, is the time for us to learn from our history.

ACKNOWLEDGMENTS

I am deeply grateful to all those at Amazon Publishing who have helped guide the two Theo Sterling novels through to publication. Many people have made important contributions to this process, but I would like in particular to thank Danielle Marshall, who has been Theo's strongest advocate and supporter, and Chantelle Aimée Osman, who has been a wonderful supervising editor. James Gallagher, Jen Bentham, Robin O'Dell, and Sarah Engel did excellent work, copyediting and proofreading the manuscript and leaving no stone unturned, and Rachel Gul has orchestrated an excellent publicity campaign. I also appreciate the help given to me by Carmen Johnson and Vernon Sanders.

I wish to thank Nan Talese and David Brawn for believing in my writing; Chris Smith, Verlyn Flieger, and Tracy and Nicholas Tolkien for their reading of the manuscript and helpful suggestions; Beena Kamlani and David Downing for their excellent and complementary developmental editing work, which has hugely improved both novels; and my agent, Marly Rusoff, for sticking with me through thick and thin.

Catherine Howley drew the excellent maps that appear in *The Room of Lost Steps* and provided me with invaluable historical assistance in relation to events in Barcelona in 1936 and 1937, and Nick Lloyd gave me a hugely helpful tour of the city and shared with me his wonderful walking museum. I also wish to thank Andy Phipps for his help with my website.

I have been engaged with Theo Sterling's story for more than eight years, and the support of my family—my wife, Tracy, my children, Nicholas and Anna, and my late aunt, Prisca—and my friends, Tom Johnson, Brett Simon, and Robert Cutter, has helped to keep me going through what has been a very long and arduous journey. I thank them all from the bottom of my heart.

And last but not least, I am grateful to my two pugs, Sadie and Roxanne, who have kept me company throughout, staying up with me through many, many long watches of the night. Dogs are truly a man's best friend.

A PREVIEW OF *THE ROOM OF LOST STEPS*

VOLUME 2 IN THE THEO STERLING DUOLOGY

1

SITGES

As spring turned to summer, Theo wandered his stepfather's house in Los Olivos, alone with his memories. His mind kept returning to that never-to-be-forgotten Sunday as he retraced his steps from the church to the stone calvary at the entrance to the village, walking behind the statue of the Virgin on her golden throne. He remembered her meeting with her risen son, the sheaf of barley in his hand, and the sound of the church bells up above. The beat of the drums, the rifle shots, the wild taratantara of the trumpets celebrating a resurrection to which even an unbeliever like himself could not be indifferent. But then the murder: the invisible thrust of the blade right there amid the joy and the glory, and fat Pedrito stretched out on the ground, staring lifeless up at the sun, his crimson blood seeping out over the starched white of his shirtfront.

Theo remembered the robe and hood hanging in the tree, the sharp press of the cobblestones into the soles of his feet as he ran up through the empty streets and squares, and the beat of his heart as he stretched every sinew of his body to get to her before she left the village forever.

He'd got there in time. Enough to see the blood on Primitivo's hands as he held his horse's reins, enough to witness the ecstatic look in Maria's eyes, and to feel the touch of her finger on his face as she leaned down to him from her saddle. *"Don't forget me!"* she'd told him.

He couldn't even if he had wanted to. It had been different during the long months in England and later in the village when Maria had been immured in the convent in the North. Despite his best efforts to keep her vivid in his mind, she had faded, becoming more an idea than a living person, and the lock of her hair a relic of a past he couldn't touch.

But now everything had changed. The meeting in the lane had lasted less than a minute, but its effect on him had been like an electrical charge. He didn't even need to close his eyes to see her face, hear her voice, feel the touch of her hand. He thought of her constantly and of Primitivo, who had saved her from a foul marriage when he couldn't. The boy was vicious; if Theo hadn't known that before, he knew it now. Primitivo hadn't needed to kill Pedrito. He'd done it because he wanted to, and because he knew the effect it would have on Maria.

The murder was the ultimate expression of the Anarchists' "propaganda of the deed." Death at Easter; religious parade transformed into stampeding terror; the arrogant cacique and Alvarez, his sidekick, struck to the heart. It was an act of grand theater and showed imagination and daring that Theo hadn't credited Primitivo with possessing.

And afterward, to cap it all, the killer had run off with his victim's intended bride. Vanished into the ether without a trace. The Civil Guard had tracked them through the mountain villages, but after that the trail had gone cold. Impatient for results, Don Fadrique and Maria's father had hired their own detectives, who had searched as far as Barcelona, but the bloodhounds found no scent, even though they were convinced that the city was the fugitives' likely destination. For decades, the starving braceros had been leaving the Andalusian countryside for the Catalan capital, hoping to find work in the mills and factories. They had taken their Anarchist creed with them, and the city was now the home of the CNT, the Anarchist trade union. It provided a refuge and support system for Anarchist outlaws who could disappear into the teeming backstreet tenements.

Theo didn't need to guess at Maria's and Primitivo's whereabouts. He *knew* they were in Barcelona, because Maria had told him that that was where they were going. He reminded himself that she had trusted him, told him that he was "one of us," but that was cold comfort if he could not follow her. And how could he do that when he had no money for the enterprise and his mother had become so nervous since the murder that she started to panic if he was gone from the house for more than a few hours?

Like it or not, he was reliant on his stepfather for financial support, and he couldn't ask him for help without telling him what he intended. Unless he lied, but he couldn't bring himself to do that. Not after all that had passed between them. He lived in dread of the day when Andrew would ask about the watch that he had given to Maria.

So he stayed where he was, tortured with an aching jealousy and sense of loss, made worse by having no one to confide in. He missed Antonio and he missed Saint Gregory's. The school had given him structure and purpose, whereas now the hours stretched out interminably, offering him no distraction from his pain. Only running helped. Pounding the paths and roads in the early morning before the sun rose too high and sent him home, he could forget himself, at least for a while.

It wasn't just Theo; everyone was restless. Night and day, the villagers argued and speculated. In the cafés where frenzied radio announcers broadcast news of violent clashes breaking out on city streets all over Spain, and in the church where Elena went every day to hear Don Vincente calling down the fires of heaven to punish the godless Reds. Everywhere he went, Theo could feel the festering hatred and division, hanging like the heat in the still, stagnant early-summer air.

He felt trapped. As if he were locked up in an airless room from which he had no means of escape, until a day came when the door unexpectedly opened and everything that he wanted seemed to drop down into his outstretched hand.

Since Pedrito's murder, Andrew had remained in the village, unwilling to leave Elena, who had become more obdurate than ever in her determination to stay put. But now something had to give. Strikes and industrial unrest were jeopardizing Andrew's business interests in Barcelona, and he knew he had to go there to deal with the problems in person.

"I can't let this go any longer," he told Elena at lunch one day in June. "And I don't want to leave you here alone. Not with everything that's happening. Barcelona is a beautiful city, and it's a crying shame that you've never seen it. I didn't marry you with the intention of keeping you holed up in a remote village halfway up a mountain with Don Vincente and a group of gossiping black widows for company. Hiding your light under a bushel."

"I like my bushel," Elena said tartly.

"No, you don't," he shot back. "The atmosphere here is toxic and you know it. You need a change. It'll be good for you. And for all of us. It isn't doing Theo any good sitting here with nothing to do all day. You'd like to go to Barcelona, wouldn't you, Theo?"

"Yes. More than anything," said Theo fervently, shocked into candor by his heart's desire suddenly being offered to him on a plate.

"I don't want to go," said Elena, clenching her small hands and pushing out her chin with that look of childlike defiance that Theo knew so well.

"You're just saying that because you're nervous of trying something new," said Andrew. "But this isn't like going to London. We can come back as soon as I've finished my business, which shouldn't take much more than a week. And once you're there, you won't want to leave. Barcelona is magical at this time of year. In the mornings, you wake up to the pealing of a hundred church bells, and in the afternoons, you can go shopping in the Paseo de Gracia, which makes Oxford Street look shabby and gray, and in the evenings we'll go to the opera on the Ramblas, and you and Theo can go to the seaside too. At Sitges, the sand is golden brown and the sea is . . ." Andrew stopped, out of breath, as he searched for the right jewel to compare in color to the Mediterranean just south of Barcelona.

And Elena laughed in spite of herself, unable to resist her husband's enthusiasm, which made Andrew laugh too. "Say yes," he pleaded, getting up from the table and going down theatrically on one knee beside his wife, just as Constanza came in with the coffee.

"I'll think about it," Elena said. "But only if you get up and stop playing the fool. I'm sorry, Constanza. What must you think of us?"

Barcelona didn't disappoint. They stayed at the Hotel Colón in palatial rooms with floor-to-ceiling windows that overlooked the great main square, Plaça de Catalunya, in which crowds of well-dressed people walked this way and that, passing amid the statues and fountains, while on the outer hub, cars and trucks stopped and started and blew their horns at each other as they came and went through the myriad of roads leading off the square in all directions: arteries running out from the city's beating heart.

The morning after their arrival, Theo stood in his room looking out, amazed by the sheer numbers of people down below. They were as anonymous to him and to each other as the flocks of pigeons that took off and wheeled and swooped and settled back down onto the marble walkways in a constant flurry of quick gray movement. He felt bewildered and energized in equal measure. The city had no connection to the slow-moving life of the village, where everyone knew everyone and nothing ever changed. It was as if he had been taken back in a time machine to the New York of his childhood.

After breakfast, he walked with his mother across the plaza and into the boulevard called the Ramblas, which sloped gently down toward the sea. Everywhere was a blur of vibrant color. In the flower market, where dahlias and tulips and white black-eyed orchids vied for the eye's attention; in the bird market, where green-and-yellow canaries sang in their tiny cages, as if yearning for a freedom they would never attain; and under the striped awnings of the cafés, where girls in pastel dresses sat with their lovers sipping ice-cold drinks through wax straws.

Waiters in tuxedos moved like dancers between the tables, silver trays balanced high on their upturned hands; sailors with their arms linked and the wide ends of their blue trousers flapping walked arm in arm up from the port; and, under the spreading canopies of the plane trees on the central walkway, performers in leotards juggled rings and clubs or swallowed fire or walked on their hands while their assistants held out their hats to passersby in hopes of reward.

The noise jangled in Theo's ears: not just the traffic but the bells of the yellow streetcars rattling under their contact lines, the barrel organs churning out popular songs, people shouting to make themselves heard. He was entranced, but the sensory overload gave Elena a headache, and she soon asked him to take her back to the hotel to rest.

Left to his own devices for the afternoon, Theo went to the concierge desk and obtained directions to Antonio's barracks from a round-faced, thick-lipped official in resplendent uniform who bore an unfortunate but remarkable resemblance to the pictures of Al Capone that used to regularly appear in Theo's father's newspaper at the time of the Saint Valentine's Day Massacre, and which had given him such terrible nightmares when he was a boy. Up close, Theo saw that the man even had a name tag above his breast pocket, giving his name as Alfonso, and he had to turn away and hold his breath hard for a moment to stop himself from laughing.

But the concierge was too polite to notice, or perhaps was just used to such reactions from American tourists, and he couldn't have been more helpful as he took out a map of the city and showed Theo how to get to the Tarragona Street barracks. At the end, Theo felt so grateful that he made the mistake of putting his hand out to thank Alfonso, only remembering when it was too late that that might not be the right etiquette for how guests were supposed to deal with employees at the Colón. However, the concierge was only too happy to shake Theo's hand and even came out from behind his desk to escort him through the revolving door of the hotel, rendering him a formal bow before he retreated back inside. Out in the plaza in the sunshine, Theo felt suddenly buoyed, having made his first friend in Barcelona.

He still managed to get lost on the way, but it didn't seem to matter, and eventually he found himself standing outside a stone gateway manned by a sentry, who stepped out in front of him and told him "No visitors!" in a commanding voice when Theo tried to walk through into the big empty courtyard beyond. At the back Theo could see the long gray wall of a building with square windows set in symmetrical rows, surmounted by a clock tower. But there was no sign of life. The place looked to him more like a prison than a barracks.

Theo told the sentry Antonio's name, said he was a friend who was just in town for a few days, and asked when it would be a good time to come back, but he soon realized he was wasting his time. "No visitors!" the sentry repeated in exactly the same peremptory tone of voice, as if these were the only words in his vocabulary, until Theo turned away disconsolately with his earlier sense of euphoria punctured like air escaping from a child's balloon.

He started to walk back down the road the way he'd come, but he stopped halfway, watching as a troop of khaki-clad soldiers appeared around the corner, led by an officer on horseback with a thin mustache and a swagger stick. He reminded Theo of Barker, even though he didn't in the least look like him. The ramrod-straight back, the sneering expression, the polished boots and buttons, took Theo back to the parade ground at Saint Gregory's and Barker shouting ridiculous commands at him and the other terrorized cadets.

The soldiers marched four abreast and Theo checked their faces as they went past, each a blank until the last row, when he caught sight of Antonio on the far side. He was gone in a moment, wheeling toward the barracks gate, but as Theo watched from behind, Antonio held out the fingers of one of his swinging hands.

Theo felt sure it was a signal of some kind. Five minutes, perhaps. And he went back and waited close to the gate, but out of view of the sentry.

Five minutes passed and then fifteen more and Theo started to wilt in the heat. He closed his eyes, wishing he'd brought water, and felt a hand on his shoulder.

"Hello, old friend," said Antonio. He hugged Theo briefly and then leaned back against the barracks wall and lit a cigarette. He looked weary, Theo thought. And not the kind of weary Theo was feeling, but a fatigue that went to the core, sucking away hope.

"You look rotten," Theo said. "Is soldiering that bad?"

"Worse than bad. And don't say 'I told you so' or I'll shoot you with my rifle, if I can get it to fire," said Antonio with a wan smile that was at least familiar.

"All right. I won't," said Theo, smiling too. "What's so terrible about it?"

"Never being alone, never getting to spend time with anyone I like, never seeing trees or grass or girls. Bad food, stupid orders that make no sense and aren't intended to . . . Do you want me to go on?"

"You make it sound like my old school."

"Except that you learned to like your school, didn't you?" said Antonio bitterly. "I'm never going to like the army."

"I'm sorry," said Theo. He didn't know what else to say, because part of him did think that Antonio had only himself to blame. He'd always acted like he had no choice about his career because he had to obey his father, but maybe he should have tried showing some backbone, like Maria. Anyone could see that he wasn't cut out to be a soldier.

Antonio looked at Theo and suddenly grinned with that look of wry amusement Theo knew so well. "I know what you're thinking and you're right.

It is my fault. I should have realized what I was letting myself in for. My father was a Fascist before Mussolini came up with the idea, and he loves the army because it's run by Fascists like that captain you saw up on his horse. Darnell's his name and he calls me *Rat* and makes my life hell because he says he can smell me."

"Smell you?"

"Smell a rat, smell that I'm not one of them. And that's true, of course. I'm not. I'm no Anarchist, but I believe that the poor have rights, and that's enough to make me a Red in their book. And there's nothing worse than a Red in the army. Not even a Jew!" Antonio laughed harshly.

"How does he know what you are?" asked Theo. "He can't smell you. That's ridiculous."

"Probably heard me talking to one of the other recruits," said Antonio. "Or got to hear about my sister and Primitivo and made the connection. News like that travels fast. It's been in all the papers."

"Is she here?" asked Theo, trying to keep the excitement out of his voice.

"Maybe. I've looked. It would've been the logical place for them to go. There are more Anarchists here than in Andalusia, but if she's here, I don't think she wants me to find her. She probably thinks I'd tell our father. Which is a joke, of course, although she's not to know that. I'd like to run away, too, but unlike her, I've got nowhere to hide." Antonio laughed. A hollow, humorless laugh that was like a window opening on his despair. It frightened Theo and grieved him, too, because he felt powerless to help his friend.

"Have you heard anything?" Antonio asked.

Theo shook his head. He didn't want to lie, but he thought that revealing his conversation with Maria in the lane would make it seem like he'd been a part of what had happened with Pedrito, and he didn't want Antonio to think of him as involved.

"I have to go back," said Antonio, grinding his cigarette out under his foot—Theo noticed that he had smoked it right down to the butt so that it had almost burned his fingers. "Are you here next weekend?"

Theo nodded.

"Good. I've got a day's leave next Saturday. Come at this time and I'll show you the real Barcelona, just like I guided you in the mountains. Remember those days? Before everything went bad? Who knows? We might even find my sister."

In the evening Elena was better, and she and Andrew and Theo took a taxi to the Liceu Opera House halfway down the Ramblas. The Colón's resident hairstylist had come to her room in the afternoon and arranged her jet-black hair in an elegant chignon and, to please her husband, she was wearing a diamond necklace that had belonged to his mother. In the refracted light of the chandeliers, the jewels shimmered and sparkled above her simple black dress, drawing admiring eyes to the symmetry of her face, in which the suffering of recent years had created an ethereal look, as if she was not of this world but rather a Madonna in a painting by Murillo or another of the old Spanish masters. Theo had never seen his mother looking more beautiful, but it was a beauty so fine that he felt it could break at any moment, and he wished they had not come.

But Andrew was elated. He passed through the lobby with Elena on his arm, introducing her to his friends. Theo was surprised. His stepfather seemed to know everyone. Standing awkwardly alone with his back to a gilded pillar, Theo watched him talking animatedly to a group of men whose affluence was evident from the oversize jewels pinned or hung on their wives' haute couture gowns. He didn't need a guide to know who they were, these merchant princes of the city. They owned the factories and the mills, and Andrew was one of them.

A bell rang overhead, and the audience passed into the horseshoe-shaped theater. It was like nothing Theo had ever seen before. Immense Corinthian columns rose to support a ceiling encrusted with gold and polychrome moldings in which eight circular paintings of Renaissance nymphs in diaphanous robes surrounded a central globe of light, while below, red velvet armchairs matched the thick weave of the carpet. Theo thought it decadent: a baroque extravaganza celebrating the city's wealth. Alone in the lobby, he'd noticed a memorial tablet on the wall dedicated to twenty patrons killed by an Anarchist bomb thrown from the balcony in 1893, and it didn't surprise him in the least that the theater should have been an Anarchist target. Sitting beside his mother in Andrew's sumptuous box, he glanced uneasily upward, wondering whether tonight might see a repeat.

He knew nothing of opera. He'd never seen one or heard one, and he'd gone expecting to be bored. But, to his surprise, he was enthralled from the moment the curtain rose, transporting him back to Seville a hundred years before. The music was alive with melody, and the Romany factory girl Carmen exerted a magnetic attraction not just on the soldiers on the stage but on him too. Spellbound while the orchestra played, he believed she was Maria. There was enough resemblance in her darting eyes and her dancing movement to sustain the illusion, and just like Maria, she insisted on her right to be free. Free to fall in love with Don José and free to throw him over when she met the glamorous young bullfighter Escamillo. Free to do as she liked, regardless of its effect on others. Theo believed in her right to choose, but he also understood José's terrible pain when he learned of his rejection and, even though he was appalled, he understood why José killed her outside the bullring. He understood how love could lead to that. Death and despair.

In the darkness, he was swept away on a tide of emotion and so felt a shock when the lights came on at the end, destroying the illusion of make believe, and the actors, stepping forward, became themselves as they joined together in a line and took their bow. The audience stood and cheered and, looking around at them, Theo felt an unexpected revulsion replacing the grief he had been experiencing a moment before. They were voyeurs, these rich theatergoers in their evening dress. Bourgeoisie watching the lawless, amoral antics of the working class through their opera glasses before they went home to their hilltop villas built on the backs of those same workers' hard labor.

The thought made Theo uneasy, a feeling that intensified when he came out of the theater and saw a man watching from the corner of a narrow street less than fifty yards away down the Ramblas. He was standing in the shadows and quickly disappeared from view when he caught Theo's eye, but the glimpse was enough to make Theo sure it was Carlos, notwithstanding the unlikelihood of meeting someone he knew in this vast city, far away from Andalusia. He couldn't mistake the daggerlike shape of the face, the pointed beard, the staring intensity in the eyes.

Instinctively, Theo moved to go after him. He had no idea what he wanted to say. "It's not what you think; this isn't me; I'm not one of them." Something like that, perhaps. But he was denied the opportunity. He'd gone only a few steps when he felt a hand on his shoulder and his stepfather called him back.

"You need to stay with us," he said. "It's not safe to go in there at night. Or even during the day, for that matter."

"In where?" asked Theo.

"The Fifth District—all this area to the south," said Andrew, pointing up and down the side of the Ramblas on which they were standing. "But particularly down here, when you get closer to the port. I'm sorry. I should have told you before."

"Why? What happens in there?"

"There are criminals, drug dealers . . ."

"Anarchists?"

"Yes," said Andrew, looking closely at his stepson, as if guessing the reason for his question. "Them too. As I've said, it's not safe."

They had reached Elena, and Theo said nothing more as they got into their taxi and sped back up the Ramblas past the cafés, which were as crowded as in the afternoon but illuminated now by thousands of tiny glittering lights.

Saturday, Theo thought. On Saturday I will see the real Barcelona.

But first he had to leave the city. Early the next morning Andrew drove Elena and Theo down the coast to Sitges. The winding road had been carved out of the cliff, with the Garraf Mountains rising precipitately above and the Mediterranean stretching away below to a distant horizon. Azure blue in the sunlight, ruffled here and there by silvery waves, it was spectacularly beautiful.

Andrew had promised golden sand, and Sitges didn't disappoint. The beach stretched brown and smooth all the way from their hotel to the picturesque church of Santa Tecla on a headland at the other end, with the clear view interrupted only by small fishing boats pulled up here and there out of the water.

Elena had felt carsick on the corniche, but now she suddenly revived. "It's perfect," she said wonderingly. "Oh, Andrew, can't you stay?"

"No," he said, smiling. "Not even for a minute. This is your holiday with Theo. I'll be back at the end of the week." And with a wave of his hand and a skid of fast-turning tires, he was gone.

Standing in front of the hotel, Theo was shocked to realize that the empty feeling that had suddenly overtaken him was in fact disappointment that his stepfather had left. For years he had blamed Andrew for taking away his mother, but no longer. Irony of ironies, he felt closer to him now than he did to her. It was the last thing he would have expected. At least superficially, they had little in common, separated as they were by age, nationality, and political outlook, but what mattered more was that they shared a willingness to at least try to see each other for who they were. At critical moments in Theo's life when he had gotten into trouble, Andrew had come to his rescue. He felt supported by his stepfather—loved, even.

Theo knew his mother loved him, too, just as he loved her, but a polarizing dichotomy in the way they each saw the world had pushed them further and further apart, creating barriers between them that he didn't seem able to overcome. Once upon a time—so long ago that he could hardly remember—they had been close. Mother and son together, speaking Spanish in an English world, gathered with the exiles in the church in Gramercy Park. But while he had grown and gone out into the world, she had stayed behind, clinging to a faith that he could not share. The faith that had given her the justification to consign her first husband to oblivion as if he'd never lived, and which she was now using to defend the terrible injustices in Spanish society that so outraged her son.

As the rift between them had widened, Theo had learned to keep important parts of his life secret from his mother. It was a process that had begun five years earlier in New York when she had practically thrown Coach Eames out of their apartment. The poor man's efforts to help her son had meant nothing to Elena once she found out he was a Communist. In the blink of an eye, he had gone from being an honored guest to becoming "a devil and a ravenous wolf." Her words were ridiculous. Anyone could have seen that, except Elena herself, who had never been able to get beyond the fear and hatred of the godless Reds that she had taken with her out of Mexico.

So, afterward, in England and Spain, it was little wonder that Theo never spoke to her of Esmond or Maria. How could he when he knew she would condemn them out of hand? And become sick if he argued with her. His mother's fragility cemented the separation between them, stifling the possibility of honest communication.

It might have helped if she had been able to relax her determination to look forward and not back, so as to avoid having to deal with experiences that upset her. But New York remained a closed subject because it reminded her of the disgrace, poverty, and sickness that had followed her first husband's suicide. She needed to forget to survive, and it didn't seem to matter to her that this meant she and Theo would lose access to their shared past. The good was thrown out with the bad. Spain was where they were now and as far as Elena was concerned, the past was another country that they'd had to leave behind to begin again.

None of this was what Theo wanted. Life was hard and confusing, and he would have liked nothing more than to be able to talk to his mother about the painful problems he was wrestling with, but he knew what would happen if he tried, and so he remained silent.

Elena, for her part, appeared blissfully unaware of his buttoned-up constraint. She acted as if everything was fine between them, and as long as they kept away from difficult subjects, she remained everything a loving mother should be: solicitous for her son's welfare and happiness, proud of his success at school, and excited by his achievement in getting into Oxford.

She told Theo how delighted she was that they were going to have a holiday together in such a beautiful place. Everything about Sitges pleased her: the hotel with its wide-open views of the sea, as if you could reach out of the windows and touch the water; the stone terrace of the restaurant where they ate their meals and where she forsook her usual temperance to order cocktails with names that made her giggle, and which came in strange, exotic colors and with tiny striped umbrellas that matched the parasols above their table; the palm trees with brightly colored birds singing in their fronds; the beach where she walked out into the sea and then came running back when the waves came in, hanging on to Theo's arm and splashing his legs and laughing.

It reminded her of her childhood, she said, when her parents took her to Puerto Vallarta for the holidays and she stood beside her father at the end of the pier and watched the pearl divers go out in their tiny boats to where there were dolphins in the Pacific, flying through the sea spray with such a weight of abandon. And sharks, too, lurking in the water, waiting.

Inevitably it was the church that Elena loved the most. Its setting was magical, rising up from the rocks at the end of the beach into weathered walls that glowed like pink quartz in the sunset. At high tide, the waves splashed up onto the stone steps leading to the door.

At Elena's request, the hotel organized a guide to take them around, and on their last day they spent a very long hour with an octogenarian man who appeared to know the date and provenance of every object in the church, down to and including the candlesticks. He took them through every appalling detail of Santa Tecla's martyrdom as portrayed on the altarpiece, while Elena listened intently and Theo inwardly groaned, longing to be released out into the sea air and the light.

As was often the case, the visit to the church crystallized his irritation with his mother and, walking back, he told her that the beach reminded him of his childhood, too, even though it didn't.

"When I went to Coney Island with Dad, we walked on the sand," he said, turning to look at her, as if he was challenging her with the statement.

And when she would not answer, he went on, refusing to let the subject go. "I don't care what he did. I think of him every day," he told her. "Don't you?"

"I can't," she said, shaking her head. "It hurts."

Theo looked at his mother. He could see that she'd pushed the memory of her first husband aside in the time it took to answer his question and was smiling expectantly now, just as she used to do years before when he was a boy in New York and the whole day was before them, theirs to do with as they pleased. As if nothing had happened—no factory, no suicide, no separation. But it didn't work. Those things had happened. They were a part of who he was, who he had become. Not to be denied.

She loved him. He could see it written in her luminous dark eyes. He felt their warmth, like a fire on a cold night, and he understood her extraordinary fragility and the precious ephemerality of this moment in time that they had together. He wanted to respond—to tell her that he loved her, too, and that everything was going to be all right. He longed to, but he couldn't, and there were no words to explain why. Or no words she could understand or accept.

He stopped, feeling like he'd hit something hard, something he could not get beyond. He picked up a stray black stone at his feet and threw it out into the sea, wishing it had been the plaster statue of Santa Tecla that his mother had bought at the back of the church and was carrying in her hand as she walked on in front of him, leaving tiny footprints behind her in the sand.

At night he dreamed that his mother was the saint. It was the same story that the old guide had told them in the church. She was being pursued through caves, and each time the pursuer got close, she prayed to God, who opened up the wall to another dark passageway, providing her with a temporary escape. But he could see the pursuer, too, enveloped in a black cloak, and he knew that it was death.

He woke trembling in the early light and went out into the hall and knocked on his mother's door, terrified that she would not answer. And when it finally opened, he put out his hands and hugged her close and whispered that he was sorry. She reached up and ran her fingers through his hair and he stood still, looking out over her shoulder through the open windows of her room toward the vast gray sea.

2

CHINATOWN

Antonio was excited. His head bobbed from side to side as he pointed out landmarks, naming streets and squares and distant hills in a cascade of information that made Theo's head spin. His weariness of the previous weekend had been replaced by a frenetic vivacity, reflecting a determination to experience to the full every moment of his day's leave from his hated barracks.

They crossed a great square populated with baroque statues and fountains and walked down a long, wide road that Antonio said was called the Paral·lel because it ran parallel to the equator. He was the guide again just as he had been in the village two summers before, although it was not long before Theo began to realize that his friend's knowledge of the real Barcelona, as he called it, was a thin veneer, concealing the ignorance of a dyed-in-the-wool country boy.

It was Theo who was at home in this urban world. He had grown up in it. The Paral·lel was a larger version of Fourteenth Street, where he had spent his childhood. There was the same spillage of shops and cafés out onto the sidewalks and the same crazy traffic—overcrowded trams with riders on the running boards hanging on for dear life and immobilized automobile drivers incessantly blowing their horns in a vain effort to get around carts laden with vegetables or coal.

In the middle of this chaos, a policeman in a fancy blue uniform stood on a box, making elaborate signals with his white-gloved hands that everyone ignored. He was like a conductor of an orchestra that had gone rogue, and Theo was reminded in a flash of the similarly ineffectual traffic cop he'd passed on that long-gone day when his grandfather had taken him through the New York streets to meet his *bubbe*.

He remembered her so clearly even though he'd met her only once: her wide-open green eyes and her foreign voice searching for the English words; the feel of her hands on his head, pressing. Leah Stern, who was dead now, gone beyond his reach.

Theo felt that same stab of loss and missed opportunity that he always felt when he remembered his grandparents, but then it was gone in a moment, swallowed up in a more general nostalgia for his hometown. Someone had painted **BROADWAY DE BARCELONA** in big white letters on a wall, and the sign made sense. It was as if the Paral·lel was consciously aping Manhattan. The cinemas were showing American films—Clark Gable and Bette Davis stared down from gigantic posters, and jazz was playing in all the cafés. Amid all the cacophony, Theo thought for a moment that he could hear Louis Armstrong singing "St. James Infirmary Blues," but when he stopped to listen, the song was gone.

This was a different world to the Ramblas. There was no grandeur or pretension or luxury—no flower or bird markets, no hats on the women made of exotic plumage. The cafés were lit by naked bulbs, not chandeliers, and everyone wore black and white and talked in those terms. The medieval church towers rising above the Ramblas were replaced here with the roofs of smoke-belching factories. Over on the right, toward Montjuïc, the three tall chimneys of the Canadenca power station were the cathedral spires of working-class Barcelona. Coal dust settled on surfaces like a thin gray dew.

At Café Chicago, the Paral·lel opened up to the north in the La Bretxa de Sant Pau, and Antonio turned left toward the Ramblas, plunging almost immediately into a warren of narrow side streets, lined on either side with tenement buildings whose height and proximity to each other prevented the angled sunlight from ever reaching the ground. The contrast to the wide, open Paral·lel was extraordinary and induced in Theo a sudden cramping claustrophobia that he had to struggle to overcome.

Some of the buildings were doss-houses with signs outside offering beds by the hour or even something called *las cuerdas*, which allowed those who couldn't afford a bed to sleep the night hanging on to ropes. Others were brothels. Theo and Antonio stopped outside one window, looking in on a scene that left nothing to the imagination. Semiclad girls in slips and petticoats sat in a line on a wooden bench, while an old woman waited behind a glass-fronted cash desk by the door with a pile of metal disks beside her. On the back wall, a calendar from the year before hung slightly askew, and farther along, a staircase rose up into gloom.

Elsewhere, women too old to find work in the brothels called out to Theo and Antonio and cursed them as they hurried past, their harsh, angry voices echoing back off the lanes' narrow walls. They frightened Theo with their lurid faces caked with rouge and their eyes heavy with mascara. The languid kimono-clad girls on Rivington Street who had adopted him as their mascot had no relationship to these desperate women struggling against the odds to keep their deaths at bay.

"What is this place?" he asked, turning to Antonio.

"The Fifth District, but everyone calls it Chinatown. Isn't it terrible?" Antonio sounded strangely satisfied, as if he had succeeded in proving a point, although what that point was Theo had no idea.

"It's worse than terrible. It's hell on earth," he replied. "Why's it called Chinatown? I haven't seen any Chinese."

"Because it's like the Chinatowns in America—foul and full of lowlifes," said Antonio. "That's the idea."

Was that why Antonio was pleased? Theo wondered. Because it showed where America and capitalism got you? Was that the idea? No wonder the Anarchists were strong in this town, he thought. Even the most patient would end up throwing bombs if they had to endure this life.

Everywhere there was the sound of coughing. Not just from people they could see but from hordes of invisible others, filling the stale, malodorous air with a miasma of germs. Theo pulled his shirt collar over his mouth and nose while keeping his eyes fixed on the ground to stop himself from walking in the filthy open drains that overflowed out onto the cobblestones.

The main source of the poisoned air was the factories that stood side by side with the tenements, spewing smoke and toxic vapors out through vents and chimneys into the rooms where families ate and slept.

Theo and Antonio looked in through the sealed window of a workshop. As far as they could see in all directions, big mechanical looms and spinning frames were being operated by lines of textile workers. Their bodies moved like the pistons of the machines, as if both were being remotely controlled by some invisible brain.

The light from the naked bulbs hanging down from the smoke-blackened ceiling was poor and the window through which they were looking was grimy, but Theo's eyes adjusted and he began to pick out small shapes moving about on the floor on their hands and knees. He pushed his face up against the glass and saw that the shapes were children sweeping out handfuls of dust and dirt and fallen cotton fiber from under the machines to stop them from becoming clogged. It was obvious that they risked being decapitated or crushed if they raised their heads or their backs too high.

"Look!" he said, taking hold of Antonio's arm and pointing at the children. "That can't be legal."

But before Antonio could reply, a red-faced man with a big stomach held in by a dirty singlet noticed their faces at the window and started toward them, waving his arms.

Now, it was Antonio's turn to pull at Theo. "Come on," he said. "That's the foreman. Let's get out of here."

"No," said Theo, holding back. "It's wrong. We need to say something."

"It won't do any good and you know it," said Antonio harshly. "Please don't get us in a fight. Trouble is the last thing I need."

A few yards away, a door opened and the clattering, thumping noise of the machines was suddenly deafening in Theo's ears. He could smell the hot, humid air thick with fiber, and he wanted to gag. The man was coming out. He was huge and his fists were clenched. Theo hesitated and then, at the last moment, just as the man was reaching toward him, he turned and ran after Antonio, sprinting down the lanes until they had left the factory and the sound of pursuing footsteps far behind.

Antonio stopped and pushed Theo hard on the shoulders, causing him to stagger back. "You're so stupid," he said. "I should never have brought you here."

"So why did you then?" asked Theo angrily.

"Because I thought you should see it. So you wouldn't think that fancy hotels and nights at the opera are what this town is really about. Just like I showed you what was real in the mountains. Remember?"

Theo nodded, understanding now.

"And because you want to find my sister," Antonio added. "Just like I do. And this is where she is. I'm sure of it."

Theo shuffled his feet uncomfortably and then looked at Antonio and held up his hands. "You're right she's here," he said. "She told me they were going to Barcelona just before she left. I should have said so before. I'm sorry."

"So why didn't you?" asked Antonio, sounding angry again.

"I didn't want you to think I had something to do with the murder."

"Did you?"

"No, of course not!"

"What about Maria?"

"I don't know. She was happy Primitivo killed him. I could see that."

"Yes, the bastard won her with his knife because he couldn't with his words. And now she's thrown in her lot with him, it's like she's crossed over to the other side. Gone where I can't follow. Sometimes I feel like I'll never see her again." Antonio bit his lip, trying to swallow his pain.

"You will. Of course you will," said Theo passionately, not because he believed it, but because he couldn't bear for it to be true. Not just for Antonio but for himself too.

"She was my younger sister and I let her down. I should have stood up for her to my father over Pedrito like you said. Not gone away and left her with nobody except Primitivo to turn to. But it's too late now," said Antonio despairingly.

"No, it's not. She's done nothing wrong. She doesn't have to be with Primitivo. She can come back," said Theo furiously, fighting his friend's defeatism. Maria wasn't gone. He wouldn't let her be gone. "We have to try and find her," he said. "You said it yourself just a minute ago."

"I know I did," said Antonio, bowing his head. "And I've tried, and I'll carry on trying, but that doesn't mean I think we'll succeed. There are thousands of people here. It's like looking for a needle in a haystack. And if we do find her, I don't think she's going to listen. That's all."

Up and down the streets and in the tiny, dirty cafés, they asked for Maria, but at best they drew a blank and at worst were met with open hostility. People who came asking questions in Chinatown were police or connected to police, and the cops were the common enemy. Finally, in one dingy bar, a man took out a pistol and spun it on his table meaningfully, and they ran. Without hesitation this time, turning this way and that as they searched for the light, until they burst out into the Paral·lel again, a block away from the Café Chicago, where they had started, and stood gasping for breath and laughing for no reason except relief.

"Enough for one day," said Antonio. "It's time to be happy." And Theo agreed wholeheartedly.

They sat at a café, eating fish with bulging eyes and mussels and scallops with the smell of the sea still inside their shells, and drinking Andalusian wine that tasted just like it had on that first evening they had spent together in the village, when Spain was an adventure Theo was waiting to begin. Before everything became so complicated and hard to unravel.

Looking at his friend across the table, drinking hard to forget, Theo wished he could go back to that night when everything had been magical and the square had been transformed into Dracula's castle just by pulling a sheet across the trees.

Afterward, they crossed the Paral·lel to the Moulin Rouge: a squat building with an illuminated windmill with rotating red sails superimposed on its facade above the portico. They bought tickets and coffee with rum in paper cups that they had to hold on to with both hands to stop them from spilling over as they pushed inside with the crowd. Soon all the seats were taken, rising in a steep semicircle up from the curtained stage. Everyone was squashed in together, shouting and laughing and smoking, utterly alive and, like Antonio, determined to enjoy to the full every moment of escape from the drudgery of their days.

Theo thought of the Liceu and wondered at the extreme contrast between the two theaters. Only a few streets separated them, but they belonged to different worlds. Plush carpet and sawdust, evening dress and overalls, the ostentation of great wealth and the degradation of terrible poverty. Could they continue to exist so close together and yet so far apart? Or was conflict between them inevitable as each fought for its own survival?

Suddenly there was a hush as the curtain rose and Conchita stepped out. Theo knew that was her name because it said so on the blackboard that was carried across the stage before each act. Dressed in a chemise and black trunks from which rolls of fat bulged out, and an oversize cross that glittered between her almost-exposed breasts, she sang bawdy songs while making eyes at and presenting her gyrating hips to the men in the front row. They reached toward her with their hands, from which she withdrew with a look of mock outrage, only to advance again. Her voice was terrible, but that was part of the joke, and the audience roared their appreciation when she came back for an encore.

"They put her in jail in 1932 when her negligee fell off," Antonio shouted in Theo's ear, but he couldn't hear Antonio's reply when he asked him how he knew, because everyone was singing along to a popular song called "La Vaselina" about a newlywed wife displaying incredible naivete on her wedding night.

The laughter was infectious. Through the acts—a kaleidoscope of sequins and corsets and glitter, of double entendre and innuendo—hysteria grew like a wind rushing this way and that through the audience, creating a violent happiness that possessed Theo like a demon.

There was a fantastic irreverence at work. In the best-received skit of the evening, the stage was turned into a confessional in which a libidinous priest even fatter than Don Vincente and wearing similar silver-buckled shoes took advantage of a beautiful female parishioner who turned out, after the slow removal of her garments, to be a man! Theo laughed so hard that it hurt and wondered afterward at his savage glee. It was as if he hated the Church now as much as the Anarchists around him, but not just for their reasons—the hypocrisy, the lies, the investment in ignorance; it was more because religion separated him from his mother, creating a gulf between them that he could not bridge.

The Moulin saved its best for last. A Romany woman in a long green dress with an elongated face and features, as if lifted from a Gauguin painting of Tahiti, walked out onto the stage, accompanied by a guitar player with a wide-brimmed black sombrero pulled low over his forehead. He sat on a stool and began to play, picking out slow notes, while she looked on immobile and impassive, gazing into a space that only she could see.

The audience fell completely quiet. No one spoke, no one moved. The sudden switch from tumult to silence astonished Theo. It was like a conjurer's trick.

A minute passed and she remained still as a statue. Until the guitar all at once accelerated and she burst into life, jumping, twisting, contorted in a feverish swirl of cloth and castanets clicking in her upturned hands. All while singing with a voice that was like a nasal howl, descending through scales that made no sense to Theo to reach a lyrical beauty that she threw away as if it was nothing a moment later.

He couldn't make sense of the words. They were distorted by the strange rhythms of flamenco, but he understood the passion. The song and the dance and the music were an expression of ecstasy and agony. Life lived on the outer rim of possibility. Carmen stabbed, bombs thrown, fire in the night. An art that this audience could embrace deep in their souls.

She stopped as suddenly as she had begun and stood looking at the audience for a moment, accepting their applause, before walking off the stage. The show was over. The lights came up and Theo and Antonio shuffled out with the crowd into the night.

They walked slowly up the wide avenue without speaking, even when they had left the reveling crowds behind.

The song had awakened a sense of foreboding in Theo that he had been holding suppressed ever since Pedrito's murder. It was dread without the knowledge of what he was dreading. A growing pressure that felt like the hour before a storm that would not break. He tried hard, but without success, to push the anxiety back into the chamber of his unconscious mind where he usually kept it contained, and the effort constrained him, so that he could not think of what to say to Antonio, with whom conversation always came so easily. It didn't help that Antonio was silent, too, lost in his own thoughts.

As they entered the street leading to the barracks, Theo forced himself to speak: "It was a good day, even if we didn't find Maria," he said. "Thank you for showing me . . ." He stopped, unable to think of the right word to describe all that they had seen.

"It's an honor to guide you," said Antonio with a trace of his old smile as he repeated the words he'd spoken to Theo when they first met two years before in his father's office. "I hope I can get away again next Saturday afternoon and we can look for her again. Will you still be here?"

"I don't know. I hope so. If I am, I'll come like today," said Theo, stumbling over his words as he felt their inadequacy to match what he was feeling.

They were in sight of the barracks now: high and gray and imposing in the moonlight.

"Do you ever feel like something is coming?" he burst out. "Something bad which we can't stop?"

"All the time," said Antonio. "And I can't see past it. I try to but I can't. It's like a bull running. It's too big."

His voice was very quiet, and Theo knew that he was thinking about the day of the storm, when they had taken shelter in the lonely cottage at the top of the village and the old woman had refused to say what she had seen in his palm. A black fate written in the lines from which there was no escape.

"It'll be okay," said Theo, even though he didn't believe it. His feeling of separation from his friend was even stronger now, but he forced himself against its weight and reached out his arms to hug Antonio, who felt limp in his embrace.

He looked at Theo and nodded, as if communicating his understanding of what Theo was trying to do, and then turned and passed through the gate and was swallowed up in the darkness.

ABOUT THE AUTHOR

Photo © 2024 Nicholas Tolkien

Simon Tolkien is the author of *No Man's Land*, *Orders from Berlin*, *The King of Diamonds*, *The Inheritance*, and *Final Witness*. He studied modern history at Trinity College, Oxford, and went on to become a London barrister specializing in criminal defense. Simon is the grandson of J.R.R. Tolkien and is a director of the Tolkien Estate. In 2022 he was named as series consultant to the Amazon TV series *The Rings of Power*. He lives with his wife, vintage fashion author Tracy Tolkien, and their two children, Nicholas and Anna, in Southern California. For more information, visit www.simontolkien.com.